Ingrid Black is a writer and journalist. She lives in Ireland.

The Dark Eye

Ingrid Black

headline

First published in 2004
by HEADLINE BOOK PUBLISHING

First published in paperback in 2004
by HEADLINE BOOK PUBLISHING

10 9 8 7 6 5 4 3 2

ISBN 0 7553 0704 6

Typeset in Plantin by Avon DataSet Ltd,
Bidford-on-Avon, Warwickshire

Printed and bound in Great Britain by
Mackays of Chatham plc, Chatham, Kent

Headline's policy is to use papers that are natural, renewable and
recyclable products and made from wood grown in sustainable
forests. The logging and manufacturing processes are expected to
conform to the environmental regulations of the country of origin.

HEADLINE BOOK PUBLISHING
A division of Hodder Headline
338 Euston Road
London NW1 3BH

www.headline.co.uk
www.hodderheadline.com

THE DARK EYE

Part One

Chapter One

I didn't even get a chance to say hello.

'You're Saxon,' the voice said soon as I picked up the phone.

'I know I am,' I answered.

'I don't suppose you know who I am?'

There was a trace of an accent there, though I couldn't place the where.

'Let me guess. Is it Elvis Presley?'

'My name is Felix.'

'I don't get three guesses then?'

'Felix Berg. You may have heard of me.'

'I haven't.'

'I'm a photographer.'

'Is that right?'

I sighed and checked my watch. Outside my window another day was dragging sluggishly to a close with nothing done, and somewhere in my apartment a clock was ticking too loudly, taunting me with time wasted. This was the last thing I needed.

'Listen, Felix, Felix Berg, photographer, whatever, what do you want? It's late, it's cold out, I need my beauty sleep. Do you have nothing better to do than call up strange women who don't give a damn who you are and tell them your name?'

'I want to talk to you.'

'I figured.'

'I want to meet. And I think you'll want to meet me too once you hear me out.'

'I wouldn't put money on that, my friend.'

There was a brief pause before he continued.

'Someone,' he said, 'is trying to kill me.'

And I thought: *Here we go again.*

I was always getting calls like this. OK, maybe always is an exaggeration, but often enough not to be surprised by them any more. It came with the territory.

Saxon: crack hunter of serial killers turned bestselling crime writer. That was me.

At least that's how they described me on cable TV.

Magnet for every crazy in town, more like it.

I'd written a couple of books about my all-too-brief years in the FBI, so it wasn't like they needed security clearance from the President to get the lowdown on me; but still they expected me to be impressed when they rattled off a few details about cases I'd worked, places I'd been, killers I'd known. Like I needed reminding. Hell, I'm as easily flattered as the next former Special Agent, but they really needed to put in some more effort.

Get a new chat-up line.

Still, as introductions go, telling me someone was trying to kill him took some beating, and I told him so.

'You think I'm joking,' he said.

'What I think is, if someone's trying to kill you, you should go to the police. I'm not some kind of private eye. I'm not any kind of private eye.'

'It's too late. They wouldn't listen to me.'

I didn't blame them.

'What makes you think I will?'

'Because you're the only one I can count on,' he said. 'You're a stranger here, like me. You don't belong. And besides—'

'Yeah?'

'You know what it's like to see into the dark.'

4

And I couldn't deny that.

I'd been staring into it longer than I could remember, so long that I could scarcely recall any more a time when I knew nothing of murder, knew nothing of death, though I guess there must have been one. A time when the darkness which lurks always at the edge of things, infecting and infesting the world we think we know, was nothing more than a rumour to me; when the dead voices still spoke a language I didn't understand and had no desire to learn.

Once the darkness has touched the mind, nothing can make it go again. And it had touched mine too often. I had seen crows pecking at the fallen in a wood in winter, snow and old blood and the shadows of branches interlacing like secrets. I had fished skulls from the sea like they were whitebait, and drawn blood out the water of a moss-ravelled well in which a woman's brutalised body had been dropped still breathing, but only barely, just hours before. I had seen the dead sealed inside walls and left folded in wastepipes as an offering for the rats, greedily unwrapped as a child unwraps its birthday gifts. I had found fingers poking out of the earth where a city decayed into rubble, nails blackened with poison, and recognised in them the handiwork of killers I almost hadn't thought existed outside my own imagination. I had searched for lost children that I knew would never be found. With my bare hands I had sifted ashes, not knowing what was dust and what was life forsaken.

I had come to know murder intimately, in all its pallors and moods, in all its hiding places, until the sight was as familiar to me as my own reflection, and I knew that dark things were all that lasted in the end, that nothing else endured. Knew that there was no end to evil, and no matter how hard we fought it there would always be more of it to fight again.

Knew too that there are some amongst us, some much closer than we know, who think no more of snuffing out a life than the horse mourns the beetle crushed under its hoof.

You know what it's like to see into the dark.

I did.

Which I guess was why I was damn fool enough to listen to some nut who called after hours looking for help, instead of putting the phone down, unplugging it from the wall, and climbing into bed. Maybe I should just get the word *sucker* tattooed on my forehead.

Where *had* I put those car keys?

Chapter Two

No, I wasn't late. I checked the clock on the dashboard. Not yet midnight. And here to prove it, rattling alongside the road, was the last train, snaking round by the side of the black water and slowing as it came into Howth. As I parked my Jeep and climbed out, I saw passengers edging out from the station and dispersing like smoke, until they were only shadows and traces of laughter and then less than that, and I thought: I shouldn't have come, no.

I didn't even know what he looked like, I reminded myself grimly.

That was a good start.

Where was it he'd said he'd be?

The lighthouse, that was it – and there it was, standing guard at the end of the harbour wall where the city gave way to the sea, blinking off, on, off.

It looked very far away, but looking at it wouldn't make it come any closer.

I locked the car and began to make my way out towards it.

In a moment it seemed I'd left Howth behind, and all I could hear was the night tide slapping against the stone and the boats in the harbour knocking together like dull bells.

That, and the flat echo of my own footsteps in the dark that made me think once or twice that someone was following me, though when I turned round there was nothing, no one else about at all, and the only other sign of life save me was some dog that came sniffing along the bollards lining the edge of the wall, strung with metal chains between, and looked at me hopefully for food before realising he was out of luck and running back towards the land.

By the time I reached the lighthouse, I was feeling unnerved. Out-of-the-way places like this always unsettled me, made me lose my bearings – the city was the only place I ever felt comfortable – and I was starting to wonder whether it hadn't been a bad idea coming out here at all. Especially when I saw that Felix Berg wasn't even at the red door of the lighthouse where he'd said he'd be. In fact, I was starting to wonder if I'd been taken for a fool.

It wouldn't be the first time.

I yawned and checked my watch.

A quarter after midnight.

I'd give it ten minutes, I thought – no, five – then I was out of here.

Put it down to experience.

I sat down on the step in front of the door and lit a cigar to keep myself company whilst I waited, and waited, and as I waited I attempted a few half-hearted smoke rings – though I'd never managed to get those right; they just died on me at birth – and pulled my jacket tighter round me to try and stay warm. The wind was turning chilly. It was April, I think I'd read on some calendar that morning. The start of spring. But winter still wouldn't give up the ghost. It cut in off the sea, hunting, hungry, camouflaged in the wind.

Looking back, I could see the glow of isolated houses like fireflies scattered across Howth Head, and a castle rotten like a tooth against the sky, stars bursting behind. Overhead, planes from the east were banking as they made the final lowering approach into the airport a few miles further inland. Across the water somewhere metal struck metal.

'Felix Berg,' I said quietly, 'your time is up.'

I didn't know if the five minutes were up, but I'd waited long enough.

I got to my feet and looked round one last time – and at

that moment the beam of the lighthouse swept round again and I saw something at the end of the pier, where the stone dropped away to the deep water that stretched out to the lightless hump of an island beyond.

Or rather, I saw two somethings.

Shoes?

That's what they looked like.

Intrigued, I tossed away the cigar and walked to the end of the pier.

The shoes were perched right on the edge of the stone, laid together neatly, laces folded back to fit inside – and there were other things there too.

Keys bunched on a keyring.

A silver cellphone.

A wallet.

And – what was this?

I took another step forward and immediately felt something crack quietly, a second too late to save it, under my foot. I looked down at a glint like ice.

The ice was broken glass. Not like the glass of a bottle, but thin and fragile like a leaf, and there was a round frame where the glass had been. It was a pair of silver-rimmed spectacles.

Irritated with myself, I shook the glass from the bottom of my boot and took one more step forward, minding where I put my foot this time.

I'd expected the wall to drop away sheer to the water, but I realised now that there were rocks below. Black rocks wound with seaweed that resisted the tugging of each wave, and scattered with empty bottles and beer cans and an oil drum and planks of wood.

And there was a final something down there.

It was a man.

Or what had been a man and was now only a body.

He lay face down, jacket twisted, trousers inky with wet, his feet bare, one arm trapped awkwardly beneath himself, the other outstretched and bent to fit the jagged shape of the rocks, his body almost as angular now as they were. And I remembered at once the caller's last words to me on the phone: *You're not the only one who's seen into the dark. And sometimes the dark doesn't like it. Sometimes the dark looks back.*

Chapter Three

Seamus Dalton. I should've known it would be Dalton. Just what I needed to round off a great evening. Scientists have trawled Africa for years looking for the missing link, and here it was in Dublin all the time, hiding out in the shape of a murder detective.

It was going to be a long night.

He was quick, that's all I'll give him, only a few minutes behind the uniforms who were now securing the scene and making the usual inept attempts at questioning. I was standing with a cop called Simpson by a row of boat sheds with metal fronts a couple hundred yards down from the lighthouse when I saw him approaching, adjusting his belt and hitching up his pants as he caught sight of me, pulling a weary face like he knew already that I was wasting his time. That was his ritual whenever we met, which wasn't often.

And I wasn't complaining.

'You know,' he said as he drew near, 'people have a bad habit of dying round you.'

'Never the right ones, unfortunately.'

He almost smiled.

'Who is it?' he said.

'We haven't been able to identify the body yet, sir—' Simpson tried to explain before Dalton silenced him with a glance.

'I wasn't asking you, son, I was asking her. In fact, why don't you go and see if you can't put up some more tape or

11

something. Make yourself useful. In fact, why don't you pop down over the wall there and take a little peek at the deceased. I'll take over here.'

Simpson didn't argue. Few of the uniforms messed with Dalton. He had a reputation for ruining a cop's evening just for the heck of it.

'They teach you people skills in police school, or does it all come naturally?' I said as Simpson backed away.

'Self-taught. Only teacher I ever needed,' Dalton said. 'Now, are you going to answer the question or do I have to put the cuffs on you, take you downtown and book you, as I believe you Americans say?'

Like he'd have the balls to do it. But he chuckled at his own joke; and when you're as funny as Dalton, you get used to laughing at your own jokes since no one else is going to.

'How the hell should I know who it is?' was all I said in answer.

'The desk sergeant said you mentioned a name.'

'I came here to meet someone is what I said.'

'Felix something.'

'Felix Berg. He told me he was a photographer. Whether it's him or not, I don't know. I think it might be.'

'Think?' He spoke the word carefully, like it was new to him.

'Yeah, think. You should try it sometime. Little practice, you might even get to enjoy it. Like I say, I *think* it might be him. I didn't want to touch anything.' Didn't want to climb down there was nearer the truth, though I wasn't about to admit that to Dalton. 'Besides, I never met him before. I wouldn't be able to ID him even if I wanted.'

Dalton seemed more interested in the fact I was out here meeting a man I'd never seen before than the fact there was a body lying on the rocks a few hundred yards away.

'What's the story?' he said. 'You suddenly get a taste for men or something? Could be my lucky night.'

'Not unless I get a taste for slugs, Dalton,' I said. 'And you can wipe that leering look off your fat face. Don't try turning this into something it isn't.'

'So what is it if it isn't what you say it isn't?'

I paused.

'He wanted to talk to me about something,' I said warily.

'Talk to you about what?'

'He didn't say.'

'He didn't say?'

'He didn't say.' I sighed. 'Look, what are you doing here anyway? Where's Fitzgerald?'

I meant Grace Fitzgerald, Detective Chief Superintendent with the Dublin Metropolitan Police's murder squad, and Dalton's superior – professionally, intellectually, evolutionarily, every sense of the word. The Chief Superintendent and I were what used to be called an item. Stepping out together. Sleeping together. Call it what you will. Had been for a few years now, ever since I arrived in the city from the States, fresh from the FBI.

Though fresh wasn't quite right. Jaded, finished, exhausted would be more like it. Fitzgerald had helped me get over it – though whether spending so much time with someone on the city's murder squad had done me much good in getting over my own weaknesses was another matter. Didn't help sometimes that she was doing what I still, in my more vulnerable moments, longed to be doing and which I knew I had little hope of ever getting back to.

Dalton knew about us, of course; they all did. No one ever said a word when Grace was around, but even then they never let you forget they knew. It didn't need words.

'The Chief Superintendent is otherwise engaged,' was all Dalton said right now. 'Busy woman. Busy woman. Stabbing down in Portobello. Murder's a growing business in the city these days, you know. Growth industry. Sorry if that fucks up your romantic plans for the evening, but that's killers for you. No consideration for anyone else. I blame the parents.'

Out of the corner of my eye I saw one of the other uniforms glance over as the sound of Dalton's loud voice reached him, like he was putting two and two together over the jibe about Fitzgerald.

'Besides, why would the great Grace Fitzgerald – out of whose rear end the sun doth shine, if you believe her fans in the local press – want to waste her time on a suicide?'

That threw me.

'What makes you so sure this guy killed himself?'

'Because I talked to one of these uniformed bozos on the radio whilst I was on my way over,' Dalton said. 'He gave me the full lowdown. Shoes taken off, phone, keys, wallet, glasses all laid neatly to one side. Classic pre-suicidal behaviour. Which,' he went on before I could protest, 'is why I find it hard to figure out why you came to the murder squad with it. You arrange to meet some guy, what purpose I couldn't say, none of my business, right? Then he throws himself in the water rather than put up with the pleasure of your company, which, you know, I understand, I can respect that. What I don't understand is why you didn't just call in the local cops. They could have fished him out of the water for you. Held your hand while you made a statement.'

'I didn't call the murder squad,' I said, doing my best to ignore his taunts. 'I called Fitzgerald. I wasn't to know her calls were being transferred. And don't you think you should leave it to the pathologist to decide how he died before jumping to conclusions?'

'Call in a pathologist, I never thought of that,' said Dalton sarcastically. 'What would we poor chumps do without your expertise as an ace crime-solver to guide us?'

I tried to ignore him. He was just trying to put me in my place. I was an ex-investigator. Ex-FBI. Ex-everything. That meant I was nothing. A civilian. The lowest of the low. I might've helped out the DMP before, if you could call it help, but it certainly had never been appreciated by the likes of Seamus Dalton. In fact, me thinking I could help was just another demerit against my name. And at that moment I knew I'd tell him nothing else.

'Let's just get this over with, OK?' I said instead.

'What's the hurry? No rush. I've got nothing better to do, and' – Dalton glanced over at the lighthouse – 'I don't think your boyfriend'll be going anywhere for a while. We might as well make a night of it. Besides, the dead are always with us. They should have more respect for me instead of disturbing my shifts with this shit. You just hold your little white horses while I take your statement and then we can both get back to doing what we do best. Though Christ knows what that is in your case.'

'I'd rather give my statement to one of the uniforms.'

'And I'd rather be in bed right now with Cameron Diaz. Come to think of it, so would you probably. Shame we can't both get what we want. Meantime' – and he took out his notebook, opened it, lifted a pencil from his pocket, put the point of the lead lasciviously to the tip of his tongue, holding my eye the whole time – 'we'll start with all the details. Do everything by the book. Keep the paperwork in order. So, name?'

I stared at him.

'Fuck you, Dalton. You know my name.'

'Sorry?' Dalton tipped his head to one side and tapped his pencil to his ear like he couldn't hear too well. 'I didn't quite catch that. You mind repeating it?'

'I said: Fuck. You.'

'Listen, this is a real pain for the both of us, but you know we've got to get the details right. All the formalities. So are you going to be a good little girl for daddy or do I have to ask Simpson to put you under arrest? Think how bad it'll look if the Chief Super's favourite bedwarmer was up in court on a charge of assaulting a police officer.'

'Since when were you assaulted?'

He reached out a hand suddenly and touched my hair.

15

Without thinking, I raised my own hand and batted his away.

'Since then,' he answered.

And he grinned his charmless baboon grin just for me.

I looked at him and realised there was no point making a stand out of it. He was pissed at being sent out here when the real action was happening elsewhere, and pissed too that I wouldn't tell him what exactly had brought me out here, and I was going to get the brunt of it to make him feel that the trip hadn't been entirely wasted. I saw it in his eyes and realised that whatever I did, he'd come out on top in the end.

He saw it too in my eyes. That resignation.

'That's better,' he said. 'I like a woman who does what she's told.'

But Dalton never got a chance to savour his victory, because at that moment the sound of quickening footsteps made us both glance up to where Simpson was hurrying back from the direction of the lighthouse towards us. He stopped a couple of paces away.

'Sir,' he began nervously.

Dalton redirected his hostility back to the cop.

'What is it now?' he said.

'It's the dead man, sir.'

'What's happened? Has he got up and started asking for a taxi home?'

'It looks like . . . like he was shot.'

Dalton was speechless, probably for the first time in his life. And there was another look on his face, a look almost of hope, excitement, the pleasure of something finally happening. And I knew what had caused it to appear.

The Marxman.

16

Chapter Four

First to die had been Tim Enright. In mid-January, for some reason no one had been able to discover, he'd driven out to the northside of the city after work and parked his car in O'Neill's Place. At about 7.30 p.m. two women returning home had found him slumped across the wheel. He'd been killed instantly by a single shot to the back of the head at point-blank range. It was a classic gangland hit of a kind that Dublin had more than its fair share of these days – there'd actually been a fivefold increase in such shootings in the city in the last five years – except there was nothing to suggest it *was* a gangland hit.

The thirty-six-year-old Enright's background had been thoroughly checked out. He'd had no dodgy dealings and no enemies that anyone could find. He'd worked downtown in the swanky Financial Services Centre as a futures trader, whatever the hell that was, running a firm inherited from his late father, and the Criminal Assets Bureau had never heard of him. The fraud squad, vice, serious crime all drew a blank. Every criminal contact the Dublin Metropolitan Police called in insisted no hit had been ordered on him, and they would have heard if it had. Nor was there anything in his private life that could be uncovered as a possible motive for his shooting. No jealous husbands, no secret gay life; his bank records showed no signs of irregular payments either in or out, there was no suggestion of blackmail.

17

Colleagues and friends alike spoke of a man with no worries, no dark side, who'd spent the days before his death preparing for a coming weekend away with his wife in Paris. He was Mr Average. All of which might have been good for his eternal soul but was fatal for the police's chances of pulling anyone in for the killing. It seemed that either his death was the result of mistaken identity, or else it was as motiveless as any killing ever can be.

The enquiry gathered dust.

A month later came the second shooting, and it wasn't Mr Average this time. Terence Prior was a High Court judge, aged sixty-seven, widowed, a pillar of respectable Dublin society, with all the right political connections and wealth to make sure that his conservative, silent-screen-era voice on most social issues was heard above that of the common herd.

Unpopular in the self-styled progressive press for jailing a woman for contempt for breastfeeding in his court, and for frequently bemoaning that he was unable to pass the death sentence on the killers of children and policemen, he had seemingly revelled in his bogeyman image to the point where even his supporters felt he'd ridden out long since on to a wide-open prairie of self-parody. He was shot in the doorway of his own house in a classy Georgian square in the south of the city as he returned from another day dispensing frontier justice to the great unwashed. Like the first victim, he was felled by a single shot at point-blank range, again from the back, this time through the heart. Same weapon: a Glock .36 with, before Enright, a clean history. The press swiftly dubbed the killer the Marksman.

That there were now two victims of what seemed certain to be a single killer – and that one of those victims possessed a well-known name to have carved on his gravestone – at least intensified the investigation considerably. What the DMP had allowed to settle into a routine gathering of evidence and statements in the vague hope that something would turn up and solve the case for them had now become more of a cause célèbre. The press were on the murder squad's backs, looking for leads, fresh angles. If her colleagues sometimes thought that Fitzgerald, simply by being one of the highest-ranking female officers in the force, got an easy press, she certainly hadn't on this one. Her life was swiftly taken over.

More resources were allocated to the enquiry, a larger team was put together, efforts were concentrated on trying to find a connection between the two victims.

There was always a connection, that was the accepted wisdom of any investigation; in fact, it was all that kept an investigation moving sometimes, the hope that some link would be found and that this link would lead to another link and that link to another, like the knee bone was connected to the thigh bone and the thigh bone to the hip bone in the old rhyme, until the whole chain was assembled and, eureka, the perpetrator was shackled to the end of it.

Only it didn't quite work out that way.

No connection was found between these two victims because there *was* no connection, that much quickly became clear. They hadn't frequented the same circles, they lived in different parts of the city, they'd certainly never met, they were different ages. It didn't seem that the killer had targeted them because of who they were at all.

At least that was the general conclusion until Finlay Hart, a slick, smirking, up-and-coming right-wing politician with a stance on most issues that made the late Judge Prior look like an anarchist, and a junior post in government which everyone in the know confidently predicted was only the first step on a rung that would lead him sooner rather than later to high office, was gunned down by the same .36 in the doorway of his office in Main Street early one morning as he arrived to begin another day's work as a master of the political universe.

At last there was a connection, and the DMP's anti-terrorist unit was not slow to exploit it. Two public figures with a stance that would not normally be expected to have the average radical leading a standing ovation had been murdered in the space of weeks, and before Hart's body had even been cleared from the steps of his office or the blood sluiced into the gutter, Paddy Sweeney of the anti-terrorist unit was angling to have the case passed into his jurisdiction, where he would no doubt make the same mess of it as he had the killing of some minor foreign diplomat a year or so back, to which he had confidently assigned a similar political motive from the start, remaining unswerving in his belief right up until the point the man's live-in male lover walked into Dublin Castle with his lawyer and confessed.

Sweeney started offering whispered briefings to the press that the killer was some freelance devotee of Marxist communist theory, and remained equally unshaken in that belief even when the fourth victim of what the press were obliging by now calling, with their usual talent for bad puns, the Marxman – and who was swiftly becoming a hero of the hour among the radical left – was identified as Jane Knox, of unidentifiable age though she'd never have seen seventy again, a one-time radical left-wing nun known as Sister Bernadette who had suffered some sort of breakdown and was now living rough among an army of stray cats on the streets round the Mansion House.

Knox was gunned down in the rear yard of the Water Margin restaurant, again with a single shot from the same Glock .36 to the head, only this time from a distance of some yards; the City Pathologist couldn't say exactly how far, and ballistics analysis was still in the Stone Age in Dublin so that couldn't help. She'd been out early in the morning looking for one of her cats among the trashcans when she was hit, and it was nightfall before she was discovered slumped across the step by one of the waitresses who'd sneaked out to the yard for a cigarette.

What kind of radical Marxist terrorist targets both wealthy right-wing judges and politicians *and* radical nuns turned dispossessed vagrants? Sweeney's attitude was give him three months and a fifty per cent increase in his budget and he'd find out – and he might have got it if Fitzgerald hadn't gone over the head and against the specific instruction of the Assistant Commissioner who nominally overseered the murder squad to keep control of the case. Ego came into it – wanting to keep Sweeney off her territory – but she was also deeply convinced that, whatever strange motivation the misnamed Marxman had, politics wasn't it.

He wasn't even making any attempt to communicate with press or police, and killers with causes rarely lost an opportunity to make their voices heard.

Sweeney had backed off begrudgingly, but he was still there in the background bitching like a girl, determined to make life as difficult for Grace outside the department as Dalton was making it inside. The only difference was she now had his balls for a souvenir of their encounter and she wasn't going to let him forget it. Not that she had time to enjoy the triumph, since the Marxman enquiry was now rapidly expanding like some malignant vermin-carried virus, consuming every moment of murder squad time to the point where stabbings in Portobello must have felt like some kind of surreal relief. She'd never been under so much pressure. A nervous public. An overexcited press. It wasn't a healthy mix.

And it wasn't helped by the fact that, for the three weeks since the last shooting, the murder squad had been in that terrible stasis which afflicts all police departments when dealing with a serial offender. They knew he would strike again, knew that even now he would be selecting, identifying, perhaps even watching his next victim. He was in what those who study such matters call the trolling phase, and all the police could do was wait, trying as best they could to predict the killer's next move, an almost impossible task, and meanwhile sifting the few fragments of clues they had so far in their own hands.

What seemed obvious was that the Marxman was deliberately trying to make sure there were no possible connections between the victims, teasing investigators occasionally with

21

the hint of a link, and then switching 180 degrees to throw them off the scent again. Everything pointed away from a pattern. The Marxman shot both men and women, from different social classes and different parts of the city; he shot them in the head and chest, from point-blank range and distance; he shot at night and in the morning.

The only solid connection, in fact, was that he only ever fired one bullet, and that each of the victims up until tonight had been killed in or through a door of some description.

Doorways: entrances to another world?

Thresholds.

A symbol of crossing over, passing through, from one state to another?

It wasn't much, but I guess every psycho needs a trademark.

I'd tried to keep the case out of my thoughts as much as I could. Tried to stay serene, detached, uninvolved. Not because what was happening didn't fascinate me. Nothing would have made me happier than to be working with Fitzgerald on such a case, to be sharing it, and I knew she felt the same, because without that connection between us there was bound to be a huge part of her world that I couldn't enter. But it was easier if I took two steps back. This was her life, not mine any more, and I couldn't pretend a place for me in it into existence.

Thus my role in the affair hadn't stretched so far beyond that of an interested spectator. Last few months I'd been writing regular updates on the case for an American crime monthly. The job paid peanuts but it kept me feeling like I was still in the loop, still had something to say. But even then we kept things separate, because she'd have been compromised if anything had appeared under my name which could be traced back to her. All I could write was what was in the public domain, so anything I did find out independently – like the fact that the Marxman always carefully picked up the empty shell casing that was ejected from the pistol on firing, which I'd learned from some young cop I'd buttonholed in a bar and spent a couple of hours pouring drink into, knowing he'd crack if I was patient – I'd had to make sure appeared elsewhere before I could use it.

And now here was Felix Berg threatening to blow apart those neat boundaries I'd erected between the two separate worlds.

As I sat there on the harbour wall, watching Dalton yell at the other cops whilst trying to belatedly secure a scene he'd been treating with contempt until a matter of minutes before – and meanwhile waiting for the car Dalton had ordered up to take me to the nearest police station to complete my statement, probably just to get rid of me before Fitzgerald arrived – I went back painstakingly over what Felix had said to me on the phone that night.

Someone is trying to kill me.

What had he known? What had he seen? Had he unwittingly peered into the dark that he had spoken of and seen the Marxman? Maybe even recognised the Marxman? That would certainly explain why someone might want him silenced, want him dead.

But why had he come to *me*?

And more importantly, how had the Marxman known where to find him tonight?

Chapter Five

It was 3 a.m. by the time I signed my statement at the station where Dalton had sent me to get me out of the way, and I was free to go. I tried asking what was going on out at Howth but the police around didn't know any more than I did. I tried calling Fitzgerald too, but she still wasn't answering her cellphone. Probably she was over at the scene. She had enough to do without wasting her time keeping me up to date anyway.

In the end I just picked up my car from the parking lot out back where it had been dropped off, which was something at least, then made my way back to my apartment on the seventh floor of an old converted warehouse off St Stephen's Green in the centre of the city, thought about making coffee, gave up, thought about Berg, then took a couple of sleeping pills, lay down on the couch and failed for a long time to sleep.

I must have dropped off eventually, because the next thing I knew my alarm was ringing and I was reaching over to switch it off before I realised it couldn't be my alarm because I wasn't in bed, and then the sound came again and I realised it was the intercom.

I stumbled off the couch to the door and pressed the button.

'Fitzgerald,' crackled a voice from the street below.

'Grace?'

'How many other Fitzgeralds do you know? Can I come up?'

'Of course you can come up,' I said. 'But where's your key?'

'I wanted to check you were awake first.'

'I am now,' I said, pondering the logic of waking someone up to find out if they were asleep, and buzzed her in.

By the time I'd found my own key and unlocked the door, the elevator door across the landing was already opening.

'You look like shit,' she said to me brightly as she stepped out.

And a good morning to you too, Chief Superintendent.

'Yeah, well, I didn't exactly have a great night,' I said.

'You're not the only one.'

But I couldn't help noticing, as she shuffled out of her coat, how great she looked however little sleep she must have got. Even with her long black hair tied up tight under control she couldn't disguise that great figure of hers, those dark eyes, the way she moved.

'I hear Dalton gave you a hard time,' she said.

'How'd you find out?'

'The officer who took you down—'

'Simpson.'

'Simpson, yeah. He's a friend of Boland, apparently.' She meant Sergeant Niall Boland, who worked alongside her in the murder squad, albeit at a fairly low level and destined to stay that way by all accounts. 'He called Boland from the station to tell him what had happened. Seems he felt bad about it. He'd heard you arguing with Dalton and suspected Dalton had crossed the line but couldn't say anything till he was sure he wasn't around.'

'Crossing the line's what he's best at.'

'Dalton's been having some problems,' agreed Fitzgerald tentatively. 'Things are changing too much and he doesn't like it. He's convinced we're freezing him out. Ever since the US trip it's been building up. Last night it just came to a head maybe.'

25

The US trip, I'd forgotten about that. After years of arguing and pitching and begging Fitzgerald had finally persuaded the head of the murder squad, Assistant Commissioner Brian Draker – a man who considered his real job to be playing golf with the Commissioner whilst simultaneously blowing off whichever time-serving paper-pusher happened to be clogging up the department of justice that month – to find the money to send some of the team on a new FBI-run training programme in the States.

A ten-week residency, the course was designed to train police officers in a series of situations from crime scene analysis to terrorism to serial murder. Sending officers there was meant to make the Dublin police department look more professional, not that that'd be too difficult, since they still had to contend with a public image of ramshackle incompetence and one of the lowest clear-up rates this side of Moscow; but cheap as the course was, it had still been a battle for Fitzgerald to squeeze the money out of Draker. Short of drawing lots, what was worse, there was no way of satisfying all the officers who wanted to take advantage of the course that the two places which were eventually agreed on had been fairly picked.

Fitzgerald, as head of investigation, was the one left to choose, and she'd passed over Dalton in favour of Sean Healy, who was, like Dalton, one of the most experienced of the squad but an altogether steadier, less prickly character. The second place had gone to Patrick Walsh, a young, ambitious police officer who'd been considered a good investment in the future since everyone in the DMP accepted he was going places. Including him.

They were good choices.

That Fitzgerald had left herself off the list – and I knew better than anyone how painful that decision had been for her – didn't make Dalton's fury any less incendiary or his paranoia any less intense, and he'd made no secret of either, spinning against Fitzgerald where he could in the department, stirring up disaffection amongst some of the other officers.

I could understand the reaction, I knew what it was like to be snubbed, but it had still been childish; it was time he got over the bruising it had caused to his delicate male ego, and I told her so. The hesitation before she answered was brief, but she did hesitate.

'Do you want me to pull him up on this?' she said.

Was she kidding? Nothing would make me happier than to see Dalton's balls nailed to the wall and him taking his rightful place in the unemployment line where I wouldn't have to deal any more with his sorry excuse for an attitude.

On the other hand – and shit, how I hated using those words – I knew how much Fitzgerald still needed him. He'd been in the murder squad nearly longer than anyone, had been there even before Fitzgerald was put in charge of all day-to-day murder enquiries, and she didn't have enough of that kind of experience around to throw it away. Dalton may have been an asshole, but he was an asshole who was good at his job. That made a difference.

'Forget it,' I forced myself to say eventually, and tried to suppress the annoyance I felt when I saw the relief in Fitzgerald's face. That was what happened when you belonged to an institution, when you were a part of it day in, day out. FBI, Dublin Metropolitan Police, Boy Scouts: didn't matter, you just ended up wanting a quiet life, no trouble, which meant you cut corners, made compromises. I'd have probably done the same in her place.

But that didn't mean I couldn't hate it when I saw it happening.

To hide my annoyance, I made my way through to the kitchen and started looking for coffee. Checked my appearance in the mirror briefly as I passed to see if Fitzgerald was right. I didn't look too bad, considering. It was only next to her I looked like shit.

But then most people did.

Still, I straightened my hair best I could. Made an effort.

'You want some breakfast?' I shot back.

'Breakfast? Do you know what time it is?'

I checked the window. The light was harsh and the noise of the traffic was rising up, horns blaring angrily. It could've been any time of day.

'Surprise me,' I said.

'It's gone three,' she said, regarding me critically with those dark eyes of hers. 'You must've been taking sleeping pills again.'

'Just a couple.'

'Why do you keep taking those things?'

'To help me sleep. That's what they do. That's why they're called sleeping pills.'

'You'd sleep better,' said Fitzgerald, 'if you had a healthier lifestyler—'

'Dined on organic yoghurt and did yoga, I know,' I interrupted her.

'You know I'm right.'

'Any fool can be right,' I said, opening the fridge door and kneeling down to take a look inside. 'The trick is knowing when it's better to be wrong. Christ, I really need to get something for the fridge.'

'What, apart from the six bottles of Bud and the out-of-date microwave curry?' she said. 'Here, I already anticipated that you'd have a problem.'

I looked up, and there she was handing me a paper bag and a carton of orange, cold, like it was straight from the fridge.

Which it was. Just not mine.

She must've picked it up on her way round. She knew me too well. A few months ago she'd turned up with one of those machines that squeeze juice for you, but I'd never got round to working out how to use it. Life's too short for clearing up orange peel was what I reckoned. If I lived up a mountain, sure, but what was the point of being thirty seconds from a hundred different stores if you still behaved like some survivalist in North Dakota, hunting and gathering your own food and drinking water from streams?

Drink the water from streams round here, anyhow, and you'd most likely wind up in hospital having your stomach pumped. And that's just the way I liked it. I'd never been one for roughing it.

I popped opened the orange and poured a glass, forgetting about coffee for now. Reached into the bag and took a bite straight out of a croissant.

'Are you going to tell me about last night?' she said.

'There's not much to tell,' I said, but I told her all the same.

About the call Felix had made to me.

About what he'd said about someone trying to kill him.

How I'd gone out there and waited and waited and got tired of waiting and then found him lying dead in the water.

She didn't interrupt; but when I finished she shook her head.

'Dammit, Saxon, the risks you take. He could've been anyone.'

'He wasn't.'

'You could've been killed.'

'I wasn't.'

'Not this time, no. But what about next time, and the time after that?'

'He said someone was trying to kill him.'

'And it seems like he was right. But just out of curiosity you walk out of here anyway whilst there's a killer running round the city taking pot shots at people?'

'There was something about what he said. About the way he said it. It intrigued me. Now? I don't know.' I stopped. My reasons for going to the lighthouse suddenly sounded weak even to me. I felt foolish. But then I'd been right. He did have something to say.

And now he'd never get the chance to say it.

29

'I guess there's no doubt,' I said, 'that it *was* Felix Berg in the water?'

'It was Felix all right,' said Fitzgerald. 'His sister came down to the mortuary to identify the body this morning. He lived with her, apparently, somewhere in Temple Bar.'

'How did she look?'

Fitzgerald considered the question.

'Kind of blank,' she said eventually. 'Cold. Face like a mask. Ice queen type. Not that I should complain. Anything's better than crying.'

It sounded callous, but I knew what she meant. I'd been in the same position when I was in the FBI and people came in to ID bodies. You find yourself just wishing they wouldn't make a scene because that makes things more difficult for *you*. It doesn't matter how many times it's happened or how much of that crap they give you about trauma counselling and the seven stages of grieving and how to guide victims' families through the gates, you still don't know how the hell you're supposed to help someone who's suffering like that. You just find yourself wishing they'd wait until they're home before breaking down.

So that it's not your problem.

'You get to talk to her?' I said.

'Briefly. She wasn't exactly in the mood for answering questions. All she said was that she left the house shortly after ten last night and didn't even know her brother was gone until the police turned up first thing.'

'Must've been a shock.'

'If it was, she wasn't giving anything away. The only thing she couldn't understand, she said, was what he was doing out there.' Fitzgerald paused, like she was wondering whether to tell me the next part. 'She was also asking about you,' she said at last.

'That's understandable,' I said. 'I found her brother's body. I was who he went out there to meet. It's only natural she'd want to talk to me. I'd want to talk to me too. I guess I should

30

go see her. Find the right words. You know how good I am at that. Not.'

I sensed a resistance in her to the suggestion.

'You don't think I should go,' I said.

'I just don't want you getting involved,' she said.

'I don't intend getting involved,' I said.

'Famous last words.'

Chapter Six

I meant what I said to Fitzgerald. I was only going to speak to Alice, I wasn't going to get involved. In retrospect I should have realised the dangers, like an alcoholic thinking one little drink won't hurt. One thing always leads to another.

All I can say is my intentions were pure.

Makes a change.

As soon as Fitzgerald had gone, I showered and changed. It didn't seem right to go and see a dead man's sister in the same clothes you were wearing when you found his body. Especially after spending the hours since sleeping in them.

Then it was down the stairs and out. Melt into the crowd. The only way to live.

The streets were full of people, drifting in and out of stores, laden down with bags. What did they buy so much of? Nothing that they needed, that much was for sure. It was just stuff to fill some emptiness inside them. Though what did I have to be so condescending about? We all need something to fill the emptiness. We all disappear into something.

With me, whether in the FBI or afterwards trying to scratch a career out of writing, it had always been work. Maybe that's why I'd been so keen to go round and see this Alice: to cover some emptiness of my own. The same emptiness that made me take refuge in sleeping pills. Still, I put it from my mind. Whatever. There's no point immersing yourself in something in order to stop self-doubt coming if you let it creep in anyway.

Besides, the city made it hard for me to feel down for long.

It's strange I have such a desire to live surrounded by people, thousands of people, when the truth is that I can't say I care for them much. What I need is the noise they make, the confusion, the carnival of aromas, that strange crackle like static against the skin that reminds you you're alive almost without you having to put in any of the effort. Dublin's a small city compared to places I'd lived before, and if it was ethnic diversity you wanted, the city as a global melting pot, then you'd be better off in Idaho. But things *were* getting better, the city was opening up slowly, and there was still that undeniable static when you walked.

The trick was to make sure you kept the right distance. That was a necessity which had caused enough problems for me in my personal life – someone was always wanting me to give away more of myself, and I'm just not the revealing type – but when it came to forging a relationship with a city, it worked just fine. We understood one another. We didn't get in each other's way. It worked just fine with Fitzgerald too. She understood my need for reticence. She didn't mistake what others saw as my apparent aloofness for a lack of caring.

I felt a little better as I made my way down through town. That was what mattered. Like I'd been kick-started into life again. Like I'd been gifted a day, or what was left of it.

By the time I'd reached Temple Bar, I felt almost human again.

A couple of centuries ago, Temple Bar was the centre for the city's lowlife, prostitutes and drunks and villains, and some might say it hadn't changed much except the villains now wore better labels on their clothes. Neglected and crumbling for decades, the area had since been turned over by the planners into affecting some pseudo-bohemian feel, like Covent Garden or Tribeca. The warehouses had been converted into expensive apartments for pretentious twenty- and thirty-somethings; the alleyways were filled with faux-ethnic shops, exotic restaurants, bars, galleries, small theatres, left-field cultural centres. Every artist in the city seemed to have at least one foot in the district, though the irony was that one toe was about all most could afford these days, few of the people who'd made the district what it was in the past years now being able to afford to live there.

It was never really my scene. Even though I'd made my living as a writer since leaving the FBI and coming (fleeing?) to Dublin, I'd never felt comfortable in those circles, still regarded them with suspicion – and the suspicion was mutual. Politics didn't help. Self-styled intellectuals in Dublin make your average New York liberal look like Howard Stern.

I'd always felt more comfortable with cops anyway, which no doubt explained how I'd fished up with Fitzgerald.

Like calling to like.

Felix Berg's place was right in the heart of Temple Bar and hard enough to find for those who didn't know what they were looking for. Maybe he liked it that way. Or *had* liked, I corrected myself. I had to weave through a maze of lanes before finding the low archway that led through a tunnel into the narrow cobbled street where Fitzgerald had told me he'd lived; and even then the door didn't have a nameplate on like the other doors, just a number nine and a buzzer.

It was a tall house, three or four storeys, it was hard to tell from the ground floor, and it looked empty. I don't know what I'd expected. Berg had been a pretty successful photo-grapher, from what Fitzgerald had told me earlier whilst I got ready, but he clearly didn't feel the need to put his wealth on show to prove it.

This was more the kind of place where you came to hide away.

I rang the bell.

No answer.

Rang again.

The same no answer.

That wasn't so surprising. If the press hadn't found out yet that it was Berg who'd been shot last night, they soon would. The DMP leaked worse than a beggar's tin roof. There was more chance of keeping a secret by broadcasting it on the nine o'clock news.

I suddenly realised that I should've called ahead to let his sister know I was coming, know who I *was* at least. It was just another example of how useless I was at doing the right thing, saying the right words. I shouldn't have come, I thought, and remembered as I did so that those were the same words I'd said to myself last night at the lighthouse.

Feeling my earlier positive mood start to dissipate, I stepped back and glanced up at the empty windows one last time to make sure no one was looking out, before turning to go—

Then I stopped.

There was a woman standing in the archway, staring at me. Dark hair pulled almost painfully tight into her scalp. Face drawn, hands clasping the collar of her coat nervously. There was something birdlike and fragile about her. Something . . . breakable. It unnerved me.

How long had she been there?

'Alice?' I said.

Chapter Seven

'You were there,' were her first words to me. There was the same trace of an accent there, but again it escaped me. 'Last night. The police told me. Can I ask you something?'

'Of course. That's why I'm here.'

'Were you sleeping with Felix?'

'No,' I said, and nearly laughed with surprise. It was the last question I'd expected. 'I'd never met your brother before. I didn't even know what he looked like.'

She didn't ask the obvious question, which was why then had I been meeting him alone in the middle of the night, and I wasn't sure I knew the answer to that myself any more. Instead her eyes still seemed to be searching me for signs that I was lying about my relationship with her brother.

For now, it seemed I had passed the test.

'You'd better come in,' she said.

Alice stepped out of the archway and brushed past me to the door, taking tiny steps like a dancer, like her shoes didn't quite fit. Something about her reminded me of the story of the little mermaid, whose every step on land felt like she was laying her bare feet on broken glass. I recalled Fitzgerald's description of her too. Face like a mask. It was that all right. She could have been anyone. Fitzgerald had told me Alice had some kind of career as an art critic, but she looked vaguely out of place in the more laid-back environs of Temple Bar, and I wondered if it had been her choice to live here or Felix's. His, I could only imagine.

She didn't look at me. Just fished out a key from her pocket, took a couple of tries to get it into the lock (was I making her nervous?), and finally pushed open the door and stepped inside to a narrow hallway with a flight of stairs at the far end leading up.

Without a word she began hurrying up them, taking off her coat and tossing it over the banister as she did so, and I had no choice but to step inside, close the door and follow.

At the top of the stairs the house opened out into one wide-open space with high windows at either end looking out on other houses and other windows with squashed slivers of sky between them. Floorboards and bare brick walls alike were painted white, and there was little furniture save for a few chairs, a couch, and one long refectory table of a sort monks might sit at, scattered with books and prints. There were no pictures hanging anywhere, nothing personal, only a single plain calendar covered with handwriting on the wall behind the long table. In fact I don't think I'd ever been in a house with less decoration.

Apart from mine.

'You want a drink?' said Alice with an unexpected brightness, breaking my concentration. 'I was going to have a brandy.'

She must have seen some apprehension in my face.

'Don't panic,' she said. 'I'm not going to get drunk and start weeping all over you. I always have a drink at this time of day. Helps concentrate the mind.'

'In that case, I'll join you,' I said, and I watched as she walked over to the table, moving aside some books, lifting a bottle and two glasses and pouring.

I hate brandy, that burn in the throat, but what was I going to do? Ask her to go and fetch me a decent malt whiskey instead?

'Sit down, won't you?' she said over her shoulder, and I did, but I felt awkward. Was this the point when I was meant to say how sorry I was? I'd never been good at that.

Breaking the news to someone that their loved one had died was different, there was a point to such exchanges, some focus to hone in on. This just felt like ritual, and I couldn't do it.

'How did you find out?' I said clumsily instead as she carried back the drinks, hands steady as a bomb disposal expert, and passed one to me before taking a chair opposite.

'About Felix?'

What else?

'There was a knock about six. I left it for Felix to answer. He was always up first, he liked the mornings, and I'd come in late last night. I was tired. But the knocking went on and on. Eventually I had to go down and answer it. It was a policeman. He asked me if I was Alice Berg. The rest,' she smiled and took a sip of her drink, 'is history. *His* story, literally. Even if we have now come to The End.' She gave a faint testing smile. 'Have I offended you?' But she didn't wait for an answer. 'Forgive me if I have. That's what Felix and I were like. Tough as stones. We weren't sentimental. That was always our way since we were children. No point changing now. There is nothing so dark that it can't be laughed at, wouldn't you agree? Nothing so terrible that it can't be mocked.'

'It's a good creed.'

'I wouldn't call it a creed,' she said with a shrug. 'But we'd been through a lot, my brother and I. We realised long ago that there was nothing life could throw at us that we couldn't overcome, that we couldn't defeat. We faced everything together. Until last night. I didn't even realise he was going out, you know. I didn't go out myself until after nine and he was still in the house then. He said goodnight. Everything was ordinary.'

I wanted to ask where she'd gone and what time she'd got back, then realised I was thinking like an investigator again, not the concerned bystander I was meant to be.

I'd have to watch myself.

As it was, Alice saved me from wondering what to say next anyway.

'The policewoman, the Chief Superintendent, told me it was quick at least,' she said.

That's what the police always say to the victim's family, whether it's true or not, because that's what any victim's family wants to hear. Quick, however, can be a grimly relative concept when it comes to death. In Felix's case, it probably had been. According to Fitzgerald, Felix had been shot through the eye, and there was a powder burn on the eye socket showing that the gun had been placed against the skin when it was fired.

It would have been quick enough.

Besides, I figured Alice wouldn't be up for a lecture on estimating survival rates for a brain with a bullet in it, so I contented myself with nodding dumb agreement.

'At least that's something,' she said. 'I wouldn't have wanted him to suffer. What I don't understand is why *you* were there meeting a man you insist you didn't even know.'

'Did the police not tell you anything?'

'They said something about . . . you wanted to tell him something, is that right?'

She didn't exactly sound convinced.

Put like that, who would be?

'It was the other way round,' I said. 'He wanted to talk to me. He called me last night. He said' – I steeled myself for the hard part – 'that someone was trying to kill him.'

I was relieved that the words sounded nowhere near as implausible as I'd feared.

'He said the same thing to me,' she admitted quietly. 'My response was to reassure him that everything was fine, that he had nothing to worry about. I thought he was imagining things. Felix could be . . . sensitive. Then the police knock on the door and tell me he's dead.'

'And now you think maybe he'd been telling the truth all along?'

'And I hadn't listened,' she said. 'Yes.'

She stared at the light on the wall, dancing, fractured.

'Do you have any idea why someone would want to kill him?' I asked tentatively.

Her face remained unreadable.

'Wait here,' she said, and she rose and went to the stairs.

I heard her footsteps crossing the bare floorboards above my head from one side of the room to the other and then back again. She had something in her hands, I saw when she returned. A clear plastic folder. She handed it to me and sat down to watch as I opened it.

I shook out the sheets of paper inside on to the couch.

They were press clippings dating back to January, when the Marxman killings began, all variations on a theme.

Victim Slain In City Street.

Marxman Claims Another Victim.

No Witnesses As Marxman Evades Police Again.

Newspapers rarely try to break bad news gently.

In each report, the name of the street where the victim had died had been underlined in stark red ink. There were psychological profiles of the killer too, from some of the quality newspapers, and magazine cuttings, one from one of the Sundays speculating that the killer was a professional hitman who had gone insane and was now doing the job for pleasure rather than money – like it was better to kill as a profession rather than a hobby; like hitmen never took the same pleasure from their work as freelance killers; like it made any difference to the victims or their families. And here too, at the bottom of the pile, were my own articles from the American magazine, stapled together in order.

'This is quite a collection,' I said. 'What did the police make of it?'

'They haven't seen it.'

'You didn't show it to them?'

'They didn't ask,' said Alice. She looked puzzled. 'I

suppose I wasn't thinking too clearly. I was just thinking about Felix . . .' She trailed off.

'You're showing them to me,' I pointed out.

'I'm trying to be honest with you. I have nothing to lose. Felix was obsessed by the killings, right from the start. He taped the news programmes whenever there was another killing and played them back constantly. Bought all the newspapers. Trawled the Net for details. He was always interested in crime, in murder, from a little boy. He read widely about the subject. He said the way to understand a city was to look at how the people in it killed one another. Have you ever heard of Weegee?'

I shook my head.

'He was a photographer. Austrian, originally. His real name was Usher Fellig. He worked in Manhattan in the 1930s for the news agencies, bringing back pictures of things that happened in the city each night, murders mainly. He had a police radio in his car so that he could get to the scene at the same time as the police. Quicker sometimes. Felix was a great admirer of his work. He said that was the way to understand a city. That was where its true nature could be appreciated. And he always wanted to understand what life in the city was about. But with these killings there was something different. He was just consumed by them, and the longer they went on, the more obsessed he became.'

'How did you feel about that?'

'I was worried for him. Felix was not' – she rummaged for the right word – 'always well. I feared he might be pushing himself too hard, working too much; sometimes he rarely slept for weeks on end. I thought he might have a breakdown. He'd had one before. At the time I thought he'd never recover. I feared this was tipping him over the edge again, and I didn't want to indulge that side of him. I didn't want to encourage it. I ignored it. But—'

I finished the sentence for her. 'The Marxman didn't.'

She nodded numbly.

41

'And now you think he knew something and that's why he was killed? Did he ever say straight out that he had information about what was happening?'

'No.'

'Could he have told someone else?'

'Felix wasn't like that. He hardly knew anyone.'

'There must have been others. Friends, lovers, other photographers. If I could talk to them, or if the police could—'

'There was no one.'

'Not even a girlfriend?'

'We had each other. It was all we needed,' Alice insisted flatly. 'That's why I don't understand why he called you. You say you'd never met before. How can you even be sure that it *was* my brother?'

'How can I be sure it was him who called?' I said. 'I guess I can't be. Not totally. I'd never spoken to him before. All I got was a call to my apartment last night. I went to the lighthouse like the caller asked. I waited. I was cold. He didn't show. I was irritated. Thought he'd been wasting my time. I was about to give up and leave when I found him.'

'His body,' she said, whispering the word with something near embarrassment.

'I had no reason to doubt it was him I was talking to,' I said. 'If you have a tape somewhere of his voice, perhaps I could . . .' But she was shaking her head already, whether because she didn't have a tape or because she didn't want me to hear it, I couldn't tell. 'What makes you think,' I said carefully, 'that it *mightn't* have been your brother who called me?'

'Oh, nothing at all,' she said with sudden agitation. 'Nothing except that it doesn't make any kind of sense, that's all. Felix never said anything to me about meeting you.'

'I got the idea it was something he wanted to keep to himself.'

'Look.' She put her glass down heavily and spoke as if explaining to an idiot how a light switch worked. 'As I told

42

you already, Felix didn't keep anything to himself. He didn't have a private life. A *secret* life. I did everything for him. Everything. I kept this house going. I made all his phone calls. Handled all his money. I made the deals; I chased up all the payments from dealers, buyers, galleries; I paid all the bills, made sure he had enough cash in his wallet when he went out. I was the one who knew where everything was when it was needed. I was the one who made his appointments. All of them.' She gestured towards the calendar I'd seen earlier on the wall. 'Sometimes I practically had to write down what he had to do each day on the back of his hand so he wouldn't forget. He was an artist, a very great one I happen to believe, so I never objected. But he couldn't do a thing without me. If he needed to be some-where, it was me who booked the flights, made all the hotel reservations; if I couldn't be there with him, I made sure he had lists of all the places he needed to go, places to eat. That was just the way things were. Felix and I were more than just brother and sister. We were two parts of the same person. The idea that there was something he wasn't telling me . . . something he could only discuss with *you* . . . well, it's nonsense.'

And her voice made it clear this wasn't something she intended discussing further.

'You know you'll have to tell the police about all this?' I said to change the subject, indicating the cuttings that were now scattered across the couch. 'About Felix's obsession?'

'I couldn't face them again,' she said. 'Going down to identify his body was bad enough. I just had to tell myself that it wasn't him, that *he'd* gone, this was only a body. I could bear it that way. I know it's a lot to ask, but would you do it for me? Just take all this stuff with you. I don't want it in the house. Give it to the police.'

'If that's what you want—'

'It is.'

43

I reached out and began to gather Felix's collection together, and as I did so something slipped between the sheets and fluttered to the ground.

I bent to pick it up.

It was a photograph, not a print like those scattered across the refectory table, but an ordinary snapshot showing . . . yes, the lighthouse in Howth. It was taken from quite far away, but it was just about possible to see that there was a figure standing before the red door.

The figure of a man.

'What's that?'

'It fell out of Felix's papers,' I said, and handed it to her. 'Did he take this?'

'He couldn't have done,' she said firmly. 'This is just an ordinary Polaroid. You can tell by looking at it. It comes from one of those cameras where each print comes out after you've taken it. Felix didn't have a camera like that. And anyway—'

'What?'

'I think this is Felix. It's hard to tell, it's so far away, but it looks like him. There, you can see a glint on the face like glasses. It couldn't be a recent shot, though. He hadn't worn his hair long like that since he went to the States.'

'You ever see the picture before?'

She shook her head.

So where did Felix get it?

Chapter Eight

One thing I knew. If I was going to get anywhere with this, I needed to find out more about Felix. Find out *anything* about him. And I knew just where to start.

Thaddeus Burke knew everything.

Which was to say, everything that was worth knowing.

He was an American too, which engendered a certain solidarity in a town that wasn't always sympathetic to Americans, and a former Marine to boot, not to mention a committed communist – a fact he'd wisely kept hidden from his commanding officers for over thirty years, not least through three tours of duty in Vietnam, where he'd been decorated for valour and mentioned in numerous dispatches. All of which I only knew because his former colleagues had whispered the details to me one night when we were drinking and he was out of earshot, not a word about his military career ever having passed his lips in my presence.

He got his name from his father – most people did – a poor man who'd left Dublin sometime in the early 1940s for New York and somehow managed to only get poorer and drink more than he'd ever done back home, leaving his son with nothing to remember him by except a bunch of old tales about the old town – which was how a black former Marine (his mother had come from Louisiana originally and had washed up in her turn on the Lower East Side, where she met Thaddeus's father) wound up in Dublin in his fifties after bagging an honourable discharge and casting off his former life like a snake shedding its skin.

Here he now ran a precarious business in a second-hand bookstore down by the quays, together with some bedraggled stray cat which had dragged itself in the back door one night when it was raining hard and which he called Hare, hence the name of the store: Burke and Hare's, so-called, he told me, after a pair of infamous bodysnatchers of the nineteenth century.

Whether Burke ever sold any books was still a matter of debate. He had fewer customers than a teetotal bar, which was what left him so much time for reading anything and everything he could get his hands on, and that seemed to be just the way he liked it. The only times I ever saw him we were generally sitting playing poker and drinking his coffee or, if I was lucky, his Scotch; someone's else's Scotch always tastes better. He seemed to pick up stray people the way he picked up the cat, or perhaps the way other people collect stamps or first editions or animal skulls, like we were specimens. He was a sucker for a hard-luck story and never seemed to turn away anyone who just wanted to talk or waste his time.

'Time I got,' he used to say. 'Money I not.'

And wasn't likely to get any either, since he specialised in stocking books the other stores didn't bother to carry, mainly because no one wanted to read them, together with more tracts of communist history and theory than even Fidel Castro would've ever wanted to read. And I rarely saw Burke reading them either. It meant he had plenty of time for poker, mind, and the place was as empty as usual when I finally arrived that afternoon after Alice's.

Closing-up time was near.

'Felix Berg?' he said when I told him what I was looking for. 'You suddenly develop an interest in photography, Saxon? You starting to take pictures?'

'Only if you let me take some nice soft-focus shots of you

46

laid out on the rug there, Burke, the way God and Karl Marx intended you to be.'

'My folks used to have some just like it up on the fireplace when I was six months old,' he said. 'What you need the updates for?'

'You not changed much since then?'

'Lost most of my looks. That's about it.'

'I don't believe it. You saying you used to be even cuter than you are now?'

He laughed, but he wasn't letting me out of it that easy.

'You be serious now. What's the deal?'

It was impossible to feign casual with Burke.

'There was a body found out at Howth.'

'I heard it on the lunchtime news. Our friend the Marxman striking again. At this rate, even I'll be packing my bags and heading for the hills. What about it?'

'That was Berg.'

I didn't mention my own part in the story for now.

'Is that right?' Burke seemed genuinely taken aback, enough so's he didn't press me when it must've been obvious I was keeping something back. 'I know his sister, you know. She comes in here sometimes looking for rare books. Out-of-print stuff. Smart lady.'

'You didn't know him?'

'No one knew Felix Berg.'

'Loner?'

'And then some. Hardly went out at all from what I heard. Not socially anyway. Recluse with a capital R. He certainly never came in here. Some people called them the Ice Bergs, they were that cold.'

'You have his books though, right?'

'If I do, they'll be back here somewheres. You just hold on now while I look.'

It was as well I'd come round now, Burke called through to me from the back of the store whilst he searched for what I wanted. If I'd waited till morning when news of Berg's death had had time to filter through to the newspapers, there wouldn't be a copy to be had in town.

'Death always does wonders for an author's sales,' he said.

'Maybe I should try it,' I said as he came back into view with a great white square of a book wedged in his huge Marine's hands. Though they always looked as though they were too clumsy for books, those hands always treated them like glass.

He laid it flat on the table.

The book was called *Unreal City*.

'T.S. Eliot,' Burke explained. '*The Waste Land*. You ever read it?'

'I've not had the pleasure, no.'

'Don't mock what you don't understand. You *should* read it,' Burke said. 'There's bound to be a copy round here someplace if you want me to add it to your tab. Eliot was a poet. He came from your neighbourhood. Boston. And he ran away from it like you too.'

'To Dublin?'

'No.'

'Then at least one of us had some sense.'

Burke smiled. 'Berg brought out three books,' he said, 'but the first two are out of print. This is the most recent. I could try tracking down copies of the others if you want?'

'I'll let you know. I'll just take a look at this first. And at these rates,' I added, catching a glimpse of the price on the inside cover, 'I think I'll pass. There are Third World countries with a smaller GDP than what he's charging for this. I don't think my credit card could cope with buying three.'

'That,' said Burke, 'is the global money market for you.'

'And as I have told you on plenty of occasions before,' I said, 'if you start preaching your pinko politics at me, I'll turn right round and walk out of here and you won't see me again this side of your damned revolution.'

'You'd be back. You know I'm right. I'll make a convert of you yet.'

48

'I told you, I got nothing to wear that goes with barricades. And you should be more careful what you say. You don't want Sweeney back here busting your balls.'

Burke had been graced by a visit a few weeks back from Paddy Sweeney when the anti-terrorist supremo was fishing for any little wriggling sardine to back up his theory that the Marxman was some leftist agitator on a mission. An outsider with a taste for Marx plus a history of familiarity with weapons, Burke was bound to beep on someone's radar eventually.

I often regretted I'd missed the encounter.

Suffice to say, Sweeney never came back.

Right now, I turned the book over and checked out the picture of Felix on the back.

It was the first time I'd seen him.

First time I'd seen him alive, that is.

First time I'd seen his face.

He wasn't smiling. He had a reedy, anxious, nervy, slightly feminine look about him. His hair, as fair as Alice's was dark, was long and needed combing. His eyes were squinting slightly through his glasses. He looked so young, he *was* young, but he looked younger still than his years. What was he when he died? Mid thirties? Yet even at that, it didn't seem like his face was ready to settle down into familiarity. It was too changeable. He had the sort of face that a particular mood could transform into something potentially unrecognisable.

I turned the book over again quickly, trying not to think about the sight of his body displayed so grotesquely among the rocks, the tide tickling his naked senseless feet.

It was hard to think of the man who had made this book ending up like that.

Murdered.

When I looked up, I realised Burke was watching me.

'Did you know this guy?' he said.

'I didn't know him, no. At least . . . it was me who found the body.'

'I get it,' said Burke. 'Look, you sit down there and take a look and I'll go get us some coffee. Forget the time. There's plenty of things I can be getting on with back here—'

'No, Burke, honestly. I appreciate it,' I said, 'really I do; but I think I'm just going to take this home and look at it there.'

'You're the boss.'

But he seemed sorry to let me go. There was his mother hen instinct again. He wanted to make sure I was OK.

It was only when I was halfway home that I realised I hadn't even paid for the book.

Was it any wonder Burke never made any money?

Chapter Nine

Once I got home, I ordered a pizza. When it came, I took it and the book out on to my balcony overlooking St Stephen's Green, Central Park's midget brother in the heart of Dublin, locked now after hours, and watched taxis pulling up outside the hotels and restaurants which ringed the green, bags being hefted up the steps, couples standing round outside glancing at menus, tourists taking a ride in the early evening sunshine on the horses and carts that worked the surrounding district, listening to the clatter of hoofs drifting up from the street.

Thought of Fitzgerald too. Tonight she'd told me she was going to visit her mother. Her mother lived someplace quiet about forty minutes out of town. Fitzgerald went to see her once a week and always came home feeling both shitty and exploited, laden with guilt at the constant criticism she had to endure from the sour witch. *Why d'you never call? Why do I never see you?* She wasn't even that old. There was nothing wrong with her, but that didn't stop her manufacturing illnesses like she was stocking them up in case of shortages later. Fitzgerald had tried taking me out there a couple of times, but it had always ended with her mother getting upset. She found it hard to accept that Grace wasn't going to get married and start producing grandchildren. She was her only child. She said she feared a lonely old age.

I wished I had more sympathy for her, but in truth she just irritated me. Griping wouldn't change one atom of the world, and I could see in her glances at me that she knew it well enough. She just wanted to punish Grace by sowing misery and weeds in her path.

I escaped from the thought of her into Felix's book, opening it on my lap.

First thing I did was read the brief biography of him at the front (there was some critical essay printed there too, but I didn't feel up to tackling that just yet).

Berg, it seemed, had been born in Stockholm, which explained the accent if nothing else. Swedish father, mother from Dublin; in looks, Felix and Alice had obviously taken after different parents, dark and light sides of the same moon. Both parents had died in a car crash when the children were still young, Alice, the elder, only twelve, Felix ten, whereupon they'd been bundled back from Stockholm to Dublin to be brought up by an elderly aunt from an obscure branch of the family in a crumbling pile out in Howth.

Felix was educated at some exclusive college in Dublin, then went on to study photography at St Martin's School of Art in London, before moving back to Dublin fifteen years ago. He'd been based here ever since. Never married, or if he had, he didn't want the private details printed all over his books. Never gave interviews.

He was also, as I'd discovered already, rarely photographed, not even by his sister, who, it seemed, was a talented photographer in her own right (she'd taken the shot at the back of this latest book), albeit that she now worked mainly as a critic, writing for various journals and academic quarterlies, turning up on TV and radio as a talking-head pundit on culture. She had also published a number of books, including ones on the American photographer August Sanders and another exploring modern theory on the use of optical and photographic effects by painters from Rembrandt to Hockney. It was all way above my head.

Felix had exhibited widely round the world: New York, San Francisco, Copenhagen, Barcelona, Munich, St

Petersburg, Sydney, you name it; and only ever in solo exhibitions. Even as a student, it seemed, he'd refused to allow his work to be exhibited alongside that of his contemporaries. He'd won numerous awards and his work had been bought by such venerable institutions as the Museum of International Contemporary Art in Brazil, the Pace/Magill Gallery in New York, the Irish Centre for Photography, as well as by private collectors in the US, London, Mexico and the Far East. The originals of his work now commanded huge prices and he was fast becoming one of the most collectable of modern photographers, not least because he refused to sell much of his work, and had recently even expended a deal of effort and money trying to buy back what he'd sold in his early years, maybe because he agreed with the critics who'd denounced that early work as violent and semi-pornographic, criticisms which had led him for a time into extended silence.

Frankly, it was another world to me. It made my head ache. But then I'd never had much time for art. I never had the patience for digging through the multiple levels of obfuscation to find whatever fragments of possible meaning were hidden within.

Same with poetry. Life's too short.

But all my doubts and cynicism faded when I finally finished the biography and just looked at the photographs. Meaning ceased to matter. The purity of the image was everything. They were unutterably beautiful and it was easy to see why these photographs had brought him such renown. All my smartass cynicism about art dissolved to nothing in their presence.

On the title page there was an epigraph in French from Baudelaire: *Fourmillante cité, cité pleine de rêves/ Où le spectre en plein jour raccroche le passant!* – thankfully with a translation below, since I don't speak French (the French seem determined to pretend to live in a world where Americans don't exist or matter, and I'm happy to reciprocate).

Swarming city, city full of dreams, where a ghost in daylight clutches a passer-by!

That summed up perfectly what Berg had tried to portray in his photographs.

They were cityscapes mainly, street scenes, shot in black and white, but with occasional splashes of colour for effect or contrast. And they were cities I knew well, or thought I'd known well before then. Dublin, naturally, and London, but also New York, Berlin, Venice, even a couple of my own home town of Boston. He'd taken one shot of Union Bridge, where I'd worked as a waitress when I was in college. Even so, he made them all seem alien; refracted through his lens, his eye, these familiar spaces became unrecognisable, sinister, so that it was only when I looked at the accompanying titles and captions and notes that I was able to place them at all.

And what made them stranger still were the figures that inhabited them.

I say figures rather than men and women, because that's what they were. It was impossible to distinguish one from another, impossible to think of them as real at all. He had taken multiple shots of the same street at different times of day and night and then superimposed the pictures over one another endlessly until one would lose count and there was layer upon layer of these strange figures inhabiting the same space, getting in each other's way, but always unaware of one another's very presence, until the image became so faded and crowded that the figures were insubstantial as phantoms – ghosts in daylight clutching at passers-by – and you could see the stones of the city through their bones and skin.

The photographs were simultaneously tranquil and hectic. On one level, the city itself became the only reality, the still point in the turning world, and on another level my head ached with the multiplicity of images, presences, lives, all clashing and conflicting with one another in a mad claustrophobia which made you realise as you looked at them how crowded and insane a city was, how lives jostled and ground

54

against one another without ceasing, even when they were unaware of doing so, and how nothing was ever really your own, everything had been claimed before, everywhere had been occupied and reoccupied repeatedly.

You were just there on sufferance till the next person took your place, and the next one took their place, and the next theirs, in endless disconnected uncaring succession.

I sat and looked at the photographs so long that the light faded into darkness, and I needed the light through the window behind me to see; but no matter how often I looked at them, I still saw something curious and miraculous, and I almost forgot I was only looking at them now because Berg was dead. The vividness of what I saw here made that idea seem absurd.

Only when I'd been through the book a score of times did I get round to tackling the essay at the front, and here finally was something truly indecipherable. Felix's images spoke with the clarity of a single pure note struck in the middle of a tuneless cacophony; seeing them was like walking out of an airless room into an open space on top of a mountain, where the air was sharp as frost. But in the essay – written, I noted, by someone called Vincent Strange – all the layers of obfuscation had been replaced on top, separating Berg's work again from the watcher and putting it back protectively into the hands of the critics, the *experts*, where it could remain unsullied by popularity. I had little time for these academic games.

Vincent Strange, though, took bullshit to a whole new level.

'Berg's exercises in existential rage,' he wrote, 'his unceasing revolt against self and society, remind one repeatedly not to take anything for granted, that what one sees is not always what is there. Reality is contingent, fluid. Nothing can be relied upon. The world is subject to constant revision. What is there is suddenly not there. What is black is white. What is he saying? That the world cannot be trusted and no one in it.'

55

The author related all this back to Felix's childhood, particularly the early loss of his parents. There was the supreme example to any child of the world suddenly proving to be less reliable, less trustworthy than they might have assumed they had a right to expect.

I wasn't particularly impressed by that automatic equation between personal history and creative endeavour. It was too trite, too reliant on the instant easy answers peddled by quack psychologists. Too often I'd dealt with killers who'd been released early from prison by the same breed of false prophets who declared their patients 'cured' of whatever it was that had afflicted them, only for them to kill again, worse again.

If they couldn't even get that right, why should they expect to be listened to when they pronounced on other complex matters of motivation? Everything was guesswork where the human mind was concerned, for all that they pretended it was science.

I guess it was just a relief to see they weren't the only ones, that art critics made the same grandiose assumptions without having the first idea what they were talking about.

Chapter Ten

Early morning found me checking out the morning editions. Felix Berg's death had made the front pages, naturally enough, of all the Dublin papers, most of the main ones out of London, and a fair few of the international editions too. My name, I was glad to see, had been kept out of it for the present, but the press had happily seized the opportunity to print once more the gratuitous details about the Marxman's previous killings, as if the public in Dublin was not nervous enough. This was still something that was happening to other people, people they knew only as names in newspapers, it was still not affecting ordinary folk in the city directly – but with each killing the sense of dread only seemed to creep closer, become more real.

As it was, the reports I read that morning told me little that I didn't know already from the biography at the front of *Unreal City*, and what I hadn't known was only dates and details and more of the same posturing affectation from critics as I'd endured last night.

Only two facts were new to me, though both were interesting. The first was that Felix had been hospitalised about a year ago after being assaulted and robbed whilst working one night. There was nothing so unusual about that. I knew from talking to press snappers that it was a dangerous business, taking pictures in the street, especially at night. There's always some junkie going to be attracted by the lure of all that expensive equipment, not to mention the drunks and thugs just looking for someone making themselves conspicuous with whom to pick a fight. He was hit on the head, suffered a fractured skull, severe concussion. Doctors said he was lucky to survive, though not any more he wasn't, I reflected grimly.

Could this be a sign that someone had had a vendetta against Felix?

The other fact I hadn't known was that there was currently an exhibition of Berg's latest photographs at the Irish Museum of Modern Art, housed out in an old building in Kilmainham known as the Royal Hospital. It had been running since New Year's Day and featured pictures taken in the city since his return from America last fall. I would have liked to head out to the exhibition straight away, partly in search of some further insight into Felix's recent state of mind, and partly too, if I was honest, just because I wanted to look at those photographs. See what he'd been working on since *Unreal City*. His photographs had dug themselves into my consciousness. Even this morning, I hadn't been able to help seeing the city through his eyes. Jostling. Crazy.

Intolerable.

But I had other plans. I was going to call in on Tom Kiernan. I called on my cellphone on the way down the stairs, and his assistant told me he was out at breakfast.

Did I want to call back later?

No, I knew where to find him.

Kiernan was infamous for always eating breakfast at a café round the corner from murder squad headquarters in Dublin Castle that was so bad the food safety officials always came to inspect it in decontamination overalls borrowed from forensics. Even the beat cops wouldn't eat there, and they were the kind who'd have eaten at Jeffrey Dahmer's diner if they were hungry enough. Everything on the menu had been dead longer than Lincoln and deep-fried until any resemblance to food as it was normally understood was purely coincidental.

*Im*purely coincidental, I should say.

'Company,' he said brightly when he saw me coming in. 'Can I treat you to breakfast?'

'Is this what you call breakfast?' I said, nodding at his plate.

'What do you call it?' he said.

'An indictable offence under all known hygiene regulations,' I said. 'But don't let me put you off.'

'You haven't,' he said, and took another bite.

I tried not to look. His plate was like a slaughterhouse. Grease had settled thickly over it like sludge on a carpet after a flood. They must use pneumatic drills in the kitchen to get the plates clean. If they ever bothered cleaning them at all.

Fitzgerald should try coming here before she passed judgement on my diet.

Then again, when you spent the day looking at what Kiernan looked at, it was unlikely that the prospect of an occasional bout of food poisoning would put you off.

Kiernan was a photographer, but his shots never wound up hanging in galleries in Temple Bar, since he worked for the DMP, specialising in what he told those who asked was 'intimate portraiture of the recently deceased', which was generally enough to make them stop asking for more details. Like all police photographers, he spent his days surrounded by images which, were they found in the possession of an ordinary citizen, would be considered grounds either for immediate arrest or at best a committal to a secure institution.

Like all police photographers too, he also constantly expressed a desire to leave it all behind and spend his days taking pretty wide-angle shots of the sun going down over Dublin Bay, and sleeping kittens; though I didn't believe it, any more than I'd believed it of all the others I'd known before him. He was driven by a determination to track down the screwballs who provided him with a livelihood as fierce as that of any police officer.

Not to mention that his professional pride probably wouldn't allow him to step aside and let the next generation take over. He was, after all, very good at what he did.

Which was why I was here now.

I'd come into contact with Kiernan first because he did an occasional sideline in photographs of the living – though he was forced to charge more for those, he said, since the subjects were invariably more difficult to handle than he was used to, and sometimes even insisted on drawing him into conversation, which he considered a waste of his time. He'd taken a shot for the flap of one of my books. And if I'd known then what I knew now about his diet, I'd probably have asked for another photographer, to avoid the risk of Kiernan's arteries exploding during the photoshoot and me having to go through it all again.

I hated having my picture taken.

'You've got that look in your eye,' he said as I sat down opposite him this morning, trying not to touch anything in case the stain never came off again.

'What look?'

'The look that says you want something. Is it my body?'

'Afraid not. I'm leaving that pleasure to the rest of the women of Dublin.'

'It's a tough job,' he said, 'but someone's got to do it. I just wish it was me sometimes. My love life's about as successful as the tip I got from Healy yesterday.'

'What is it with the murder squad and women? You've got almost as many failed relationships behind you as Zsa Zsa Gabor. Boland's divorced. I hear Walsh hits on anything in a skirt. Dalton will never be able to keep a woman unless he builds a cage for her in his cellar – and I wouldn't put it past him.'

'That's where you're wrong,' said Kiernan. 'Sergeant Boland has a new lady friend, last I heard. And I for one hope it works out and they get married so that I can make a few extra shillings from the wedding photos.'

'There's no such thing as shillings any more.'

'You're telling me. Nothing stays the same.'

I was silent for a moment, thinking about Kiernan's news. It just proved to me how little I saw Sergeant Niall Boland these days. We'd worked together on a case when he'd first joined the murder squad and I'd got to know him pretty well. Liked him too, though he had the kind of taking-it-easy approach to policing that was guaranteed to get me kicking the furniture. Now I couldn't remember the last time I'd seen him around. That was what came of me keeping myself to myself these days. I should give him a call.

'What is it you want, anyway?' said Kiernan.

'I have a Polaroid of someone. I want to know who it is. Any suggestions?'

'Ask the photographer?'

'Ordinarily I would. Only problem in this case is he might be dead.'

'Bit tricky,' acknowledged Kiernan. 'Are we talking about the illustrious Felix Berg?'

'Might be. Did you know him?'

'Knew his work.' Kiernan shrugged. 'Not bad if you like that la-di-da vibe.'

'I should have known better than to expect one photographer to have a good word to say about another one.'

'Is the caped-crusading crimefighting world any different?'

'I guess not.'

'There you are then.'

I took the photograph I'd discovered in Felix's papers out of my pocket and handed it across the table to him. He wiped his hand on his pants before taking it from me.

Manners maketh man, don't they say?

'Is this it?' said Kiernan. 'Well, I think I could do something with it maybe. Scan it into the computer and fiddle about with the focus and the filters and the light.'

'That's all very interesting, I'm sure, but I don't want a

lesson in your professional technique, Kiernan. Can you do it? That's all I want to know.'

'Of course I can do it. You know your problem? You think we're still all cavemen age here. I know this ain't Quantico, Special Agent, but we have been known to have access to some of the benefits of modern technology. Hell, we even have electricity sometimes when the Chief remembers to put up the lightning rod round the back of Dublin Castle.'

I smiled. I guess I asked for it sometimes.

'In fact,' he said, 'are you doing anything right now?'

'Apart from getting ready to throw up after watching you eat that crap? No.'

'Then let's see if I can't sneak you back to my lab and lock the door behind us, get the secretaries gossiping about me for once, and see what we can do. What do you say?'

'Point the way, big boy. I'm all yours.'

Chapter Eleven

'He said the trick was,' I told Fitzgerald, 'to blow the photograph up as far as he could—'

'Who's he?'

'Tom Kiernan.'

'You've been borrowing my crime scene photographer?'

'He said he wasn't busy. Are you listening? He said the trick was to blow the picture up without losing the focus of it altogether. Don't go far enough and the image remains indistinct, go too far and it collapses into splodges and splurts. I don't know how he did it. You know what I'm like with technology. There's no way I'd get into the FBI these days, recruits all need skills I haven't got. Proficiency in a foreign language. Computer science. Information technology. Military experience. I'd be flipping burgers for a living.'

'The burger world's loss is crimefighting's gain,' said Fitzgerald wryly.

We were sitting in her office at Dublin Castle. Rooftops dissected the sky outside her window and the day was clear. A half-bright sunlight was striking off the edge of the table.

I could almost believe springtime was right round the corner today.

She'd sent for coffee, but it must have been coming via Colombia because it looked like there was less chance of it putting in an appearance than the Assistant Commissioner at a crime scene.

'I'm just telling you what he had to do to the photograph to make the image come out,' I said. 'This was the best he could do.'

I tossed the printout Kiernan had given me half an hour ago across her desk.

Fitzgerald picked it up and gazed at it.

'It looks like Felix,' she said.

'It is Felix. At least, I'd be ninety per cent sure it's Felix. Enough to stake my left leg on it, but then I've always been the gambling type.'

'I'd stake your left leg on it too,' Fitzgerald said. 'But what of it?'

'Only that this shows he might've been being watched. Followed. And that he knew it.'

'It proves nothing of the sort, as you well know. It's only a photograph. The fact that someone other than Felix took it is irrelevant.'

'Even if it was the Marxman?' I said.

'It wasn't the Marxman.'

'How can you be so sure?'

I couldn't understand why she was so resistant to exploring a possible link here after all the frustration she'd endured on the investigation to date.

I thought she'd have been pleased with my help.

'Because of this.' She picked up a folder that had been sitting face down on her desk and tossed it across the table. 'It came this afternoon. It's the autopsy report on Felix Berg.'

I picked it up, peeled back the cover.

Scanned through it quickly.

I didn't need to wade through all the details of the toxicology readings and blood samples and analysis of the stomach contents. I read out the only part that mattered.

'*Death by self-inflicted gunshot wound.*'

I could hardly believe what I was seeing. According to Alastair Butler, the City Pathologist, the only possible verdict was that Felix had placed the gun to his own eye and fired the trigger. The angles were all correct for a self-inflicted injury. He had gunshot propellant residue on his hands. There were no signs of defence injuries or marks consistent with any kind of a struggle. He had one small, clean, shallow recent cut on the back of his hand, and some post-mortem tearing to the skin caused by the body striking the jagged rocks, and that was it. He'd also, I noticed, glancing back through the blood samples – looking for flaws? – had three times the recommended alcohol limit in his body when he died.

Getting himself smashed to gather the courage to put the gun against his eye?

He'd been dead less than an hour by the time I found him.

'But it doesn't make any sense,' I said, my voice struggling to come to terms with what the report was saying. 'He *told* me someone was trying to kill him. Alice showed me his file filled with clippings about the Marxman. I have it with me here in my bag. I was going to give them to you. And now you're saying he killed himself? There must be a mistake.'

'There's no mistake,' said Fitzgerald. 'Butler knows what he's doing.'

'Did you find a note?'

'Not everyone leaves a note.'

'But the bullet went in through the eye,' I said. 'Suicides don't shoot themselves in the eye. There are sites of election. The temples. The forehead. Not the eyes.'

'That's just statistics. There are always exceptions. Just because most suicides don't shoot themselves in the eye doesn't mean this one didn't or couldn't. Besides, you can't have it both ways. You can't say there's something fishy about the way he died because he shot himself through the eye and therefore it must have been the Marxman, and then ignore all the evidence which points away from the Marxman's involvement. Like the same fact that he was shot through the eye. The Marxman's never done that before. He always shoots from the rear. Besides, the gun was placed directly against the skin before being fired. If the Marxman was able to get that close to Felix, wouldn't he have struggled, lashed out, resisted?'

'But . . . you never said anything about finding a gun.'

For the first time, she looked a little uncomfortable.

'That's because we didn't,' she admitted.

'You didn't find a gun?'

'Dalton thinks it may have sprung out of his hand when he fired the bullet and ended up in the water. It happens. I've sent out divers to take a look through the water near the pier. If they find anything, we should be able to make a match.'

'So what you're saying is you have no actual evidence Felix even had a gun?'

'We have evidence that he fired one, and that the bullet from the one he fired passed through his eye socket and part of his brain and ended up embedded in his own skull.'

'What kind of gun *was* it?' I said, sighing with frustration and flicking back impatiently through the notes, looking for a verdict.

'We're not sure yet. Some old pistol from the war or thereabouts, looks like. Made a bit of a mess of his face. We haven't been able to make an exact identification.'

'But you're still going to leave it at that?'

'What else can I do? I'm a murder detective, and what Butler conducted this morning was an autopsy on the body of a man who committed suicide. We're actively looking for the gun. Meanwhile, there's no evidence to suggest that any foul play occurred. I can't investigate every suicide that happens in the city; do you have any idea how many of them there are?'

I was shaking my head in disbelief. I couldn't think straight.

'I'm sorry, Saxon,' she said. 'It's not that I don't want to help you out, but there's nothing here to give any cause for suspicion about how Felix died. Besides, I took time out today to call Miranda Gray—'

'Who?'

'She was Felix's therapist. Dalton found out about her when he was putting together his report on the death.' It took all my self-control not to snap out some insult, irritated more than I liked to admit that Dalton had managed to find out something I didn't know. That just seemed to defy the normal laws of nature. 'She says Felix was suffering from bipolar depression and had done for years. She said he had a breakdown last year.'

'Alice told me.'

'She also said she wasn't surprised that he might have committed suicide. His life seemed to have been quite complicated. Alice's too.'

'What does she know about Alice?'

'She's her therapist too.'

'His and hers matching shrinks. Cosy. Does she have king-size couches so they can have joint sessions?'

'She couldn't tell me much, obviously,' Fitzgerald continued, ignoring my sarcasm, 'but she'd had worries about Felix for a while. She even read out some of her notes to me. Felix often talked about the lighthouse. He'd lived near there as a child. She said he saw it as something permanent and reliable in his life after his parents died, he said he found it comforting, he used to look at the light each night from his window before he went to bed. She could understand him going there if he was troubled, unhappy, in need of solace. And you know how it is with suicides, they often—'

'Go back to places that mean something to them when they decide it's time to die, I know,' I said testily. 'Whatever happened to patient–doctor confidentiality?'

'Don't be petty. Any other time you'd be bitching if she didn't give us some details. And you should be glad I took this trouble for you.'

'I am glad. Really I am,' I said. 'But where would Felix have got a gun?'

'Anyone can get a gun in Dublin if they know what they're looking for.'

'Point taken. But this wasn't just any gun, you said so yourself, it was some kind of antique. From the war. Where'd he get it?'

'The firearms unit are looking into it. If they find anything out, I'll pass it on to you. It's really not up to me. I have other things to do. Like the Marxman enquiry, remember? He's probably out there now, fishing for his next victim, as we speak. Laughing at us. Four dead bodies is bad enough without adding a fifth to the tally on little more than a screwy sister's conviction that her brother was the victim of the Marxman.'

'Is that Miranda Gray's professional diagnosis? That Alice is screwy?'

'Not in so many words.'

'Well, I'm not convinced. There are too many points of coincidence to simply let it go. Felix's interest in the case. His call to me. He was trying to tell me something, I'm convinced of that. Even the fact that he was shot through the eye, it's too symbolic, like he was being punished for something he'd seen, something he shouldn't have seen.'

'And from your experience, you also ought to appreciate how difficult it is to stage a murder to look like suicide.'

I wouldn't listen. I was floundering for some rope to grasp on to.

'Did no one even hear a gun going off?'

'No, but it's a quiet neighbourhood. They're not like you. They hear a gun going off and they're more likely to think it's a car backfiring.'

'Whereas I hear a car backfiring and instantly start trying to figure out what calibre it is,' I said quietly, and I wasn't proud of it. 'What about witnesses?'

'There were a couple, but you're not listening,' said Fitzgerald. 'It doesn't matter if there were a thousand people on the pier that night. You could tell me the massed ranks of the Dublin Symphony Orchestra were playing hide and seek in and out of the boats and it wouldn't make any difference.

If there's no evidence Felix Berg's death was anything other than a straightforward suicide, then there's no evidence.'

'Indulge me. What did the witnesses see?'

'Only you. I'm serious. You stand around on your own long enough and you're bound to be noticed.'

'How'd they describe me?'

'Small, dark, smoking a cigar, couldn't stand still. I'd recognise you anywhere.'

'They didn't mention the fabulously good-looking and sexy part then?'

'It was dark.'

'Oh well, I've had worse notices,' I said, and I could feel a panic rising in me as the threads which held together my interest in the death of Felix Berg started fraying, coming apart. 'I don't get it, is all. If Felix did kill himself, why the elaborate charade to make me, Alice, everyone, think he was murdered? Why tell me someone wanted to kill him?'

'Who knows what was going on in his head? Maybe he just needed to make a drama out of his death. Maybe simply dying like everyone else wasn't good enough for him. Maybe he wanted to make himself the centre of attention even in his absence, keep the world guessing, and who better to rope in than you, famous writer, former FBI agent? Maybe he just wanted an audience and figured you wouldn't come all the way out there on the back of an invite to the opening and closing night of his one-man suicide show. Or,' she added in a tone that made me look up and take notice, 'maybe he planned on taking you along for the ride.'

'You think now he wanted to shoot me too?'

'It's a possibility.'

'It's ridiculous is what it is.'

'You don't know what's ridiculous and what isn't. You don't know the first thing about Felix Berg. What he was thinking. What he was capable of. And that's why you need to just let this go. I mean it,' she said firmly. 'You say you're only going to talk to Alice and not get involved, and the next minute you're reacting badly because there might be nothing to Felix's death after all. I'm worried where it's going to lead. I don't want you to be dragged into something.'

'I'm not going to be dragged into anything. I'm just curious.'

'You know what curiosity killed.'

'I'm not a cat. I'm restless, is all. I need to be doing something to stop me seizing up. I wasn't made for sitting round at home watching daytime TV.' I flipped the cover and handed back the autopsy report. 'And you know me. I need to *know*. Felix called me; he arranged a meeting; and when I got there, he was dead. That must mean something.'

'Suicides are sick in the head. What they do and say doesn't mean anything. Sometimes things don't make sense. You know that. Sometimes you never find out what's going on, it never adds up. You just have to clock it up to experience and move on. That's one thing I have learned. A case doesn't always tie up, there are always loose ends, things that don't make sense. Sometimes you have to accept that you'll never get all the answers.'

'I've never been able to do that,' I said. 'It's not in my nature.'

'That's why you're always getting into so much trouble,' she said.

70

Chapter Twelve

'Not everyone leaves a note,' Fitzgerald had said, and she was right there, I thought as I left her office and started walking back to my apartment through the incessant crowds.

Sydney certainly hadn't.

Sydney just got out of bed one morning, didn't even bother getting dressed, walked down to the railway line at the back of her house, lay with her head on the rail for a pillow, and waited for the morning train from Boston to Washington DC to come along.

Sydney was my sister.

Had been my sister, I should say. Now she was only a memory in my head, and even that was fading. It got harder and harder each year to remember what she had looked like, and I had nothing to remind me. I don't keep photographs from my past, since most of the time the past isn't something I want to remember. Besides which, I never thought I'd *need* a photograph to remember Sydney by. I always assumed she'd be around.

No one ever understood why Sydney killed herself either, and what made it worse was that no one but me seemed to care about finding out. She was the only one of my family I really had any feelings for. My folks and I had never got along. I had an elder brother who was so stuck up his own ass with self-importance that he'd lost all contact with the real world years ago. Sydney was the baby of the family. She looked up to me. Didn't judge me by some fake standard like

71

they did. She accepted me for what I was, same way Fitzgerald did.

She'd been married about a year when she died, and I knew it hadn't been easy for her. Her husband fooled around almost from the day they got together. Turned out later he'd even been banging one of the bridesmaids. A true romantic. What games he played with her head after they were married I'll never know, but no matter how I tried to persuade her to get out, get a new life, within that year she seemed to lose all sense that she could escape from his influence, all sense of her own strength. The Sydney I'd known vanished before my eyes as he gradually stole every last part of her and locked it away where she couldn't retrieve it any more. In the end, Amtrak must have seemed like her only salvation.

A case doesn't always tie up, there are always loose ends, things that don't make sense. Sometimes you have to accept that you'll never get all the answers.

Fitzgerald wasn't to know how those words cut me. I'd never told her about Sydney. She knew I had a brother, because he sent me an occasional Christmas card (he didn't get one back), but Sydney wasn't something I felt able to share with anyone, not even her. I'd certainly never bought the illusion that talking about something makes it better.

Only one person knew about my dead sister, and that was Lawrence Fisher, a criminal psychologist I'd first met when I was writing a book about profilers and whose advice Fitzgerald had sometimes sought since in relation to cases she was working on. I counted him among my closest friends, not that that was saying much, but even so, the only reason he knew about Sydney was that he'd once spent a couple of semesters teaching out in Boston and by chance had met people who knew me, knew my family. I'd sworn him to secrecy on pain of, well, pain. I always found that direct threats worked best with Fisher. Men are such cowards.

No, Fitzgerald wasn't to know, but could I really let it happen again? Let someone die on me and never find out why? With Sydney I'd been trying to dig a tunnel to Newfoundland with a sugar spoon, knowing her husband had been to blame for her suicide, convinced that he'd actually insinuated the idea into her head and manoeuvred her subtly towards it, that he was as guilty of her death as if he'd tied her to the railway track himself and driven the train. But the tunnel of logic kept collapsing in on me; no one would listen; they preferred to read Sydney's last act as a symptom of some internal fragility rather than the crime I knew it was.

Now along came Felix and it was all happening again.

History repeating itself.

Was I going to let it?

I never made it back to my apartment that morning. Some impulse instead sent me walking out towards Kilmainham, up St James's Gate and into Military Road, and through the gates into the grounds of the Irish Museum of Modern Art. I was standing at the door almost before I knew I'd been headed that way, but once I realised where I was it made sense.

Briefly I wondered if they might have closed down the exhibition of Felix's latest work out of respect. Then I remembered what Burke had said. Death was good for the box office. There were too many bad reproduction postcards and overpriced coffee table picture books to be sold. These places were businesses, after all. I only needed to look at the notices on the board outside to realise that. Finest seventeenth-century building in Dublin . . . restored in the year yadda yadda . . . coffee shop . . . guided tours . . . excellent conference facilities . . .

Christ, who reads this stuff?

For a while I hung around, finishing a cigar, taking my time, thinking about Sydney and wishing I could remember

73

something about her that could erase the image of her leaving the house in her nightclothes and walking so acceptingly to her death, but there was nothing.

As I stood there, other people began to arrive, and I heard Berg's name whispered repeatedly. Were we all such ghouls? Did death always have to generate this instant celebrity?

I followed them inside, down a long corridor with bare walls interrupted on one side by windows looking out on to a bright, quiet inner courtyard.

By the side of the door at the end of the corridor was a simple white card with four words typed on it.

New Studies. Felix Berg.

Nothing more. No explanation or analysis, which was a relief.

I stepped inside.

Immersed myself once more in Felix's head.

There weren't as many pictures as I'd expected – only twenty-one, I counted, which was not much to show for his first major exhibition since *Unreal City* – but the photographs themselves were incredible. Here was a complete reversal of all the work that had taken my breath away last night as I sat looking at his book on my balcony.

The swarming city with its ghosts in daylight had vanished, but they had left behind them an atmosphere more unsettling and unnerving than ever. The multitude had been replaced by a city of such eerie emptiness that it made you feel lost, lonely, abandoned just to look at it. There was nothing lifelike in them at all, only an utter emptiness, like the world had been abandoned as surely as the *Mary Celeste*, like the watcher had woken and found the world had suddenly become empty and depopulated, and the effect was startling.

The photographs I'd looked at last night had seemed mysterious and shadowy, but now, compared with these, they became in my memory almost too busy, too crowded.

Too corrupted by the very things they were repelled by. The new photographs had a stillness, a tranquillity, like Felix had captured something of the possibility of silence and solitude – and loneliness – that existed within the most crowded city.

How he'd even managed to take some of the shots I simply couldn't begin to understand. All of the pictures had been taken in Dublin, but it was a Dublin from which all trace of life had been plucked. Here was Cornmarket at what looked like mid-morning in the rain, but not a soul in sight. How could he have taken such a shot? Cornmarket was never empty. Here was Greek Street and Westland Row and Golden Lane and Lincoln Place, and the pathway outside Tara Street station, and there was Merrion Square and Earlsfort Terrace, Wicklow Street curving into Exchequer Street, all lit with a steely winter light, and all frozen, embalmed almost, in that same sinister atmosphere of depopulation.

Or were they? The more I looked at these photographs, the more I began to notice something I hadn't seen before.

There *were* people in the pictures.

Glimpses mainly, faces, details, but there all the same.

Here was a face peering out of a window streaked with rain.

Here was a shadow, elongated thinly by a weak afternoon sun, of a figure who must have been standing just out of shot – and the reflection of another, broken into shards on the surface of a puddle. Here was a figure glimpsed distantly in the street, back turned.

In another shot, a trailing foot could just be seen as its owner turned a corner.

Or a hand clutching the edge of a door as it closed. And this? A snapshot placed under the leg of a chair, the face of the person in the shot obscured. They were always there, almost invisible but never quite vanishing, just on the edge of being known, of being seen.

Like they were being watched or, perhaps, were watching Felix.

And I thought: Was that how he'd felt in those final months?

Observed?

Shadowed?

There was something strange about these New Studies, though, and it took me a long time to work out what it is.

Then I saw.

There was snow in some of the pictures.

It was heaped against railings and burying steps and lying along the edges of walls and window ledges and the otherwise bare branches of trees, and in one shot there was even a line of tiny weaving footprints imprinted on it.

And it hadn't snowed this winter.

I knew that for certain because I have always been something of a connoisseur of snow – it must be my New England genes – and there's little enough of it falls on Dublin that it has to be savoured when it finally comes, the memory stored away for leaner times.

I read somewhere once that the mildness of the winters here has something to do with the Gulf Stream, but I don't know about that and never considered it worth my while finding out. Even if I knew why there's little snow, it still wouldn't make more snow come.

All I knew was that there hadn't been a snowflake on the city all winter, so how could Felix have taken some of these pictures since his return from the States in the fall? More likely, I thought, they'd been taken the previous winter, when, unusually, there'd been almost a week of snow and I had relished every second of it, and probably it didn't matter much.

If he wanted to pass off old work as new, after all, it was none of my business. They were equally impressive whenever they were taken. Summer, fall, winter: who cares?

But as I looked closely to check that I was right about the

weather, I noticed something else that was less easy to dismiss. A blurred street sign reading *O'Neill's Place*.

The air caught in my throat.

That was where Tim Enright had been gunned down by the Marxman.

A coincidence?

Quickly I began to scan the other photographs to find what I was looking for.

Grosvenor Square.

Main Street.

The Mansion House, in whose shadow Jane Knox had died. A bitten sickle of moon was clinging on to a black sky above the line of buildings.

They were all there.

In each of the places where the Marxman had struck, Felix Berg had taken a photograph and hung it here on the wall as part of his latest collection.

And maybe there was nothing very remarkable about that. He was obsessed by the killings, Alice had told me so herself. What was more natural than that he would take a shot in the places where the Marxman had taken his own shot before him? He thought murder was the key to understanding a city. But this exhibition had opened on New Year's Day.

Before the Marxman even killed his first victim.

I stood and stared at the photographs, checking, double-checking, making sure I was right, that there could be no doubt, before turning round and making my way back to the main lobby to find a telephone.

I called Alice.

'It's Saxon,' I said soon as she picked up.

'If you've called to commiserate with me on my brother's untimely suicide,' she said sarcastically, 'don't bother. Some detective who was there that night – Seamus Dalton, is that his name? – called about an hour ago to give me the results of the autopsy.'

'I wasn't calling you to commiserate. *I* don't think things are as simple as the police believe.'

There was a long silence before she answered, so long that I began to suspect she must've hung up.

'You'd better come round,' she said at last.

Chapter Thirteen

The front door was slightly ajar when I got to Alice's house. I nudged it gently with my foot, stepped into the hall. Behind the door lay a scrap of paper, folded twice and apparently pushed through the letterbox. Glancing up to make sure no one was there, I crouched down and hastily unfolded it. Inside someone had written: *Alice, call me. Please – Gina*.

I heard a noise upstairs and guiltily replaced the scrap of paper on the floor.

'Alice?' I raised my voice.

A face appeared at the top of the stairs.

'It's you,' she said. 'Close the door and come on up.'

I shut the door and walked up the stairs to the first floor, wondering if Alice had left it open for me, and if she had, why she hadn't seen the note on the floor.

Unless she'd wanted me to see it too.

The first thing I noticed when I got upstairs was that she was carrying some clothes over to a bag on the table and laying them neatly inside, pushing them down with her hands to pack them tightly before returning to fetch more from a room off the main living area.

She was wearing dark glasses, though the sun wasn't bright.

'What are you doing?'

The words were out of my mouth before I could remind myself I had no right to be asking her questions.

She looked at me for a moment, judging what lay behind the question perhaps, then said simply: 'I'm going away for a few days. I've had reporters bothering me since they learned that Felix was dead. The phone hasn't stopped ringing, they've been knocking at the door, looking for me to say something about Felix. Some of them even offered me money. For what, I don't know.' Her face creased with distaste. 'Did you not see them outside?'

'I didn't see anyone,' I said truthfully.

'You didn't?'

Alice's face showed surprise. She laid down the clothes she was carrying on the arm of the couch and crossed the room. Standing a little back from the windows, she peered out into the lane below. She looked puzzled, almost alarmed.

'They must have gone,' she said. 'For now.'

I couldn't help wondering if Felix's death had made her a little paranoid. Not to mention why she would leave the door ajar if she was being bothered by reporters.

'You should say something to Grace . . . the Chief Superintendent,' I said to her. 'She might be able to get someone detailed to watch the house and keep the reporters away.'

Not that Fitzgerald would thank me for saying so. The DMP was stretched enough as it was without offering protection from the paparazzi to bereaved art critics.

Alice shook her head anyway.

'I can deal with it myself,' she said, and for the first time I glimpsed the frost lurking behind the apparently timid, controlled façade. Alice. There was ice in her very name. 'Besides, I'm not sure that having them around wouldn't almost be as bad as the press.'

She returned to her packing. She was taking rather more than I'd have expected for the few days she'd said she was going away, but I reminded myself again that it was none of my business. And it must be tough being here after what had happened to her brother. I could understand the need to escape. I'd felt it after Sydney died too.

'I wouldn't go too far if I was you,' I contented myself with warning mildly.

'I'm just going to find a hotel. Book in under a false name. Get some rest.'

'The police might need you again, is all.'

Something in my voice must have alerted her, despite all my efforts to sound casual, because she said: 'Who are you? Really? You told me when you came yesterday that you weren't *in* the police.'

'I'm not.'

'Well then, all I can say is that you certainly talk like you are sometimes. What are you even doing asking all these questions about Felix?'

'I'm not with the DMP,' I said, 'but I did use to be a special agent with the FBI, and I'm close to Grace Fitzgerald, the Chief Superintendent you met when you went to identify Felix's body. Old habits die hard, I guess you could say. I just want to know what happened out there in Howth the other night. Why Felix called me.'

'The police already think they know what happened,' she said disparagingly.

'You don't think Felix killed himself?'

'Of course I don't believe Felix killed himself,' Alice said. 'Why would he have done such a thing? He wouldn't have thrown away his life, his gift, like that. For nothing. He wouldn't have left me alone. He didn't even *have* a gun. And he wouldn't have known how to use it even if he did get his hands on one. That's just one more thing which makes all this so absurd. First they say he killed himself. Then they say he had a gun. What are they going to tell me next? That he was wearing women's underwear when he died?'

'The autopsy report said he had gunshot residue on his hands,' I said.

'I'm not an expert,' Alice said. 'All I know is that my brother wouldn't have killed himself. And you hinted on the telephone that you thought so too.'

'I'm just trying to play devil's advocate,' I said. 'Trying to see it from the point of view of the police.' I hesitated, knowing I was treading on dangerous ground. 'You did say the other day that Felix wasn't sleeping, that he was pushing himself too hard.'

'He was often like that,' she confessed. 'Just before *Unreal City* came out, he suffered a breakdown. And then, last year, he started showing some of the same signs.'

'Was this after he was attacked in town?'

'You know about that?'

'It was mentioned in the obituaries,' I said. 'But there was nothing about him suffering a breakdown afterwards. I was just putting two and two together.'

'It's not the sort of thing we wanted getting out. Being attacked affected him badly. He was suffering from severe headaches, he was in a deep depression, it seemed like he was lost to us. We felt we needed to keep it secret. Vincent—'

'Sorry?'

'Vincent Strange. He's a friend of ours. He's devastated by all this. He handled the sale of a lot of Felix's work. He owns a gallery here in Temple Bar.'

That was where I'd heard the name. He was the genius who'd written all that garbage at the start of Felix's book about reality being contingent.

'He and I got together and decided the best thing was to take Felix away somewhere till he got better, so people wouldn't talk. I took him out to New England, moving around: Connecticut, Rhode Island, New Hampshire. We were there about six months. It was difficult at first, but slowly he began to pull himself round, to get a grip on things again, enough that we felt it was safe for him to come back.'

'When was this?'

'October. And we found him a new physician here, he was on a new cocktail of medication, he was better than he'd been for a long time. He opened his new exhibition. And then shortly afterwards the damn Marxman started his own work and Felix became, like I told you, obsessed, and it seemed like all our good work was being undone.'

'You say he was better than he'd been for a long time,' I said. 'Was that why he wasn't taking photographs any more?'

The silence was forty below.

Her look made forty below seem tropical.

'Who told you?' she said.

'Lucky guess,' I replied. 'I went round to see the photographs in Kilmainham. That's where I called you from. That's *why* I called you. I happened to notice there was snow in some of the pictures, but there was no snow in Dublin between his return in October and January when *New Studies* opened. He couldn't have taken them when he said he did.'

'Are you going to . . . say anything about it?'

'Why should I? I like them. Doesn't matter to me when they were taken.'

'You're right about the dates,' she said. The frost was melting somewhat now she could sense I wasn't out to damage Felix. She even stopped carrying clothes over to her case, and came and sat down opposite me, leaning forward slightly like she wanted to make sure I understood what she was saying. 'He told me himself that they were taken last winter. He hadn't taken any pictures since he got back from the States. Not since he started to get better. He said it was gone. His creative urge. His eye. He said he was seeing things differently now and he didn't want to take any more photographs.'

'Not ever?'

'He said it had been a burden to him for years and he didn't want to do it any more.'

'The only problem being,' I said, 'that he had an exhibition coming up?'

'Vincent had arranged it for him. Felix didn't want to let him down. And he said he needed the money. He'd spent plenty of it during his breakdown the previous year. If he was going to start a new life, he needed more money. I told him we'd be OK, I have money enough of my own, but he took out the old photographs and pretended they were new. The gallery never noticed. They were just delighted to have anything from Felix, even if there were so few. They liked them very much. Said they thought they were among his best work.'

'Maybe someone else liked them too,' I said. 'Maybe even liked them too much.'

'I don't follow you.'

'Have you seen them?'

'Naturally,' she said. 'He never let me see his work before it went on show, he never showed it to anyone before he was totally happy with it, but I went with Vincent to the official launch, and then back by myself a few days later to have a closer look.'

'And since then?'

'Have I been back, do you mean? No. Why?'

So I told her how the photographs were taken in the same locations as the Marxman killed his victims, and whilst I told her I watched as she took a small bottle of pills out of her pocket, shook three on to the palm of her hand and lifted them to her mouth.

I wasn't sure if she even realised she was doing it.

Had the doctor prescribed her them after Felix died?

'That's impossible,' she was saying. 'The exhibition opened on New Year's Day. The Marxman didn't kill his first victim until mid-January. You must be mistaken.'

'You're looking at it the wrong way round,' I said. 'The important thing is not that Felix was obsessed by the Marxman killings, but *why* he was obsessed. What was it about these particular murders that drew him towards them? There are plenty of murders. Too many murders. What was different about these murders that made him fixate on them? I think it was that he knew the locations of the shootings were the same ones hanging on the walls out at Kilmainham with his name on them.'

'You're saying the Marxman went to the exhibition, saw the pictures, and deliberately killed those poor people in the same places? Why?'

'That I don't know. But I do know that it's the only answer that makes sense. The only answer that explains why Felix became obsessed from the start. The Marxman shoots Tim Enright in O'Neill's Place. Felix thinks that's a strange coincidence, but not so significant. Then Judge Prior is killed in Grosvenor Square and he starts to notice a pattern. By the third and fourth killings, there's no doubt. How could he *not* become obsessed? He never gave you any indication that's why he was so consumed by the Marxman?'

She shook her head in bewilderment.

'You never noticed, even in passing, the same link yourself?'

'No. You've seen Felix's photographs. You could be looking at your own house and not know what it was. He made everything seem alien. Unrecognisable. He had the gift for taking things and making them his own. Refashioning them through his own eyes. Often I *never* knew where they were taken. He wasn't one to talk about his work, and he always went out alone to take the shots. After nightfall, more often than not.'

'The Marxman obviously recognised where they were,' I said.

Alice got to her feet again and walked back to the suitcase she'd been packing, putting in the last pile of clothes and letting fall the lid, zipping it round briskly, then starting on the straps.

Keeping her hands busy whilst she thought.

'Did you tell this to the police?' she said as she worked.

'I called the Chief Superintendent.'

'What did she say?'

'That she'd send someone round to take a look,' I said.

'There's a but there.'

'There's always a but,' I said. 'The Chief Superintendent said that even if the Marxman did choose the places to kill based on Felix's photographs, then that only explains why Felix was obsessed, not who the Marxman is, and that's all she cares about. She said it is not like it's practical to put surveillance on all the remaining seventeen locations out of the twenty-one photographs in the vague hope that the Marxman might turn up one night. She also said that what I'd told her just added to the argument that Felix killed himself. If he thought the Marxman was using his pictures as a template, she said, then Felix might've felt responsible in some way for what was happening, and it was his guilt which drove him to the lighthouse.'

'How many times do I have to say it? Felix would not have killed himself. Do the police not even care that there's a killer out there being inspired by my brother's work?'

'As far as they're concerned, it's a public exhibition. Hundreds, thousands of people have been and gone through the door at Kilmainham since New Year's Day, and the Marxman could've been any one of them, even assuming it isn't just a coincidence.'

'You don't sound convinced.'

'I don't believe in coincidences,' I said. 'Felix was obsessed with what the Marxman was doing, we know that. Obsessed enough that he wouldn't let it alone. At the end he said someone was trying to kill him. Between those two events isn't it equally possible that he tried to find out who was using his photographs and why, and in the course of that discovered something so important that the Marxman's only option was to neutralise the threat? He may have liked the idea of using Felix's photographs as a template, but he wouldn't like it if Felix turned the tables on him. The hunter would start to feel hunted.'

Though that still didn't explain why he should have gone to all the trouble of staging such an elaborate crime scene. Or how he'd managed to leave no trace of what he'd done.

'Is there anything you remember,' I pressed, 'that suggests Felix was being stalked or followed or harassed in any way? It needn't be anything dramatic. Unexplained phone calls would do. Letters. Strangers hanging round the door. Anything.'

'No,' Alice said, 'nothing – oh.'

She stopped.

'What is it?'

'There *was* something,' she said, looking appalled. 'I remember now. And when I say it was something, I mean it was nothing . . . at least, at the time I thought it was nothing, but, well, we *were* broken into about two, three weeks ago.'

'Here?'

'We were in Berlin for the launch of a retrospective of his work. When we got back here a few days later, a back window had been forced open, a few things were gone. Little things. Worthless things. A watch, money, some jewellery. We tried not to make too much of it. Lots of houses round here have been burgled.'

'That was all that was taken?'

'Not exactly,' she said. 'That's why it came back to me when you asked about Felix being harassed. He told me some photographs were missing. And a journal.'

Was I right then? *Had* the Marxman broken in looking for evidence of what Felix knew about him? More to the point, had he found it?

'Did you report the break-in?' I said.

'For what it was worth. The police never catch anyone. We just got a locksmith in to fit us up with a better security system and tried to forget about it. But it was unnerving all the same. I tried to laugh it off, but I felt Felix knew more about it than he was telling me. I never suspected for a moment, though, that it had anything to do with the Marxman.'

'Maybe it didn't,' I said, but I doubted my clumsy attempt at reassurance had worked. I wasn't convincing myself, let alone Alice.

It was like someone wanted to know what Felix had known.

'Do you still think it wasn't Felix who called me that night?' I asked Alice.

'I can't help hoping it wasn't.' She sighed. 'Since our parents died, all we'd ever had was each other. I know I should have listened to him, believed him, I'll never forgive myself for not being there for him, but I still hate to think of him shutting me out like that.'

'He probably wanted to protect you from whatever danger he was mixed up in.'

'I wouldn't have wanted to be protected,' she rebuked me. 'I'm not thirteen years old any more. If he was in trouble, I would have wanted to share that burden with him.'

'Even if it led to your death too?'

'Even then. At least we'd be together.'

Chapter Fourteen

For the rest of that day I was holed up in my apartment, trying to write my piece on the Marxman for the next issue of the US crime magazine Felix had found so fascinating. The deadline was coming up fast and I needed to get down whatever fragments of fact, rumour and conjecture I could assemble at short notice into something vaguely resembling sense.

It wasn't easy. I didn't even know where to begin. Since I'd written my last piece, Felix had died, and that changed everything. Changed everything for me, that is.

And yet his death had nothing to do with the Marxman, according to the police, according to all the evidence, so it wasn't something I felt comfortable writing about. I could mention the fact that there had been a killing and that it had been initially attributed to the Marxman, but beyond that what could I say? Should I mention Felix's call to me that night?

Should I describe his photographs?

Should I say that Alice was still not convinced her brother took his own life?

The important thing, as in any investigation, was to strip away the leaves and leave the bare skeleton of the tree visible against the sky behind.

See it as it was.

Here that wasn't possible. What I was confronting was more like a forest, and I couldn't see which tree it was I was meant to be looking at. The branches tangled together like barbed wire.

In the end, I took the easy way out and concentrated only on sober facts, details, background, those things you use to fill in the gaps between real meaning, and left myself out of it; I still wasn't ready to talk about that night at the pier, I still needed to take a step back from it. As a result, the piece felt faked, forced. I just knew that anyone who read it would know I was hiding what I really thought. It just died on the page, the words coagulating like blood, and I spent as much time on the balcony smoking cigars as I did at the keyboard.

At least the writing gave me the chance to pull together what I knew so far.

The downside was I realised what I knew wasn't much.

By the time I'd thrown something together and sent it down the phone line into the world, it was nearly midnight and the moon was bright as a new coin above the city.

Would Fitzgerald still be at Dublin Castle? I hadn't heard from her since I called to tell her about the photographs and she'd been unenthusiastic in response. I didn't know what she was doing now. She sometimes snatched sleep in her office when she was working late, but the Marxman investigation was a stagnant pool and I couldn't see her doing that tonight. I thought of calling her at home, but what if she was in bed already? I couldn't disturb her. No, I'd drop by her place. If the windows were dark, I'd just sit there a while and imagine her sleeping, then come home, or drive around all night, why not?

I didn't feel like sleep.

I took the Jeep out and drove through moon-bright streets towards the sea.

Where Fitzgerald lived was right across the road from the strand, with a view over to Howth Head on the other side of the huge horseshoe of Dublin Bay, some soulless estate where the houses all looked alike and huddled together in horror of the world around them, where the cars in the driveways gleamed each Sunday like new and the men all played golf.

Hers were the only lights still on, and I'd pulled into the cul-de-sac before I noticed the car parked outside her door.

Sean Healy's.

I thought about knocking but didn't. *I* wouldn't have minded going in and joining them, but it might only make things tense for her. Not because of our relationship. Healy was a good friend of Fitzgerald's; they'd always had a close relationship, with none of the tensions and stand-offs she faced from some of the other men in the murder squad; he was older, and he didn't feel threatened like they did. She didn't need to keep anything hidden from him. Even so, I didn't know who else might be there or what they were talking about.

If it was work, it might be awkward. Either Fitzgerald would have to compromise herself by talking business in front of me, and that'd look bad if it got back to the station; or else I'd wind up sitting in the garden whilst the grown-ups discussed grown-up things.

I'd understand; but I'd be irritated too.

So I reversed out again and made my way down alongside the strand before turning round and making the circuit again to see if he'd gone yet.

Then I made it again when he hadn't.

The third time I was tired of driving, and just parked by the side of the road where it was darkest and I had a view of the house. I switched the radio to the first station I could find that was quiet enough, and waited. I was getting quite a talent for waiting.

The radio was playing Billie Holiday, and it made me melancholy.

It was meant to.

And then I started to feel sorry for myself, that someone was in there with her whilst I was outside in the night, in my car. It was absurd the way we virtually had to make appointments to see one another.

91

But then that was my fault. Fitzgerald often said we should get a place together, somewhere we could both feel comfortable, and I was the one who constantly put off making that commitment. Not because I had any doubts about my relationship with her; it was something more vague, indefinable than that. Maybe it just came down to the fact that I'd always preferred to live alone and couldn't imagine now doing anything else, or maybe I was avoiding making a commitment to the city. There was always something standing between me and just accepting the fact I was here, even as the years merged into each other and I showed no sign of getting out or even knowing where I'd go if I did.

Buying a house with Fitzgerald would be one more obstacle removed to my becoming part of the city rather than a perpetual outsider, which was how it had always been.

How I liked it.

I wasn't sure I was ready to give that part of me up. To stop resisting.

Fitzgerald reckoned I made too much of it. A house was just a house, she said, it meant no more or less than that. It'd be somewhere to spend more time together, and it didn't make sense to keep two places going when Dublin was such an expensive town to get by in.

I knew she was right, and we'd even gone so far as to start looking for a place, but I was always finding excuses why each place wouldn't do. It was too far out from town, there was nowhere for me to work, the street was too quiet, the neighbour's dog was barking when we went viewing. I was betraying her in a way, because buying a house with me was bound to attract even more attention to our relationship, single her out as being different in the department again, but she was still willing to do it, still willing to face all that crap.

When it came down to it, however, I always pulled back. My attachment to my apartment was still too strong to break, and I couldn't imagine living anywhere else, with different views, different sounds, a different set of coordinates to map into my head.

Eventually we'd quietly let the project drop, though I knew from the times I stayed round here that she still picked up brochures from real estate agents now and then; I'd found them stuffed down the sides of cushions or filed casually amongst the household bills, like letters from a secret lover. I really hated myself for being so pathetic sometimes.

Chapter Fifteen

I must have dozed briefly as I sat there that night, thinking, listening to the music, for the next thing I remember Billie Holiday had gone, travelling lightly on her way, and all I could hear was the loud beep of a car alarm being disengaged and I looked over to see Sean Healy and another man I didn't recognise walking back to the car.

Someone else connected with the murder squad, I guessed.

Young. Not bad looking. Definite swagger about him.

They'd obviously been at Fitzgerald's for some kind of briefing, and she was now at the door, seeing them off. She watched them climb in and reverse out of the drive into the road just like I'd done a half-hour ago, before stepping inside and closing the door behind her.

I tried to make myself as inconspicuous as possible as they drove past on the other side of the road, then followed their headlights in the wing mirror back towards town.

I was pretty sure they didn't see me.

Soon as the road was clear, I turned on the engine again and pulled over to the space they'd just vacated, hopped out and went up to ring the doorbell.

Fitzgerald answered almost immediately.

'Forgotten something?' she began, then stopped when she saw me. 'Saxon.'

'Grace.'

'I thought you were—'

'Healy, I know. I saw him leaving just now. I was parked across the street for a while out of sight, waiting for them to go. Who was the other one?'

'That was Patrick Walsh. I told you about him.'

The cop who'd been on the training course in the States with Healy, much to Seamus Dalton's annoyance. That explained the swagger then.

I followed Fitzgerald through into the kitchen. There were files scattered across the table, three cups half filled with cold coffee and a half-eaten packet of biscuits, a radio tuned to the same station I'd been listening to murmuring low.

Results of an evening's work.

'Have you eaten?' she said. 'I could fix you something.'

'I'm good,' I said. 'Don't worry about me. You're always trying to get me to look after myself better.'

'Someone's got to do it.'

'It's you you should be worried about. You look all in.'

'You think I'm bad, you should see Healy. He's spending all hours on the Marxman case, plus we still have plenty of other cases to be dealing with. It's not like normal everyday murders just stop happening because there's a higher-profile case going on. He's been on the go since six this morning, and then this afternoon Draker calls us all in to discuss some hare-brained scheme for a gun amnesty and he expects us to put in all the preparation for him on it. Like we haven't got enough to do with the Marxman as it is.'

'An amnesty?'

'You know, criminals get to hand in their weapons without fear of having them DNA-tested. The press and TV get lots of nice pictures of guns being pulverised. Plenty of headlines about making the streets safer to walk. They had one in London recently, that's where Draker got the idea. He's certainly never had an idea of his own. Lasted a month and they got twenty thousand guns handed in, handguns, assault rifles, machine guns, air pistols, half a million rounds of ammunition, even a three-foot cannon, and all applauded by the usual array of do-gooders, community workers and probation officers.'

'Why is he suddenly doing this now?'

'There's talk of the Commissioner retiring. Again. Draker seems to think if he can get a few good press cuttings about how he's making the city safe, he'll up his chances. Plus I think he wants to punish me for going over his head to get the case off the anti-terrorist boys. You know how much he would've loved to offload it on to them and let them take the flak.'

'He doesn't deserve to be Commissioner.'

'I don't care if he deserves it or not. I'm backing him all the way. Anything that gets him out of my personal space has to be a good thing.'

'Then *you* can apply to become Assistant Commissioner.'

'I wouldn't get it if he had his way, which he would if he was Commissioner; and I'm not sure I'd want it. I'm not a political animal, never have been, and they're the only kind who last long in those positions.' And she was right about that. 'What are you doing out here, anyway? Just want some company, or is there something on your mind?'

'Just company.'

'Then let's have a drink. Beer?'

'Sounds perfect.'

She lifted a bottle out of the fridge, popped the lid and handed it to me in what looked like one smooth action. She was well named. I never had that kind of poise. That balance.

'A gun amnesty would certainly be a good way for the Marxman to dispose of the Glock if he starts getting cold feet,' I observed as we walked through into the sitting room and sat down on the couch. 'No questions asked. No ballistic or forensic tests. Convenient.'

'I've thought of that already,' she said. 'And if Draker thinks I'm going to not put any Glock that comes in through testing, he can think again. There've been few enough breaks on the case as it is without letting a possible lead go just because he thinks it'll look good on his CV. This isn't Texas, after all; any old psychopath couldn't just walk in off the street and pick up a gun so long as he has enough change in his back pocket.'

'Any old psychopath couldn't do that in Texas either,' I said, putting the bottle down on the floor and tugging roughly at my stubborn boots in an effort to pull them off. 'You're just letting your patronising Old World prejudices show through there.'

'The point is that there're plenty of guns in the States and there aren't here,' said Fitzgerald, 'so if I get something that looks like it's even been in the same room as the Marxman, I'm putting it in for tests, Draker's bullshit amnesty or not.'

'Which is why the Marxman probably wouldn't risk disposing of the gun that way. He'd suspect that's what you'd do. In fact, if he hears about an amnesty he'll probably start suspecting you've set it up deliberately to catch him. Screw these boots.'

'Here, let me.'

She knelt down in front of me and pulled at the remaining boot until it slipped off.

'What about you?' she said as she laid the two of them side by side on the hearth, reminding me for a moment of Felix's shoes perched at the edge of the pier in Howth.

The last thing I wanted to be reminded of here, now.

'You mean, have I made any progress on connecting Felix to the Marxman? Not an inch,' I said. 'And I know, I know, you warned me. You're probably right. The photographs probably mean nothing. I'm reading too much into everything as usual. But I'm still convinced there's something and I intend to keep niggling at it until I find what it is. There. I've warned you in advance, so you can't grouch later when I won't let the subject drop.'

She smiled, but didn't pursue the subject.

Didn't want to get into a fight.

'What does Alice think?' she asked disingenuously.

'To tell you the truth, it's hard to know what Alice thinks about anything,' I said. 'She's a hard woman to get to the heart of. She's an enigma wrapped inside a riddle inside a . . . whatever it is that old proverb says.'

'Sounds like someone I know.'

'Maybe that's why I like her,' I said, 'though I know she's not being completely straight with me.'

'You like her?'

'Maybe liking's putting it too strongly. Let's say I recognise a fellow soul. A fellow secretive type. I think she just needs some time to come round. But to answer your question, she still thinks her brother didn't kill himself. She's not buying the autopsy report.'

'Relatives of suicides often refuse to accept their loved ones killed themselves,' she said. 'They take it as a rejection of them, and most of the time they're right. I remember when I was first in uniform, I was stationed out in Monkstown near the harbour and we were constantly being called out to pull the suicides from the water where they'd jumped. That was bad enough, but it was dealing with the families afterwards that was the real hard part. It was like opening up Pandora's box. Every emotion comes spilling out. Anger. Disbelief. Denial.'

Tell me about it, I thought. I'd spent years blaming myself for what happened to Sydney. Though it wasn't like Pandora's box with my family. The emotions weren't desperate to get out there. You could've unlocked the box and left the lid open and tried enticing them out with candy and threats and promises and they'd still have preferred staying right where they were in the corner, in the dark, hiding.

'Look,' Fitzgerald went on when I didn't answer, 'I'm not going to start nagging you again, you're a big girl now, but you shouldn't let feeling sorry for her, if that's what it is, lead you into something you'd be better off staying out of. No one ever killed themself because their life was uncomplicated.'

'I do feel sorry for her,' I said. 'I think she's lost right now

98

without her brother. Doesn't know what to do. Doesn't know what to think. I know how she feels. I tried calling her again earlier this evening, but I forgot she's not at the house any more. In the end I just left a message saying if there was anything I could do, to call me.'

'Should I be worried?'

'She's not my type.'

'What is your type?'

'I like them taller.'

'Everyone's taller than you.'

'Miaow,' I said. 'That hurt.'

'Well, I'm just glad she'll be off my back now,' Fitzgerald went on. 'She's been bugging me all day, calling and asking when I was going to release Felix's body. Healy's been getting calls from her too. I don't know what she thought we were going to do with it – lose it? I don't get her. She tells you her brother was murdered and then she can't get the body back from the police quickly enough, as if he was some ordinary car smash victim.'

'What did you tell her?'

'The truth. That the body was not my jurisdiction. That only the coroner could release it.'

'And is he going to?'

'No reason not to now the death certificate's been completed. It's usually just a matter of procedure after the autopsy so long as there's no ongoing police enquiry. It could be six months till the inquest, longer. It wouldn't make sense to keep his body till then. She'll have Felix back soon enough. And then I hope that's the last I ever hear from her. I'm trying to let Dalton deal with her as much as I can. Seems he's taken quite a shine to her.'

'Like she doesn't have enough problems.'

'Anything that keeps her away from me, I'm not complaining. In fact,' she said, 'maybe I should send Walsh round to see her instead. I hear he's quite the charmer where women are concerned.'

'Now I'm the one who's worried.'

'You needn't be. I never sleep with my inferiors,' said Fitzgerald with dignity. She reached over and took a swig of beer, then swallowed it quickly as she started to laugh quietly. 'Though, I don't know how I forgot to tell you this, he did ask me out to dinner.'

'Get away.'

'Couple of days ago. Just came right out with it.'

'Asking out his own Chief Superintendent. I'm in awe. That boy has some nerve. He'll go far. Though not with you, I hope. What did you say?'

'I told him his behaviour was entirely inappropriate and that if he crossed the line one more time I'd have him transferred to traffic duties. That cut him down to size, though privately I was quite impressed. Like you say, it takes some nerve to ask your boss out.'

'Is that why you've never asked Draker out?'

'That and the fact I wouldn't want to spend the night with anyone who made the prospect of being hanged, drawn and quartered seem attractive by comparison.'

'I guess I'll take that as a compliment.'

She smiled and reached out and took the bottle from my lips again, and it felt good to see her so relaxed; and I was suddenly lightheaded with gladness that I'd come round, that I'd waited outside till Healy and Walsh had gone and not driven home and gone to bed alone. Or maybe it was just the taste of beer after missing dinner that was making me lightheaded.

Whatever it was, it couldn't last.

Before she'd had time to take another drink, there was a ringing from the phone in the hall, and Fitzgerald swore under her breath as she put down the bottle and went to answer it.

I listened to her voice through the doorway.

'Yes . . . yes,' I heard her murmur. 'Yes, I know it. I'll be right there.'

'Is that what I think it is?' I said when she reappeared. Fitzgerald nodded.

'Seems that our friend the Marxman may have struck again,' she said. 'Struck for real this time, I mean. And this time there're two dead.'

Chapter Sixteen

I lay in Fitzgerald's bed, watching channels flash by – late show, war film, subtitles, soccer.

Then there it was. A shot of a street somewhere in Dublin, a live relay from the scene of the latest attack. Neon lights made a fog of the night. The air was green. *Two dead in latest shooting. Is it the Marxman?* ran the caption along the bottom of the screen.

It was a sign of how big the story was becoming that the stations had switched their usual schedules for rolling news. Or maybe it was just that this time the shooting had happened right in the centre of town, meaning reporters didn't have to walk too far from their favourite bars to where the action was, glad they had something to wallow in now that Felix Berg's death had turned out to be a dead end, not even murder at all, much less the Marxman.

I turned up the sound to hear what was happening.

The scene of the shooting was some Gothic monstrosity called the Church of Our Father in the north inner city. It was a big, ugly, dour building with metal grilles on the smoke-blackened stained-glass windows. I knew the look of it vaguely from my circuits of the city, though I'd never been inside; in fact I'd never taken much notice of it at all. But then Dublin was full of churches; religion was one thing there'd never be a shortage of here, it was the one part of the old city that kept peeking out through the bright postmodern face, clinging on in people's consciousness like a bad smell round a rubbish tip. I tended to ignore it as best I could. I'd had enough of that stuff in my childhood. I didn't need it now.

From what reporters on the scene were able to tell, the first victim had been making his way home from a night's drinking in town and had stopped in the doorway of the church to relieve himself, as drinkers often did, sometimes not bothering to avoid the down-and-outs who were sleeping in the doorway at the time. He'd been shot once in the back, through the heart, from a distance of about ten feet – an impressive effort from our friend the Marxman.

The blood had arced on to the antique wooden doors in a delightful pattern. The TV lights picked it up in close-up, like some undiscovered Jackson Pollock, before the police managed to get the screens up and herd spectators far enough away.

He'd fallen forward head first and died where he lay.

What had happened next was unclear.

About a hundred yards away lay another body. A young woman – little more than a girl really, according to eyewitnesses – in her late teens or early twenties, unidentified so far, who had apparently been making her own way home from a night out. She was wearing red stilettos and a cheap black glittery cocktail dress and clutching a red bag with nothing inside but a house key, some money, and a cloakroom ticket from a club in town.

It was the usual story of a woman killed for walking home late at night rather than taking a taxi, though in her case she'd died, so first impressions indicated, because she'd walked inadvertently on to the scene as the Marxman was taking aim at the first victim.

The initial couple of shots meant for her seemed to have missed, the first hitting a nearby wall, the second shattering a window; and he must have been running to catch her up as he fired, for the third shot had hit her in the right hip and felled her as she ran too, and the next two were delivered from close range as she lay on the ground looking up at the killer, the gun placed directly against the front of the forehead, the trigger pulled. A paramedic who attended the scene was quoted as describing the two circular contact wounds, close together, that he'd seen on her skin, powder burns surrounding them like a halo round the head of a saint.

Other than that, it was difficult to tell much of what was happening. Once the crime-scene tape went up and a small battalion of officers arrived, counting their overtime already, to keep out the curious, there was only so much that could be said, that could be seen.

I saw the City Pathologist turn up just ahead of the van from the mortuary, and recognised faces from the murder squad as they passed grimly through the cordon. There was Sean Healy. Patrick Walsh. Tom Kiernan arrived on his motorbike and walked through the cordon with his helmet under one arm and his camera slung over the other shoulder.

Still no sign of Dalton getting in on the action.

As if on a loop, I watched footage of one reporter trying to buttonhole Fitzgerald for a quote as she arrived at the scene what must have been only forty minutes after leaving the house. I smiled as she just brushed past him as if he didn't exist and disappeared into the darkness behind the screens. *Detective Chief Superintendent Grace Fitzgerald of the Dublin Metropolitan Police arriving at the scene of the latest shooting*, read the caption underneath.

It was a curious sensation watching her out there whilst I lay here in her bed, her pillow behind my head, the smell of her perfume in the room.

Over the next couple of hours, as I switched channels looking for anything new, I found only the same confused reports, endlessly repeated, the same small snatches of fact spun frantically in the hope that they would transform into something more valuable. But then the news reporters were masters at making gold from straw; they could keep this kind of thing going for hours, like jazz musicians given a hint of a riff and letting themselves spin off into some crazy innovation that soon took on a life of its own and left its old shell behind.

In place of reliable information, reporters filled in the gaps by talking to residents, oblivious to the fact, or maybe not giving a damn, that if any of the witnesses they spoke to really did have genuine evidence to impart about that night's double shooting, then it was only going to be contaminated by this endless retelling for the benefit of the cameras and the furiously scribbling pencils of the assorted hacks.

Had the bystanders seen anything?

You bet.

Some claimed to have seen a man running in the direction of the river, though their descriptions of him varied considerably. Black guy, strongly built, said one, and a few backed him up. Well, it was the sort of neighbourhood where, when anything happened, they were inclined to think that a strongly built black guy had been to blame, even though any black guy, strongly built or not, would have been unlikely to move through these streets unnoticed. Dublin was changing fast in that respect, but it was no melting pot. Burke would be lucky not to be arrested by morning. Another reckoned the man was white, and so thin as to be almost skeletal in appearance. He had a beard. He had none. He wore a coat. He was in shirtsleeves. Yet another said she'd seen a woman backing away from the scene.

Another had heard a scream. When? He couldn't say.

As the stories were retold, they were consistently embellished, like travellers' tales round a campfire, so that dugongs became mermaids and rhinoceroses were unicorns and nothing was what it had been in the first innocence of the experience, until one man who lived in a house across the way from the Church of Our Father quite seriously declared that he'd been knocked to the ground by what he thought was the killer and distinctly remembered how he had a scar running down the left-hand side of his face; and it was only when he'd told it three times that it transpired this all happened the night before the shootings even happened.

If it happened at all.

This was why it was important for the police to be on top of things. Why hadn't the witnesses been isolated? Why hadn't their statements been taken before they had the chance to cross-pollinate their own memories with the seeds of whatever fantasies they picked up floating through the fevered air? Why hadn't the police—

I stopped myself. There I went again, telling other people how to do their job. It had always been my weakness. This is none of your business, I told myself firmly. I wasn't police, I was only someone lying in a policewoman's bed and feeling redundant.

So I listened instead to a discussion with the ancient trembling priest in whose church doorway the man had been shot, who agreed, with that unrivalled talent for piety and platitude all churchmen have, that it was a terrible tragedy altogether and the truth lay with God and all things would come back to God in the end and God would make it right. He would also, he said, be holding a special prayer service for all the community to help them come to terms with this awful event, when, no doubt, his congregation would swell way beyond its normal size as those content to be ungodly the rest of their lives suddenly decided that there were benefits to godliness, not least the chance to share a piece of this action which had intruded so dramatically into their dull lives, and not forgetting a chance to appear on TV.

It was always the way.

I shouldn't be so cynical, but between the Church and the inevitable grief counsellors who would follow, trawling for trauma to nurture like fishermen trawl for eels, I swear it was a wonder anyone managed to stay sane any more in the days following a tragedy.

The TV itself didn't help. They kept up a rolling banner of news along the bottom of the screen. *Is anyone in the city safe?* asked one. *Where will the Marxman strike again?* There were numbers to call to vote on who was to blame for the crisis.

Studio discussions were planned for the morning. Folk in the city had stayed pretty calm, considering, since the shootings began, but then the murders hadn't really impinged on most people's lives, and the shootings had been spaced out far enough till now that any risk of panic had had time to subside again; but the more victims who died, the less chance there was of keeping a lid on collective emotions.

I decided finally that the only thing I could do was switch the TV off. A huge weariness was flowing over me. There was little that could be done about murder when it became no more than a diversion, an entertainment, for everyone involved save the victims and their families.

When that happened, we were truly lost.

As the screen dissolved to grey, and the chatter of the news channels was replaced by the sound of traffic passing sparsely along the road outside, and the faint wash of the sea, I tried to tune my mind to a different frequency by thinking of Felix Berg, but that hardly helped either. I was pretty sure the Church of Our Father hadn't featured in any of the photographs out at Kilmainham. Did that mean Fitzgerald was right to dismiss Felix's other pictures as coincidental? That his call to me really had been nothing more than a despairing self-dramatisation that had nothing more to do with the Marxman than Sydney's death did?

If so, it ought to have been a comforting thought, but somehow it wasn't. One thing I'd realised as I lay here alone tonight was that I didn't want my own part in all this to end. Fitzgerald was out there, cold and sleepless probably, and envying me, but I envied her too. And I was sure she'd have felt the same if our positions were reversed. I still needed my own crime scenes, my own investigations, otherwise what was I? Nothing. Nothing at all.

Chapter Seventeen

Strange's gallery was in Temple Bar too, not far from where Felix had lived. I hadn't bothered telling him I was coming this morning, since I didn't want to give him the opportunity to refuse to see me.

I didn't have any reason to believe he *would* refuse to see me, but why take the chance?

The gallery was called Post.

Postmodern? Postindustrial? Posthumous? The sign wasn't saying, and why should I care? It was in an old building, the front of which had been removed and replaced entirely with glass, so that all three floors were exposed as though by X-ray. The walls were as white as Felix's and Alice's and there were hardly any photographs on them, which meant that there was plenty of blank wallspace to see. The floor was of huge sandstone tiles.

I could see a man through the window, sitting behind a long glass desk, talking into the telephone. It could only be Strange.

He sat there with a sense of total proprietoriality, lord of all he surveyed, wearing a huge fur coat which made him look like a bear, or like he'd wandered in absently from an old Edward Gorey print, and he had the most bizarre moustache I'd ever seen, like he'd grown it for a wager one time and forgotten to shave it off once he'd collected his winnings.

An old-fashioned coatstand stood incongruously behind him.

I tried the door.

It was locked.

So I knocked to get his attention.

He glanced up, and I think was about to ignore me when a flash of something – recognition? – crossed his face and he pressed a button below his desk to activate the door.

It clicked opened and I pushed inside.

By the time I'd closed the door behind me, he'd returned smoothly to his telephone conversation, so if he had recognised me he obviously didn't think I deserved any further acknowledgement. I stood looking at the photographs on the wall instead.

Talk about disturbing.

Female nudes, black and white, very tasteful, except that the photographs were cut off savagely at the head each time. In one of the shots, a woman lay with a knife flat on her belly, the point angled towards her navel; in another the indent of a heavy chain could be seen deep on the skin of her buttocks and the chain itself lay coiled like a sleeping snake on her back. In another, she'd cut herself and the blood was painted on her skin in a coil the same way as the snake.

Title: *Self Portraits*.

It made me appreciate Felix's photographs all the more.

'Do you like them?'

The voice was almost in my ear and I turned swiftly. There was Strange at my shoulder. I hadn't heard him approach, which on that stone floor was some achievement.

Then I glanced down and noticed he was barefoot.

'Not really,' I said, answering his question. 'I prefer art that doesn't look like it's likely to turn up in the courtroom sometime soon as Exhibit A. Who took them?'

'The artist prefers to remain anonymous.'

'I don't blame her.'

'You find this work sinister?' Strange seemed surprised, as though the idea that there might be something odd about a woman posing with daggers and chains around her torso had

109

never occurred to him until that moment. 'It's very daring. Some people do find it threatening.'

'Conventional people, you mean?'

'Not everyone understands,' he put it more gently.

'Artists always blame adverse reactions to their work on the hang-ups of the audience. Does it never occur to them that some people might find their work freaky not because of the viewer's own bourgeois preconceptions, but just because it *is* freaky?'

'Freaky's not a word I'd use,' Strange said with a smirk. 'It's challenging society's ideas about femininity, about violence, about the body. If it's disturbing, that's because it's meant to be. The watcher's meant to explore why they feel disturbed, what makes them feel threatened. That way they might learn something about themself. Alternatively, you can always look upstairs, there are other photographs there that you might like better.'

'That's OK,' I said. 'If this is what you put on the ground floor, I'd hate to see what you have hidden up there. Besides, it's you I came to see. My name is—'

'Saxon. Yes, I know. Alice told me about you.'

'Did she describe me too so you knew it was me at the door?'

He didn't answer the question directly.

'She said you might call round,' he said. 'Won't you take a seat? I'm afraid I can't offer you any coffee. There seems little point having a machine here when there's a perfectly delightful place selling the best cappuccinos in town just around the corner. In fact, why not forget the seat and let's take a walk round there now? Get some fresh air.'

In the middle of the city?

'You don't mind shutting up the store?'

'I won't have to close the gallery,' he said, ignoring my attempts to needle him. 'My assistant is upstairs, and it's not as though we're open to the public anyway. This is a private gallery, viewing is by appointment only. I'll just give her a call and tell her where I'm going.'

'Don't forget your shoes,' I said, and retreated outside and waited whilst he murmured into the mouthpiece of his phone and slipped his feet into moccasins.

'I half expected you before this,' he said when he finally emerged and pointed me in the right direction, and I couldn't tell if he was disappointed I hadn't come round sooner. 'Alice told me you were interested in Felix's death. What happened to him was a terrible tragedy. He had a great talent – no, talent isn't right. Rock stars have talent. Felix had genius. A mastery of image.'

I said nothing. I hoped he wasn't about to deliver another critical appreciation; I'd read enough of his pretentious essay in Felix's book.

'But then Alice is a remarkable woman too,' he went on to my relief. 'A very great critic. There aren't many great critics. There are reviewers who can look at a photograph and throw together a couple of hundred or thousand words of praise or blame for some art magazine, but a critic is a rarer thing. You know what Jean Anouilh said about art?'

'I'm afraid not.'

I didn't admit that I didn't know who the hell Jean Anouilh was.

'He said the object of art was to give life a shape. And the object of the true critic is to give art a shape beyond what you can see only with the eye; it's about making connections, and Alice is the best there is. Even when she writes about bad art, she's worth reading, she always finds the right and true thing to say. Indeed, you might say that the mark of a good critic is one who is as worth reading when they're talking about bad art as they are when they're talking about great art, wouldn't you agree? It must be hard for her right now,' he went on when I didn't respond to his question. 'She and Felix were very close.'

'So she tells me.'

'It's hard to imagine them being apart,' Strange continued. 'The prospect of life continuing without Felix, day after day, must be intolerable for her.'

'She's told you that?'

'Not in so many words, no. She doesn't need to.'

We'd reached the cappuccino place and ordered our drinks, and while we waited I looked around at all the people drifting aimlessly through the square.

Swarming city, full of dreams.

'That's why,' said Strange, 'I think it would be best if you left her alone. If you didn't keep getting her hopes up that there's more to Felix's death than meets the eye.'

'He called me,' I said. 'He said someone was trying to kill him. Then he died. Maybe you could just shrug something like that off. I can't. Besides,' I went on as he tried to dismiss my words with a flutter of his fingers, 'I haven't been getting anyone's hopes up. Alice doesn't believe her brother killed himself. That is to say, she doesn't believe that he *simply* killed himself. It's Alice who's encouraged me all along to keep digging.'

'That's not the way she tells it.'

'How does she tell it?'

'Alice says you've been bothering her about Felix.'

'Me bothering *her*? That's crazy.'

'You're bothering me. Why's it so crazy you'd be bothering her too?'

'In what way am I bothering you?'

'Asking questions.'

'Asking questions doesn't count as bothering in my book,' I said. 'Don't you want to know how Felix died?'

'I know how he died. He committed suicide. The police told me exactly how it happened. I spoke to the detective in charge. And Alice knows it too.'

'Is that another thing you know without her needing to tell you?'

'That was something she told me. Not in so many words.

In those exact words. She doesn't think for one moment Felix was murdered. I mean, at first we all did. Thought it was the Marxman. But not any more. Now we know the truth. I spoke to her last night on the telephone and she told me she was ready to put all her initial doubts about his death behind her.'

I was about to protest when I realised there was no point. If he was lying to me, he wasn't going to suddenly stop because I got antsy. And if Alice had been lying to me or lying to Strange, then either way she must have her reasons.

I sipped at my coffee.

It was good.

He was right about that, at least.

I sat down next to him on a low wall.

He gazed out across the square like it was his.

'Did you at least know that Felix was obsessed by the Marxman?' I tried asking.

'Felix?'

'Yeah, Felix. Alice showed me a thick file of cuttings he'd taken from the newspapers about the case. He'd been following it from the start.'

'I'm not going to call you a liar,' Strange said with a thin smile. 'If you say that Alice showed you a file of cuttings, then she showed you a file of cuttings. All I'm saying is that this is the first I've heard about it. He never shared any such obsession with me.'

'Would he have done?'

'Felix was my friend. He was *more* than a friend. We were both strangers here, we weren't from here, so we knew what it was like not to fit in.'

'You're not from Dublin?'

'I was born in South Africa,' said Strange, 'and sent here to school. You never really fit in. That's why Felix and I understood one another so well. Why we connected. I admit we hadn't seen as much of one another lately as in the past. He was following more of his own path, he didn't need my guidance as much as he once had. And he'd not been well. Alice told me she'd mentioned that much to you. So if he did have this obsession which you claim, then he wouldn't necessarily have told me about it anyway.'

'Why did he call me that night if he didn't know something?'

'I don't know, I really don't,' he said, shaking his head sadly. 'Felix was complex. I admit that. I don't know what was going through his head at the end. I am just sorry I couldn't have been of more help to him in easing whatever pressures he felt were bearing down on him.'

'What about the break-in?' I pressed.

'What about it?'

'Seems to me that the burglar was looking for something. He left plenty of valuables lying about the place, camera equipment, the safe was untouched. All he took was a few worthless pieces to make it look like a bona fide job – *and* some photographs and a journal. Doesn't that prove someone had it in for Felix?'

There was a silence.

'I have the journal,' said Strange at last. 'It was never stolen. Felix gave it to me for safekeeping. The photographs too. He asked me to look after them.'

'Why?' I said, trying and probably failing to hide my disappointment.

'I suppose the break-in made him realise that they were vulnerable, that they might be stolen, and he didn't want that to happen.'

'What was so precious about them that he feared losing them?'

'I don't know, I didn't ask.'

'You didn't ask?'

'If a friend asks for help, you don't ask why, you either help or you don't.'

'*I'd* ask why.'

'Well, I didn't.'

And Fitzgerald thought Alice was tough work.

'So where's the stuff now?' I said, knowing already what his answer would be.

'I'm afraid I can't tell you that.'

Yeah, that was the one.

'If that journal has something to do with why he died, which could explain why—'

'You're back to this again. You know, I'm beginning to think that it's you who has the obsession. What could his journal have to do with his death? He killed himself.'

'Alice doesn't think so, whatever she might have told you. Don't you think you owe it to her and Felix to explore every avenue before chalking his death up to a simple suicide?'

'Alice is under terrible strain right now. As her friend, I do not believe that keeping investigating this matter is what is best for her. Especially when I've already told you that she has said not one word to me or any of her friends to make me think she disbelieves the police's version of what happened in Howth.'

'She told me that she did.'

'I only have your word for that.'

And I could see how pointless it was asking him any more questions.

I drained the last of the coffee, crushed the paper cup and threw it in a perfect arc towards a nearby garbage can.

I missed.

Strange looked suitably disapproving.

'OK, one more thing and then I'll be out of your hair. Did Felix ever tell you anything, anything at all, that even suggested he might've been afraid?'

'Nothing that I can remember,' said Strange stiffly.

'You saw no sign he was anxious?'

'No.'

'I don't just mean the last few weeks.'

'I told you. Nothing. At least . . .'

'What?'

'I shouldn't have said anything. It's just . . . I feel foolish even bringing this up, and you're probably going to react entirely the wrong way, but Felix did once tell me that he used to share a house with a murderer.'

'And that's what you call nothing?'

'Wait a moment now. Don't be getting carried away here. It was just idle talk, he never told me more than that. It was a conversation we had years ago when I first met him, and I mean years. He simply told me he used to share a house with a murderer. He wouldn't tell me any more about it. I don't know where it was or when. I don't know anything.'

'Was the murderer ever caught?'

'I don't think so.'

'Did he tell the police?'

'I don't know! I can see now that I shouldn't have told you. It has nothing to do with Felix's death. It was all a long time ago. Long forgotten.'

'In my experience, murder is rarely forgotten.'

'All the same,' he replied, 'I'm not letting you see the journal or the photographs, if that's what you're angling at. I can't. Felix gave them to me under strict instruction. They're safer where they are. You give me any reason to think that Felix's death was anything more than an unfortunate tragedy, and I'll hand them over to the police. Until then, I will keep my word.'

'And if something was to happen to them in the meantime?'

'Happen? Like what?'

'If there was a fire, or if they were stolen. It happens. It might look suspicious if you had possession of them and suddenly they were gone. And say Felix *was* killed for the secrets contained in the journal, in the photographs? Who might be next?'

Strange looked momentarily disconcerted; the possibility had clearly never occurred to him before that keeping Felix's secrets might be a dangerous business, although if he was

116

telling the truth about never doubting that Felix had taken his own life, why should it have? But he still shook his head firmly. Felix's secrets were staying exactly where they were.

'Your choice,' I said.

Chapter Eighteen

Strange may not have been for giving way, but it would still make me a whole lot easier in my mind if I knew where he was keeping Felix's possessions. And I had a hunch I could find out. I'd instilled a measure of doubt in his head. Now all I had to do was wait.

Sure enough, about a half-hour after Strange and I had parted company at the door of his gallery, he was on the move again, still wrapped in that distinctive fur coat of his.

He went to the end of the lane, turned left into Crown Alley and then through the tunnel at the bottom and over the Ha'penny Bridge to the other side of the river. He didn't look round once as he walked. He wasn't expecting to be followed.

Along Bachelor's Walk and then he crossed the busy junction at the bridge and made his way, still following the river, down towards the Custom House.

Strange lived out along the coast somewhere on the other side of town, I'd already checked that out, so I knew he wasn't going home, and I doubted he'd be crossing over to the northside for any reasons of pleasure. The northside would hold few attractions for a man like Strange. He didn't look like the sort who liked roughing it.

So where was he going?

I must admit I rather enjoyed following him through the streets, keeping him in sight, keeping my distance. I was out of practice; there hadn't been much opportunity for this sort of thing since I left the FBI; and there was no denying I missed it. I felt my senses growing more alert, my eyes sharper. Maybe I'd missed my vocation. Maybe I should've been a stalker.

That ridiculous fur coat of his made it simple, not to mention a total self-absorption which made him not even consider the possibility he might be being followed or watched.

He turned aside before we reached the Custom House and followed the curve of the road round to the left towards the police station on the corner.

Surely he wasn't going there?

No, he passed by, and turned up the next busy street.

Now I knew where he was going.

Soon he disappeared into a gloomy subway under the railway bridge and up the steps inside to the high-vaulted concourse of Dublin's Central Station, where hundreds of passengers waited alongside piles of luggage, listening to the crackling announcements, squinting up at the board showing arrivals and departures, enduring the endless waiting, waiting, waiting that was the inevitable lot of the practised traveller.

I didn't have to worry Strange would notice me here.

I stood by a long board showing timetables whilst he strode down towards the row of lockers that lined one wall near the entrance to the platforms.

There was a line of people queuing here for the gates to open on to the platform, but I could see him through the gaps between bodies, delving into his pocket for a key.

He slotted it into the hole and opened the door. I was too far away to see what he could see. I only saw him reach in, touching the things inside as if reassuring himself they were still safe, still there, then he closed the door again and twisted the key to lock it shut.

A brief glance round, then he turned and walked back the way he'd come, down the steps, and out. I followed to make sure he really had gone, then hurried back up to the station.

There was the one he'd unlocked.

I tried the handle out of habit, but of course it didn't move. It wouldn't have been difficult to prise it open – as Fitzgerald frequently reminds me, I have a greater range of anti-social skills than I have any right to feel proud of – but there was no point taking a risk right now. I had my answer. The rest could wait. To everything there is a season.

'Sure I know Strange,' said Burke when I told him what I'd been up to. 'Know *of* him, anyway. Started out as a painter – watercolours, I think – but he never made it.'

'A failed artist.'

'The only thing worse than a failed artist,' agreed Burke, 'is a successful one. That's why he turned to being a dealer, and now he's swimming in money. Drowning in it. Least that's what I hear. We ain't exactly moving in the same social circles, you know. Though Vincent Strange, now, he has friends in high *and* low places. I see his picture all the time in the social diaries at the weekend. You know the way it goes, glass of shitty white wine in one hand, couple of well-dressed women with more tits than brain cells in the other.'

'You don't like him.'

'Well spotted. You should be a detective.'

'I'm too old. I'd never pass the medical.' I stretched out a hand to stroke the cat that had hopped up on to my lap as soon as I sat down, despite all my best efforts to push the brute out of my way with my foot. The damn thing wouldn't take no for an answer and I figured it was bad form to drink a man's whiskey and then kick his cat, so I usually let it have its own way. 'What was that reference to low places all about, anyway?'

'There've always been rumours about Strange,' Burke said.

'A faint whiff of scandal?'

'More like a stink,' he said. 'You remember Freddie Sheehy?'

'Some gangster shot a couple of years back by his own

120

boys. They'd stolen some painting from a big house out in the wilds somewhere and he tried to double-cross them.'

'The very one,' said Burke. 'It turned out that Strange had had more than a few business dealings with Sheehy. They were all above board so far as anything's above board with a man like Sheehy, but still it didn't look good. Especially when a picture appeared after Sheehy's death in the newspapers of him and Strange out at dinner with the good old boys, playing at the Godfather, brandy and cigars, the whole caboodle. I'm surprised you don't remember.'

'I don't follow the local news.'

'Unless it's something gruesome like last night's little entertainment. Well, the upshot was,' said Burke, 'that it was all hushed up nicely, no questions asked.'

'Is this where the friends in *high* places come in?'

'Strange went to school with Grace's friend the Assistant Commissioner.'

'Draker? No shit.'

'Expensive place out by Howth where the children of the ruling classes get shielded from the likes of you and me. Then, when they grow up and take their rightful place at the top of the tree, they spend the rest of their lives making sure no one else climbs up and none of *them* fall down. Strange's certainly had a few helping hands keeping him on his branch.'

'You're not going to start giving me some speech about the workers, I hope.'

'I'll spare you this one time, girl, since I'm in a good mood. Save it up for a rainy day.' Then he said, almost as an afterthought: 'He collects guns too, you know.'

Talk about leaving the best till last.

'Isn't that slightly – how shall I put this? – illegal in Dublin?'

'Nothing's illegal if you know the right people, and I'd say we already established Strange's credentials there. Let's just say he gets the necessary permits, or no one ever gets round to asking. I mean, I'm not talking Uzis or Kalashnikovs here,' he added.

'What kind *are* you talking about?'

'Antiques. I'm no expert in that kind of medieval shit. World War Two guns, is what I heard, stuff going right back to the Civil War. Winchesters, duelling pistols, Remingtons, I dunno. I get some of the magazines coming through here sometimes, you should see the squirrels who come in here looking for them. They should wear badges: I Got No Penis, Let Me Look At Pictures Of Guns Instead. Me, I saw enough of them in the army.'

'Penises or guns?'

'Both.'

I was thinking. Wondering first if Fitzgerald had thought of checking the mailing lists of US gun magazines coming into Dublin. Finding someone with a fixation on weapons was a possible angle for the Marxman. But mostly I was just wondering about Vincent Strange.

About the gun Fitzgerald's divers had pulled that morning from the water near where Felix had died. *An old pistol from the war*, Fitzgerald had said they were looking for, and that's just what it seemed to be. It was being tested right now for Felix's prints.

Felix was afraid in the days before he died. Afraid enough to go looking for a gun to protect himself with? Alice said he didn't have one, and that he wouldn't have known how to shoot straight with one even if he did, but there was plenty else he had kept back from her; why not this too? And where was Felix more likely to get some quote old pistol from the war unquote than from a man who collected them and who'd been one of his closest friends?

I was thinking about all that when my cellphone went off, startling Hare and making him skitter like some frightened mouse off my lap and into the back room. Just when it seemed as if he was settling in for a long session. Thank God for technology.

The call came from Niall Boland, I discovered when I answered it. I'd called him earlier before heading for Strange's, figuring he might be as good a source of information about the shooting at the church as I was likely to get at short notice, but the phone had gone unanswered. I hadn't heard from Fitzgerald since she left her house last night either, and I could feel myself getting slowly more uptight with being out of the loop.

This must be how a drug addict feels when he's running low on supplies.

'I got your message,' he said now. 'You wanted me?'

'Just checking if you were free for breakfast.'

'Sorry. I had the phone switched off. Probably just as well. I'm supposed to be on a diet. Cassie says I could do with losing a few pounds.'

More like a few hundred pounds, I couldn't help thinking.

Boland was what you could call the solid type.

'Cassie's your new girlfriend, right? What's she like?'

'She's not my ex-wife. That's good enough for me. Listen,' he said, 'if you want to talk, you can always come out jogging with us if you like.'

'You and Cassie?' I said, trying to imagine Boland jogging.

'No, me and Walsh,' Boland said. 'He's in training for the Dublin marathon. Reckons he can set a new record for the DMP. He's got me out training with him. I get to ride a bike and work the stopwatch, he does all the hard work.'

'Sounds like a good arrangement.'

'I'm meeting him in half an hour down by the quays. You're welcome to tag along.'

'I might just do that,' I said, though there was no might about it. The prospect of seeing Niall Boland on a bike was too good to miss.

Chapter Nineteen

I didn't have far to walk from Burke and Hare's to Grattan Bridge, where Parliament Street crossed the river and became Capel Street and where I'd arranged to meet Boland. Spring had gone into cold storage again today and the wind was little daggers off the river; and the daggers felt all the sharper after an hour by Burke's oil stove.

Thankfully, I didn't have long to wait before Boland came along.

I saw him cycling, puffing hard, up the sidewalk that ran along the river towards me, wobbling slightly in the wind. The cold had made his face ruddier even than usual, and the helmet he'd jammed down on to his head looked two sizes too small.

Then again, most things looked two sizes too small on Boland. He had a lumbering, thickset quality about him which, like many men his size, hid a surprisingly gentle, shy nature. I'd always liked him, though I'd never met anyone worse suited to being a murder detective. He was still the rookie on the team after switching a while back from Serious Crime, and it was beginning to look like he'd stay that way for ever. He spent most of his time down in Records, shuffling files, which made him useful to me, since there was no one better at digging up information, but didn't exactly blow away his colleagues.

He even managed to look out of place in the city, like his mind had never got used to being hemmed in by stone and longed for an uninterrupted sky, but it was combined with a baffled expression which made it clear he couldn't work out what was wrong.

He raised a hand and waved when he saw me waiting, then quickly brought the hand back down to the handlebar when the bike started swerving towards the traffic pouring down the quays in the opposite direction. Cars honked in warning, or it may have been plain annoyance.

Boland seemed to have that effect on some people.

Behind him came a leaner figure in sneakers and sweats and a hooded top with *Tennessee State University* written across the front. He had the hood up and his head was down as he ran, and the contrast between him and Boland's square, solid frame, thick hands and clumsy manner couldn't have been more pronounced. They were from different planets.

'Saxon,' said Boland with a gasp when they reached the bridge, and the other man stood catching his breath, hands resting on his thighs, 'this is Patrick Walsh.'

'I know,' I said, because I recognised him from last night at Fitzgerald's house. I held my hand out towards him. 'The Chief Superintendent's mentioned you. Said you're good.'

'I do my best,' Walsh said with a lopsided grin, returning the handshake, and I could see his eyes appraising me, wondering if I was worth the effort, especially since he was bound to have heard plenty about Fitzgerald and me in Dublin Castle.

The usual locker-room talk.

Not that it had stopped him making a play for Grace.

Boland was checking his stopwatch.

'You were faster that time,' he said appreciatively.

'I hear you're after the record,' I said.

'No point doing something if you don't want to be the best,' Walsh replied.

'That's Saxon's philosophy too,' said Boland. 'Are you two related?'

'Where you from?' Walsh asked me.

'Boston.'

'Boston, Mass., or Boston, Georgia?'

Was I supposed to be impressed?

'You're such an expert, you should be able to tell by my accent.'

'Course I know,' he said. 'I was only teasing.'

'Is that right?'

'I've seen you before,' he said.

'Have you?'

'Last night. Sitting in a Jeep opposite the Chief's house.'

So much for my being inconspicuous.

'You're an observant boy, Patrick.'

'That's what they all tell me, babe,' he laughed.

Babe?

This once, I decided to let it go.

I wasn't sure what I thought about this Walsh. He was pretty forward; we'd only just met and here he was talking to me like we were old friends. I've always had a bit more old-school reserve, frequently mistaken for indifference, hanging over me. It's not that I minded him talking to me like that, it just took some getting used to.

Besides, Fitzgerald had said he was a good cop. That was all that mattered to me.

As I waited for my mind to make itself up, I asked Boland what he knew about what had happened last night. I'd never been one for making small talk.

'You'd better ask Walsh about that,' Boland said. 'The Chief gave me the night off. I haven't even been out to the scene. Patrick can give you all the details.'

Though I wasn't at all prepared for what he told me.

'A copycat?' I said more loudly than I intended. Then lowered my voice as a few passing heads turned sharply in our direction. 'How the hell do they figure that?'

Walsh held his hands up in supplication.

'Not so fast. Bear with me, babe. I'm just telling you what

126

the theory was. The Chief reckoned we were getting too quick to see everything as the work of the Marxman.'

Paranoid, I wondered if she'd had me in mind when she said it.

'Plus,' he went on, 'there were points of difference.'

Not those again.

'The pattern's always been the same up till now. One shot, one victim. Disappearing without a trace. Clinical. This time it got messy. So messy that the gunman didn't even pick up the shells before making his getaway. *And* the first victim turned out to be one Charlie Knight. Known as a bit of a hitman himself. Serious Crime say he's carried out at least nine contract killings for various gangsters round the city over the last three years, and those are just the ones they know about, and yet he's never been charged with a single offence, not so much as an unpaid parking ticket. They call him the Grim Reaper in underworld circles.'

'So the thinking was someone finally took a hit out on *him*?'

'Had to happen eventually. The fact that he was standing in a doorway with his back to the gunman when he was shot could've been a mere coincidence.'

'You said that's what the theory *was*. What happened to change it?'

'The shells happened,' said Walsh. 'Soon as the firearms boys had a look, they IDed them as coming from the same type of weapon as the previous victims. Whether it's the same one exactly we'll have to wait for the usual tests. But—' He opened his hands in a shrug.

'How many gunmen can there be running round Dublin with a Glock .36?' I finished.

'You're reading my mind.'

'What about the girl?' I said.

'Looks like she just got in the way and had to be disposed of.'

'At least there's no change of tactics then. I was worried

127

last night meant he'd graduated to killing two at a time,' I said. 'Does she have a name yet?'

'Tara, wasn't it?' said Boland.

'Early,' said Walsh. 'Tara Early. Sixteen. She lived round by Summerhill in a flat with her older sister. Moved there a couple of months ago because she wasn't getting on with her parents. They didn't like her boyfriend, apparently. She'd only just left school and had started working at a supermarket round the corner from where she lived. She'd been out for the night with her mates in town, spending her first week's wages, seeing which bars would serve them underage. They said she left about eleven. She must've been on her way home, cutting through the back streets, when she came across the Marxman at work, maybe let out a cry, got *noticed*, and it was goodnight Vienna.'

It was that simple. Murder could be so trite, so petty. And I thought of something I'd once heard someone say: 'It's not the bullet with my name on it that worries me. It's the one that says "To whom it may concern".' That one had certainly found a home in Tara Early.

To cover my growing sense of gloom, I suggested we start walking back towards Dublin Castle. We crossed the road and began climbing up Parliament Street.

The gates of the castle were dead ahead at the top of the hill.

'I was talking to a friend of yours this morning,' Boland said to me as he pushed his bike and Walsh trotted briskly alongside, making jabbing motions at the air like a boxer.

'Yeah, who?'

'Alice Berg,' he said.

'You were talking to Alice?'

'The Chief asked me to give her a call. She said Alice had told you something about how she still thought her brother was murdered, have I got that right?'

I nodded. Fitzgerald had mentioned last night maybe

sending Walsh round to deal with Alice. Then the Marxman obviously intervened and Walsh had better things to do.

Boland, though, was always available.

God bless Fitzgerald, still thinking of me in the midst of the Marxman case.

'You get anything from her?'

'Are you kidding me?' said Boland. 'She's one of the most infuriating women I've ever met.'

'That include your ex-wife?' said Walsh.

'You leave my ex-wife out of it. Only I'm allowed to insult her. This Alice now, she's something else altogether. I couldn't get a squeak out of her. She's a brick wall in the shape of a woman, I swear, she wouldn't tell me anything. Soon as I mentioned what happened to her brother she clammed up like, I don't know, a clam with laryngitis. It's as if she thought I was trying to trick her into saying the wrong thing, when all I was trying to do was get her to say something that'd shed some light on why her brother killed himself.'

I wondered if that was how he'd put it. Little wonder she clammed up if he did. It wouldn't exactly have endeared him to her.

'If it's any consolation, I've had much the same experience with her,' I said. 'One minute she's insisting she knew everything about her brother's life and the next she's admitting she knew next to nothing.'

Not to mention spinning a whole different line to Vincent Strange, always assuming he was telling the truth. I wondered how many different versions of Alice there were.

'I met this Berg's girlfriend, you know,' announced Walsh unexpectedly.

That threw me.

'Felix had a girlfriend?'

'Is there something wrong with him having a girlfriend?'

'Alice swore to me he didn't have one, that's all,' I said. 'She said they only needed each other. How'd you find her?'

'She turned up yesterday morning wanting to see his body,' said Walsh. 'I didn't know who she was at first. I just told her that, for one thing, she was in the wrong place to see anyone's body, and, for another, she'd need the permission of the next of kin. She stormed out. Said she had as much chance of getting permission from the next of kin as she had of getting laid in a monastery. My kind of woman. I'd give her permission to see *my* body any time.'

'What's her name?' I said.

'Gina Fox.'

Alice, call me. Please – Gina.

So that's what that was about then.

'I'm glad to see I'm not the only one the sister was holding out on, anyway,' said Boland.

'I think Alice is starting to realise Felix had a whole secret life she knew nothing about,' I said, 'and she's afraid of where it might lead.'

'So now this foxy Gina gets written out of the official history,' said Walsh, 'like all those communists who made the mistake of falling foul of Stalin? Is this Alice going to airbrush her out of the family photo album too?'

'She's trying to protect him.'

'I'd say he's a bit beyond protecting now,' said Boland bluntly.

'She's thinking of his reputation.'

'*He that filches from me my good name,*' declared Walsh, pausing briefly in his dancing, '*robs me of that which not enriches him and makes me poor indeed.*'

Boland and I stopped walking and stared at him.

'Shakespeare,' he said with a bow. 'I used to want to be an actor. I learned that speech once for a part I was reading for. Othello. I didn't get it. Didn't get hardly any parts, to tell you the truth, which is probably how I ended up joining the police.'

We'd come to the lights at the top of the hill and waited for a gap in the traffic. I saw Boland's eye take in the flashing sign for a café further down the road towards town.

Saw him glance down at his watch.

Wrestling with temptation.

I couldn't help wondering what would become of him. Increasingly, he was like some slow, doe-eyed dog which sat around waiting to be kicked.

All detectives needed to have a spark, a sense of, yes, mission; it was nothing to be ashamed of, and murder squad detectives needed it more than anyone. They had to believe they were different from the rest, that they were better, and sometimes they took it so far they disappeared up their own asses with arrogance. But they still needed it, otherwise they were just making up the numbers, and Boland was drifting pretty close to that state these days.

His get-up-and-go had got up and gone.

The very fact that Fitzgerald had let him keep his night off even after the Marxman struck again, and sent him off today on errands to Alice when Felix's death wasn't even in her jurisdiction any more, was proof how little she needed or respected him.

She wouldn't have done it if Boland wasn't depressingly dispensable.

I caught Walsh's eye and he winked at me, grinning, like he knew what I was thinking and he thought the same, and at that moment I despised his conspiratorial grin, and despised myself for having invited it by being disloyal to Boland in the first place. Whatever he lacked in investigative nous, he more than made up for with a good heart, and I needed to believe in that sometimes.

What was equally depressing, though, was that Boland didn't even seem aware of the silent communication passing between Walsh and me. Or if he did, he was doing a remarkably good job of hiding it, and I'd never noticed that propensity in him before. He had one of those bluff, honest, open faces that just expose all the thoughts inside no matter what.

He caught me watching him and took his chance.

'Didn't you say you wanted to get something to eat?' he said.

'I thought you were on a diet?'

'One bacon roll can't hurt.'

'No,' I said. 'I don't feel like eating any more.'

'More for me then,' he said cheerfully.

At least he was still hungry for something, I found myself thinking unkindly.

Chapter Twenty

A girlfriend. It wasn't much to go on, but it was more than I'd had that morning when I woke.

Before we parted, Walsh gave me her number on the strict understanding that I didn't reveal it came from him; I think he still had plans of his own for calling her up and asking her out, and didn't want his chances ruined by me; but as it was, Gina didn't even ask.

Still, she took some persuading before she'd agree to talk to me.

'You're not the police?' she said. 'Then I don't get it. What do you want me for?'

'I'm—' What could I say? 'I'm a friend of Alice,' I put it feebly.

'Oh,' she replied. 'Alice.'

'She asked me to look into Felix's death. You knew him. I just thought—'

'I didn't know him that well,' she said. 'Well, not as well as I thought I knew him.' She sounded bitter, and I was immediately intrigued. 'Look, come round if you really want, I'll talk to you, it can't do any harm. But I don't see what help it's going to be either . . .'

It took a while to find the address she gave me. It was a basement apartment in a quiet street not far from Appian Way on the southside of the city. Potted plants round the door, a windowbox with flowers. Not my kind of thing at all. She probably had cuddly toys in her bedroom too. She was dressed like I expected from the outside of the apartment too. She had on some kind of shapeless shift with a bright summer pattern, and wore a string of beads round her neck interlaced with tiny silver charms, and she had that weird frizzy hair that never stays combed down for long; it spilled freely long and red past her shoulders.

Seeing her, I wasn't surprised it hadn't worked out with Felix. He didn't seem the type to go for a woman with such a vague, hippyish, New Age vibe about her; though to be fair, she seemed sharp enough when she introduced herself and let me in.

Inside was more austere than I'd expected from the outside too. The walls were bare, exposed brick and plaster, painted white – that seemed to be the required style with artists – and there was little save an iron-framed bed against the wall, the sheets and quilt all white too, and a table scattered with photographs. Her own, I guessed, and self-portraits mostly, some of her tastefully in the nude on the bed here in this tiny room – and there, through a window, I saw a yard and a stone wall painted white too with a covering of ivy, and that was in the background of some of the other nude shots.

She must be popular with the male neighbours.

And maybe some of the female ones too.

Among the photographs were also still lifes: of a watering can and a wooden staircase heaped with books and a window with a cracked pane of glass like a spider's web, as well as shots of a white cat stretched out in a patch of sunlight, and the same cat chasing a leaf. I was glad to see no sign of a cat round my feet, at any rate, since I wasn't in the mood for befriending another one. Hare was more than demanding enough.

Gina was silent for a while, letting me look at her pictures.

'Do you want a drink?' she said at last.

'That depends what you mean by drink,' I said.

'Never fear, I'm not going to offer you herbal tea or homeopathic tonic, if that's what you're worried about,' she said, as if reading my thoughts. 'I've got a bottle of wine here somewhere, you can drink it with me if you like.'

I liked.

The day was still chilly, so I was surprised when she lifted the wine and two glasses, carrying them all in one hand, each finger occupied, whilst with the other hand she pushed down the handle of the door and led me into the yard.

Traces of music, low and well behaved, drifted out from an open window above. Voices came out to join them at intervals but the words were indistinct. Somewhere up there too was the sound of a guitar being played badly, the same few chords over and over, as Gina laid the glasses and wine down on an iron table where there was room for just two chairs and we each scraped one back noisily and sat down.

'You don't seem like the sort of person who'd be friends with Alice,' Gina said to me once she'd poured the wine, sparing me the difficulty of deciding how to begin.

'You didn't get along?'

'I only met her once. That was enough. Enough for Alice too, from what Felix said.'

'She didn't take to you?'

'Ask her.'

Touchy subject. I let it drop. I could always come back to it later.

'How did you meet him?'

'It was my idea. As you saw inside, I'm a photographer too. I sent him one of my photographs. I'm not denying it, I was looking for my first step on the ladder. I wanted to have someone looking out for me. I thought if he liked my work, liked me, then it would help me get a foothold in the art world. Maybe get my own exhibition, space on someone's walls, a dealer, who knows? If you don't look out for yourself, no one else will.'

'Why Felix?'

'Why did I choose him to send my stuff to, you mean? Because I liked his work. Genuinely admired what he did.

His work was different from everyone else's. I know *everyone* thinks their own work is unique, but I really do think mine has a quality not everyone would appreciate. I thought he might. So I wrote to him, didn't know if I'd hear from him again, but he called me one night, we talked, and arranged to meet next day.'

'How long ago was this?'

'About a year ago?' she said, considering, slipping on a pair of sunglasses, reminding me of Alice. They both seemed to retreat behind sunglasses when the light hardly merited them. 'Yes, that'd be right. Maybe January last year. We arranged to meet in a hotel the following afternoon. We had drinks. I showed him my photographs. Some of them are quite, well, erotic I suppose. You saw them. It obviously had an effect on him. We ended up spending the rest of the day in a room at the hotel, making love. I didn't get the impression it was a surprise to him that the meeting ended that way.'

'Do you think he arranged the meeting in a hotel with sex in mind?'

'He was a man, he probably did everything with sex in mind, even putting up a shelf. Not that I can imagine Felix putting up shelves. But no,' and here she gave a small smile half of pleasure, half of mischief at the memory, 'I must confess that the hotel was my idea.'

'You planned on seducing Felix?'

'I wasn't averse to the idea. He was a good-looking man. I didn't think it would hurt, I thought if he felt something for me, he might . . . you know.'

'Make you a few introductions?'

'That was the idea. Afterwards, I agreed to see him again and for a few months we spent a lot of time together. I even used to go out with him sometimes at night when he was taking pictures. I suppose those are the moments I cherish most.'

'Did you ever go out with him when it was snowing?'

'I don't think so. I'm sure I'd remember. Why'd you ask?'

136

'No reason. Curiosity.'

She frowned at me slightly over the top of her sunglasses. I didn't blame her. Curiosity. Did I think she was stupid?

'And did he?' I said quickly to change the subject. 'Introduce you to the right people, I mean?'

'Vincent Strange was one. Have you heard of him?'

'Our paths have crossed.'

'Then you'll know all about him. Big shot. Big house. Big head. Important gallery. Frightfully well connected, don't you know? He'd been a supporter of Felix's from his early days. I hoped he might do the same for me but nothing came of it. Felix, though, I was growing rather fond of. The sex wasn't up to much, but he was sweet, and he seemed to have a genuine interest in my work. Always encouraged me. First one who ever had. I was touched. I was feeling vulnerable at the time, I suppose. I don't have any family. My sister died when I was young; both my parents are dead; I'd only recently arrived here from London, I hadn't made many friends, I was doing some crappy commercial photography work to make ends meet. So when Felix showed me some affection, I was glad of it. It wasn't just sex. Sometimes he didn't even want to make love. He just came round here and we lay on the bed and talked. Sometimes he put his head on my shoulder and slept.'

'So what went wrong?'

'Nothing, as far as I was concerned,' Gina said. 'No quarrels, no drifting apart, none of the usual clichés. He just called one day and said we shouldn't see one another again.'

'What did you do?'

'I'm not the begging type,' Gina replied from behind her sunglasses, unreadable. 'I wasn't going to throw myself at him – though I know what you're probably thinking. That that's exactly what I did at the hotel that first afternoon.'

'I wasn't thinking that.'

'Doesn't matter if you were. It's all over now. I called him a few times, turned up once at Strange's gallery when I knew

he'd be there, but he was distant, preoccupied, almost—'
She stopped herself clumsily.

'What were you going to say?'

She spoke the next words slowly. Reluctantly, I thought, though she might have just wanted me to think they were reluctant; they might have been exactly the words she wanted me to hear all along.

'I was going to say he seemed almost afraid to talk to me, but that wouldn't be what I meant. That is, it's what I thought at the time, but maybe I just needed to believe there was some other reason he was dumping me rather than the fact he'd just tired of me.'

'Were you surprised when he broke off your relationship?'

'Surprised is putting it mildly. I was spitting fire. Look, I've been dumped before, it's not exactly a new experience. But usually for some reason, you know? With him, I couldn't figure out what I'd done wrong. I thought I deserved an explanation at least.'

'Why did you think he'd ended the affair?'

'Oh, there's no real mystery about it,' said Gina. 'He told me eventually. He said it was Alice's fault, said she didn't think I was right for him. As if she was his mother or something. And more than just a mother, if you know what I mean. I don't think she thought anyone was good enough for Felix. Except her.'

There was something about the way she said this that made me aware she meant more than she was saying. I left a silence for a moment, then said: 'When I was talking to Alice the other day, I sensed something in the way she spoke about Felix. Something—'

'Not quite right?' she jumped in. 'That's what I thought too. They were way too close for brother and sister. There was too much of an intimacy there. Wasn't normal. She may come across as some kind of vestal virgin – doesn't take any lovers, there's never any gossip or scandal about her name – but if you ask me, that's because she already had what she wanted in Felix. Had in every sense of the word, if you know what I mean. It's no wonder she was so jealous when I started getting in the way.'

'And did you sense Felix felt the same about her?'

'He was always talking about her,' she confessed. 'How Alice had done this and Alice had said that. Always checking things were OK with Alice. We couldn't have a date or go anywhere without making sure it was OK with Alice, and obviously it pretty quickly started to be not OK with Alice.'

'Must've been awkward for you.'

'You go out with someone, you don't expect them to be running home each night to their sister, or be constantly talking about her when they're in bed with you. It's bad enough when they talk about their former lovers. When it's their sister, it starts to get a bit creepy.'

'Why did you put up with it?'

'I had no right to expect anything of Felix, he was an occasional lover and if I ever allowed myself to think there was more to it than that, then I knew I was just daydreaming. I was still nothing next to him, a minor thing in his world, Alice's world, Strange's world. But I did think we had something, we fitted together, so when he was able to throw it away so easily on what seemed to me so flimsy an excuse, then I was disappointed in him. He wasn't the man I thought he was. He hadn't lived up to what I hoped he'd be.'

So that was what she'd meant on the phone by not knowing him as well as she'd thought. And maybe she hadn't. Maybe I hadn't either. Was there something in Felix and Alice's relationship that I hadn't picked up on before? And did it matter if I hadn't?

Lives are messy, after all. Doesn't mean there's any connection between the messiness of the life and the mystery of the death.

I took another sip of wine and replaced the glass, watching

the light dance on the unsettled surface for a moment before settling into the reflection of a window up above.

'Did you ever see him again afterwards?'

'After we split up? Sure. I was at a party, some friends of friends of friends of Strange. Don't ask me how I got an invite, but I turned up. And yes, I probably was half hoping I'd bump into Felix. I hadn't completely given up, though weeks had passed without a word. I was wandering round looking for someone I knew when I saw him with a woman. They were standing in a dark corner and I was sure they'd been kissing. I was annoyed, I suppose, that he'd been there with another woman so soon after dumping me, and I just walked out of the party. It was only afterwards, when Strange introduced me to Felix's sister, that I realised she was the woman at the party. She just smiled at me smugly, as if she'd won.'

'How did you hear Felix was dead?'

'Strange called me. He knew Felix and I had been lovers. He said he thought I was owed the courtesy of a call. It's not as though Felix and I were destined to be together or anything, but I at least deserved that, otherwise I'd have heard about it on the late news.'

'How did you feel?'

'I just felt dreadfully sorry for him. I went round to the police, wanting to see his body, but they said I couldn't without Alice's permission. I even left a note for her at Felix's house but she never had the courtesy to get back to me. Same old Alice.'

'She's had a lot on her mind.'

There I went, defending her again; I'd have to knock that on the head.

'I don't mind admitting I was scared too,' Gina said. 'When something like that strikes so close to home, it makes you think no one's safe. But then I heard this morning that it wasn't the Marxman at all, and then I just felt ashamed that I hadn't realised he was in such pain, enough pain to – I don't need to say it – to do something like that. It was a long time since we split up, so there's no reason why I should have known. I felt bad, that's all.'

'You've no doubt he killed himself?'

She looked at me like she didn't understand the question.

'What's it got to do with what I think?' she said. 'Strange told me about the autopsy report. The papers this morning said the police were no longer looking for anyone else in connection with his death.'

'Alice doesn't think Felix killed himself,' I said. 'She still thinks he was murdered.'

She shook her head sharply.

'I wouldn't listen to anything that bitch tells you. She is one seriously screwed-up lady. Trust her to turn Felix's death into some major drama for her. It couldn't just be suicide. Is that why she has you asking questions? What are you, some kind of private detective?'

'Nothing like that. I'm the one who found Felix's body,' I told her. 'He called me that night, asked to meet me. He thought I could help him, but I never got the chance to find out what it was he wanted to tell me. He sounded – troubled.' I didn't mention how he'd said someone was trying to kill him. 'My only interest is in finding out what happened.'

'You found him?' She seemed genuinely taken aback by the news. 'I heard on the radio that a woman had found him, but I thought it meant some local in Howth.'

'I asked for my name to be kept out of it,' I explained.

'Least they respected it. More than the police obviously did when I said I didn't want to be involved.' She took another sip of wine. She must be on to her third glass by now. 'It doesn't matter,' she added quickly. 'I don't mind. I haven't had much chance to talk about Felix since he died. And I suppose that explains what Miranda Gray was doing here too.'

'Felix's therapist has been here?'

141

'She turned up yesterday. Asking what I knew about Felix's death. She said she was worried about some stuff Alice had said to her. Gray used to treat them both, you probably know that already. She used to see him every Monday and Friday afternoon. When we were together, I'd drive him round to her consulting rooms and wait outside in the car whilst he went in for his session. She used to see Alice straight after. Cosy set-up, don't you think?'

'And now she's digging. I wonder why?'

'She said she was concerned for Alice,' said Gina. 'Not an emotion I find myself sharing, I must say.'

My eye was distracted momentarily by a bee which had landed on the edge of the table and was now walking unsteadily about, one of the first of the new spring.

I hate bees. I was stung once as a child and still remembered it, the panic I'd felt and how my mother had berated me for making such a fuss. She wasn't a woman who believed in people making a fuss, not even frightened children. And maybe she was right. There were easier ways to deal with pests than panic, and I moved my hand quickly as I sat there to flatten it against the table. But Gina was too fast for me. By the time I had moved, the bee was already dead and she was wiping her hand on a cloth to clean off the remains.

She laughed lightly.

'More wine?'

Chapter Twenty-One

The last thing I expected when I got back to my apartment some hours later was to find Alice sitting on the stairs outside my door waiting for me; and I wasn't sure I was in the mood for talking to her either. My head was the worse for wear with wine. Gina had ended up making pasta and showing me more of her photographs, opening another bottle. And then another one after that. She was hard to keep up with, and I'd got out of the habit of drinking seriously during the day, which Fitzgerald would no doubt say was a good habit to get out of.

Now here was Felix's sister expecting *what* of me?

And what would I get in return?

More evasions?

A woman like Alice needed delicate handling, and she'd caught me at the wrong time for diplomacy. Hence I was a little abrupt as I asked how she'd gained entry to the building.

'The doorman let me in. I said we were friends.'

Hugh. I should make a note reminding me to kill him.

'I went round to the house,' Alice explained, 'and yours was the last number that had called. I tried ringing you back, but there was no answer here, and I knew you didn't have a new contact number for me. So I came round.'

A simple enough explanation.

Except I didn't remember giving her my address.

Still, I could hardly leave her sitting on the steps.

'You'd better come in,' I said.

I unlocked the door and ushered her inside, chiding myself as I started giving the apartment a brief once-over to see if it was tidy. Like I cared whether it was tidy. I must be picking up some civilised habits from Fitzgerald; I'd have to put a stop to that.

'How's the hotel?' I said.

'I don't think it's going to work out,' said Alice. 'I don't know what I'm doing there really, apart from running up a huge bill on my credit card in the mini bar. I can't run away from Felix simply by leaving the house. I can't stop *thinking* about him simply because I can't feel his presence in the room like I do at home.'

'At least the suicide verdict means the police can release the body,' I replied. 'Isn't that what you want? Grace Fitzgerald says you've been asking about it pretty insistently.'

'My brother's body was collected from the morgue this afternoon,' Alice said with a stiff nod, either not noticing or ignoring the harder edge to my response than I'd allowed myself to indulge on our previous meetings. 'That's another reason I came round,' she continued unruffled instead. 'I wanted to give you this.'

She took a card from her pocket and handed it to me.

Invitation to a funeral.

My social life really needed improving.

'This is fast,' I said, looking down at it.

'There's not much point dragging it out,' said Alice. 'I'd rather get this over with as speedily as I can and then start getting on with my life again. If you can call it a life.'

But I wasn't in the mood right now for feeling sorry for her. I was tired of hearing different versions of what she'd said, what she thought. My sympathy for her was leaking away through the gaps between them all.

'You didn't need to bring this round personally,' was all I said.

'I wanted to. I wanted to make sure you got it. Also, I . . . I wondered how you were getting on with investigating the circumstances of his death.'

'You're not letting this go?'

'Not until I'm satisfied that Felix died by his own hand, no.'

Died by his own hand: she talked sometimes like she'd been a Victorian governess in a previous life.

'I don't think I can help you,' I said, and she didn't make any effort to hide her disappointment. And, annoyed with her though I was, her look scratched at me because I knew what it was like when no one would help. When no one would listen.

Sydney's death had taught me that lesson.

'But yesterday you said—'

'I know what I said yesterday. It's not that I don't want to help. I told you, I still think there are plenty of unanswered questions about Felix's death. I can't get it out of my head, his call to me that night. Can't stop thinking that maybe I could've done something, if I'd asked for more details, if I'd got to the lighthouse quicker. But you're not being straight with me. If you want your brother's death investigated, why don't we start with Gina Fox?'

She flushed, and a flash of something crossed her face. Anger?

'How did you find out about her?' she said tightly.

'It wasn't hard. You can't ask complete strangers to investigate your brother's death and then not expect them to find out he had a lover.'

'*Had* is correct. That slut was no longer part of Felix's life.'

'Made sure of that, did you?'

'You've been talking to her, I can tell,' she said. 'I can recognise her lies. They're infectious. Is that where you've been this afternoon?'

'It's really none of your business where I've been.'

Her next words were careful.

'I didn't like Gina, it's true. And I told Felix exactly what I thought about her, that she was using him, that she was bad for him. But it was his decision to break up with her. He was a grown man. What do you think I did – threaten to stop his pocket money if he saw her again?'

It wasn't as easy as that. A couple in as long and complicated a relationship as Felix and Alice could make demands of one another without anything needing to be said, much less threats made. Just the thought of displeasing the other, of pushing them away, of losing them, of being alone, could be enough. But I held my silence. Alice knew all that as well as I did, and she knew that I knew it. She didn't need me to spell it out to her.

'That still doesn't explain why you didn't get around to mentioning the fact that Gina existed,' I said.

'She and Felix split up nearly a year ago. I had no reason to suspect that Felix's death had anything to do with her, and I certainly didn't want her brought back into my life. Gina Fox is not a pleasant woman. She was jealous of what Felix and I had together.'

'According to her, it was the other way round.'

'What?'

'She thinks you and Felix were . . . how shall I put this? On closer terms than brother and sister normally are. She thinks you couldn't cope with the fact that Felix wanted to be with her, be in her bed. That he took her with him when he was taking photographs.'

'That's another lie,' said Alice. 'Felix always worked alone.'

'That's not how Gina remembers it.'

'And does Gina remember how, after Felix told her he wanted nothing more to do with her, she put us through hell? I remember. The late-night phone calls. The abusive letters. It didn't matter where we were. We'd turn around and there she'd be, following us, watching us.'

'You think she was dangerous?'

'In the right circumstances, yes.'

'All the more reason then to tell me about her after Felix died, surely?'

Down came the mask again.

'I'm not saying she had anything to do with my brother's death,' she said.

'Aren't you?'

'No.'

I put my fingers to the bridge of my nose and pressed them hard. My head felt foggy. I wanted to lie down. Wanted silence. Wanted not to have to play this game any more.

'You see, Alice, this is the problem I have. You say you want me to find out more, and then you turn monosyllabic on me. Not cooperative. You can't ask people to help you if you won't give them anything to go on. If you won't make the journey easier for them.'

'I don't mean to be uncooperative. It's just . . . I don't want to say anything that . . .'

'Makes Felix look bad, I understand that. But what's more important? Keeping Felix's secrets, whatever they were, or finding out what really happened that night, finding out if someone *was* trying to kill him, like he said, if he *had* seen something he shouldn't?'

'Don't you think I want to find out?'

'I think you haven't thought through yet what you want. All I know is there's something going on. You're digging, you get me digging; now Miranda Gray's digging.'

'What's Miranda got to do with this?' she burst out. I could see it was news to her that her therapist was looking into the circumstances of her brother's death as well.

'Your therapist went round to Gina's place yesterday fishing for information.'

'She didn't tell me she was going to do that,' Alice said quietly. 'But Miranda cared a lot about Felix. Maybe she doesn't believe Felix killed himself either.'

'On the contrary,' I said. 'She told the police that Felix's suicide was totally in keeping with what she'd learned about him during their sessions together.'

'That's ridiculous. Felix wasn't suicidal.'

147

'She said he was suffering from depression. You told me he'd had a breakdown.'

'There's a big difference between a breakdown and suicide.'

'Tell that to Miranda Gray.'

'I will. That's exactly what I'll do. She's no right to be telling the police anything about Felix. She was his doctor. She was bound by an oath to him.'

'Even after he was maybe killed?' She didn't answer, so I pressed on, probably foolishly. 'Who says she was digging into *Felix*'s state of mind anyway?'

I was probably slitting my own throat. If I really did want to find out more about Felix's death, I needed Alice on side. But she was irritating me too much to pussyfoot around.

'What do you mean by that?' she said.

'What if she was trying to find out what's going on in *your* head? Find out why, for instance, you'd tell me your brother was murdered, then tell Strange you said no such thing.'

'Is that what he says?'

'He says you told him that I was bothering you, trying to get you to believe all sorts of wild stories about Felix's death. That I was playing with your mind.'

She seemed confused.

'I . . . I don't know why he said that,' she said at last. 'I'm sorry if that's what he told you. It's not true. I *told* him Felix had been killed, but he just told *me* I was being silly, that I was upset. Not thinking straight. Just like *I* told Felix. You do believe me, don't you?'

'I don't know what to believe,' I said honestly. 'When I try to put the pieces in order, I'm not even sure I know anything about you. What secrets you might be hiding.'

'I liked you,' said Alice. 'I thought we could be friends. I really did. I see now that I was wrong. I won't bother you again, if that's how you feel about me. That I'm a liar.'

'I didn't say that.'

'Not in so many words. You didn't need to.'

'Alice, don't be silly.'

The words were wasted. She was gone. The door slammed, and I heard the clattering echo of her footsteps fading down the stairs, and I kicked myself.

Metaphorically, that is. I wouldn't trust myself to stand up straight after all that wine if I did it literally. But I certainly deserved to be kicked.

I considered running after her, but what would be the point? The fact was, I realised as I stood there listening to her footsteps vanish down the stairwell, I was tired of Alice, tired of Felix, tired of it all. I wished I'd never heard of them. Wished Felix had never called me that first night. It felt like he'd locked a collar round my neck and thrown the key into the black water where even the beam of the lighthouse couldn't find it; and no matter how deeply I swam, I'd never find it. All I'd do was forget where the surface was.

Part Two

Chapter Twenty-Two

'Any excuse to wear black,' Fitzgerald said as she watched me getting dressed on the morning of Felix's funeral.

'And I have the mood to match,' I replied.

I wasn't looking forward to this. I didn't like funerals at the best of times. No one likes funerals, of course; it's not like people go to them for fun. But I dislike them to the extent that I'd normally go into hiding to avoid having to attend one. I'd actually left town on the day Sydney was buried and hadn't come back for a week. I'd flown to St Paul because that was where the next flight was headed when I got to the airport.

It's because you're afraid of your own mortality that you avoid funerals, some smartass once said to me. Screw that. I'm not afraid of my own mortality. If there's anything I'm afraid of, it's having to watch other people's grief. Strong emotions of any kind, I guess, including my own. I prefer people to keep their emotions to themselves. The only reason I was going to this funeral was because . . . well, I still wasn't quite sure.

Because I couldn't let it go, I guess, whatever I might've let Alice think.

'How do I look?'

'Like you always do.'

'That bad?'

I went through into the kitchen to pour myself some coffee. It was bright out, but still as cold as it had been, if not colder.

It was easy to forget when you saw the bright sunshine some days that the air didn't feel the way the sun was pretending. I wished the weather would make up its mind. The last thing I need is a climate with an identity crisis.

I took a cookie from the barrel and ate it in silence. It was something to do more than anything. I didn't feel like eating.

'What time is it?'

'Quit worrying,' said Fitzgerald as she came out from the bedroom and started getting her own papers together for work. I must've asked her that question a hundred times already that morning. 'You'll be fine.'

'I won't know anyone.'

'You know Alice.'

'Yeah, and she's the one I want to avoid. I don't even know if the invite still stands. She's not been returning any of my calls. And what if she starts asking me again about Felix? What do I tell her?'

'The truth,' said Fitzgerald. 'You tell her the truth.'

'You make it sound so simple.'

To her, it was.

I envied her that certainty.

The funeral was at eleven at a church in a part of the city known as Harold's Cross, though why I'd never bothered to find out. It was just about far enough to justify getting the Jeep out, but I'd already decided to walk that morning, to give myself a chance to prepare. Down Leeson Street and over the canal, turning right on to Grand Parade.

It was a quiet morning, one of those days which never seem to have mustered enough energy to get started but are just ticking off the hours until sunset.

Within half an hour of setting out, I was there.

Early, of course, which meant no one else had arrived. So I wandered through the graveyard, round the back of the church, smoking a cigar, reading the epitaphs on the overgrown graves, and thinking mournfully of all those other lives of which nothing now remained but a few words on slabs bought and paid for by loved ones who were now long forgotten themselves. Some had been dead centuries, and it was these graves, strangely, which made me most sad. At least those killed in recent weeks and months had someone to remember them by, someone to keep the graves tended. The ancient dead had nothing.

I looked up at the old church, at those elaborate arches carved into the stone, and at the stained-glass windows stained further by traffic fumes, and couldn't figure why Alice had picked this one of all places for her brother's funeral. Had he left instructions? And what was it here that had appealed to him if he had? However it had looked when the stones were first pulled into place, now it was dreary and shabby and hunched. Another couple of years and it would likely be another bingo hall, fixtures and fittings torn out to be sold off for scrap.

Oh, pull yourself together, girl. What business was it of mine what the hell they did with it? It wasn't like the church meant anything to me, or I gave any thought to God and the angels – though I surely gave as much thought to them as they ever gave to me. I'd scarcely been inside a church since I was a kid back home in Boston, when I practically had to be dragged to the altar, enduring interminable masses in the hope of warding off sin.

And a fat lot of good it had done me.

A fat lot of good it had done Sydney too, who'd believed all that crap.

My only experience of religion since then had been of the kind killers used to inflame themselves into action. Theological pornography was how I saw it. And if it gave comfort to them, had been my thinking, what could it have to offer me? I kept my distance from God and expected Him to have the same consideration for me. It wasn't much to ask.

All the same, it was depressing to see these old places falling into dissolution. Another part of the fabric of the city being thoughtlessly unpicked, like a child pulling a thread in a shirt to see what happens and then watching as the shirt unravels.

By the time I got round to the front of the church again, I was relieved to find that others had started to arrive, sparing me in the process from my own unoriginal thoughts.

Reporters and photographers lingered too near the gates, most likely waiting for any well-known faces who might turn up to pay their respects to Felix, but there weren't many of them. There would've been more had it still been thought that Felix had died at the hands of the Marxman, but that angle hadn't lasted longer than it takes for a butterfly to reach old age.

And what was another suicide to interest them?

Especially the suicide of an artist. That was what tortured artists were supposed to do, wasn't it? Maybe Felix was just obeying the script in that respect too.

I acknowledged with a nod the few faces in the press pack with whom I was on speaking terms, and then went inside, pausing for a moment in the aisle to look at the coffin up front, finding it hard to believe that the man I'd found sprawled on the rocks out at Howth only nights ago was now lying in there, cold, decaying already, the lid screwed tight over his head. Then I took my seat at the back of the dimmed church and tried to make myself inconspicuous. The scent of incense made my head light. I almost felt high.

A few people must have guessed who I was, or maybe they were friends of Alice, because I received the odd acknowledgement of my existence. Over there were some faces I recognised from local TV, others whose pictures looked vaguely familiar from the newspapers, a couple of policemen in uniform. But I didn't know any well enough to speak more than a half-dozen words to. Most of the mourners I couldn't even have told apart.

There was no sign of Gina Fox.

Only Strange stood out. He'd come wrapped in his fur coat, turned up at the collar, and entered the church with the sense of ownership I'd seen in him whilst we sat drinking coffee in Temple Bar. Maybe he treated everywhere in Dublin like it was his own.

Today he took a seat near the front and started to talk rather too loudly to people nearby, so that intermittent disconnected words drifted over the hum and whisper of the rest of the mourners right to the back where I sat, before in my imagination hitting the wall like a wave and returning to join the conversation up front again.

I felt I could've surfed down there on the crest of them.

After about ten minutes, Alice arrived. She didn't look around as she came in, so she didn't see me, just made her way to the front and took her seat. She was dressed simply, head bare. It didn't look like she'd been crying, but she looked exhausted, pale, washed out.

I was relieved when the service started and I could measure out the ordeal in readings and dubious music. Then came the eulogies. A magazine editor who'd commissioned Felix for a series of photographs spoke about how well respected Berg was in his field; Strange discussed Felix's place in the present art scene, his themes, his legacy. There was something mechanical about their words. Warmth didn't exactly beam out of them.

Alice had clearly chosen not to speak about her brother at all.

She simply sat there, staring ahead.

When they carried the coffin out, I stayed seated and didn't bother following as the church emptied. I could hardly remember why I'd come at all. There was no reason for me to be here. Outside I heard the cries of crows as they settled in the trees round the churchyard, and thought I heard bells, muffled, remote, somewhere above.

How many peals for a life?

Could I light up in here, or were there fire alarms? That would be all I needed, setting off an alarm in church during a funeral. Even I had to draw the line somewhere.

I closed my eyes and laid my head on the back of the pew, worn wood biting hard into the soft skin at the nape of my neck. Then I snapped them open again as I heard the sound of the church door opening and footsteps materialised, clicking quietly on stone.

A shadow, lengthened by the sun behind, tapered down the centre of the aisle.

'Alice?'

'Saxon, I thought it was you.'

'Shouldn't you be—'

'Out there watching them lower the body into the ground?'

'That's the general idea.'

'I suppose so,' she said coolly. 'Not much point coming to see the play if you leave before the final act. But to hell with that, and to hell with Felix. He didn't give a fig for convention and neither do I. I've been feeling sick now for days. I don't know what's wrong with me, but I do know this is the last thing I need. This' – unable to find the right word, she gestured around her at the church – '*show* was all his idea, not mine. I didn't even know this was what he had planned until the solicitor showed me his will. He always told me he wanted to be cremated when he died. I don't even like this church.'

'Why'd he pick it?'

'Beats me. Our aunt, when she died, left one third of her money to the restoration fund here, which, as you can see, didn't do much good. She'd have been better off throwing it straight on to the fire; at least it would have kept us warm before it was all gone. She was married here, you see, years ago, years and years, centuries. The marriage didn't last long. He ran off with a nightclub singer, leaving her with a few thousand pounds' worth of debt – and this was the days when a few thousand pounds' worth of debt meant something – not to mention a bad case of, well, family rumour never put a name to it, but some unfortunate disease, let's put it that way. As a result she could never have children of her own.

158

Instead she took us in when our parents died. She obviously never forgot about the husband, though, otherwise why leave a third of her fortune to this place?'

'You didn't approve of her charitable instincts?'

'Forced to choose between Felix and me having the money, or this hole, then yes, I think I'd choose us. But a will is a will. It's clearly a family tradition to leave surprises, though I wish someone had told *me* about it. I must remember to rewrite my own, telling the beneficiaries they have to personally scatter my ashes on the summit of Mount Kilimanjaro if they want the money; it'll serve all the bastards right. It must have been Felix's idea of a joke to make me come here, but I don't see why I should have to go along with it.'

'The thought of his funeral probably seemed so far away at the time that he didn't think about it.'

'*Remember thou must die*: that's what they always told the emperors. They used to employ people to whisper that in the king's ear so that he never forgot he was mortal too, for all his apparent power. Felix had a habit of forgetting he was mortal.'

She stopped suddenly and looked round as if she'd heard something, but it was only the door of the church creaking shut again after her entrance. She'd been standing up to that point, but now she edged into the pew next to me and lowered her voice.

'About the other day . . .' she said.

'Don't say anything. That was my fault,' I replied. 'I was frustrated at everything going nowhere. Half-answers. Loose ends. I shouldn't have been so tough on you.'

She shook her head.

'You were right. I should have told you about Gina from the start. I let my feelings get in the way. I wasn't thinking about Felix, I was thinking about me. And I haven't been feeling so hot. I don't know what's wrong with me.'

'You don't have to explain.'

'I do, so that you can see I have no hard feelings. I told you I wanted us to be friends, and I haven't changed my mind.

You must come round to the house. I'm back there now. And soon. I realise now I had no right to expect you to take the same interest in what happened to Felix that I had. That I *have*. It's just . . . the whole thing . . . didn't add up. Still doesn't.'

There it was, the subject I'd feared.

The truth was, I'd been thinking about little else. Alternating between Fitzgerald's clear logical conviction that Felix's death had nothing to do with the Marxman, and my own continuing doubts, and always my thoughts returned to his voice on the phone that night.

Someone is trying to kill me . . .

But before I could decide whether to admit as much to Alice, and thereby risk opening up again that Pandora's box which Fitzgerald had warned me about, the door of the church suddenly slammed open and a voice called out harshly: 'Alice?'

Bear-like Strange in the fur coat appeared round a pillar.

And this time the bear had come with a sore head.

'You're here,' he said testily, holding out his hands in a gesture of impatience at Alice. 'Everyone's asking what's become of you. What are you doing in here?'

'Saying hello to Saxon.'

His eye caught mine briefly, but he barely took me under his notice. It was like he wanted to pretend he didn't remember me, make me feel too insignificant to warrant a place in the memory bank of so august a human being as Vincent Strange.

'Hello doesn't take three-quarters of an hour.'

'It didn't. Don't exaggerate, Vincent,' Alice said with a sigh. 'And stop fussing. I'm coming.' And she put her hand on the pew in front and pulled herself to her feet, refusing the hand he stretched out to help her. To me she said: 'Another time.'

'I'll call.'

'I'd like that.'

And then the bear bore her away, and I realised she'd said nothing about why, if she wanted to be friends and she was back in the house, she'd returned none of my calls.

I waited a while longer before leaving, by which point the mourners had all drifted away; the press pack was following, even the crows had dispersed.

Only a single figure still waited by the gate.

He looked up when I stepped out and offered a smile.

'It's about time. What were you doing in there? Confessing all your sins? No, couldn't have been or you'd still be in there.'

'Fisher, you fat old fraud,' I said. 'What are you doing here?'

'I knew you'd be pleased to see me.'

Chapter Twenty-Three

'So you know Miranda Gray?' said Fitzgerald.

It was late afternoon, and we were sitting at a table in the window of a restaurant in Coppinger Row. It was still cold, which was why the tables outside were all empty, and people walked by huddled inside overcoats, shuffling over intermittently to look at the menu.

'Know her in every sense of the word, isn't that right, Fisher?' I said.

'Please, you're making me blush,' Lawrence Fisher said, though of course the only colour in his increasingly fleshy cheeks was coming from the wine we'd ordered to go with the pasta. 'Miranda and I went to university together, both studying psychiatry. She was a very brilliant student. We had a little thing going on for a while, though we both got over it. It's long past now. Our paths diverged.'

Hers into a lucrative private practice treating rich artists who'd come to the conclusion that their misery was not just a symptom of the human condition shared by everyone, but something utterly unique to them and well worth spending thousands trying to cure – an optimistic view of the benefits of therapy which their therapists did nothing to dissuade them of – whilst Fisher had gone into criminal psychology, spending years in prisons interviewing killers, honing his research, before he'd leapt on the opportunity afforded him by a book I'd written on offender profiling, in which he figured prominently, to shuffle off the constraints of a normal job and embrace modern media stardom instead.

He now wrote two books a year, and appeared in numerous TV programmes and videos, many of them bearing his name (*Lawrence Fisher's World of Criminal Masterminds* was a particularly risible example I'd caught a glimpse of whilst switching channels late one night, though I had to admit I'd enjoyed it thoroughly), whilst salving his conscience for having given up that less lucrative but unarguably more worthwhile former position by working, often unpaid, for Scotland Yard, and the Dublin Metropolitan Police too when he could, as a consultant on a string of obdurate cases

He was overworked, overfatigued, overweight, and I had never once seen him lose his temper, or heard of it happening. Whenever he felt his patience fraying, he often said, he just thought of his large house in Highgate, his second home on the beach in north Cornwall, a third in France, and the school fees he had to pay for his five children.

Zen calm descended instantly.

Not that the Zen calm had stopped his beard going greyer than I remembered since we'd last met.

What I liked about him was that he didn't pretend he was doing anything other than blundering his way through, doing his best. His best was as good as it got, as it happened, but still he didn't play the infallible card like some of them did, didn't pretend that he was the Pope with a direct line to unquestionable truth. Nor did he cod himself that the creeps he worked with could ever be cured, which was another tick on his bonus card to me. Psychologists generally thought they had the answer to everything. They seemed to think that if they could just figure out what traumas or deprivations lay in a killer's childhood then all their subsequent distorted development could be understood, and fixed, like a car mechanic taking a engine apart and fitting the pieces together again so that it ran smoothly.

It was a lie, and a dangerous one, but they stuck to it.

'I've always kept in touch, though,' he was saying now about Miranda Gray. 'Christmas cards, postcards from holiday, phone calls, the occasional lunch when we were in the same town at the same conferences.'

'Olive approves, does she?'

'How many times do we have to go over this? My wife's name is Laura, as you well know. And what's there not to approve of?'

'I've heard those conferences can be awfully full of temptation.'

'You heard right. The late nights, the heavy drinking, the heady excitement that comes from listening all day to ten-thousand-word papers from some crackpot out of Eastern Europe who wants to prove a link between the shape of a man's toenail clippings and his criminal tendencies. It can all get too much and we just rip each other's clothes off and leap into bed. It's an orgy out there. But I've a bad back these days. Not to mention that I'm a very happily married man who couldn't afford the child support payments if my wife caught me misbehaving. Hence I am a veritable paradigm of virtue.'

'So how come you're here in Dublin with her?'

'It was chance,' Fisher told Fitzgerald, 'as I've been explaining patiently to Saxon all afternoon. I'd contacted Miranda to tell her that a TV producer I knew was looking for fresh talking heads for some new programme he was making and that I'd recommended her and she should look out for his call. I could tell she was concerned about something. We got talking. She told me that one of her patients had committed suicide.'

'And you came hurrying over here to save her, her knight in shining armour?' I said.

'If you insist on seeing it like that.'

'Hold her hand? Offer a shoulder to cry on?'

'Saxon, you make it sound almost lascivious.'

'I'm just trying to see it through Daphne's eyes.'

'Will you stop bringing my wife into this? *Laura* knows there's nothing going on between Miranda and me. That spark died long ago, to be replaced by a small flame of mutual respect, admiration and friendship. She's had a tough time, it's hard when a patient dies. I thought a bit of mutual support would be in order, especially with the funeral.'

'Is that what they call it now? Mutual support? Maybe we should be honoured you're wasting your time here with us then,' I said. 'Shouldn't you be at her place consoling her?'

'She's working until late,' he said with dignity. 'We've arranged to meet after. Not that it's any of your concern. And not that there's much I *can* say besides offering my commiserations. It happens all the time. Dealing with suicides is an occupational hazard for a therapist. The prisoners were always hanging themselves when I worked in the jails.'

'No loss there then,' I said under my breath.

Fisher gave me a disapproving stare.

'Did Miranda tell you who it was had died?' asked Fitzgerald.

'Not at first. There was no reason to. I hadn't even known Felix Berg was Miranda's patient, how would I? It was private, confidential patient-and-doctor stuff. But once he was dead . . . well, there wasn't the same need to protect his privacy.'

'Which is *how* she came to let slip something very interesting,' I said to Fitzgerald, 'which is *why* I suggested we meet here so you could hear it for yourself.'

'Thanks for sparing me the trouble of telling her in my own time,' said Fisher.

'Stop griping and just tell her.'

'Well?' said Fitzgerald.

'Miranda told me,' said Fisher, 'that Felix Berg confessed to being the Marxman.'

I don't think Fitzgerald could've been more amazed had Fisher told her he was having an affair with Seamus Dalton. She looked between the two of us without saying a word, almost as if she was trying to decide if this was some tasteless joke.

'I know it sounds incredible,' Fisher said, 'but that's what he told her. I couldn't believe it myself. Of course, I'd been following the case in the newspapers. Now Miranda was telling me one of her patients was confessing to being the killer. Shortly after the second shooting she had a session with Berg and he came right out and said *he'd* killed Terence Prior. That he'd been waiting in the shadows at his house and simply shot him.'

'Did he say why?'

'He said he felt like doing it. Straightforward as that. When he was in America – Saxon here tells me he'd had a break-down and was out there recuperating or something – he told Miranda he'd started frequenting gun clubs and got a taste for it. He'd managed to smuggle a gun back into the country and had decided to start killing.'

'Like you do,' I said grimly.

'But it's absurd,' said Fitzgerald.

'Naturally it was absurd, that was the point. Miranda was in a turmoil, wondering what she should do. On the one hand she had to respect the professional relationship between them. On the other hand she couldn't simply ignore what he'd said. Two people had died at this stage. What if Felix really was the Marxman and he went on adding more victims to the total? Besides which, she realised she herself was in danger. Either he *was* the Marxman and might soon decide that she needed to be killed before she could expose him, or else he *wasn't* the Marxman, in which case what game was he playing? Was he delusional? Was he potentially violent? Either way, she felt uncomfortable.'

Fisher lifted his glass, noticed it was empty and flagged down a passing waiter with that immediate authority which men seem to have in public spaces. What is it that makes waiters ignore women? Do they take exams in it or does it just come with regular practice?

'I don't mind telling you,' he continued whilst he waited for the bottle to come, 'that Miranda is not the sort to flirt with danger. She comes from a very good home, middle class, father was a consultant surgeon, mother organised lunches for various charities. Don't get me wrong, she became a therapist out of a genuine desire to help troubled people—'

'Rich troubled people,' I corrected him pettily.

'But she never pretended she was getting down and dirty with the real crazies. She preferred dealing with neurotic and, yes, Saxon, well-off people telling her each week that they felt their mothers didn't love them. Now suddenly, this.'

'So she turned to you.'

'Not at first. Mainly because she knew what my profess-ional advice would have been. I'd have told her to take it directly to you, privately if she didn't want to betray her confidences with Felix, and let you decide how to handle it; and she tells me now that she hadn't reached the point at which she felt able to do that. You have to understand, she's one of the old leftist hippie crowd, she thinks the authorities would've come down hard on Felix and she'd be responsible. So she waited. She only involved me after Felix was dead.'

'What was she doing in the meantime?'

'A spot of amateur sleuthing,' said Fisher with a wry smile. 'Very like Miranda, let me tell you. She found as many details as she could on the Marxman, became quite an expert, and then cross-referenced that information with what she knew about Felix.'

'And what did she learn?' pressed Fitzgerald.

'That when the first victim was killed, Felix was in Stockholm.'

'So it couldn't have been him?'

'Exactly. He may have spent all the time in the world hanging out in gun clubs in the States but even that couldn't

167

teach him how to fire a shot in Stockholm and have it hit a futures trader in the back of the head in Dublin. So she was reassured, she hadn't wanted him to be the Marxman obviously; but she was also puzzled, because why had he told her that he was? And then, just as she was beginning to look back through his notes and see if there was anything there that might explain why he'd come up with this elaborate fantasy, he was found dead in Howth and she was presented with a new dilemma: was he killed because he had known who the Marxman really was? Had he been trying to tell her obliquely?'

'It was a high-risk strategy,' said Fitzgerald. 'What if she'd come straight to us with the information about Felix? He might have been arrested, certainly he'd have been questioned. It wouldn't have been great publicity for a successful artist.'

Fisher shrugged. 'Maybe he thought he knew her well enough by then to know that she wouldn't. Or maybe he couldn't think of a less risky alternative. Or maybe he secretly wanted the police involved, but couldn't think how to make it happen.'

'What about simply handing over whatever information he had?'

'Say a stranger walks in off the street tonight and says he knows who the Marxman is,' Fisher said. 'What would be the reaction of the desk sergeant to that?'

'He'd probably have him hauled away in a white van.'

'Exactly.'

'Point taken. But it's still a stupid risk. So what's your theory? Same as Saxon, that Felix had found out something he shouldn't have known and died as a result?'

'I know what you're going to say,' said Fisher. 'Saxon already told me about the autopsy report. I've spoken to Miranda about his depression. There's nothing suggesting anything other than that Felix shot himself. But you must admit it's intriguing.'

'Intriguing is one thing,' said Fitzgerald, 'but I still can't see anything for the pair of you to get so excited about. Felix Berg was clearly some sort of fantasist, wanting to turn everyone on with the idea that there was a big mystery about his life, so that when he did die you'd all not be able to believe things were as simple as they looked and you'd keep digging, digging, digging for some darker, less prosaic hidden secret. Which is exactly what you've all been doing, Saxon, Miranda Gray, now you too, Fisher.'

'We're just telling you,' I said. 'No need to get antsy.'

She was thoughtful for a moment, sipping on her wine.

'What if he *hadn't* had an alibi for the first death,' she said after a moment. 'In light of his confession, what would you make of Felix Berg as a suspect?'

'The accepted wisdom,' said Fisher, 'is that artists – and by artists I mean the whole range, poets, painters, composers – don't become killers.'

'Why?'

'Why is that the accepted wisdom, you mean? Because there's never been an artist who was known to have committed a premeditated murder. Some have been driven to kill in certain circumstances, by rage or jealousy; but not the kind of murder you're talking about.'

'No, I meant why *don't* they become killers?'

'Because, you could say, murder is largely a crime of self-esteem. A man or woman who kills repeatedly is doing so because their own self-image is so indistinct, so threatened, that killing is the only way they can gain a sense of self. A false and twisted sense of self, admittedly, but it suffices. Till the next time. They have this huge drive and urgency and a sense of belief about themselves and nowhere to channel it. Artists have another channel to disperse their energies. They don't need to kill in order to express their desires. Or,' he went on, picking at his pasta, 'you could just say artists don't kill because they're self-actualisers.'

'Come again?' said Fitzgerald.

'Self-actualisers. Have you ever heard of Abraham Maslow?'

'Can't say I have.'

'Maslow was an American psychologist who conducted a study in the 1950s into people he thought were the best exemplars of mental health. He identified certain characteristics that they shared. A highly developed sense of the ridiculous. An ability to listen to their own feelings rather than the dictates of authority or tradition or majority opinion, though without flouting those norms for its own sake. A respect for other people.'

'That's you ruled out on the last one then, Saxon,' said Fitzgerald.

'Very funny.'

'The main thing they held in common, Maslow concluded, was an ability to see the world as it was, not simply how they wanted it to be, so they were more detached, more rational. More able, what's more, to tolerate ambiguity and uncertainty. This is exactly the quality which the kind of killers like the Marxman lack. They cannot accept the world as it is; absolutely cannot tolerate ambiguity. Nor can they laugh at their own weaknesses and failings. And since creativity tends to be more pronounced amongst self-actualisers, and self-actualisers are unlikely to become killers, then it follows that artists can't be killers.'

'Sounds like bullshit to me,' I said.

'You and me both,' agreed Fisher. 'No group is collectively immune from the tangle of impulses that go into making a serial murderer. Not psychologists, not artists, not police, not anyone. Felix could have been your man as well as anyone. In fact, there are things in his work which could have singled him out as above averagely likely, I'd have thought.'

'Such as?'

'You can see from the Marxman's MO that he isn't picking out specific targets. That's why you're finding it so difficult to catch him. Usually there is something linking a killer's chosen victims that says something about him. That's the Rosetta Stone of profiling. There's always a link. So a man who kills blonde single mothers, or bank managers in their forties, has a specific psychology and history which orients him towards those targets. The Marxman, though, whatever the press might have thought initially about his political leanings, doesn't seem to have any of those targeting mechanisms in his head. He kills across a whole spectrum of society indiscriminately, or seemingly indiscriminately.'

'He doesn't feel anything then? He thinks like a paid hitman?' said Fitzgerald.

'Not like a paid hitman at all,' Fisher demurred. 'To kill people for a living requires a certain psychopathic disengagement that suggests an inability to regard other people as being as real as yourself; but even so, a paid hitman only kills the people he's paid to kill. Your hitman, your Marxman, is doing something quite different. He genuinely hates the people he kills, but for nothing in particular, just the fact that they exist at all. He hates people in general; he's almost like a spree killer whose rage towards the swarming masses expresses itself in one violent outburst, in which he seeks to kill as many of that mass as possible. The only difference is that the Marxman is spacing the spree out, taking it one at a time. His rage is controlled, directed. Even the fact that he prefers to take only one shot shows his need for control, though obviously that went a little askew at the church recently.'

'How would all this fit in with Felix?'

'I don't know anything about Berg's state of mind, I can only go on his work, and the photographs in *Unreal City* could certainly be seen as dissociative in the same sense. Berg seemed to see individuals as a faceless, indistinguished mass, not as individuals; he set himself apart from them in a way that would make it easier to kill them if that was what he decided needed to be done. He wouldn't be killing anything important, only an insect, an ant.'

Fitzgerald frowned.

She had a good frown.

'I wish it *had* been him,' she said. 'That would mean it was all over.'

But she knew things were never that simple.

Chapter Twenty-Four

Fitzgerald and I went from the restaurant straight to the theatre. They were showing some revival of a play I hadn't even wanted to see first time it came out. I didn't care much for the theatre, to be honest. If it was up to me, we'd have taken in a movie instead, or just gone home; but Fitzgerald was always trying to improve my mind – introduce me to culture was how she put it – and I didn't complain too much because it was a chance to be together. And the theatre had one advantage over the movies. They stopped the show halfway through so you could get a proper drink. As it was, we skipped the second half anyway since Fitzgerald agreed that they shouldn't so much have revived this play as smothered it with a pillow.

Like your mother, I wanted to reply.

But I didn't. I was on my best behaviour. My sense of humour got me into too much trouble in this town as it was.

Instead, we found some bar and drank whiskey, and I could tell she was tiptoeing round me because she didn't even complain about me smoking like she usually did. In fact, we were both tiptoeing round one another, since my interest in Felix was still there between us and I knew she was afraid that seeing Alice that morning might have reactivated something in me which she would have preferred to go cold, while I wanted to stay off the whole subject to avoid getting annoyed again that she wouldn't see what I was convinced I could see, that Felix's death was connected in some as yet imperceptible way to the case she was working on.

There was nothing to be gained from revisiting that old quarrel.

In the end, she ordered herself a taxi and headed home, saying she had to be in work early – and I didn't point out that if she wanted to be in work early, then my apartment was surely the best place to start the morning's journey.

I simply finished my drink then made my way back through the winding streets to my apartment. It was quieter than usual. I hardly passed anyone on the way. The latest killing seemed to have had that effect on the city. Everyone was waiting and fearful.

The door was unlocked when I got back to my building, the lobby deserted, no trace of Hugh the doorman; and the elevator was broken again, which meant I had to climb the stairs. It's at times like this that an apartment on the seventh floor starts to seem less desirable.

All I wanted was to crawl into bed and leave thinking for the morning.

But I immediately sensed something was wrong when I reached my door.

There was a tension in the air.

Something was disturbed.

It was only when I took the key from my pocket and tried to slip it into the lock, and the lock moved backwards as if flinching, that I realised what was wrong.

The door was open, like the one downstairs in the lobby.

Was someone inside my apartment?

I reached instantly for my gun before realising I didn't carry one any more. No one carried a gun in Dublin.

Except the Marxman.

I guess I should have left it at that and come back with reinforcements, but that was never my style. Why do the sensible thing when you can do a stupid one instead?

So I pushed the door with one hand until it swung back

fully and I could see all my living room in shadow down to the glass doors at the far end leading out on to the balcony, and they were open too; and with the other I reached for the light switch and clicked it on.

Instant light flooded the room.

Everything leapt out in sharp relief.

The chair toppled on to its side, the upholstery torn at the back.

The drawers taken out and upended.

Papers fluttering in the breeze from the open balcony.

Books scattered everywhere.

My one painting pulled down from the wall and slashed.

Even the cupboards in the kitchen, I realised as I stepped forward into my apartment and gazed round in incredulity, had been searched. Jars had been swept out and smashed on the floor. Bottles broken. And it was the same in my bedroom.

Shirts, pants, jackets, underwear, all thrown crazily across the floor; the mattress pulled back and torn cleanly with the blade of a knife; a lamp lay on its side.

On the floor of my bathroom lay a smashed scent bottle. The shower curtain had been pulled off its rings. The sink was filled with bottles pulled down from the shelf above.

Someone had clearly been searching the place – but for what?

The same thing they'd been looking for in Felix's house?

And here, in the closet at the end of the corridor, was the trunk where I kept my work. The manuscripts of books I'd never managed to complete; research notes which had accumulated over the years with the inevitability of debts; newspaper cuttings, videos, tapes, photographs; my own yellowing articles, and various editions of my books, hidden away here out of sight where I wouldn't have to be reminded of them every day.

The trunk had been discovered by the night's raiders too, and its contents disgorged and pawed over and ripped till it looked like a wolf had attacked them whilst they slept.

I'd always been wary of people I didn't know well enough being in my apartment, which was why I was so careful about who I invited here, why I'd been so nervous when I let Alice in. In the early days of our relationship I hadn't even allowed Fitzgerald to come back here, which she'd considered pretty strange but accepted as part of my alien charm.

Having my own space was important to me. That was one of the reasons why I'd always resisted getting a place together.

But knowing a stranger had been in here, looking through my things, touching my possessions, rummaging around in my world – and me not even knowing who it was – was something more nightmarish still. It felt like a violation. Don't psychologists always say the home is an extension of the self, after all? That was why there was no such thing as a pure crime against property; there was always a personal assault involved too, even if it was only an assault on the mind. And what did 'only' mean in that context anyway? It made me wonder too why I'd never taken more precautions to stop it happening. I knew the principles involved in making small spaces defensible against burglary, and yet I'd never even bothered in my own apartment. I guess I'd never imagined that I'd need to. More fool me.

The only consolation was that I kept so few of the personal mementoes that other people gather around them for company that I was able to think of that absence as a barrier between the intruder and myself. It would have been different had he been able to look at private letters, diaries, photographs – but I collected nothing like that. Like Billie Holliday, I was always travelling light, and I was reminded again of why I preferred it that way.

You didn't get hurt.

I returned to the living room and closed the balcony doors, then lifted the chair back into its rightful place and sat down on it, wondering who it was had been here.

I could have written the whole thing off, told myself it had been kids looking for money, a random burglary. Like Alice said, people were always getting burgled, especially right here in the centre of the city. But I couldn't fool myself that easily.

Whoever came here tonight had been looking for something.

Something to do with Felix.

I couldn't prove that, but I knew it was true. Whilst I'd been following Strange and imagining myself very clever, someone else had been shadowing me. Not only that, but shadowing me much more successfully. They knew who I was, for one thing.

Knew where I lived.

And that realisation was as frustrating as it was unnerving. I hated anyone having an advantage over me. I needed to know what I was up against.

I couldn't say how long I sat there contemplating the trashing of my apartment, but gradually my eyes must have become accustomed to the mess because I suddenly noticed something I hadn't seen before. It was attached to the hook where my one painting had been hanging when I left the apartment that morning to go to Felix's funeral.

My first thought was that it must be a note.

Then I saw what it really was.

A photograph.

Another snapshot like the one I'd found hidden among Felix's Marxman papers, only this one needed no enlargement to see who it was in the picture.

It was me.

It had been taken this morning at the churchyard as I idled among the gravestones, passing time before the funeral. I could see the line of the wall that ringed the cemetery along the bottom of the picture, meaning that whoever had taken it had been standing in the road at the time. My eyes were turned away from the camera, regarding nothing, and I was frowning; I always seemed to be frowning in pictures, I think my face was just designed to look unhappy.

The photograph had been pressed firmly on to the hook in the wall so that it looked like the point was protruding through my skull, tangled by my own hair.

My visitor sure had a neat way of making a woman feel good about herself.

Chapter Twenty-Five

Conor Buckley had started out with offices in some crumbling, rat-gnawed Victorian hole down by the quays that shook gently when the trains went by, shivering stone overlooking its shivering reflection in the water at its feet. Now he'd fled the heart of the city for some soulless glass and steel monstrosity in the growing financial district, where his fortress sat indistinguishable from the ranks of banks and insurance companies massed alongside it.

There was no point me trying to get past security. Besides, I could tell by looking for his Mercedes in the parking lot that Buckley couldn't have arrived yet. Not unless he'd started taking the bus, and there was more chance of Warren Beatty taking a vow of chastity.

So I waited in the parking lot.

Yawning mostly.

I hadn't got much sleep last night. Clearing up made me realise how Sisyphus felt, pushing that rock eternally uphill; and then, when I'd finally brought some semblance of order to my apartment, sleep wouldn't come anyway. The thought of a stranger rifling through your underwear drawer isn't exactly the best relaxation known to woman.

When I cornered him that morning, Hugh couldn't tell me any more than I knew already. He'd knocked off early, one of the other residents in the building must have left the door downstairs open, or maybe fallen for some story and let the intruder in . . .

What he had for me instead of explanations was a letter from Buckley.

Hence the waiting.

Buckley was a lawyer, excuse me whilst I wash out my mouth, and the worst kind: a defence attorney. He'd once represented a killer I was trying to nail, which didn't exactly endear him to me either. It wasn't so much that he represented him – everyone is entitled to a defence, right? – so much as that he didn't seem to care much whether the guy in question was guilty or innocent. For me, that's kind of a crucial question.

I didn't have to wait long before Buckley's Mercedes pulled in.

He was driving, and there was some woman in the passenger seat admiring her reflection in the overhead mirror, like she had to make sure she looked good enough before getting out in case there were paparazzi waiting with cameras.

Buckley hadn't changed much, I saw as he climbed out. Short and round and bald like Mussolini – that's who I always thought of when I thought of Buckley, which, I am glad to say, wasn't often. Ever since I'd known him he'd been stuffed to the same bursting point with self-satisfaction at having made it. He was the archetypal working-class kid with a grudge. Clever, that went without saying, but a man for whom intelligence could never bring as much satisfaction as deviousness, or justice as much as beating the system. It was said of him that he regarded each case he won as another blow to the Establishment. I didn't go in for that kind of amateur psychology, but it didn't seem far off the mark in Buckley's case.

Perhaps I'd introduce him to Burke and they could plot the revolution together.

Except Burke would despise the oily creep as much as I did.

His passenger climbed out too and she was all legs and blonde hair and . . . well, that was about it. Philosophy major?

I doubt it. She was carrying a few files, so I guess she must've been his secretary; but I doubted Buckley had hired her for her typing skills.

'Saxon,' he said when he saw me. 'Is that a bad attitude in your pocket or are you just displeased to see me?'

'Spare me the feeble banter, Buckley,' I said. 'I want to talk.'

'I'm busy.'

'Don't tell me. You're due in court.'

'Within the hour,' Buckley said with a smug smile. 'I'm representing some young gentleman who had the misfortune to be found at the airport with five kilos of cocaine in his hand luggage.'

'Let me guess. He didn't know what was in there. He was the innocent pawn of an evil international trade.'

Buckley pretended to be astounded.

'Have you been sneaking a peek at my intended defence, Special Agent?'

'Just a wild guess,' I said. 'You know, you must have the unluckiest clients in Dublin. They're always being arrested for things they didn't do.'

'They're not that unlucky if they have me to represent them,' Buckley said slickly. 'Which reminds me. Since I'm going to be tied up in court protecting my client's constitutional rights, I'll have to skip lunch with my wife. Be a good girl, Simone, and call to tell Margaret I'm running late, will you?'

The blonde with the legs and teeth smiled with the sort of smile you normally only see in toothpaste ads and went off to do whatever it is blondes with legs and teeth do.

'I think I took the wrong path in life,' I said, watching her go. 'I should start studying law. Try out as a defence attorney. Find some guilty scumbag to represent, you know, get a big office, an unemployed supermodel to answer the phone.'

'You mean Simone? She's something else, isn't she?'

He grinned. Cat who got the cream.

'Where'd you find her?' I said.

'I won her in a backgammon game.'

'I believe you. I'll bet she's a great help all those nights you have to work late.'

'A man has to have a hobby,' said Buckley. 'Think of it as one of the perks of the job.'

'I'd rather not think about it at all, if it's all the same to you. Right now I'm more interested in finding out what the hell this is about.' I reached into my pocket and pulled out the letter Hugh had handed me that morning. 'You mind explaining why I got a letter on your headed notepaper on behalf of Vincent Strange warning me to stay away from him?'

'You've been putting the frighteners up him. I'm not saying you don't have your little reasons, be they professional or extracurricular, but enough is enough. He wants you to stay away, to stop harassing him. What do you Yankees say? Cut him some slack.'

'I haven't been harassing anyone.'

'Whatever you say, Saxon, whatever you say. It's not you that's been calling him up every hour through the night then hanging up. It's not you who had his gallery broken into and ransacked three nights ago. It's not you who's been sending him photographs with his face defaced. It's not you who's been seen hanging round his house.'

So I wasn't the only one, I thought.

Always presuming Strange was telling the truth.

'Don't you think I have better things to do?' I said.

'Let me think.' No pause. 'No.'

'Look, Buckley, I don't know what you call evidence in this town, but you can't accuse me of harassing Strange just because he says I am. What evidence does he have?'

'He says you turned up at Felix Berg's funeral yesterday.'

'I got an invite. From Berg's sister.'

'You have a copy to prove that?'

'You think I keep all my funeral invites filed neatly under C for Cadaver?'

'Well, Strange says you didn't get one. According to him, you were gatecrashing.'

'He's a liar.'

'Is he lying too about you buttonholing Berg's sister in the church and trying to get her to hire you to look into her brother's death?'

'Did she say that?'

This was getting more surreal by the minute.

'He also says,' said Buckley, 'that this isn't the first time you've given him grief. Apparently you've also been bugging him for some stuff he has of Felix Berg's.'

'I went round there once about a week ago. I didn't even know Strange had Felix's stuff until he told me. I asked if I could see it. He said no. End of story.'

Apart from following him round to the locker at the station, but I thought it best to leave that part out.

'He also said you made some vague threats about what might happen to him if he didn't hand it over, about how people were dying. Does that part sound familiar?'

'OK, so I may have tried to put a little shiver of doubt into him, but I certainly didn't start ringing him up and putting the phone down. What do you think I am – nine years old? And I certainly don't make a habit of sending defaced photographs through the mail.'

'Then forget it. You've got nothing to worry about, have you? All you have to do is stay clear of Vincent Strange and nothing more will be said about it.'

'You know,' I sighed, 'I'm beginning to think the Marxman shot the wrong legal eagle.'

'What's the matter, Saxon?' he said. 'Am I not your type?'

'Buckley, you're not even my species.'

Chapter Twenty-Six

'What a creep. Can you believe him telling me to keep away from Strange? Like I'm some kind of stalker or something.'

'You know what Buckley's like,' said Fitzgerald mildly, hardly even glancing up from the file she was reading on her desk. 'I hear complaints about him in here every day. He gets up people's noses. He *likes* getting up people's noses.'

'Doesn't it piss you off?'

'Of course it pisses me off, but what good is being pissed off going to be? He's a defence lawyer. That's what defence lawyers are like. You should let it go. Just back off on Strange like Buckley advised and then nothing more will come of it.'

'Back off on him? All I did was talk to him.'

'Then let me rephrase it. Forget him.'

'I can't forget him. Strange checks out for too much of this.'

'Too much of what?'

'Too much of everything. I've been finding out plenty about him,' I said. 'Such as his criminal connections. He's been under investigation for years by the Criminal Assets Bureau. They've never got anything on him, but they obviously don't think he's clean otherwise why would they keep on at him? And did you know he collects guns? He has stuff shipped in and out of the country all the time. All along you've been wondering how the Marxman got hold of a Glock semi-automatic. It'd be easy for Strange.'

'You're not trying to say Strange is the Marxman, are you?'

'Why not?'

I finally had her attention.

Fitzgerald pushed the file away and leaned back in her chair.

'Because,' she said, '*I* had him checked out too. Strange's name was bound to come up once firearms were involved. Everyone with a licence in the city, or who's ever applied for one, or who's ever been suspected, questioned, convicted or sentenced for a firearms offence, or who's ever been involved in the military in any way, has been questioned, sometimes many times over. And Strange has rock-solid alibis for at least two of the killings.'

'But—'

'I know you think I don't know what I'm doing here—'

'That's not true—'

She raised a hand to stop me. 'But I *am* able to do that much at least. I checked all the shipments he's taken in the last year and none of them match up. Sorry, but he's clean.'

Suddenly I felt ashamed. Fitzgerald was under enough pressure on the Marxman case without having me throwing bricks at her too. Maybe she'd made some bad decisions, but the only people who never make a bad decision are those who never make a decision at all. She had to go with the percentages. She couldn't just go chasing after her instincts like me.

But ashamed or not, I still wasn't willing to let it go.

The state of my apartment last night was reason enough.

'What about the old gun that Felix had? Alice said he didn't even own a gun. Doesn't it make sense at least that he got it from Strange?'

'Saxon,' said Fitzgerald slowly, 'I'm going to tell you something. I shouldn't be telling you, but I will because I don't want you shooting off down the wrong path and then accusing me later of holding out on you. You're right about Strange. He *did* give the gun to Felix.'

'You know that?'

'Felix went to him about three weeks before he died. Said he was frightened of something, that he felt in danger. He begged Strange for a gun to protect himself with.'

'And Strange gave it to him?'

'He was reluctant, but Felix Berg was a friend, not to mention one of Strange's most valuable artists. He wanted to help. He never imagined Felix would shoot himself. If he'd known he was in any way suicidal he'd never have handed over a gun. At the time he just thought that having one would calm Felix down some. Then, when Felix killed himself, he felt bad. He went to Draker and told him what had happened.'

'And old friend Draker made sure it was covered up.'

'What would have been the point of pursuing it?' said Fitzgerald reasonably. 'It wouldn't have brought Felix back. It wouldn't have been in the public interest to prosecute Strange for a simple mistake.'

'Now you sound like Draker.'

'There's no need to be bitchy, Saxon. Don't you think I have better things to do than pursue a man like Vincent Strange on minor charges? I'm trying to run a murder enquiry. I've been in here since six a.m. I have a list of suspects that's starting to look longer than the Dublin phone book. I have surveillance on five possible candidates for the Marxman. I have the press demanding answers. The families demanding answers. The Commissioner demanding miracles.'

'But doesn't that make you want to investigate the circumstances of Berg's death more closely? Doesn't Felix asking for a gun prove that his life was in danger?'

'No, it doesn't, because there's still no proof that he *was* being threatened,' Fitzgerald said. 'How many times do we have to go over this? All you have to go on is the fact he told you that he was—'

'And Strange too, apparently.'

'You're dragging Strange in as a witness now? Thirty seconds ago he was your prime suspect. Felix probably only told Strange he was afraid so that Strange would give him a gun. A gun that he could shoot himself with. Telling Miranda Gray that he was the Marxman just emphasises that you can't trust anything he told you. You're chasing after shadows.'

And for a moment I was too exhausted to argue. Was I the only one who wanted to keep Felix Berg's death on the agenda? Fitzgerald wanted it dropped. For the newspapers it had been a one-day wonder. Strange still insisted there was nothing in it despite the fact that his supposed close friend had asked him for a gun only three weeks earlier because he was afraid.

As for Alice, she still wasn't answering my calls, I must have left a half dozen since the funeral, despite saying she wanted us to keep in touch yesterday.

I didn't know who to believe any more.

What to believe.

Maybe if I told Fitzgerald about the break-in she'd believe me; but what good would that do? It would only be one more thing she had to think about, worry about.

She had enough of those as it was.

'Why didn't you tell me?' was all I said eventually.

'Tell you?'

'About Strange. About the gun.'

'I'm telling you now.'

'Before,' I said, 'when I was running round like a fool after him.'

'If it had gone any further I would've done. But I couldn't tell you, you're not . . .' She trailed off uncomfortably, and I knew what she was going to say.

You're not police.

Like I needed reminding of it.

It was my theme tune almost.

OK, so I wasn't police, but that didn't mean I couldn't pursue my own enquiry, that I had to sit around waiting for the *real* police to do their job. If I waited for that, I'd be some old woman in a condominium in Miami watching Court TV all day before they came up with anything. I could picture the scene. *You want to know what I remember of the Berg case, Officer? Wait right there while I put my teeth in and I'll tell you all about it.*

'I just don't get why you're so adamant.'

'To not play Felix Berg's little game?' she said. 'Because after what he did, he doesn't deserve people running round after him, acting out this posthumous drama for him. Suicides are selfish bastards. I get enough of that emotional blackmail crap from my mother.'

'Has something happened?'

'Only the usual. I had her on the phone this morning telling me how she has nothing to live for any more, only a daughter who's never there, and no chance of ever having grandchildren running round her feet, and how lonely it is being old.'

'She can't expect you to live your life only to satisfy some need in her.'

'I know that. But it doesn't stop her dropping hints that she might just leave the gas in the oven running one night, or take a swim off the beach.'

'Did you try to talk her out of it?' I asked.

'I'm not going to plead with her,' Fitzgerald said. 'It's her life. That's what she wants me to do. Get involved in some big negotiation so she feels important. She's trying to frighten me into feeling guilty, and I have nothing to feel guilty about. There's nothing more I can do for her than I do already, just as there's no more you can do about Felix. It wasn't your fault that he died. It's not your fault that you can't tell Alice why.'

'I know that,' I said.

Just like I *knew* Sydney's death wasn't my fault either.

But did I really?

* * *

188

I went down to Records. I shouldn't have been wandering about Dublin Castle unaccompanied, but since no one was stopping me I didn't feel any need to play jailer on my own movements; and it wasn't like there was anyone waiting for me at home.

Or waiting for me anywhere.

Niall Boland was at his desk.

'I was getting ready to call you,' he said.

'You got something for me then?'

'Might have.'

Strange's cryptic remarks that day at the gallery about Felix once sharing a house with a murderer had intrigued me. I'd wanted to know more. Maybe this, sparse though it was, might provide a lead at last. And where better to get the information than from Boland? I'd asked him to see if he could get me a full list of all the places Felix had lived.

I hadn't expected him to come up trumps so fast, though.

I'd lost count of the number of places I'd lived in my life, from a string of student lodgings in Boston to one winter spent up in Montreal with an old boyfriend, Steve, in an apartment where the only thing that stopped it falling down, I sometimes thought, was the ice that coated everything. One shock heatwave and I swore the place would fall apart. Then there was a house in Boston where I'd lived for three months with my first serious girlfriend, Arabella; and the fact that I'd ever dated a woman who shared DNA with people who could give their kid a name like Arabella horrified me now. She wore cotton print dresses and smoked too much weed and listened to Joni Mitchell all the time. It drove me nuts, I had to get out of the relationship just so I didn't have to hear *The Hissing of Summer Lawns* on vinyl one more time. The only real hissing I ever heard when I was with her was the air escaping out of her brain when she smoked too much dope. I'd got back together with Steve for a while after that, for which I'd never forgive her; though to give him credit, it was his goading which drove me to apply for the FBI as I

189

wandered rootless and destination-less, it seemed to me, through my twenties. Christ knows where I'd have ended up if it hadn't been for that.

I wasn't cut out for the Housewife of the Year awards, after all.

As for when I was in the FBI, I'd lived out of a suitcase effectively for five years; I did buy a tiny place outside of Saratoga in upstate New York, but hardly ever went there. After a couple of years in Dublin I'd sold it at a loss to get it off my hands.

And those were just the places I could remember off the top of my head.

Felix's life had been less nomadic. After the childhood home in Sweden, there were only a handful of places that he'd lived. The aunt's house out in Howth; an apartment he'd rented in Clerkenwell in London when he was an art student at St Martin's; back to the Howth house after his aunt died; then finally he and Alice had sold up and moved into Temple Bar. And that, apart from one summer spent back in Sweden and the months out in New England last year after his breakdown, was that.

Was the answer hidden somewhere in there?

Maybe.

And maybe it was the Howth house where it lay.

Boland had come up with two names.

The first was Paul Vaughan. The son of some famous theatre director in the city, he'd been Alice's boyfriend at the time Felix was studying in London. He had even moved in with her and Felix shortly after the aunt died and Felix returned from London, and stayed about a year and a half before he and Alice broke up. Three years later he was killed in a road accident whilst taking a bend too fast on his motorbike. According to reports at the time, he'd been so badly mangled they could only identify him from his clothes and his driving licence.

The second name was Paddy Nye – another

photographer, interestingly, though by popular consent nowhere near as gifted or successful as Felix. Boland hadn't been able to find any listings of exhibitions of his work. Quite what he was doing living in the house in Howth was not clear, but he hadn't stayed long, three months at most. Afterwards, he ran his own studio for a time, working for various magazines, surviving mainly on the jobs Felix passed over and passed on to him, and publishing a single book, self-financed, of black-and-white photographs of Ireland's Eye, the small uninhabited island a half-mile off the coast that I'd seen an outline of the night I found Felix's body. Now Nye and a wife he'd acquired along the way owned a store selling photographic equipment out in . . . guess where? Howth.

'He doesn't seem to have been in contact with Felix or Alice in the intervening years,' Boland said. 'I checked the list in this morning's newspaper of mourners who'd attended Felix's funeral and his name wasn't there.'

'Unless he turned up under a different name.'

Howth.

It seemed a promising enough place to start. Every road seemed to have led there from the moment Felix had lured me out in that direction on his last night.

Had he been trying to tell me the place was somehow significant?

Had he wanted to *show* me something?

'I found something else too,' Boland said before I left.

He showed me the file he'd uncovered in the archives.

A fifteen-year-old girl by the name of Lucy Toner had gone missing from her street in Howth one hot August around the same time Berg was living there. The police at first had treated her disappearance as a straightforward missing persons case, and even told the family she'd probably run away (those were less sophisticated days), and it was only when a dog was seen digging furiously at the bottom of the girl's own garden three days later that they finally realised the truth lay closer to home. Lucy had been sexually assaulted and strangled, though the actual cause of death was asphyxiation brought on by her mouth being filled with earth.

Not a pleasant way to die.

'And this was where?' I said.

'Just round the corner from the Bergs' house,' said Boland.

'Was anyone ever picked up for it?' I asked.

'Oh yes,' said Boland. 'A man by the name of Isaac Little. He was – is – a paedophile who'd recently finished a prison sentence for touching up little girls. He lived about three doors down from Lucy. When his house was searched, police found he'd set up a little den on the second floor so that he could look down into a children's playground nearby. He used to go up there and play with himself while he watched them. There were stains everywhere. On the carpet, walls, furniture.'

'I get the picture. What happened to him?'

'He confessed eventually, though retracted the confession the day before he was due in court. He's protested his innocence ever since.'

'What about Lucy Toner's family? They still live in the area?'

'No. The whole thing was a mess. The family owned some kind of general store near the sea front. The father was a musician of sorts, he died of cancer about a year before the daughter was killed. The mother was in and out of mental institutions her whole life, and after the murder just seemed to go totally to pieces. She finally drowned herself a couple of days before Isaac Little's trial was due to begin. Off the pier in Howth, no less.'

'Killing yourself there must be a Howth tradition.'

'A younger daughter went totally off the rails herself, ended up in care. An elder brother dropped off the map.'

The usual unhappy fallout of a senseless murder. I'd seen it happen a thousand times.

But did it have anything to do with what was happening

now? Had Felix suspected Little was innocent, that someone in the house at the time was the real killer?

Was that what he meant about sharing a house with a murderer?

If so, then it didn't take much guessing where I had to start.

Apart from Alice, there was only one member of that household still alive.

Chapter Twenty-Seven

I decided to take the train rather than the Jeep. It seemed I hardly ever took it out of its parking space now. The streets were clogged with traffic these days, like a storm drain in a back yard with leaves in fall. Was it getting worse or was I just getting less tolerant? All I knew was that by the time I got out to the harbour my nerves would be strung so tight the wind coming off the water might make me snap like a frozen blade of grass.

I got to the station in good time for the next train north, fished change out of my pocket for a ticket, then climbed the stairs through the flow of people coming the other way until I emerged at the top into a warm wind.

A train was turning the corner, and I climbed in the first door that presented itself, found a seat by the window and sat back for the journey, staring out of the dirty window, ignoring the other passengers. I wanted to think, and anyway I hate starting conversations with strangers, because when they hear my accent they always want to know more about me, where I'm from, what I'm doing here. I have no answer to that last one.

People always want to know stuff, that's the problem, and I have no desire to tell them. Why are they so interested in my life when it isn't even that interesting to me?

The train moved slowly through the city. Looking out, I saw overgrown railway sidings with out-of-service engines standing idle and rusting, stretches of trackside scrub giving way to grey yards and gardens marked by lonely, pathetic trees; chimneys, churches; lock-up garages scrawled with unimaginative graffiti; bridges black with smoke. The spaces all strewn with litter and stray scrags of dogs and children, all equally bored, with nothing to do, until gradually the grubby outskirts of the city, as bleak as any of the downtown projects I'd been in back home, began to fall behind, not keeping up in more ways than one, and the train came in sight of the sea and I saw the grey water slapping listlessly at the edges of the land where the city came to soak its feet.

The light was metallic and uninviting on the water.

Then there we were.

The end of the line.

Howth.

I climbed out and began to make my way along the harbour road, walking a way before realising I didn't know where the hell I was going. I'd been thinking of the last time I'd been here, the night that Felix died. Now I shook my head, told myself to concentrate.

I took out the scrap of paper on which I'd written down the address Boland had given me, then looked around till I found a map near the harbourmaster's office.

It was one of those maps they put up to point tourists in the direction of whichever attraction will be most pleased to take their money. Castle this way, boat trips out to the island that way, and when you're done the tea shops are over there. Now beat it back to wherever you came from, suckers. And don't have a nice day now.

But at least it gave the names of the roads and I was able to get a rough idea of the right direction. I glanced back and saw the houses rising up . . . what was it now? Church Street, that was it, and then winding on further up the side of Howth Hill. Somewhere in one of those narrow lanes was where I'd find Paddy Nye. I crossed the road and began to climb.

It didn't take long to find the place I was looking for, though it would be easy to miss if you weren't looking for it.

Nye Photographics read the sign across the front, and in the window sat a range of cameras in front of pictures of gap-toothed kids in technicolour.

A bell chinged as I pushed the door and went inside.

There was a woman standing behind the counter. Small, pretty. The wife, presumably. She smiled when she saw me, but the smile vanished faster than a snowflake landing on a furnace when she realised I wasn't there to buy anything.

'You want to speak to Paddy?' A sigh. 'Very well. Wait here.'

She ducked out of a doorway at the back of the shop and I could hear her footsteps receding down a corridor. Left alone, I could hear only the ticking of a clock that I couldn't see and a murmur of slightly raised voices. Cameras stared at me from behind glass.

A few moments later she was back, and she had Paddy Nye with her.

At least I presumed it was Nye. Tall, curly-haired, with a kind of vigorous, hearty look about him, the hiking type, checked shirt and jeans with a belt.

He stared at me with little interest.

'Can I help you?'

'That's a question only you can answer. My name's Saxon,' I said.

'If you're trying to sell something . . .'

'Nothing like that. I want to talk about Felix Berg.'

There was no hint of emotion in his voice as he replied.

'I have nothing to say about Felix,' he said.

'Not even though he died down there in the harbour about a week ago?'

'What does that have to do with me? Felix and I lost contact a long time ago.'

'You don't care what happened to him?'

'As a matter of fact, no. Should I?'

'You were friends.'

'And like I told you, that was a long time ago.'

His eyes shifted and he looked back over my shoulder suddenly as the outline of a man appeared on the other side of the glass, looking in, his hand reaching for the door handle.

Nye Photographics did have some customers then.

A glance passed between Nye and the woman, then he said to me: 'Come through. We can talk more freely out here.'

He led me through the same doorway at the back of the store and down a narrow tiled corridor to another door leading out into the garden. Because the house was built on the hill, the garden was almost precipitous, dropping down in steps towards another house below. We were flying above it, almost looking down the chimney. The view ahead was entirely of the sea, dazzlingly blue once the water left the land and flecked with white this morning, with the harbour and the boats like a child's toys, and beyond that – Ireland's Eye, clear, bright.

There were a couple of chairs here. Evidently he'd been sitting reading when I called. A cup of coffee sat by the chair on the stone flagstones; I could smell the heat rising from it. A book lay open on the ground next to it.

He didn't ask me to sit down.

'That's some view,' I said.

'I'm glad you like it.'

'That's Ireland's Eye, isn't it?'

He turned and regarded the island briefly. In this light it looked almost close enough to have tossed a stone on to it.

'I tried to get hold of a copy of your book,' I lied, 'but . . .' I tailed off.

'You couldn't find it. I'm not surprised. It wasn't exactly a bestseller.'

'You like it out there?'

He nodded. 'Ireland's Eye is the only reason I still hang around this dump. If it wasn't for that place, I'd have been gone years ago.'

'It must mean a lot to you.'

197

'Not just to me. My wife' – and here he nodded back towards the house – 'feels the same way. It's a patch of wildness right on the edge of the city. An escape from all this noise. It couldn't be much closer without touching the land, and yet when you're there you could be a thousand miles from civilisation. If you call a city civilisation. I like that contrast. I like the fact that it's there, just waiting to be explored. Your own and yet belonging to everyone. We have a boat. We often go out there. Even spend a few nights out there sometimes.'

He stopped, looking a little embarrassed.

'What did you say your name was again?'

'Saxon.'

'Well, Saxon, I don't want to be rude, but I really have no interest in getting involved in anything to do with Felix Berg. I was friends with him a long time ago. It's not a part of my life I want to revisit.'

'I don't want to cause you any trouble,' I said. 'It's just Felix's sister asked me to find out why he killed himself, and I discovered that you were his friend, that you shared a house together here in Howth some years back. I thought maybe—'

'That I might know something about his life now? I haven't seen Felix for ten years, longer. That is, I haven't seen him in the flesh. I've seen his picture.'

'You didn't stay in touch?'

'I didn't stay in touch with him. He stayed in touch with me. If you can call it that.'

'Stayed in touch how?'

He gave a small, embarrassed laugh.

'For years after I stopped being part of Felix's circle, I used to get stuff sent to me. Catalogues of his latest exhibitions, newspaper clippings about his success, photographs of him meeting various important people at functions in the city.'

'You think it was coming from Felix?'

'I know it came from Felix. That was Felix's style. He liked to make people feel small. Remind them that they didn't have his talent, his success. Put them down. That's what he was doing by sending me all that crap. Trying to destroy my confidence. Even when I published my first and so far only book of photographs he sent me a copy of a bad review that appeared in one of the art journals. Just in case I hadn't seen it.'

'Did you ever confront him about it?'

'What would've been the point? Felix liked to play games. Liked to be cruel. If I'd let him know that he was getting to me, it would simply have made him worse. It was better to stay quiet, wait and hope he got tired of it, let it stop of its own accord.'

'And did it – stop?'

'Not entirely. I didn't get messages every week, no, but they still came intermittently. I learned to recognise the packages and throw them out without looking inside.'

'Is that why you didn't go to the funeral?'

'What makes you think I got an invite?'

'Did you?'

'I did,' he conceded. 'I read about what happened to Felix in the paper, next thing I get an invite to his funeral. I didn't bother answering it.'

'You didn't feel the need to speak to Alice even?'

I meant nothing by the remark, but he snapped back instantly.

'So you know about me and Alice. Big deal. That was ancient history too. It all happened way before I met my wife, and I haven't seen her for years either.'

'I wasn't trying to . . . do you mean you and Alice were lovers?'

'Isn't that what you were getting at?'

'No,' I said honestly. 'I thought she was Paul Vaughan's girlfriend.'

He pulled a face like he pitied me for knowing so little.

'Yeah, she was Paul's girlfriend. And mine. And Christ knows who else's. She'd have moved us all into the house if there'd been enough room. Had us all waiting our turn. I can see you're surprised. You don't seriously buy that prim and proper act she puts on these days, do you? I remember what she was like. I think she screwed just about every man who was vaguely connected to the art scene in Dublin in those days. Including Felix himself, I shouldn't wonder. Oh. I can see that part isn't news to you, anyway.'

Was my face so easy to read?

'You sound bitter.'

'Things didn't end well between Alice and me. I was in love with her. I wanted her for myself. I didn't like the fact that her bedroom was busier than Grand Central Station during rush hour. In the end I couldn't stand it any more. I had to get out before I went as crazy as Paul, before she had me eating out of her hand the way he did.'

He gazed towards Ireland's Eye, eyes screwed tight in a frown, like he was remembering and didn't like what he remembered.

'But I still don't see what any of this has got to do with what happened to Felix. He killed himself, didn't he? I don't know why and I don't care. It's nothing to me.'

'Alice still thinks he was murdered,' I said.

Nye laughed.

'She *would* think that. Alice always had a flair for the melodramatic. Simple things were never good enough for her.'

'That's what Gina said too.'

'Who's Gina?'

'Doesn't matter.'

'Does Alice think *I* did it then?'

Where did that come from?

'She never mentioned you,' I said.

'Really?'

'Not a word.'

I couldn't say for sure, but he looked almost disappointed.

'So where'd you get my name?'

'I was rooting around and it came up. I'm just trying to find out as much as I can about Felix, so that I know him a bit better. Finding out who he used to live with is part of it.'

'It's not about that crazy story he used to tell, is it?' he asked.

'Crazy story?'

'About one of us being a murderer. He always used to tell us that, have us looking askance at one another. Alice was the same. She had a million stories. Like the time she told me she was being stalked. I learned to stop believing them after a while. If anyone was a murderer it was her and Felix. I wouldn't be at all surprised to find that they'd bumped off the old dear who brought them up so that they could get their hands on the inheritance.'

'I was thinking more of Lucy Toner.'

'Who?' he said quickly.

'The young girl who lived round the corner,' I said. '*She* was murdered.'

A nod.

'I remember it now. Some pervert went to jail for it, isn't that right?'

'He says he's innocent.'

'Don't they all?'

He wasn't wrong there.

'It's just another piece of old history,' he said. 'Felix, Alice, now this girl. I don't know what lies and fables Alice has been feeding you, but I don't care. I left all that behind me a long time ago. This is my life. The shop. My wife, Tricia. My young son. Nothing else counts.'

And his gaze wandered out again towards Ireland's Eye like a drowning man clinging on to a rock. And Ireland's Eye shimmered mysteriously in the bright light and ignored him.

Chapter Twenty-Eight

Lawrence Fisher rang as I was on the way back to town to ask if I wanted to meet for dinner.

'What happened to Miranda? You two have a lovers' tiff?'

'Don't start that again. Besides, she's going to be there too,' Fisher said. 'And I already called Grace and she says she can make it. What do you say?'

'How can I say no?'

Any chance to pick Miranda Gray's brains about Felix, after all.

We arranged to meet at some restaurant called Nemo's. I hadn't heard of it, but Fisher gave me directions. He had no idea what the food would be like since Miranda had booked the table, but he had high hopes. The booking was for nine.

That left plenty of time for calling in on Burke. I stopped on the way to pick up doughnuts and a couple of cartons of bad coffee.

'You not got a home to go to?'

'Is that how you greet all your customers?'

'Most of them, yeah.'

'No wonder you never sell any books.'

I passed him the coffee and he looked at it like it was poisoned, which, once I tasted it, I realised mightn't be far off the mark. The doughnuts got a better reception. He picked one out and devoured it in two bites, then reached for another, brushing the sugar on to his pants.

'You know something? These aren't bad,' he said as he ate. 'Are they for free or do you want something in return?'

'Only a book.'

'You're in the right place. By?'

'Paddy Nye.'

'Never heard of him.'

'Nor me till this morning. He's a photographer. Friend of Felix's. He published a book about Ireland's Eye a few years back. It's an island,' I said when he looked blank.

'I know what it is,' he said. 'I just don't think I have anything like that. Do you think I keep a copy of every book that's out there? I ain't got the room. Every loser's published a book these days. I can't keep track of them all. Life's too short.'

'It was a book of photographs,' I said.

'Look, give me the name of it and I'll look it up on my computer. Everything's catalogued in there somewhere. In print, out of print, wanted, unwanted. If it exists it'll be in there. Just leave it to the magic fingers.'

Burke lifted another doughnut and strode over to his desk.

'It's called *Eye*,' I told him.

'*Eye* by Nye. Catchy,' said Burke, and he clicked some buttons. 'Here you are,' he said after a couple of moments. 'Published ten years ago, privately financed, long out of print. I could try and track it down for you if you like, but it could take weeks. Expensive too. Tell you what. Seeing it's you, I won't charge you the usual search fee.'

'You're all heart.'

'Hold up,' Burke added. 'There's another book listed here by one P. F. Nye. Wonder if it's the same man? I might even have this one in stock.'

He got up from behind the desk and made his way to a wall on the other side of the store, pushing down his bifocals from the top of his head so he could scan the shelves better.

'This is the section I keep for local stuff, city guides, maps, that sort of thing,' he told me as he looked. 'There's a whole series of local history too, published by some two-bit company in the city. According to the catalogue, there's a P. F. Nye who's written one of their efforts. Reckon I might have one left in stock . . . ah, here it is.'

He pulled out a thin volume, more a pamphlet than a book, and tossed it over to me.

'*The Ireland's Eye Murder – A Re-Examination*,' I read out. 'What's this about?'

'I keep forgetting you don't know all this stuff,' he said. 'In fact, sometimes I wonder why you even live in this city when you got so little interest in it.'

'The natives love me so much they keep begging me to stay.'

'Is that what it is?' he said. He pointed a finger at the book. 'This is about a famous murder happened out on Ireland's Eye in the last century. Last but one, I should say; I keep forgetting. I can't remember all the details. Some man killed his wife, or the police said he did and he didn't; and he might've been hanged or he might've been let off, I ain't sure.'

'You'd make a great expert witness.'

'I never said I was an expert,' said Burke. 'Look, why don't you just take a little beady look at it and see if it's any use to you?'

I looked at the book. It was pretty cheaply produced, with a sepia print from the nineteenth century on the cover showing Ireland's Eye as seen from Howth Harbour. The author's name was indeed P. F. Nye, and there were no other details about him save the phrase: 'The author lives in Howth and is a well-known local historian.' Was he indeed?

I opened it up and began to read, whilst outside the traffic snarled past and customers came and went, talking to Burke in whispers, like some people did in bookstores.

The book concerned a young woman who was found dead in an area of Ireland's Eye known as Long Hole in 1857. She was found lying on a sheet, with a cut on her breast and blood issuing from her ears. Initially it was presumed that she'd drowned – and to be honest, I couldn't think why, especially since drowning could be a notoriously difficult cause of death to diagnose even now – and only later was her husband arrested and charged with strangling her. He was found guilty and sentenced to life imprisonment, not hanged at all, and got out after twenty years. Killers usually do in this part of the world.

Seems that the murder of this young woman had been something of a cause célèbre ever since among local historians, most of whom believed the dead woman had indeed simply drowned and her husband was the victim of a miscarriage of justice. Nye was of the same mind, though as far as I could see that didn't explain how she'd come to be laid out neatly on a sheet afterwards. The sea didn't usually tidy up the corpses it created.

Still, it hardly mattered now. What interested me more was where Nye's interest in miscarriages of justice came from. Could it be from the conviction of Isaac Little?

I wanted to speak to this Little, I realised as I sat there, and for that I was going to have to rope in Boland again, suppress my guilt at using him, and see if he could pull some strings to get me a pass into Mountjoy to see Howth's not-so-favourite son.

I was about to reach into my pocket and pull out my cellphone to do just that when I got that indefinable, inexplicable feeling you get when you know you're being watched.

It was probably just the damn cat, I thought, glancing up – but I found myself looking straight into the eyes of a man in the far corner of the store.

He was standing with his body turned towards a shelf of books, and one of those books was lying open in his hands, the fingers of one hand poised with a page held between them like he'd started to turn it and then forgotten what he was doing; and his head was turned straight towards me. He was so surprised by my looking up and catching him watching me that for a moment he didn't even turn away, and when he did it was only briefly, another furtive glance to the side quickly following. I wondered how long he'd been looking at me.

He was tall, dressed in a smart pinstriped suit, gleaming shoes, with an overcoat draped over his arm. His hair was cut short and at his feet sat a briefcase. A tie was knotted obediently at his throat. Get close enough and I'd probably see he had perfect fingernails too. He didn't look the kind to be browsing in a store with revolutionary pretensions like Burke's, and maybe that accounted for the awkwardness in him as he stood there. Either that, or he was now aware I was watching him in my turn as he'd watched me. His face was fixed with the same look, as if he was desperate not to give anything away, like he was counting down the seconds until he could close the book, replace it on the shelf and leave.

Sure enough, a moment later he shut the book – but he didn't replace it on the shelf. Rather he bent down to pick up his briefcase, and then carried the book to the counter, where Burke was trying to work out his monthly accounts on a tiny calculator, his massive fingers making a mockery of his attempts to press only one button at a time.

Burke received the book from the pinstriped man, opened the flap to check the price, and put it inside a paper bag, before taking the folded banknote that was offered and handing back the right change; and all this time, I was waiting for the next glance.

Now?

But no. The stranger didn't look up again, not even on his way out as he passed my chair. He simply opened the door and left.

I got to my feet and crossed to the window. Looked out through the reversed letters of Burke and Hare's names at his back as he retreated down the quay in the direction of town. If he looks back over his shoulder, I thought, I'll know I'm right.

Yes.

Just as he was about to move out of sight amongst the crowd, he looked back once, straight at the bookstore window, straight at me.

Our eyes met.

Then he was gone.

I was right.

I only wished I knew what I was right about.

Right maybe that what had happened was significant.

'You eyeing up my customers now as well?' said Burke behind me.

'He was watching me,' I said, still staring out at the street in case he came back.

'Watching isn't a crime,' said Burke. 'You're worth watching. Is a man not allowed to look at a woman any more without being accused of being a rapist? He's not to know you're of the other persuasion.'

'I don't mean watching me like that,' I said.

'What kind of watching do you mean?'

'I don't know,' I said, and for once I meant what I said instead of just saying it to deter further questions. I didn't even know if I'd have thought there was anything peculiar about him watching me if it hadn't been for what had happened last night in my apartment.

But last night *had* happened and I couldn't change that. It was bound to affect how I saw things for a while. Bound to make me suspicious.

'You have any idea who he is?' I asked Burke, returning thoughtfully to the desk and laying down Nye's pamphlet.

'Never seen him in here before, now that you mention it, but he did buy a book, so I'm prepared in the spirit of international brotherhood to give him the benefit of the doubt.'

'What are you on about, international brotherhood?'

'He was buying a copy of the *Grundrisse*.'

'Come again?'

'*The Foundations of the Critique of Political Economy.*'

207

'Burke, would you cut it out and just tell me what the hell you're talking about?'

'Karl Marx, sister. He was buying a book by Karl Marx.'

'And do you get many people in pinstripes buying copies of books by Karl Marx?'

'More than you'd think,' said Burke. 'Working where they do, they see the system from within. They know it stinks.'

'Something certainly does,' I said.

Chapter Twenty-Nine

Was Miranda Gray what I had expected? Hard to say. I hadn't really expected anything. She was tall, distinguished-looking, long red hair, clothes expensive but understated, the kind of woman who always knew how to dress and look good while making it seem like she never gave it a second thought, or even a first thought. The kind of woman I always felt vaguely inadequate next to, as if they'd some secret no one had ever passed on to me.

Whereas me, I just threw on the first thing that came to hand.

And, as Fitzgerald often teased me, it showed.

'Where's Grace?' said Fisher when I met him at the door.

'There's been some kind of break-in at the mortuary,' I said.

Another break-in.

Was I getting too paranoid in thinking they might be related?

'It was probably just kids,' I explained, 'looking for drugs. But the place is a mess, they really turned it over apparently, there are autopsy reports scattered everywhere. The pathologist's having kittens. Grace had to go and make sure nothing important was missing.'

'How long will it take?'

'Could be all night from the sound of it.'

'A table for three it is then,' said Fisher.

All in all, what with Fitzgerald not being here and Miranda Gray looking like she'd walked out of a Noel Coward play, I was more than a little wary, and it was a long time after we sat down to dinner before I started talking to her properly. Till then, I just let Fisher do all the work, and he was good at that, putting people at their ease. It must come from spending so much time in the company of psychopaths.

With those people, you *needed* to put them at their ease if you weren't going to end the meeting being carried out in a body bag.

I scanned the menu while he talked.

Fish, fish and then some more fish. And what was this? Well, what about that? Fish again. There was a certain consistency about the menu, I'll give it that.

The awkwardness soon passed once we'd ordered, and Miranda turned out to be easy enough company. I'd feared enduring a few hours of shop talk between the two psychologists, or worse, that they'd start shooting the breeze about people who meant nothing to me.

In fact, Miranda only seemed to want to talk about Alice.

'Fisher tells me she's got you looking into Felix's death,' she said.

'I wouldn't put it like that,' I said. 'I have my own reasons for being interested.'

'You've got me intrigued.'

'Maybe I'm just intrigued too,' I said, because I certainly wasn't going to start talking about Sydney. Fisher wouldn't have told Miranda about her, would he? 'It's not like I have anything else to do with my time.'

'Life been dull since you left the FBI?'

'It was the one thing I was any good at,' I said, 'but in the end I couldn't hack it and I had to leave. I should've taken six months off, a year, then gone back. Instead I wrote a book and burned my boats and ensured they weren't able to take me back.'

'Is that a common habit of yours?'

'To raze the ground behind me where I go? You bet. But it's not something I think about, and,' I said, 'it's certainly not something I want to talk about with a psychologist.'

'Saxon disapproves of therapy,' said Fisher.

'I think it's self-indulgence,' I admitted. 'I mean, don't you get bored sometimes listening to other people's relationship problems? How their mother didn't love them, and they feel like a failure, not to mention all that interpretation of their dreams?'

'It's not so bad,' Miranda laughed. 'They're not all so predictable. The dreams or the people. And there are one or two perks of the job.'

'Like the pay,' grumbled Fisher. 'When I think of all the years I spent in prisons, slaving away sixteen hours a day for next to nothing, when I could have been pampering to the Freudian hang-ups of rich narcissists with a need to pretend they're in the middle of some personal drama. They should try getting a job and then they wouldn't have time for all that.'

'Fisher, you're starting to sound like me,' I said.

'Don't worry about him,' Miranda said with mock sweetness. 'He's a disgrace to his profession. I think he prides himself on it sometimes. It's not as if you starved all those years, Lawrence. Not judging by your waistline anyway.'

She smiled indulgently at him before reaching out and squeezing his hand.

A small look passed between them and I couldn't help wondering again if the relationship was as really in the past as Fisher had told me.

It sounded weird hearing someone call him Lawrence, I knew that much.

'Do you mind if I ask you something?' I asked her.

'Fire away.'

'Who started coming to you first, Felix or Alice?'

'Alice. I knew her years ago when I lived out in Howth.'

'You're from Howth too?'

'Not originally. My people came from London, we moved over here when I was a teenager, lived in Howth just round the corner from the Bergs. But I was long gone by the time I started seeing her in any professional capacity. And she was coming to me a year before Felix even set foot through the door. Even then it was a long time before he relaxed, opened up, and really started to get something from the sessions.'

'Did she persuade him to come?'

'I got that impression,' Miranda said. 'She's a great believer in psychoanalysis. Reads all the right books, asks all the right questions. Keeps me on my toes, I suppose.'

'She sounds like hard work.'

'Harder than some patients. She's highly intelligent. Much more so than Felix was, I should think. Perhaps I shouldn't say that. Felix was intuitive, creative, good at lateral thinking. Alice is more single-visioned, deeply intellectual. She's a formidable woman.'

'Were they having a sexual relationship?' I shot at her.

'Sleeping together?' said Fisher, and he sounded shocked, bless him.

'Don't be such an innocent,' I said. 'Happens more often than you think.'

'Not in my family it didn't,' said Fisher. 'But then you haven't seen my sister. I'd turn gay first. No offence,' he added hastily.

'None taken. Well?' I said to Miranda.

'I'm sorry. I don't think it would be right for me to go into that.'

'Professional ethics are a new concept to Saxon,' said Fisher. 'You'll have to give her mind time to adjust to the novelty. But even if they were' – he gave a little mock shiver – 'sleeping together, what would that have to do with whether he was killed or not?'

'A thought, is all. Say they were having a relationship, would that make it harder for Alice to accept that Felix had killed himself? Would it make her angry, bitter, jealous, looking round for someone else to blame to erase her guilt at not having seen it coming?'

'Not bad,' said Fisher. 'You should be a therapist.'

'I'll take that as the insult it wasn't intended to be.'

'I can see what you're getting at. It's a fascinating theory,' said Miranda. 'But . . .'

'You can't give away client details? I understand.'

I said the words, but I didn't feel them in my gut. I *didn't* understand. Solving the mystery of Felix's death was more important than not breaching her confidentiality with Alice, surely? On the other hand, it mightn't look right for a therapist to sit at dinner swapping tales of her patients' sexual complications. Might not be good for business.

'Do you think *Alice* would ever kill herself?' I said.

'I wouldn't have thought so. She doesn't have the usual predictive traits. She's pretty tough. But then you never know. I could see that Felix was fragile, close to some edge, but I was still surprised by what happened. It's always a shock when a patient kills themself. It's like a slap in the face. They're telling you that you can't help them.'

'Is that why you were round at Gina's house? Looking for answers?'

She took a sip of wine before answering, looking pensive.

'You have to remember that I saw him for an hour twice a week,' she said. 'What did I really know about him? If I was going to understand what had happened, I needed to talk to people who spent their lives alongside him. Knew what books he was reading, what movies he watched, what jokes he laughed at. People who slept with him.'

'Like Alice?'

She smiled.

'There you go again, trying to get me to be indiscreet.'

'Don't you therapists ever swap stories of your patients?'

'Only with other therapists,' said Miranda. 'That way we keep the craziness in house.' And she and Fisher laughed together like the old friends they were. Once more I felt excluded, like I did when I was with Fitzgerald's circle. It's like I didn't belong anywhere, just as Felix had told me that first night on the phone. I was the perpetual ghost at the feast.

Outside looking in.

I decided to try a different tack to stop myself drowning in self-pity.

'Did you tell Alice her brother confessed to being the Marxman?' I asked.

'Fisher! You told her that?'

'Sorry.'

Fisher looked as sheepish as a small boy caught stealing candy.

'And there you were giving lectures on professional ethics to Saxon. You could do with a few reminders yourself. Don't bother defending yourself.'

'I wasn't going to,' he said. 'All I was going to say is that I told Saxon and Fitzgerald in good faith. They want to know what happened too.'

'Oh, I don't mind really,' said Miranda quietly. 'Secrets can be corrosive, and I don't want to have to be keeping his. Besides, if Lawrence told you that much, Saxon, then he must have told you that I did some other digging and found out it couldn't have been him.'

'Did you tell Felix you'd found out it couldn't be him?'

'No. I couldn't. He must have had his reasons for saying such a bizarre thing to me, it might have been counter-productive to push him too far. My approach was to let him talk about it when he felt ready. He didn't return to the subject again anyway.'

'Did he ever confess to anything else?'

'Any other murders, you mean? Absolutely not. Why would he?'

'Wouldn't someone who was the type to make false accusations against himself be more likely to make a number of fabricated confessions?

214

'I see what you mean. Not in Felix's case, no.'

'One set of murders is enough for anyone,' said Fisher.

'And did you ever tell Alice what he'd said?'

'Absolutely not. One time I was in town shopping and I saw Alice at a café table outside and went over to say hello. She was reading a newspaper report about the Marxman, and we talked about it for a while. Saying how terrible it was. How no one was safe any more. You know, the usual things. I tried to be casual about it, as if I was just asking out of curiosity. I said Felix had once mentioned it, and she said he would, he was obsessed by it.'

'You still didn't think that could prove he was involved?' said Fisher.

'I told you, he had at least one alibi that I could discover. Alice told me herself that he was out of the country at the time of the first shooting. I decided in the end that his obsession must be a sign of something else in him other than guilt. You've seen his work. The dislocation, this sense he had of people as an undifferentiated mass, his horror at the lack of individuality in modern society. A shooter like the Marxman – pardon the lingo, but I've been doing some reading on this in my spare time – would see human beings like that too. I decided that perhaps Felix simply sensed a sort of philosophical connection there and wanted to explore it, wanted to know why he expressed his alienation artistically whilst another with the same viewpoint turned to murder. But I'm only speculating. Psychoanalysts are always being accused of not seeing the wood for the trees, of reading too much meaning into simple things, of always thinking they must represent something else. Felix could have simply been interested in the Marxman because he was on the news so much. You can't open a newspaper or turn on the television without seeing something else about it.'

'And is that what you think now?'

'No. Not now. Now I think he did know something, that he was trying to tell me what it was, that he wanted me to

215

press him further, but I never gave him the chance. My therapist's detachment must have seemed to him like disinterest. I let him down.'

'That's what Alice thinks about herself too,' I said.

And Miranda was silent again as we returned to our dinner.

A short while later, she rose to go to the restroom.

'What do you think of her?' Fisher asked me as we watched her weave between tables to the door.

'I think you make a lovely couple.'

'Be serious, Saxon.'

'I am serious. If Laura could see you now, I think she'd be a very worried lady.'

He didn't deny it. All he said was: 'Do I have to keep reminding you of the purely platonic nature of our relationship?'

'Frankly, Fisher, yes. You do.'

Chapter Thirty

On the way out to the car from Nemo's, I rang Fitzgerald at Dublin Castle again. I hadn't heard from her since she called to say she couldn't make it to dinner.

The phone must have rung a half-dozen times before being picked up.

'You still not finished yet?' I said.

But it was Boland's voice that answered.

'Saxon, is that you? I've been trying to reach you. I thought you might want to know.'

Something about his voice – some edge of panic – made ice form like fur in my veins.

'Boland, what is it? What's the matter?'

'Haven't you heard? The Marxman's shot another one.'

'What? Where's Grace?'

'She's at the hospital.'

'She's what?'

'The hospital.'

It was like my head wasn't working properly, I couldn't make sense of what he was saying. Fitzgerald had been shot? I just about managed to get out of him that she was down at St James's before telling him I was on my way.

'But Saxon—'

Impatiently, I pressed the cellphone into silence.

I didn't have time.

I had to get to her, and quickly.

I dashed down the last steps to the Jeep, jumped in,

reversed out into the street, ignoring the angry protests of other drivers, broke the first set of lights and was on my way.

A huge Victorian building near the river, St James's Hospital was home to the main emergency department for Dublin city. I'd never been there but I knew that there was a large parking lot out front, and vehicles were lined up nose to tail along the road leading to it. I had to go slowly to avoid knocking anyone down, and going slowly was making me more anxious.

If anything was to happen to Fitzgerald . . .

All I could think of was how I'd told her that morning that she was starting to sound like Draker. I'd meant it to wound her, and it had. Now it sounded so childish.

In the end, I abandoned the Jeep in a side street and hurried round to the front entrance. At the edge of my sight I could see the police cars ranged about, lights flashing on top like some reassuring pulse, but my only thought was to make for the door.

To get inside.

I was halfway up the steps when I felt a hand grab hold of my sleeve, and I was turning angrily to shake off whoever it was who had grabbed me when I saw it was Patrick Walsh.

'Hey, babe. I thought it was you. What's the big rush?'

'I need to see Grace,' I said.

'The Chief's upstairs,' he said, puzzled.

'I know,' I snapped. 'That's why I'm here. Boland called to tell me what had happened.'

'Then he obviously didn't tell you what was going on,' said Walsh. 'Did you think . . .?' He trailed off. It must have been obvious from my face what I'd thought.

'You mean she's OK?'

'She's talking to someone, that's all,' he answered. 'Christ, no wonder you looked so shocked. You thought something had happened to *her*?'

'Boland said something about the Marxman . . . I guess I didn't give him a chance . . .'

I remembered his last words: *But Saxon*—

Just like me always to jump to the wrong conclusion.

'Come on,' Walsh said, 'let's find somewhere to sit down. I'll explain.'

He led me back towards his own car, and I sat in the passenger seat with my legs sticking out while he stood leaning on the door, watching the hospital entrance in case he was needed. Relief had taken hold of me and I almost felt like I wanted to giggle.

'She's up there with Healy,' Walsh said. 'They brought the guy in about half an hour ago. He was shot down by the river this evening. He'd just finished a job near there – he's some kind of magician, apparently, does tricks at children's parties, pulling rabbits out of hats, you know – and had nipped into a bar called the Louis IX or something along those lines on the way to the station. On the way out, according to witnesses, a figure in black stepped up close behind him, put his hand on his shoulder, and shot him.'

'Was it the Marxman?'

'Once again, we're not sure yet. Certainly looks like it.'

'But what are you all doing *here*? Why aren't you at the scene?'

'The guy's not dead,' said Walsh.

'He's alive?'

'Unless the hospital food's killed him since he arrived,' said Walsh. 'Sorry, bad joke. He's going to be fine.'

'Who is he? Did he say?'

'He told the paramedics his name was Brook, told them where he lived, asked them to call his wife and tell her he wouldn't be home for dinner. The things people think of when they've been shot. But the really interesting thing was what he told them after that. He said whoever shot him whispered something to him before he pulled the trigger.'

'What did he whisper?'

'*I am the dead hand.*'

219

'Then he shot him? How did he manage to make it to hospital, let alone live this long afterwards, if he was shot in the back at point-blank range?'

'He was only shot in the shoulder,' said Walsh.

'Then he mustn't have meant to kill him,' I said. 'He couldn't have missed at that range. Doesn't matter if you've never picked up a gun before in your life, you'd still get it right if you were up that close. That must mean he wanted this victim to live.'

'I know. That's why the Chief's up there interviewing him now. She wants to find out as much as she can about the attack. He's in a lot of pain, though, or so he says. Doctors have him sedated. Maybe he's just a bit freaked out by it all. Traumatised, isn't that what they call it? It's not every day you get shot on your way home from work.'

I looked back at the hospital. The windows were all lit up. In one of them, Fitzgerald was cooped up with a possible answer to the mystery.

Ten minutes ago I'd thought she was dead. Now I envied her. Sitting in Walsh's passenger seat hearing everything at second hand was no substitute for being on the inside.

I got to my feet and turned away from the hospital, not wanting to look any more.

'What makes you think it was the Marxman this time then?' I said.

'There was a single shot, in the back, the victim was shot in the doorway as he came out of the bar, after which the shooter coolly picked up the shell. The MO's all pointing in the right direction. More than that, the bullet looks the same.'

'The surgeons got it out of him then?'

'Didn't need to. It went right through his shoulder and out the other side. It broke up a bit when it hit the wall but they could still see it was the same as the others.'

'If it was the Marxman, that's the first time he's touched one of the victims,' I said thoughtfully. 'There might be something on Brook's coat. Was he wearing a coat?'

'He was in shirtsleeves. He'd been entertaining a small army of five-year-olds for the past hour and a half, he didn't need a coat to keep him warm. The shirt's been bagged up and taken away by forensics, but by the time the paramedics and doctors had done with him he'd been pawed over by a dozen different hands. They had to cut off his shirt to get at the wound and staunch the bleeding. If you ask me, forensics will be practically useless.'

'It's something all the same,' I said.

But Walsh wasn't listening. He was watching the steps of the hospital, where voices had been raised suddenly. I turned my head to look, and there was a small group of cops barring the way to a young man in a white coat who was trying to reach the door.

He had his hands raised like he was trying to show them he came in peace.

Angry voices drifted over.

'I'm a doctor. I told you. I got a call telling me to come in.'

'Do you usually bring a camera in to work with you, *Doctor*?'

'I only brought it because . . . because one of the nurses is having a birthday party later . . . She asked me if I'd take some shots . . .'

'Looks as though the press have found out about the latest victim,' said Walsh with disgust. 'I'd better go sort it out. You be OK here until I get back, babe?'

'I'll be fine.'

Fine as long as he stopped calling me babe, anyway.

I watched as he ran over to the scuffle, then turned my back on it, uninterested.

The circus was taking over. It always did.

Didn't mean I had to watch the show.

Instead I lit a cigar and cherished the familiar scent. A huge exhaustion had descended on me and suddenly all I wanted was to take a couple of pills and slip back into darkness, a proper dreamless oblivion this time, not the fitful, feverish state I'd been enduring lately, when I woke almost more wiped out than I'd been when I went to sleep.

What was it I always dreamed about these nights?

Dark water.

Drowning.

A lighthouse.

The turning beam red like blood.

Didn't take Miranda Gray to figure out where that came from.

There wouldn't be any sleep for a while yet tonight, that was for sure. My brain was trying to process all these new fragments of information. Put some order on them.

Find a shape.

Another shooting . . . a victim who had survived . . . If the Marxman wanted this victim to survive, then it was for a reason, and the only reason it could be, as far as I could see, was because he wanted him to pass on the message.

I am the dead hand.

The dead hand.

It was such a meaningless statement on the surface of it, but it must mean something. Was that what the Marxman had said to all the victims before they died? But no, he hadn't been close enough to some of them to whisper anything.

This one alone then had been meant as a message.

But a message saying what?

I felt frustrated. All the anxiety I'd experienced earlier after taking the call from Boland had been channelled now into thinking about the Marxman, and wondering despairingly how any of this related to Felix Berg. I'd spent so long trying to make two sequences of events entwine themselves into a single thread, and now I could feel them separating again in my fingers.

I couldn't see how Felix Berg and this magician could be connected.

I am the dead hand.

I stood and watched ambulances come and go, come and

go, because the world didn't stop for just one victim. It didn't stop for a thousand. My thoughts were evaporating.

Thinking about all this was like trying to sculpt water, and I was relieved when the door finally opened and Fitzgerald emerged. Healy must have still been inside.

I saw her pause briefly at the top of the steps, savouring the air the way she did on my balcony sometimes after a long day, composing herself.

It was all I could do not to laugh out loud with the sheer pleasure of seeing her alive. It was torture not being able to walk over to her. I could still taste that sick feeling of panic I'd felt when I thought she was lying here dead, or dying. Fitzgerald dead was not something I could imagine imagining, and I didn't want to try imagining it in case I found that I could, in case I got that image fixed in my head somewhere, as permanently inscribed as something on a computer hard disk, where it's there for ever even if you think you've erased it.

Whereas myself dead I imagined all the time.

A world without me didn't seem so very different.

Didn't seem so bad.

But a world without her . . .

She stepped down and listened as a young policeman came up to give her a message. Nodded. Then looked up and caught sight of me standing by Walsh's car, waiting for her to see me. She smiled and meant it, before walking over, out of range of the other cops.

'Hey,' she said quietly, which said it all.

'You have any luck in there?'

'He doesn't remember much. He had his back turned the whole time, we're just trying to see if he can remember anything more about the voice. Could be the first real piece of evidence we've had about the killer. But what's to remember about a whisper? He can't even remember if it was a man or a woman, young or old; he can't remember an accent.'

'Better than nothing.' I tried to be reassuring.

'It's certainly better than sorting out the autopsy reports down at the mortuary with Alastair Butler clucking like a mother hen over her chicks,' she said. 'But there's bad news too, unfortunately. Healy thinks he knows what that stuff about the dead hand means. He says it comes from some old quote: *The dead hand of history lies like a nightmare on the brains of the living.*'

There's profound.

'What's so bad about that?' I said.

'What's bad is that it comes from Marx. And I don't mean Groucho.'

'Terrific,' I said casually, thinking about the guy in Burke's bookstore and then reminding myself that I couldn't go round reading too much into the fact that someone who was looking at me had bought a book by Marx, especially since at the time we were both in a store that specialised in selling books by Marx, about Marx, inspired by Marx.

You go to a cheese store to buy cheese, after all.

'Terrific's right,' Fitzgerald said. 'Just when I thought I'd seen off Sweeney for good.'

'Has he heard yet?'

'He's already been on the phone to the Commissioner, saying this proves his theory that the shootings are political and that the anti-terrorist unit should take over operational control of the investigation at the soonest opportunity.'

'How is shooting a guy who pulls rabbits out of top hats and ribbons out of his ears for a living meant to be political?'

'You're preaching to the converted here, Saxon – but try telling them that.'

'The killer's only trying to throw another red herring into the net. Literally red in this case. He only has to read the newspapers or watch TV to see that there's bad blood between the murder squad and the anti-terrorist branch over this. So he chucks a little bit of his own communist manifesto into the mix to stir things up, and—'

'Hey presto, as our friend Brook might say.'

'He has Sweeney on the case on another reds-under-the-bed hunt.'

'Which suits the Marxman just fine. So-called Marxman, I should say. He's no more interested in Karl Marx than I am.'

Fitzgerald stopped suddenly and frowned.

'What is it?'

'Nothing, I don't think,' she said, but she was looking across the road at the usual crowd of curious onlookers who had gathered there at the first sight of a police light.

Word gets out fast.

I turned my head to look at them too, but it was dark now, they were only faces.

'Did you see someone?'

'I thought so,' she said. 'For a moment there, I thought I saw Alice.'

Chapter Thirty-One

Fitzgerald held a press conference for the early morning news shows.

Following a definite line of enquiry . . . a number of promising leads . . . confident of being able to report development soon . . .

She was a good liar.

The fact that the killer had passed on a message in this way was good. Silence was what was worrying. And if this was a sign he really did want to make contact, be understood, then there was hope he could be caught out that way too. But there was still a long way to go. When no obvious motive existed, catching a killer was made all the harder.

Sometimes impossibly so.

I had different plans for the day. I was driving north through the city towards Mountjoy Prison. Healy had taken me to one side at the hospital shortly before I left and pressed a piece of paper into my hand with a name and number scrawled on it. Boland had told him I was looking to see Little; Healy knew the right people. It would only be half an hour, he said, but the way I saw it, a half-hour was still a half-hour longer than nothing.

I'd told Fitzgerald where I was going, but she'd simply raised her hands palms up in front of her chest to silence me.

'I don't need to know,' she said. 'In fact, I don't even want to know. I'd rather have deniability. You do what you have to do. Just be careful, yeah?'

'Aren't I always?'

'I won't answer that.'

Little himself was apparently eager to meet me. He didn't get many visitors, Healy said. Correction. He didn't get any.

I approached the gates with that vague feeling of dread I always got from prisons, and there was something especially miserable about Mountjoy. It was the Leonard Cohen of prisons, all hopelessness and misery and gloom. The very stones were stained so black that water couldn't have made any difference. The guards frisked me when I gave them my name to make sure I wasn't bringing him in any contraband (though the only drug I'd be interested in bringing in to someone like Isaac Little was cyanide, and only then if I could administer it myself). Then I was scanned to make sure I wasn't taking in any weapons, and looked at in that suspicious way they have to make sure . . . well, I'm not sure what that was for.

Did they think they could detect malign intent just by looking?

Eventually they decided I was harmless enough and led me hurriedly into the building, down one corridor, into another, corridor leading to corridor, until we entered a small windowless room.

Not the usual room for visitors, that was for sure, but then I was out of hours for visiting. There was only a table, two chairs, not even water. A page was pinned to the wall showing a shift rota. There was a green No Smoking sign above the door.

A dead spider was tangled in its own web in a corner.

'If there's anything you need,' said the guard, 'just ring this' – and he showed me the button under the table that activated the alarm. 'Try not to press it unless you really need to. You're not supposed to be here. I'll try and keep an eye on things through the grille.'

Then he was gone.

I lit a cigar, then noticed again the No Smoking sign. They were probably worried the inmates would get cancer and sue the prison authorities for exposing them, frail, delicate creatures that they were, to the horrors of passive smoking.

Besides, I didn't want to set off any fire alarms.

I stubbed the cigar out regretfully.

And waited.

It seemed an age before the door opened and Isaac Little came in.

The guard sat him down on the chair.

'No nonsense now, Isaac,' he said.

'With these?' Little lifted up his cuffed hands. 'Chance'd be a fine thing.'

He was a surprisingly scrawny man, wizened, husked, sort of shifty in his movements, with thin bony hands, fingers like some variety of medical probes, a mouth studded with bad teeth, scrags of stubble sticking out from his grey chin; he scratched at the growth with his joined hands like he thought he had company there. His hair hung lank as pond weed, and he sniffed constantly as he sat there. Eyes never still. His skin was blotched and poor and dry; he kept licking his lips with slight lizard movements of his tongue but they never seemed to get any less dry. White trash, I'd have called him if I was back home.

What did they call him here?

No need to call him anything.

He was Isaac Little.

That sufficed.

He repelled me, and I knew I'd have to struggle to contain it. I'd met worse than him, and yet there was something revolting, repulsive, rotten about this specimen.

His soul gave off a stench, and it wasn't even a stench of evil; it only aspired to evil, and had settled in the meantime for a third-rate wickedness. It's a cliché of policing that child sex offenders look just like everyone else. Little didn't. There was something noxious that came from his eyes that made me feel infected and dirty just to see it. He was the sort you'd pull your child to your side to avoid if you saw him oozing down the street.

It was hard to think he'd ever been allowed near a child when the maliciousness in him was such a palpable aura hanging round him. Had he always been like that, I wondered, or had he simply allowed his true self to cultivate itself since being locked away, when it didn't matter any more, when there was no reason to pretend, ready to assume the right mask again when free?

His eyes looked me up and down, but the lechery was half-hearted. I guess I was too old for him. About thirty years too old, to judge by his file.

I recalled the charge sheet Boland had read out to me over the phone that morning.

Interfering with a minor. Inciting a child to engage in sexual activity. Arranging or facilitating the commission of a child sexual offence. Causing a child to watch a sexual act. Paying for sex with a child. Indecent exposure. Voyeurism. Unlawful carnal knowledge of a girl under the age of fifteen years. Knowingly producing, distributing and printing and publishing child pornography. Knowingly possessing child pornography.

Truly it's a wonderful world we live in.

He'd also worked in a care home for the mentally handicapped for two years, and the offences there had racked up too. Inciting a person with a mental disorder or learning disability to engage in sexual activity. Causing a person with a mental disorder or learning disability to engage in sexual activity. Inducement, threat or deception to procure sexual activity with a person with a mental disorder or learning disability.

Prior to his conviction for the murder of Lucy Toner, however, Little had committed no known acts of violence against a child except insofar as all his offences were acts of violence. That didn't mean he wasn't capable of violence – murder often came out of nowhere, no prior warning, like lightning from a clear sky – but it made me wonder.

'What do you want?' he said eventually.

No small talk then. Suited me fine. I didn't exactly relish the idea of finding topics to break the ice with this man. What would we talk about – Mid East affairs, the stock market, the most effective ways to groom a child for the purposes of sexual depravity?

The usual subjects for polite dinner-party conversation.

'I want to ask about Lucy. You remember her?'

'Of course I remember her. I killed her, didn't I?' Sarcasm dripped off his tongue like poison from a syringe. 'Laid down the little honey in the sand and smothered her with one hand up her panties, yes indeed, soft and warm, what a glorious morning it was to be alive.'

He grinned at me, trying to shock me.

I kept my face impassive.

This was a part of the job I'd always found difficult. Fisher could do this sort of thing without a thought: meet killers, perverts, treat talking to them like it was shooting the breeze with a stranger at a bus stop about the weather. Any hint of disapproval and they'd curl up like porcupines with the prickles pointing out. You had to befriend them, get in under their defences; that was how you found stuff out.

I'd always been bad at that because I found it harder to shield how I felt; they always caught a glimpse of it and hostility came between us. It was there now, and I knew we could both sense it, but Isaac didn't curl up porcupine-style. I could only guess it was a long time since someone had come out here and talked to him, and he wanted to see where it might lead, what he could get out of it; he wasn't going to risk it this soon.

He had *some* self-control then.

It was just a pity he'd never showed it in the presence of children.

'I don't believe you did that,' I said as carefully as I could manage.

'I know. I was told. That's the only reason I agreed to see you.'

'So do you want to tell me what you really did that day?'

'Stayed in bed most of the time. I was on this medication. Sleeping all the time, just getting up to eat, take a slash. I got up about four, went down to the kitchen for something to eat, I didn't see no one all day, then I went back to bed. Next day the police were hammering at the door and I was being pushed about by some inspector looking for promotion who seemed, for some reason, to have taken a dislike to me. Seemed to think I'd murdered some girl down the road.'

'You absolutely sure you hadn't?'

'It's the sort of thing I'd remember. I've got a good memory for little details like that. Faces. Phone numbers. Murders I've committed.'

'You said you were on medication.'

'On medication, yes. Out of my head, no. I've never harmed a child in my life.'

'Apart from raping them, you mean?'

He flinched.

'That's your word,' he said.

'What word would you use instead?'

He paused a long time before answering.

'I loved those kids,' he said, 'and they loved me. You wouldn't understand.'

'Because I'm not a pervert, you mean?'

He sat up straight. 'There's a certain pride in being a pervert, as you call it. The niggers and the queers all call themselves that now, don't they? They've claimed the word back for themselves. Why shouldn't perverts take pride in what they are too?'

'Perverts of the world unite, you have nothing to lose but your chains.'

'Something like that.'

He grinned, and the bad teeth declared themselves open for business.

I could see him now, in a band.

Pervertz With Attitude.

Number one with a bullet.

Only not straight between the eyes, unfortunately.

'Look, we're just wasting time here,' I said. 'I came because I'm interested in Lucy's death. You said you didn't do it; I believe you. I want to know who you think did.'

'I know who did it,' said Little.

'Yeah?'

'It was one of those young ones in the house up the street. Hippie types. Plenty of money. Used to live in some kind of commune.' A joke had come to him. 'Free love, man.'

'And what makes you think it was one of them?'

'Because he told me. Felix. The photographer.'

'He told you?'

'Yeah, he wrote to me soon after I was convicted. Sent me a letter right here. Said he wanted to come and speak to me, said he had something to tell me, that he knew I was innocent.'

'Just like me.'

'He wasn't quite so hot.'

I ignored him.

'You let him come?' I prompted.

'Why not? I knew his sister. I got into some trouble when I first moved into the house there. I'd just got out of jail. I'd done some time for robbery, I'd turned over a chemist's somewhere—' He wasn't looking at me now. Didn't he think I'd read his file and knew the real reason he'd been inside? 'When they found out who I was, I got some hassle from the neighbours.' Fancy that. 'They didn't like the fact I was lowering the tone of the neighbourhood. Bringing property prices down.'

'But Alice didn't join in?'

'She brought me stuff. Food. Wine she'd made herself. Books. Used to drop them round.'

Proper little Florence Nightingale.

'She ever tell you why she was doing it?'

'She said she believed everyone had the right to a second chance. That I'd paid for my errors and now needed to be encouraged to live a virtuous life again.'

I honestly thought I was going to puke.

'You didn't tell her then about the stash of pictures of naked children you had upstairs, and the nice view of the playground?'

'What can I say? It didn't come up in conversation.'

I'll bet it didn't, I thought, and was amazed again how intelligent, educated people like Alice could be so naive, swallowing that bullshit about redemption and second chances. A second chance for monsters like Isaac was just a second chance to ruin more children's lives.

'I'm surprised she didn't come by this place herself,' I said. 'For morning coffee and biscuits, you know.'

'I thought you were on my side here,' he whined unpleasantly in reply.

'Not thinking you killed that little girl isn't the same as thinking you're some sort of hero or that I have to pretend all the other stuff didn't happen. You can't deny you presented a bit of a target for the police. They were bound to come up with your name, and once they did, all the other evidence was just sitting there. You had no alibi, an unhealthy sexual interest in children. You can't expect everyone to be as understanding as Alice. You still haven't said why she hasn't visited you here.'

'Felix told me she was upset,' said Isaac with a trace of sulkiness, 'that she'd moved away. He'd be coming instead now, he said, but he had her full support. His exact words. He told me on his first visit.'

'Did *he* bring homemade wine and cookies too?'

Evidently not.

'He told me he knew for a fact that someone in the house where he lived had killed the girl and he was going to help me prove I was innocent. He was gathering information, he said, and soon as he had enough he'd come forward. He said he'd told the police about his suspicions but they didn't want to know, but that he had money, lots of it, and he was going to use it to hire people to find out what had really happened, lawyers, PIs, the lot.'

'He didn't care that you were a menace to children?'

'He cared about the fact that I was innocent.'

'Yeah, you said that already. So what happened?'

'I heard from him a couple of times, he told me he was getting close. Then nothing. I sent him a couple of letters asking him to get back in touch, but he never answered.'

'What did you think had happened?'

'That he'd been warned off by the police. They do that, you know. Or paid off. Either by the police because they wanted to keep me in here, or else by the real killer. I figured maybe he'd found out who did it and had decided to cover up for them because that would cause less trouble for him than letting me rot in here.' His voice was rising. 'Then I thought maybe he'd just been leading me on, getting some kind of kick out of building up my hopes.'

'And now? What do you think now?'

He considered the question.

'I think he knew damn well who killed the little bitch and just stopped trying to help me for his own reasons.'

'You know he's dead now, don't you?'

'I heard about it,' he said dismissively.

'No great loss to you?'

'When someone tells you they're going to help you, then ignores you for years, you kind of lose any attachment to them you might have had. He shot himself. Big deal. I just wish it was me who'd plugged him. He was probably sticking his nose into other people's business again and they had someone go put a bullet in him. Fuck him.'

There was something in that. Felix digs into the death of Lucy, and is frightened off when maybe he gets too close. He investigates the Marxman killings – and winds up dead.

Maybe he made a habit out of curiosity one time too many.

Ran out of lives like a cat.

'The way I see it,' Little said, 'is that there's karma and everything comes back to haunt you. You don't help those who need help and then in the end there'll be no one there when you need them. Instead you get back what's coming to you sevenfold, right up the ass.'

'And is that what you think happened to Felix?'

'I fucking well hope so, lady, I fucking well hope so.'

Chapter Thirty-Two

By the time I left Isaac Little and returned to the world of light, I'd seen enough of him to last a lifetime, and I wasn't sure I could face the prospect of another visit.

Besides, I figured I'd got as much out of him as I was likely to get, meagre though it was. Was I prepared to put myself through the ordeal of another six, ten, a hundred sessions breathing the same air as him just in the hope that he might come up with something, some nugget, which would make it all worthwhile?

Little, needless to say, was eager for me to return, and I forced myself to make enough of the right noises to keep him happy without disgusting myself totally.

He knew I despised him, and that I wouldn't have cared if he'd spontaneously combusted in front of me, but still he wanted my attention. I despised him all the more for that, as if there wasn't enough to be contemptuous of him for already. My one hope was that I was only raising his hopes of release in order to dash them. Nothing was more guaranteed to destroy a long-term prisoner's spirits. If I was lucky, I'd get the balance just right and the wiry little bastard would succeed in hanging himself from the bars on his window.

My fear, however, was that I'd find something that proved he was indeed innocent, and then what? He was too much of a danger to children to feel any cosy liberal satisfaction about overturning a miscarriage of justice. I only needed to remember his charge sheet to know what I might be helping to let out on the street again. And there'd be other offences to add to the list if he ever got out, because someone like Little never stopped, they were addicted to corrupting innocence. I wasn't sure I could have that on my conscience.

It wouldn't have lost me any sleep to keep someone like Little in prison for something he didn't do – keeping him inside was what mattered – but what if that meant keeping the killer of Lucy Toner on the outside?

Wasn't that just as bad?

My thoughts grew progressively darker as I made my way back across town, taking a short cut down towards Bridge Street only to find that it wasn't so short as I'd hoped and some hold-up had that part of the city by the throat and showed no signs of letting go.

To pass time, I called Boland on my hands-free set.

'Hello?'

No one ever seemed to pick up their own phone any more. This time it was a woman.

And she didn't exactly sound delighted to hear my voice.

'Who?' she repeated when I told her who I was.

'I only want to speak to Boland a moment.'

A sigh.

'Hold on.'

She passed the phone over with a cold whisper: 'It's a woman.'

'This is Boland,' came Boland's puzzled tone.

'Boland, it's me, Saxon.'

And I heard his muffled tone on the other end of the line as he covered the mouthpiece with his hand and murmured: 'It's not a woman, it's Saxon.'

Thanks, Boland.

I really needed that vote of confidence.

'Who's that anyway?' I said to him.

'Cassie. Who did you think it was?'

'She's living with you now?'

237

'Not for long once she hears you on the other end of the line.'

'She's nothing to worry about from me. I'm not even a woman.'

'You heard that?' said Boland.

'Every self-esteem-boosting word.'

'Well, you know what I meant. It's an awkward time.'

'Serves me right for calling at an awkward time then. Though,' I said, glancing at the clock on the dashboard, 'this is the first time I ever heard midday called awkward.'

'Did you get in to see Isaac Little OK?' he sidestepped.

'That's what I want to ask you about.'

I told him what Little had said about Felix and Alice being his best buddies.

'I don't know about Alice,' Boland said in reply, 'but you're way off on Felix. He never made any representations on behalf of Little. He was interviewed as part of the investigation and he said nothing about his suspicions. Not then, not afterwards.'

Why was nothing ever straightforward?

'You dug out the records?' I said.

'Soon as I knew you were going into Mountjoy to see him. There's nothing in the case notes or interview files about Felix saying one word about Little. Not to say he was innocent, nor that he was guilty. In fact, he claimed he didn't know him at all.'

'Alice certainly knew him if Little's to be believed.'

'That's a big if,' Boland pointed out. 'The guy's a child abuser. Those men are accomplished liars. They're worse than politicians. You can't believe a word they say.'

'But what would be the point of spinning me a line about Felix?'

'You're asking me? I don't know. To make his case for wrongful conviction look stronger, to make you feel sorry for him . . .'

'He's a shock coming if he thinks I'll feel sorry for him,' I said.

Then again, why hadn't he asked me *why* I was so interested in his case, since I made no attempt to hide my contempt for him? It wasn't like I was fussing over him like he said Felix and Alice had been, fretting like anguished liberals about his bruised civil rights.

Was Little playing some game with me too?

'What about the other people in the house?' I said. 'Paul Vaughan? Paddy Nye? Did they say anything at the time about knowing Little?'

'Paul Vaughan was never interviewed. At first he wasn't available, and by the time he was, Little had been charged, and it was all just formalities. Nye's only statement was to confirm Felix Berg's story that they were together at the time of the killing.'

'So if Nye killed the little girl, then Felix covered up for him?' I said.

No reply came.

'Boland, are you there?'

But somewhere over Dublin, the signal had obviously fizzled out.

It was probably snarled up in traffic too.

I leaned on my horn and joined the chorus.

It was another hour before I got back to my empty apartment.

First thing I did when I got in – second thing, actually; the first thing was to check that the place hadn't been turned over again in my absence – was listen to my messages.

Fitzgerald was first, checking how I'd got on with Little. Next was Fisher to tell me where he was staying, since he'd agreed, he explained, to hang around for a few days longer and try to help the police make sense of last night's message (and see some more of Miranda Gray too?). Then came Miranda Gray herself to say how much she'd enjoyed dinner and we should do it again sometime. And finally . . .

It took me a second to recognise the voice.

Gina.

239

Felix's former girlfriend.

And she was crying.

'I feel such an idiot now,' she said as she stepped back and let me inside. The room was in shadow. A fan on the desk was blowing out cool air, and the pages of a book fluttered quietly like a dying bird. 'It was probably nothing. Really. You needn't have come round, I'm fine.'

'Is that why you have the drapes drawn? Because you're fine?'

She smiled faintly.

'I just felt . . . felt as if I was being watched.'

'Can I see it?'

She crossed to a dresser and pulled open a drawer, reached in, took out the envelope which had arrived at her house that morning.

'I didn't know who else to call,' she apologised, 'and I remembered you being here, and how you gave me your number . . . and I went and dug it out and . . .'

'It's OK,' I said, because I was afraid she was going to start crying again, and crying always made me uncomfortable. 'Just let me see it.'

She handed the envelope to me.

Gina.

That was all it said.

'It wasn't posted then?'

'It was dropped through the letterbox whilst I was out. The mail had already arrived. I'd gone to get milk. When I got back . . .' She couldn't finish. Her hands were shaking. 'Whoever it was must have been watching me,' she concluded in a whisper.

The envelope was crumpled and torn at the top; I pulled the edges apart and fished inside with my finger. There was a photo, a single snapshot, like the one that had fallen out of Felix's cuttings file and the one that had been attached to a hook on my wall.

240

This one showed Gina, dressed exactly as she was now, emerging from the gate at the top of her steps, a bag slung over her shoulder, sunglasses pushed up her head. The vision was partly obscured by a motorbike parked outside the gate, but there was no mistaking it was her. It had to have been taken right across the road, next to the phone booth.

'Whoever it was must have been waiting for me to come out, taken the picture, waited for it to develop and come out of the camera, then put it in the envelope, crossed over the street and dropped it through the letterbox for me to find when I got back.'

Only pausing, I thought but didn't say, to slash the front of the photograph with a knife.

Right across Gina's face.

'How long were you out?'

'It couldn't have been more than five minutes. Ten at most. The shop's only at the end of the street,' she said.

Plenty of time.

'And you didn't see anything as you walked back?'

'I wasn't looking, but no, no, I didn't.'

'No strangers? Strange cars?'

'You can see for yourself, it's a busy road. People coming and going. There are always strange cars and bikes parked up here. It's only supposed to be for residents, but no one takes any notice of signs. I wouldn't have spotted anyone. Anyone I didn't know, I mean.'

I put the photograph back into the envelope and made to give it back to her.

Gina moved her hand away.

'I don't want it,' she said. 'You take it. Burn it. I don't care.' She look up suddenly, and flinched as the window started rattling violently as a truck went by.

It was, as she said, a busy road.

'I'll pass it on to the police if you like,' I said.

'Do you have to?'

'Threatening letters . . . photos . . . Of course they should be told.'

Because it rarely ends there, I could have said, but what would have been the point? She was frightened enough as it was. Besides, it wasn't like I took my own advice.

And she wasn't listening anyway.

'Who is doing this?' she pleaded, still staring at the window. 'What do they want?'

'I don't know,' I said, 'but I heard Strange was sent one like it.'

'Was his cut up too?'

'I didn't see it,' I said. 'I only heard about it. I heard it was defaced, so I guess it was the same. He thought it was me who'd sent it to him.'

'You? Why would you do such a thing?'

'Why would anyone?'

Gina was thoughtful for a moment.

'You know,' she said, 'it's almost a relief to know other people have been getting them too. I thought it was only me.'

Though would she feel so relieved if she knew this photograph might be only the first? According to his lawyers, Strange had been getting them regularly.

And now I'd started too. Felix, Strange, Gina and me: there was a pattern there. Initially I'd thought it had something to do with the Marxman, because of Felix's obsession, but what if the link was something else entirely? Something much closer to us all?

And then I thought about Alice, who wasn't taking her telephone calls.

Who wasn't answering when I called round.

Was she afraid too? Was she getting these pictures?

'I should try Alice again,' I said without thinking, and felt Gina bristle immediately.

'Alice,' she said scornfully.

'I know you two don't get along, but this could affect her, she deserves to know . . .'

242

'Maybe she knows plenty about it already.'

'What are you saying?'

'Nothing. Nothing. Oh, you know what I'm saying. I can't deny it crossed my mind that it was Alice who did this. She's the only person I can think of who hates me enough. Who would want to make me suffer. And you know . . .'

'What?'

'Well, it just seems such a *woman* thing to do,' she said.

And she was right.

Spiteful letters.

Anonymous hate mail.

Women were masters of the art.

All I could think of suddenly was Fitzgerald glimpsing what she thought was Alice in the crowd of onlookers opposite St James's Hospital the previous night.

And there was something else.

Something that had been bothering me.

I felt for my cellphone, before remembering I'd left it in the apartment.

'Can I use your phone?' I said to Gina.

If she was surprised, she didn't let it show.

'Of course,' she said, 'it's right there.'

'I see it.'

She retreated to another room whilst I picked up the receiver and dialled.

'Tell me something, Strange,' I said when he picked up. 'Who *did* take all those charming sado-masochistic shots you have on the walls of your gallery?'

'Who's this speaking?' he demanded.

'Surely you haven't forgotten me already? And after I got such a charming letter from your lawyer too.'

'This is Saxon, I presume.'

'I'm touched. You remember. There's hope in our relationship yet.'

'You're making a big mistake,' Strange said. 'I warned you to stay away from me.'

'You warned me to stop *harassing* you, is what I remember. Since when does a friendly phone call constitute harassment?'

'I'm putting the phone down.'

'No you're not. You're going to tell me who took those pictures in your store.'

'Gallery. And as I believe I told you before, the artist wishes to remain anonymous. I do not discuss my artists' private affairs with anyone. And certainly not with you. How dare you call me and—'

'It's Alice, isn't it?'

Silence.

'Alice Berg took the photographs,' I said.

'You're cracked,' said Strange. 'I'm putting the phone down right now.'

'Is that so you can call her and warn her that her secret identity has suddenly become a bit less secret?'

There was no answer. Our voices hadn't got tangled up in the signal-crowded skies above the city this time. This time Vincent Strange really had hung up.

Chapter Thirty-Three

Could Alice really be mixed up in all this somewhere? Could she be sending threatening photographs to Strange and Gina? Could she have been involved in the death of her brother?

She was certainly holding out on me, on Strange, on everyone.

Changing her story.

Telling Fitzgerald that she wanted her brother's body released as quickly as possible, and telling me she wanted his death investigated as murder. Keeping back the existence of Gina. Stonewalling Boland when he tried to find out more about Felix. Then there was her appearance outside the hospital last night when the latest victim of the Marxman was brought in.

What had she been doing there?

I had no evidence even that the file she had showed me of cuttings on the Marxman case had belonged to Felix at all. What if the file were hers? What if it was a catalogue of her own strange obsessions? The photographs sent to Strange and Gina reminded me too of the taunting mail Paddy Nye said he'd received for years. He'd always believed it was Felix behind it, but Felix couldn't be behind the slashed photographs now, because Felix was dead.

He couldn't have broken into my apartment.

What if it had been Alice all along?

Hadn't she befriended Isaac Little? Hadn't Miranda Gray

said how Alice read all the 'right books' on psychology? Who better to play these sorts of mind games?

Hadn't she turned up at my apartment when I hadn't even given her my address?

I recalled Nye's bitterness about her too. How he'd said he wouldn't be surprised if she and Felix had killed off their aunt for the house and legacy.

And the more I thought about it, the more another suspicion whispered at me.

Could she even be the Marxman?

That idea was so incredible I could scarcely put it into words for a long time; but it made a mad sort of sense. If Alice had been the Marxman all along, it would certainly explain why Felix had been so obsessed.

Why also he'd been willing to cover up for her.

Until that final night, when maybe he'd decided to bring the game to an end, to tell me what he knew – and she'd found out about it. Where had Alice been that night? She'd never given a satisfactory explanation. Had the police ever checked out her story?

But then why *would* they check it out? Felix wasn't murdered, according to Butler's autopsy report, he killed himself. She didn't have to prove where she was.

Besides, was this all I had on her – that she'd acted suspiciously?

Acting suspiciously wasn't a crime.

Acting suspiciously wasn't the same as murder.

And yet, I wondered, was I now just dismissing the possibility because she was a woman? I remembered a case Fitzgerald had worked on last year. Some thuggish drunk had been beating his wife for years: knocked out her teeth, branded her with a hot poker, kicked her so badly once that she lost the child she was carrying. One night he picked up a glass of beer and smashed it against her face. By the time she got to hospital she needed eighty-three stitches and had lost the sight in one eye. Between being smashed in the face with the glass and getting to hospital, however, she'd responded by picking up the nearest kitchen knife and sticking it so far into her husband's throat that it came out the other side and skewered him to a cupboard door.

She got off on a plea of self-defence and diminished responsibility due to years of spousal abuse, and Fitzgerald and I had quietly cracked open a bottle of champagne to celebrate.

Those are the kinds of easy connections we like to make when it comes to women and violence, but there's a block in our heads that seems to make us unable almost to think of women as being capable of other kinds of violence, of stalking, abducting, murdering, and *enjoying* it, rather than simply being its innocent victims; but it's not like there aren't plenty of examples.

The problem is that, faced with what is inexplicable, what is horrible, we are lost. A cultural conditioning kicks in which means we don't pay such murders by women the same attention that we would if they were by men. These women just don't fit our concept of what a killer is, what a woman is. And even when we do find evidence of the same instincts and predilections in a woman, we dismiss them, make excuses – say she must have been under the spell of a domineering man, or deranged, unbalanced by her hormones; by how life has treated her *as* a woman – anything other than confront the reality of what this woman has done.

Anything other than admit that maybe women just do it for the same reasons men do.

Because they're bored.

Because life doesn't feel real, and reality is insufficient.

Because of a burning will inside them. Because killing heightens the deadened senses, shakes them up, makes the world itself sit up and take notice.

Because it just turns them on.

Everywhere, now, psychologists are studying male killers, trying to understand them better, find the formula for the disease that had wormed its way into their brains; and that made sense statistically, because in all arenas of law enforcement it's men who pose the greatest threat.

Even so, it doesn't mean women killers can be safely ignored.

A victim is a victim.

Dead is dead.

And it could be argued that women need to be studied *more* for the very reason that they are so elusive to understanding, so complex. Male killers are simple creatures, by and large. Not simple to catch, but simple in their motivations, however depraved.

Women killers are harder to fathom.

They are colder.

More dispassionate.

That was what struck me most that evening as I dug out books in my apartment – including one by Fisher; was there anything the man hadn't written about? – and tried to read my way out of trouble. Struck me most because it matched so closely how I thought of Alice.

She just rang all the right bells.

Commonly these killers were careful women. Precise. Methodical.

Quiet in their strategies.

Alice was in the right age range too. Most female killers didn't start until after the age of twenty-five, and they continued for a much longer period than their male counterparts.

Of course, there were huge differences too, which made the whole idea that Alice was the Marxman seem absurd.

Women, for example, tended to kill within specific target groups. Lovers. Children. The old. They were unlikely to attack adult strangers, the very group most at risk from male serial killers – and the very group which had been targeted by the Marxman.

Female killers also tended to stay closer to home.

The Marxman roamed, predator-like.

The cooling-off period between killings was also much greater for female than male killers, which was part of the reason they went undetected for longer.

The Marxman was killing quickly.

Female killers took fewer chances.

The Marxman took plenty.

Women were also less likely to employ weapons to kill. Guns were only the fourth most frequent instrument of violent death used by women, behind lethal injection, suffocation and, every woman's favourite, poisoning. And the statistics I found were for the United States, where guns were much more readily available. In Dublin, where guns were rarer than Confederate bumper stickers in Manhattan, the numbers must be correspondingly infinitesimal.

But all this was just statistics. Number-crunching. I could've come up with a hundred reasons why the moon shouldn't stay up in the sky, but the important point is, it still does.

And each time I nearly talked myself out of thinking bad thoughts about her, I kept remembering Paddy Nye's words to me out in Howth: *You don't seriously buy that prim and proper act she puts on these days, do you?*

Did I?

Chapter Thirty-Four

When I woke on the couch the next morning, surrounded by books, I almost felt ashamed of my thoughts the night before. How could I ever have believed Alice was involved in something like this? It was nonsensical . . . laughable . . . and yet there was no denying there was something not quite right about her. Maybe I should go round to see her.

Within half an hour I was knocking at her door in the narrow cobbled lane.

I didn't quite know what I intended to say to her, especially after what I'd said to Strange about the pictures in his gallery. It wasn't as though I had any evidence against her.

Even if she had taken those pictures – even if it was her in them – what of it? She was a damaged woman. Who could say what her behaviour really signified?

Fact was, I hardly knew her at all.

But I felt my doubts growing anew as the door remained unanswered.

Had she fled? I remembered seeing her packing that morning I went round to the house. She'd told me she was back, but that might have been another lie. But why should she run? It wasn't as though the net was closing in on her. I wasn't even sure there *was* a net.

It felt like there was nowhere left to turn for answers. Alice's other friends remained vague notions in my head rather than real people. Some names she'd mentioned came back to me: Isobel, Maud. I guess I could have tracked them down given time, but time was something I didn't have; and what excuse could I give for asking questions anyway? Why should they tell me anything? She'd probably warned them about me already.

Like she warned Strange.

The only one I could think of who might be able to help was Miranda Gray, and I called her on the number she'd left for me on my answering machine.

I half expected her not to be available either, I was getting over-sensitive maybe, but she picked up almost instantly and said yes, coffee would be great. About eleven?

Her consulting rooms were in Merrion Square, so it wasn't like she had far to come.

As it was, she was late arriving at the café, and came in flustered, trailing elaborate explanations for not being here sooner, as busy professional people often did.

'There's no need to explain, it's not a problem,' I said in reply, but mostly it was because I didn't care to hear about her problems juggling her diary. 'No Fisher today?'

'He's hanging round with the Dublin Metropolitan Police,' she said. 'He obviously finds them better company than me. No need to tell you that. You know Fisher. Any chance to get involved in a spot of murder. I'm sure you didn't come here to talk about me anyway,' she added. 'What is it? You sounded troubled on the phone.'

'I hope you're not going to start psychoanalysing me,' I said.

'Merely making an observation. I'm right then?'

'It's Alice,' I said.

'If it's Alice, let's get the coffee first.'

She took her coffee black, espresso with an extra shot. And she took it with a sticky bun which she bit in to greedily when it came. I hadn't put her down as the sweet tooth sort; she'd skipped dessert last night – unless Fisher had been dessert. There I went again, speculating, interfering. I needed to remember all this was none of my business.

'Have you seen Alice lately?' I said when we were seated.

'Not seen, no.'

'I've been trying to contact her since the funeral. There're a few things I need to clear up with her. But there's never any answer to my calls, and there doesn't seem to be anyone in the house.'

'That's odd. She called me – let me think now – two days ago to cancel our usual appointment.'

'She's back working already?'

'That's the sort of woman Alice is. Throws herself into her work. She's difficult to read. I didn't think anything of it. She'd cancelled before. Although . . .'

'Yes?'

'It's nothing. Only that she usually reschedules her sessions immediately when she has to cancel. This time she just said she'd be in touch when she was ready.'

'What did you read into that?'

'Nothing at the time,' she said. 'Now . . . well, I wonder now if she's decided to end her sessions with me.'

'Would it bother you if she did?'

'Now you're trying to psychoanalyse *me*. You should know better. Therapists ask awkward personal questions, we never answer them.'

'Like cops.'

'I never thought of it like that, but I can see the similarity, yes.'

'How did she sound?'

'Alice? I didn't speak to her. Elaine, my secretary, did.'

'Did she tell you what Alice said?'

'To be honest, I wouldn't trust Elaine to know what day it is. She's new. And not very bright. I didn't ask. She just said Alice had asked to pass this week and that she'd written it down in the appointments book. That's about the limit of her competence, I'm afraid.'

'Why did you hire her?'

'I felt sorry for her. Her parents both killed themselves

when she was young, she doesn't have any family, she was new in town. I suppose I'm just a sucker for hard-luck stories. I ended up giving her the job. It's not as if it's very challenging work.'

'I wonder if she's OK,' I said.

'Elaine? She's fine, just a little scatterbrained.'

'I meant Alice.'

'Oh, Alice. Well, I can make some calls if you like.'

I liked.

Miranda immediately took out her cellphone and started ringing round a few of Alice's friends, whilst I ordered more coffee and eavesdropped. How she knew them I couldn't guess, unless it was that she'd met them whilst digging into Felix's secret life, first to satisfy herself he wasn't the Marxman, then to satisfy herself that he really had killed himself.

Alternatively, maybe they were friends of hers too. Dublin's a small town. In the concentric circles in which Miranda and Alice moved, everyone tended to know everyone else. They liked to keep an eye on one another, the better to keep them in their place.

Whatever the reason, it helped us discover fairly quickly what we needed to know. After the fifth or sixth call, I lost count, it was obvious that none of Alice's friends had heard from her for two days at least. Some she'd even phoned to tell them she wouldn't be around for a while, or to say she was with other friends, friends who likewise had been told another story, until the whole story curled back on itself like a serpent with its tail in its mouth.

'Perhaps we should call the police,' I said eventually, when she'd exhausted her list.

'And tell them what?' said Miranda. 'Alice is a grown woman. She doesn't have to answer to her friends for her movements.'

'But if her vanishing is out of character . . .'

'That's just it,' she said. 'It isn't. She often shoots off for days at a time, she's a great one for travelling. She could have flown anywhere for a few days for some peace and quiet – London, Paris, Stockholm. She does it all the time. You know what the police are like. The first thing they'll ask me is whether she's done this before, then when I say yes—'

'They'll refuse to do anything.' I sighed bitterly, knowing she was right. The police had very unimaginative minds sometimes. 'All the same, there must be something we can do. She might have, I don't know, fallen down the stairs, or anything.'

I still didn't want to tell her what I really feared, that maybe Alice had more to hide about the Marxman than she was letting on, partly because it wouldn't be right to encourage suspicions to fester when I had nothing but my own over-excited imagination to go on, but mainly, I think, because I didn't want to look foolish. I didn't feel confident enough yet to share my suspicions about Alice's possible role in all of this.

I needed to make them seem less idiotic to myself first.

But looking at the therapist's face, I saw I didn't need to raise any fears about Alice being implicated in the Marxman killings to make her see how urgent it was we find her.

The suggestion about her falling down the stairs had been enough.

'Do you really think she might have?' she said.

I didn't say anything. I didn't need to.

'I know how we can find out,' Miranda said firmly. 'I have a key.'

That was unexpected.

'Why?' The question was out of me before I could stop it.

'Alice gave me a spare last year, when she and Felix went to the States. She asked me to keep an eye on the place, make sure it hadn't been burgled or the pipes hadn't burst, send on the mail, that sort of thing.'

Miranda obviously believed in giving her clients the personal touch.

'You still have it?'

'I never got round to returning it.'

'You have it here with you now?'

'I think so. But,' she looked slightly concerned, 'do you really think we ought to let ourselves in? What if she's there? What if she simply doesn't want to answer the door? How will it look if we just waltz into her house?'

'She'll understand,' I said, though in truth I didn't know any more if Alice was the understanding sort. 'She'll realise you were concerned about her.'

'But what about—'

'It's a risk we have to take, Miranda. How are you going to feel if you leave it now and find out later you could've helped?'

She was thinking, thinking.

Eventually: 'You're right.' And she lifted her purse off the arm of the chair where she was sitting and began to rummage through it, cursing at the mess as she did so.

'It's not here.'

Finally in frustration she tipped the purse upside down, and the table was instantly covered with all the accumulated junk that women seem to carry about with them, though I can't say I'd ever got into the habit. Spare change, ballpoint pens, receipts, credit card, car keys, phone numbers written down on scraps of paper and immediately screwed up, packets of disposable handkerchiefs, a tube of extra-strong mints, sugar lumps wrapped in paper picked up at various cafés and forgotten about till they melted: she seemed to have everything here.

Everything except the key.

'It must be in here somewhere,' she murmured as she sifted the mess with her fingers.

I was beginning to lose patience when she finally exclaimed in triumph, producing the key with a half-embarrassed flourish.

Quickly she swept the rest back into her purse and we got up, leaving the second espressos untouched, and made our way through the traffic and the roadworks to Temple Bar, me for the second time that morning.

There was no one in the lane, still no signs of life at any of the windows.

We knocked again, and when again there was no answer I looked through the letterbox, while Miranda smeared a space in the grime of the window on the ground floor and peered inside. It was clear we could've stood here all day and no one would come.

'Miranda.'

'Here, you do it.'

She handed me the key and I inserted it into the lock. A turn, a click, and the door was open. I pushed against a small pile of letters which had settled on the floor behind it.

The hallway was dark.

All was silence.

'Alice?' I called.

There was a faint echo of her name, then silence once more.

'Alice? I'm here with Miranda Gray, are you there?'

There's something unmistakable about a voice calling in an empty house.

'She's not here,' I said to Miranda.

And I whispered even that.

Still I felt the need to keep calling Alice's name as we quickly searched the ground-floor rooms, through to a long kitchen at the back with a vaulted glass ceiling, frozen hard with light. There was a knife on a chopping board and two upturned halves of a wrinkled apple and a bottle of wine; a radio was turned low playing music.

I switched it off.

We climbed the stairs to the first floor, where the sitting room opened out just as I remembered it, except that the table was now bare, all photographs gathered away.

'What's upstairs?' I said.

'A bedroom,' said Miranda.

'Just the one?'

She understood the look I gave her.

'I never enquired as to their sleeping arrangements.'

'I'm going up to look,' I said.

'I'm coming with you,' Miranda replied. 'I don't want to be down here on my own.'

And I knew what she meant. There was something unsettling about the house now in its emptiness. Something eerie. The place felt haunted. I had a sense of being watched and at the same time a sense of Miranda and me being the only things here alive.

Bare stairs gave way to bare floorboards, and here was a small landing and a door and another flight of bare steps to another landing, another door.

One glance at each other, then we began to climb that too, feeling like intruders, terrified of being caught, but also half hoping we were because at least it would lift the sense of dread which had descended on us.

At the top of the stairs, with no more flights to climb, I turned the handle of the door and entered another huge room, a bedroom this time, with one bed in the middle, a low futon with only a sheet laid across it, and floorboards painted black, and a Japanese hanging lantern-style light suspended from the ceiling. There was lots of photographic equipment here too, spotlights and cameras, all pointing at the bed.

But no Alice.

'She's gone,' said Miranda.

She didn't even seem to have noticed the bed or the cameras. Or maybe this wasn't exactly a surprise to her. Wasn't such a surprise to me either, to be honest.

She was just staring round bewildered, as if she'd forgotten what we came for.

'Come on, there's no point hanging round now,' I said.

It was only as we made our way back downstairs that I remembered the other door down here. There was a key protruding from the lock.

I caught Miranda by the edge of her sleeve to stop her returning downstairs and pointed towards it. Made her wait while I turned the handle.

It wasn't locked.

I went in.

It was a bathroom, of course there had to be a bathroom. Large, stone-flagged, white-walled like the rest of the house. Straight ahead there was a circular pattern of dipped tiles in the floor, centred on a plughole, with a shower nozzle hanging directly above from the ceiling – and beyond that a claw-footed iron bath painted white, and above it a bare sash window open halfway, a mild breeze trickling in, a shimmer of light reflecting on the glass like . . . water?

I stepped straight across the centre of the open shower to the edge of the bath and looked down. Water filled it almost to the brim; it was a wonder it hadn't spilled over.

The only movement in the water was the shiver of wind on the surface, and it seemed inexplicable it should be so still, because lying naked on the bottom of the bath, staring upwards, eyes wide open, was Alice.

Chapter Thirty-Five

For the second time in little more than a week, I found myself waiting to give a statement to the police on the discovery of a body.

Miranda Gray and I were downstairs, in the small bare front room. I was standing at the window watching officers come and go, and Miranda was sitting in a corner, upset, and talking, talking. Cruelly I was tempted to borrow a phrase from Oscar Wilde and remind her that to lose one patient was unfortunate, but to lose two was starting to look like carelessness.

Mostly I was wondering whether Vincent Strange had called Alice last night. If he'd told her what I'd said about the photographs in his gallery. How that might've affected her. Could the fear of discovery have been enough to make her kill herself? *Had* she killed herself?

It was like history repeating.

Eventually Fitzgerald turned up with Sean Healy, and with them Alastair Butler, the City Pathologist, and they went upstairs, talking quietly together. They were up there more than half an hour before the pathologist came downstairs alone and went out into the lane.

I hurried out of the door after him.

'Butler?'

He turned round with a look of offended surprise. He had the kind of face, I always felt, that made Stalin look like a barrel of laughs by comparison.

'Saxon, isn't it?' he said stiffly.

He knew perfectly well what my name was, but he'd never liked me. On the few occasions we'd met before, he'd barely even looked at me. Partly I guess it was because of my relationship with Fitzgerald; he was pretty traditional in that respect. Partly too the fact that I'd been close to the previous pathologist. Butler was a man who believed in keeping his distance. If he was married, he'd be the sort to address his wife by her full name over breakfast.

'Well?' I said.

He gave me the familiar raised-eyebrow treatment.

'Well?' he repeated, like it was a foreign language.

'How did she die?'

'I really don't think I should be discussing that with you, do you?'

'Why the hell not?'

'You are not authorised to have that information.'

I cut him short sharply.

'Come on, Butler, don't be such a tightass, I'm not asking you to betray your country. I knew Alice. I found her body. I only want to know how she died.'

'And I have already told you that I can't disclose that.'

'What's the matter with you?'

'I really do not wish to have this unseemly discussion,' Butler insisted. 'Now, if you'll excuse me' – and he turned once more to leave.

I was reaching out to catch his arm and prevent him moving further down the lane when another voice behind me spoke my name like a warning.

Butler looked round at the sound of the voice too and saw my hand stretched out, and then we both looked at Fitzgerald, who was framed in the doorway.

'I'll catch up with you later, Chief Superintendent.' The pathologist nodded to Fitzgerald, and left, his footsteps rattling military-style through the arched tunnel back into Temple Bar.

'Grace—'

She didn't even let me start.

'What are you trying to do here, Saxon?' said Fitzgerald. 'Butler's not like the rest of us, you know. Not only is he a stickler for the rules, but he also doesn't know you. Hasn't had time to get used to your less than subtle ways. He won't stand for it. If he complains—'

'I only wanted to know—'

'How Alice died, I realise that. But there are other ways of finding out than grabbing hold of the City Pathologist at a potential crime scene and demanding he tell you something that you know he never will. Christ, you're not twenty-two any more. Haven't you learned by now that there's a time and a place for everything? That there are different ways of getting what you want?'

'I'm sorry,' I said. 'I'll call him. Apologise.'

'No. You've done enough damage this morning. Just forget about it, and tell me instead what you and Miranda were doing here in the first place.'

I told her briefly about not being able to contact Alice, and how Miranda had a key.

'You do seem to have a habit of being in the wrong place at the wrong time,' she observed wryly when I'd finished.

'Tell me about it. So how *did* she die?'

'Butler reckons suicide.'

'Another one,' I said. 'I'm growing kind of tired of hearing that.'

'You have any better suggestions?'

'Miranda was Alice's therapist. She says Alice wasn't the suicidal sort.'

'Then why don't you get her to explain why there are no signs of a struggle, no bruising?' That all sounded depressingly familiar too. 'It just looks as if Alice took as many tablets as she could find whilst still being able to walk – there were half a dozen empty bottles lined up against the window in the bathroom – and then slipped into the bath. Died fairly peacefully, Butler thinks. We should all be so lucky. And there's another thing.'

'What?'

'She was pregnant.'

'You're joking.'

'No. Obviously we'll have to await the autopsy results to confirm, but there's a home pregnancy testing kit in the wastebin, and it's showing positive.'

'She told me at the funeral she felt sick,' I remembered.

I don't know what's wrong with me, she'd said.

'And that's not all. Come on.'

She led me back inside the house and up the stairs, where the police were still searching the sitting room. On the table was a bundle of photographs. Two of the cops were standing leafing through them, and looked embarrassed when they realised Fitzgerald had reappeared.

'Don't you have something more useful to do, boys?' she snapped, and they murmured apologies and stared at the floor as they edged away. Fitzgerald glared after them and then reached out and handed me one of the photographs from the pile they'd been looking at.

Leering at, maybe that should be.

It was a picture of Alice. Naked. She was lying on the bed I'd seen upstairs. Head thrown back, eyes closed. There were other pictures. Alice standing naked under the shower. Lying face down on the couch in this same room. Sprawled across the floorboards. And there were pictures of Alice and Felix naked together, Alice and Felix making love.

Not the kind of shots you'd show to the aunts at Thanksgiving, put it that way.

'So they *were* sleeping together,' I said.

'You think he was the father of her baby, if she was pregnant?'

'I asked around about her,' I answered. 'She was a pretty private person, but I couldn't find evidence that she'd taken any other sexual partners lately apart from Felix. In the past she seems to have made her way through plenty, but there were none recently.'

It didn't take a genius to imagine what had happened here.

Alice had discovered she was having a baby.

Felix's baby, maybe.

Couldn't handle it.

Took an overdose.

Ran a bath.

Case closed.

So much for my suspicions about her last night.

'Did Butler say how long she's been dead?' I asked.

'Not more than twelve hours was the closest he'd say.'

'Shit.'

'Is that a problem?'

I didn't tell her just how far I'd taken my suspicions of Alice last night, but I did confess that I'd called Strange to ask if the sado-masochistic photographs on his wall were Alice's work, and how, if he'd called Alice and she feared exposure, then maybe—

'You called Strange?' said Fitzgerald before I could finish. 'After Buckley's warning letter? You weren't supposed to go near him.'

'Strange reminded me of that too, funnily enough.'

'There's nothing funny about it. What are you going to do if he tries to slap a restraining order on you? That's going to look fantastic. The press will have a field day.'

What could I say?

'Look,' she said, 'I'll speak to him. Someone will have to tell him about Alice anyway. Might as well kill two birds with one stone. I'll find out when the last time was he spoke to Alice. And come to think of it, screw him anyway if he complains. And screw Butler too.'

'But you just said—'

'I know what I said about Butler. Have you never heard that it's a woman's prerogative to change her mind? But I have more important things to worry about right now than whether the City Pathologist thinks his toes have been trodden on. I'm tired of tiptoeing round all these precious little male egos each trying to protect their patch. So he'll gripe a little. Let him gripe. Butler's not the point. I can handle him. This isn't about him. It's about you. You can't carry on blundering about the city like an elephant in Doc Martens. I care too much about you, Saxon, to have you putting yourself in these situations all the time.'

'Will you still feel the same way if he makes a complaint?'

'Officially, you mean? He won't. Trust me. I have to work with him every day. He's not going to make a big thing out of you asking him an improper question at a crime scene when he knows the very next day that he and I'll have to be making polite conversation over a corpse. He's too professional to let this morning get in the way. He's probably already shrugged it off as little more than he'd expect from an uncouth American.'

'Chief?'

Fitzgerald turned round. Healy was standing at the bottom of the stairs.

He beckoned her over.

They spoke for a moment, their heads bent together, whilst I looked through the remaining photographs of Alice and Felix and tried not to listen.

'Saxon, I have to go,' Fitzgerald said presently. 'I'll catch up with you later.'

And she was gone.

'What was all that about?' I asked Healy.

'Something came up,' he said noncommittally.

'I guessed that. What is it this time?'

He looked uncomfortable.

'I can't say.'

'Not you too,' I said.

Healy glanced round quickly, making sure no one could overhear.

'You'd better not say this came from me, understand?'

'I understand.'

Healy lowered his voice.

'Mark Brook is dead,' he said.

'What? I thought the wound was nothing?'

'It *was* nothing. But he discharged himself this morning, said he couldn't stand being cooped up in hospital any more, and returned home. About an hour ago his wife drove round to the chemist to pick up a prescription for painkillers for him, and when she got back she found him in the doorway.' *The doorway*. 'He'd been shot. Same kind of bullet as the one that hit him in the shoulder, only this one was right through the forehead.' He groaned with frustration. 'Why in God's name didn't we see it coming? Why didn't we realise the Marxman would go after him?'

There was nothing I could say. Why hadn't *any* of us realised Brook was still in danger? That once he'd delivered the message he was meant to deliver, the Marxman would want him dead like all the others? And more than that, how had he managed to get so close?

'Surely the press were swarming all round Brook's place?'

'He was barely out of hospital. They hadn't found out where he lived yet. Witnesses said a motorcycle pulled up, the rider got off, knocked on the door, Brook answered, and bang.'

How had the Marxman known where to find Brook so quickly?

Inside information?

'You track down the motorbike yet?' I said.

Healy nodded.

'It was stolen this afternoon, together with the helmet, from outside a house on the South Circular Road. The genius who it belonged to had left it sitting outside his front door with the keys still in the ignition. Some people deserve to be burgled.'

'You don't suspect him?'

'No, apparently he'd already reported the bike gone by then. In fact, a patrol car was round at his house and officers were taking a statement at the time the shooting happened.'

'At least you have the first sighting,' I said. 'The Marxman must be getting confident, striking in the middle of the day in a residential neighbourhood.'

'He still got away with it. He was wearing a helmet. He's hardly going to be picked out of an identity parade, is he? Oh, but there *was* one bit of luck.'

'What?'

'He dropped the gun.'

'You're only telling me this now?'

'Give me a chance. Soon as he'd shot Brook, it seems he climbed back on, kicked the motorcycle into gear and roared off back towards town. Only he roared off a bit too fast, because he misjudged the next corner and nearly went flying. The gun fell out of his pocket. Couple of witnesses said he stopped and was making his way back for it, then realised there were too many people around. Ballistics have it now. It'll be a while before they can say for sure, but they're pretty confident it's the same gun he's been using all along.'

Healy's news was shocking, but for the first time in weeks I felt happy for Fitzgerald. This was the first real break she'd had in the case. This was her chance to bring the cycle to an end, to get them all off her back: Draker, Sweeney, the press. Throughout the last months, the murder squad had made little headway finding out where the Marxman had got the gun, but if today he'd lost his preferred weapon, then that might mean he'd be on the lookout for a new one.

'We'll put the word out straightaway,' Healy agreed. 'Make sure every criminal in the city keeps an eye out for anyone trying to buy a gun. Anyone suspicious, anyone they don't know, we have to make sure they get in touch with us. Make it worth their while.'

'It'll be worth every nickel if it brings in the Marxman.'

Unless he already has a backup gun, I thought, or an alternative source of supply.

But I said nothing.

No point being negative.

There was a first time for everything.

Part Three

Chapter Thirty-Six

I dreamt the sea came to take Dublin, lifting itself up in the bay like a sleeper climbing out of bed and collapsing sideways into the harbour and down the length of the river as it wound through the city, past North Wall and Custom House Quay and Bachelor's Walk and out towards Islandbridge; and the walls that had held out against the sea for so long suddenly gasped and cracked and gave up the ghost, and the salt water sneaked out into roads and quickly began to spread. As I watched, it stretched itself through Abbey Street and Mary's Lane and College Green and Temple Bar, Winetavern and Fishamble and Sycamore, flowing over doorsteps and flooding the houses behind, coming indoors without knocking and slowly edging up the stairs until the roofs were boats and many more were submarines with chimneys for periscopes peeking out; and still it went on rising further until it had made an island of Dublin Castle, and then Cornmarket was gone and the Coombe, and St Stephen's Green was a bay, salt water splashing at a stone shore, and I was standing on my balcony looking out at this sudden, quiet sea stretching out to where Mountjoy away to the north had become Alcatraz, marooned on its stark rock. And before I knew what I was doing, I was diving off my balcony into the water below, which was strange since I can't swim, and the water was so cold it stole the breath from my body, and I found I *could* swim because I was pushing underwater, supple as a fish, down through sunken roads, and I was the only swimmer. And Baggot Street was a sea trench, with lights still lit in windows, and sparkling plankton drifted like blossom, and the water was pulling leaves off trees and filling the sea with them as though it was autumn and it was the wind which had tugged them off rather than the tide, and I was swimming in and out of open windows and up stairways, round the spires of drowned churches like I was flying, through alleyways, peering into secret places, passing like a ghost, like a fragment of some child's dream that had got left behind when everyone fled from the rising waters. And the more I swam, the more the houses became like rocks, encrusted with seaweed and barnacles and hollow within like grottoes, and I realised I needed to breathe suddenly, and I rose, rose, my chest bursting with the effort of it, until I felt the air fill my lungs, and I was shouting with relief – till I looked and saw the city was gone and I was far, far out to sea, and it was dark, and all I could see in the distance was the lighthouse at Howth, blinking off, on, off; and even as I kicked for home, I knew it was too far to reach.

My body was stone.

And then I woke with a gasp – afraid – and I knew there was someone in my apartment. I could hear breathing. Or was it only mine?

Listen.

Listen.

Yes, I could hear them now, moving about in darkness on the other side of the door.

I slid out of bed and tiptoed across the floorboards, placed my ear next to the door and listened – hearing nothing again – before turning the handle and edging it open, slipping through the crack like a shadow and down towards the sitting room, where all was still and unlit and the moon coming through the great window fixed unearthly shapes to the walls like waves frozen in ice, reminding me again of my dream.

Turning the corner, I saw the room was empty as it should have been and began to think I must have imagined hearing someone here – only imagined that my previous unwelcome visitor had returned – and then there was a small, furtive movement and I saw the outline of a figure silhouetted against the light from the moon.

'Don't move,' I said quietly. 'I have a gun.'

'You'd better not have,' said a familiar voice, 'or I might have to arrest you.'

'Fitzgerald? What are you doing here?'

A light snapped on, hurting my eyes fleetingly, and there she was, sitting in a chair on the other side of the room, still wearing her coat, her arms folded across her chest.

'I'm sitting in a chair with my coat on and my arms folded,' she said.

'I can see that,' I said.

'Then what did you ask for?' She smiled. 'Do you have any ice cream?'

'What time is it?'

'Will my answer affect your answer to the ice-cream question?'

'Of course not.'

'Then it's after two. Now, what have you got?'

'Chocolate chip, last time I looked.'

'Yum. Don't forget to bring a spoon.'

'You want *me* to get it?'

'You're nearer to the fridge. Plus, you're up.'

I fetched her the tub of ice cream and a spoon, and perched on the arm of the chair next to her whilst she peeled back the lid and helped herself.

'I was having a dream,' I said.

'That's what happens when you go to sleep.'

'I dreamt the whole city was flooded. The sea was everywhere. I was swimming.'

'You?'

'I can't really remember it now.'

'That's dreams for you,' she said. 'You can't rely on them to hang around.'

'You're in a strange mood,' I said. 'Flippant.'

'You complaining?'

'Simply observing.'

'I'm delirious with sleeplessness, that's all,' Fitzgerald said as she held up a spoonful of chocolate chip for me and I bent my head to taste it. 'Nothing ten hours in bed and a new job wouldn't fix. I've just spent the night with Fisher in his hotel room, raiding his minibar and trying to figure out once more the connection between the victims. There's always something connecting them, isn't that what the experts say?'

'That's a cliché,' I said.

Fitzgerald gave a laugh.

'What's so funny?'

'Your line about clichés is exactly what I said to Fisher,' she told me, 'and he said: *I knew I'd read it somewhere. It must have been in one of Saxon's books.*'

'Charming. You two get any actual work done as well as bad-mouthing me?'

'Not much. That is, we got a lot of work done, but we didn't get any results. Much better to have it the other way round. Most of the time we just spent pondering what significance there was in the bar where Brook was first shot being called the Louis IX.'

'I never had you down as an expert on old French kings.'

'Don't underestimate me. You don't know what I might be an expert on. Go on, ask me a question about Louis IX. Any question.'

'It's late, Grace, come to bed.'

'Any question,' she insisted.

'Any question?'

'Any.'

'OK then. What year was he born?'

'Twelve fourteen,' she answered instantly.

'Died?'

'Twelve seventy. In between he became King of France at the age of twelve after the death of his father. Had eleven children. Went on two crusades. Spent hours in fasting and penance and prayer. Patron of architecture. Renowned for his charity. He fed beggars and washed their feet. St Louis in Missouri and San Luis Rey in California are both named after him—'

'You've made your point,' I said. 'Where'd you learn all that stuff?'

'From Fisher. He's been doing his homework like the good little profiler he is. Or what is it they call them now – behavioural investigative analysts?'

'Does Fisher really think there's something in the bar being called the Louis IX?'

'Not really. But he has reached in a handful of days on this case the stage it took most of us weeks to get to. What is technically called the scraping-the-bottom-of-the-barrel phase. He's looked at every connection between the victims he can think of. Their names. Star signs. What the weather was like at the times they were killed. He's practically looked at what colour socks they were wearing and where their great-grandmothers lost their virginity.'

'I never realised before that was an indicator for psychopaths.'

Fitzgerald spooned another helping of chocolate chip ice cream out of the tub, and didn't even notice as a drop fell off and landed on her coat.

'We missed you,' she said. 'Could've done with your input. Did you not get any of my messages?'

'I got them,' I said. 'I just wasn't sure I'd be much use to anyone tonight.'

'Is it still Alice?'

She was all I could think about these days.

Alice in the water.

How long had it been since I found her?

Four days?

Five?

I'd lost count.

All I knew was that I couldn't get the final image of her out of my head. It reminded me of some painting I'd once seen of a young girl floating down a river, dead, surrounded by flowers, the water sparkling. And somehow that painting and Alice had become mixed up in my head too with an imagined memory of Lucy Toner lying dead in the ground at the bottom of her garden in Howth, her tongue heavy with soil, and an image of Sydney sleeping with her head on the rail, because asleep was always how I needed to imagine her in those moments.

That Alice had been pregnant when she died – ten weeks gone, according to Alastair Butler's autopsy report – only made it worse.

It was like Felix all over again. Only no, not like that. With Felix it never felt right that he'd killed himself, despite his depression, his breakdowns. Alice had had none of the predictive traits, and yet it *did* feel right when I told myself she'd taken her own life.

The words didn't knock their head against the ceiling of credibility.

'You did warn me against becoming emotionally involved,' I said.

'It's easier said than done. I'm not blaming you. Here,' she added, finally noticing the ice cream on her coat. 'Hold this while I get a cloth.'

She handed me the tub and got up to go to the kitchen.

She'd only taken a couple of steps when she stopped abruptly.

'Hello, what's this?'

She bent down and picked up something that was lying behind the front door.

It was like an oversized playing card with a painted picture on one side. Someone must have pushed it under the door earlier, only it was so dark when she came in that Fitzgerald hadn't noticed it. The picture showed a young man walking under the sun, in an old-fashioned tunic and yellow boots, holding a flower, a knapsack on a stick over his shoulder, a dog dancing at his feet. He was stepping off a cliff where a rainbow waited to catch him. Two words were printed along the bottom. *The Fool.*

'I know what this is,' she said. 'It's a Tarot card. And see, there's a number on the back. Looks like a telephone number.'

I took the card from her and looked at it.

'This is Gina's,' I said.

Chapter Thirty-Seven

'And she began to lay the cards face up on the table very, very slowly,' Fitzgerald told Lawrence Fisher next morning as we sat in her car in the parking lot at Dublin Castle, the psychologist in the passenger seat up front whilst I was stranded in the back with Patrick Walsh. 'The Moon. The Star. The Hanged Man. The Devil. The Wheel of Fortune.'

'God, I always hated that show,' I said.

'And once she'd laid them all out, she explained even more slowly how Tarot cards were the oldest form of prophecy, and how the cards were originally chapters in a Book of the Dead written in Egypt by the god of wisdom, and how they were copied down on to tablets of stone and then the tablets were copied on to cards, and how each card stands for some aspect of your life or personality or destiny, and how Felix had given her this pack and how he often made decisions based on the way the cards were dealt. And then she told us her theory.'

'Which was?'

'That the Marxman was killing people according to the Tarot cards.'

'No way,' said Fisher.

'That's what she'd come round to my apartment to tell me,' I said, 'then, when I didn't answer the door' – I avoided Fitzgerald's eye in the rearview mirror asking me the sleeping-pills questions again – 'she put the card through my door with her number on it because she didn't have any paper on which to write a note.'

'According to her,' Fitzgerald took up the story again, 'each of the victims represented one of the picture cards of the Tarot. Mark Brook was The Magician. Judge Prior was Justice. Jane Knox was The Hermit. Charlie Knight, aka the Grim Reaper, was Death. Finlay Hart was . . . shit, what was Finlay Hart again, Saxon? I've forgotten.'

'The Emperor,' I reminded her.

'The Emperor, that was it,' she said. 'Apparently, that one represents authority.'

'What about Tim Enright, the first victim?' said Walsh.

'She admitted she didn't have a clue which one he was meant to be,' I said. 'Her best guess was The World because it symbolised material wealth. Didn't he work in finance?'

'She even reckoned,' Fitzgerald added, 'that that was what the Marxman meant by whispering in Brook's ear about being the dead hand. It was nothing to do with Karl Marx. He just meant he was the one who dealt the hand of cards that dealt out death. Dead hand.'

'And what did *you* say after she told you all this?' Fisher asked.

'Say? It was hard enough keeping a straight face, never mind saying anything,' said Fitzgerald. 'Tarot cards, I ask you. It's not even original. I was just worried that when she'd finished with the Tarot she was going to get out a ouija board and suggest having a seance to contact the spirits of the victims.'

'So,' I said, 'we just thanked her for her help and then—'

'We made a break for it,' finished Fitzgerald.

And Fitzgerald did catch my eye in the rearview mirror this time and we found ourselves slipping into laughter again, like we'd done last night in my car after escaping from Gina's basement apartment. An escape was what it felt like.

'I don't know what's so funny,' Walsh said in all seriousness as he looked between Fitzgerald and me with a blank expression. 'I think it's pretty neat.'

'Neat?'

'Yeah, neat. What have you got against it, babe?'

'What I've got against it, pretty boy,' I said, trying not to catch Fitzgerald's eye a second time in case she set me off again, 'is that it's total bullshit. And quit calling me babe.'

'Children,' said Fisher soothingly. 'No squabbling there in the back. Besides, maybe your friend Gina has a point.'

'You're not saying *you* buy into all that mystic mumbo-jumbo, are you?' I said.

'Buy into it, no. But I wouldn't call it mumbo-jumbo,' Fisher answered. 'The Tarot has it uses. I even studied it in college as part of my psychology course.'

'They study this crap at college?'

'It was background for Jung's investigation into the collective unconscious,' Fisher explained patiently. 'The symbols are supposed to represent states of being or qualities which we encounter as we go through life. Miranda still uses the cards in her sessions. Sometimes a patient can be encouraged to read meaning into them, and the meanings they find help them understand what's going on inside their heads, helps them make sense of the world. It's similar to interpreting the symbols that pop into the head in dreams; it says something about one's psyche and the way that psyche adapts to deal with life's shocks and knocks.'

'Maybe her patients would make a lot better sense of the world if they didn't have all these Jungian, Freudian, what-everian delusions floating about in their heads.'

'Let's not go there again,' said Fisher. 'I think we all know your uncompromising views on therapy, Saxon. And I said I studied it at college, I didn't say I used to sacrifice virgins and dance naked round standing stones every time there was a full moon.'

What an image.

'I'm just surprised you bothered with it at all,' I said.

'Well,' said Fisher, 'you're only Jung once.'

It was a joke that deserved to be ignored.

'OK,' I said, 'let's say for argument's sake – and it's a pretty feeble argument, but let's say it anyway – that the Marxman was addled enough in the head to choose his victims according to the Tarot cards. What difference would it make? All it means is you'd have to check out every New Age looper in town, talk to all the places selling scented candles and incense and books of spells, anyone offering horoscopes and feng shui consultancies in their back room or running night classes in astral projection. It'd be a nightmare and it'd still add up to zip, it still wouldn't tell you who you're looking for or who he's going to shoot next.'

'You know something, Saxon?' said Fisher. 'Your brain isn't working half so well as it used to. You need to trade it in for a younger model.'

'You're saying there *is* something in this?'

'Not in the way Felix's girlfriend meant probably. But even red-haired cranks can inadvertently stumble on the truth by accident. And don't jump down my throat again, I don't mean the Tarot. I mean Tim Enright. She was right to single him out as unusual.'

'But Enright was no one,' I said.

'That's the point,' said Fisher. 'Look at all the other victims. They were all someone. They were all known. All public figures. Terence Prior. Finlay Hart. Charlie Knight. Mark Brook. Even the vagrant woman used to be *someone*. But Tim Enright wasn't a public figure, he'd never been *important*, so why was he shot too? More than that, why was he shot first? The Marxman could have started with any one of the victims. The judge, the politician. That would really have been making a statement. That would have gained him attention right from the off. But he didn't. He started by killing an unknown, anonymous man. With a whimper, not a bang. Gina got that part right at least. Tim Enright doesn't fit.'

'So what you're suggesting,' I said, trying to work my way through his chain of logic, 'is that his significance to the Marxman couldn't have been in the public sphere, so it must have been in a private one? That Enright might have even known the Marxman?'

'I'm suggesting it's a possibility,' said Fisher.

'Couldn't he just have been getting in practice by shooting Enright?' asked Walsh.

'That was my thinking initially when Fitzgerald asked me to look into this whole thing,' Fisher admitted. 'That Enright's was an opportunistic killing and only afterwards did the Marxman realise he didn't need to stop with one murder. He could go on. And on. Now I'm not so sure. If the Marxman did know Enright in some way, and planned the killings in advance, then isn't it equally likely that he feared Enright exposing him and hence had to dispose of him right at the start? *He* had to be got rid of to make everything else possible, to give the Marxman the space to be himself.'

'Then we need to start by finding out more about Enright,' said Fitzgerald.

She lowered her window and called over to Boland, who'd been left standing by the wall all this time, playing lookout, and he trotted over with a bundle of files in his arms that Fitzgerald had asked him to bring along in case she needed to refer to them.

'What have you got on Enright?' she said.

Boland squatted down and began flicking through the files one by one.

When he had got to the end without luck, he flicked through them again.

'Give me a minute, Chief. It's in here somewhere.'

'In there isn't much use to me.'

'Damn, I could've sworn it was . . . ah, here it is.'

He tugged out the correct file finally and put it into Fitzgerald's outstretched hand, and there was silence as she turned the pages slowly, reading.

'It's basically as I remember it,' she said. 'His whole bloody life story's in here. School, college, work, professional qualifications. In other words, nothing much.'

I leaned over and lifted out a page torn from a magazine whose edge was peeking out from among the other papers. It showed a glossy picture of three men sitting behind a desk, Enright in the middle, all sporting fixed grimacing smiles and casual sweaters with vivid patterns which they wore with that self-conscious embarrassment of men normally to be found dressed only in three-piece suits and ties. Below was a caption: *Celebrating Ten Years Of Success.*

'What's this?' I said, glancing at it quickly then handing it to Walsh.

'It's from some local business magazine which did a profile of Enright's company about six, eight months ago,' Walsh said dismissively. 'The usual corporate PR whitewash. Boland took it out so we had a good picture of the victim for the file.'

'Other than the one taken at the autopsy, you mean?'

'It wasn't his best side.'

Enright smiled out of the picture with the melancholy innocence of the unknowing.

'Don't forget he worked in the city,' said Fisher. 'That means he must have had a score of clients on his books. That could be an angle worth pursuing.'

'We've been down that road already,' said Walsh. 'Enright didn't have any fallings-out with his clients. No disagreements or rivalries. No one had a motive to want him dead.'

'Someone did,' Fisher reminded him mildly. 'It doesn't have to be a disagreement, anyway. Perhaps quite the opposite.'

'A closer than usual professional association, you mean?' said Fitzgerald. 'It's a possibility. Walsh, get on to it. Get me a full list of Tim Enright's clients going back . . . call it three years. Look for any discrepancies or unusual patterns in his dealings, his accounts, his diary. And speak to his colleagues again. There must be something they can remember. Boland, you see if there's anything else about Enright in the records that hasn't come up yet.'

'Will do, Chief.'

'You can come with me if you like,' said Fisher, turning round in his seat as Walsh and Fitzgerald climbed out of the car again. He obviously realised I'd become redundant once more as the official DMP machine geared up. 'There're a few people I need to try and see before this afternoon. And before you ask, no, I don't mean witch doctors.'

'I appreciate it, Fisher,' I said, 'but there's somewhere I need to go.'

'You going to tell me where?'

'No.'

'Thank heavens for that. I'd have been disappointed if you had. You wouldn't be the same Saxon we all know and love if you suddenly started being forthcoming.'

'I aim to please.'

'Isn't that the Marxman's motto too?'

Chapter Thirty-Eight

'You should be careful,' I said. 'Last person I arranged to
meet secretly like this wound up lying face down and dead in
the water with a bullet hole in his head.'

'That's not funny,' said Vincent Strange.

'Who's laughing?'

Strange was where he'd said he'd be when he called
earlier out of the blue, in St Stephen's Green, standing by
the worn bronze statue of one of history's dead rebels about
whom I knew nothing and cared less, wrapped in his
favourite fur coat and looking his usual conspicuous self.
He simply didn't possess the gene for blending into the
background.

'You're probably wondering why I called,' he said.

'I haven't got around to wondering yet. I'm just giving
thanks it wasn't another letter,' I replied. 'Still, this is better
than hiding behind lawyers, isn't it? Much more civilised.'

'I wasn't hiding behind Conor Buckley,' Strange said with
a pained expression. 'It had been a difficult few days. At the
time I didn't want you bothering me, that's all.'

'Who was bothering you? I just wanted to ask a few
questions about Felix.'

'I saw it differently.'

'Buckley made that plain enough.'

He was avoiding my eye. I could tell he was nervous,
debating whether he'd done the right thing. It didn't take
much of a genius to figure out why. He must want something

from me, and we didn't exactly have the kind of relationship where he'd feel comfortable asking for a favour.

You couldn't even call what we had a relationship to start with.

'Let's walk,' he said. 'I can't stand here like some idiot.'

I wanted to say: *Why change now?*

But I kept my mouth shut.

I was on my best behaviour.

Whatever reason he had for calling, after all, it had to be a good one to make him overcome his natural inclination to treat me like something unpleasant he'd found beneath his shoe.

So we started walking.

Taking a stroll round the park like any other courting couple. The oddest-looking courting couple you ever saw in your life, but love is blind, isn't that what they say?

I liked it here. In summertime, when the air was warmer, I often stepped out from my apartment only a few hundred yards away, and ate lunch sitting on one of the benches that lined the pools. The trees would be rich with foliage, birds sang through the relentless howl of traffic, the sound of children laughing drifted over from the playground elsewhere in the park.

There were always plenty of people doing the same, office workers taking time out in the middle of the day, kids bunking off school, old folks taking a stroll, remembering the place as it used to be. Today was quieter, because the summer had yet to get going; it was taking its time, and the air still had an edge to it that encouraged people to think they'd be better off indoors. The paths were wet with a rain I realised I hadn't noticed falling that morning. The trees still looked as if coming into leaf was a struggle many of them might not bother making this year.

I knew how they felt.

'Is this about Alice?' I said.

'No. At least, maybe. Oh, I don't know. Do you think she killed herself?'

'As a matter of fact, I do.'

'You didn't think Felix had.'

'That was different.'

'Different how?'

'Felix had no reason to kill himself, as far as I could see. Far as I can still see. There was no reason for him to do what he did. Only problem was that no one would listen when I went looking for answers.'

'If you mean me . . .' began Strange.

'You were one of a number.'

'I had my reasons.'

'For lying to me?'

'I didn't lie to you. Or rather, yes, I did lie. When I told you that Alice said you were bothering her, for example. And that she didn't believe Felix had been murdered. She did believe it. She even asked me for my help in finding out who it was who had killed him.'

'Why didn't you give it to her?'

'Because I believed that it was absolutely the wrong thing for her. I was worried about her, it wasn't good for her to be obsessing about Felix; he'd killed himself. I felt that if I encouraged her, it might only make her more fragile, and what would be the point? He killed himself, the police knew that, I saw the pathologist's report. Those were facts that couldn't be ignored. I couldn't encourage Alice to go chasing after what seemed to me a fantasy.'

'And do you still think that's what it was? A fantasy?'

Strange stopped walking. We'd come to a bridge over a lake in the centre of the green. He leaned now on the side and stared down at the water. A swan floated by, looking up hopefully for crumbs, then dipped its beak into the water for food that wasn't there, momentarily headless.

'I don't know any more,' Strange said. 'All I know is that something is not right. That's why I needed to talk to you. That's why I came here today looking for your help.'

'I'm still waiting.'

At first he couldn't say it.

Couldn't form the words, same way I hadn't been able to when I wanted to tell Alice about Felix's first phone call.

And when he finally did force the words out, I understood the difficulty.

'A man contacted me two nights ago,' he said, 'and asked me to supply him with a firearm.'

'I didn't realise you'd branched out into gun dealing,' I said. 'Is the art market a bit slow at the moment?'

'I presume that's another attempt at a joke?' said Strange, lifting his elbows off the side of the bridge and starting to walk again. 'Frankly, I find the suggestion that I would sell one of my guns offensive. I'm a collector, not a criminal.'

'Who was it?' I asked, following him.

'You may find this hard to believe, but he never got around to giving me his name.'

'You say contacted. You mean . . .?'

'He telephoned me. At the gallery. I never saw his face.'

'Did you recognise the voice?'

'I'm fairly sure I've never heard it before.'

'Then it seems like congratulations are in order. You're one of a select group. Only two people have heard the voice of the Marxman – and the other one died shortly afterwards.'

His reply came out almost like a yelp.

'Who said anything about the Marxman?'

'Come on, that's what you think, isn't it?' I said. 'And after what happened to Felix, I don't blame you. Who else would come to you for a gun? Ordinary criminals don't usually ring up art dealers when they need weapons. They have alternative supplies. The Marxman doesn't. He can hardly go through the usual channels when half the criminal world's waiting for his next move so they can cash in on the reward. You're not saying you think it's a coincidence you got a call within days of the Marxman losing his favourite Glock? Has it ever happened *before*?'

'Of course it's never happened before.'

'There you are then.' The trees roared above us suddenly with a wind from out of nowhere. For a moment it drowned out the noises of the city and I could almost imagine we were lost deep inside a forest. 'What kind of gun was he looking for?'

'Not a Glock, if that's what you're thinking,' Strange said, managing to make the word Glock sound almost comic. 'He just said he wanted a gun. He wasn't fussy, as long as it was working and couldn't be traced. That, and the ammunition to go with it.'

'What did you say?'

'I said no. I told you, I'm not a gun dealer.'

'Good boy. I would've expected nothing less from a law-abiding citizen like you,' I said. 'So what exactly are we talking about it now for? Why didn't you go straight to the police?'

'Well,' said Strange, 'that's the awkward part. When I said no, the caller threatened that if I didn't provide a gun under the specified conditions of secrecy, or if I went to the police, then he would reveal certain information about me which I would rather keep private.'

'This information being?'

'You don't honestly think I'm going to—'

'Tell me? Yes, I do. Unless you fancy being a front-page lead in tomorrow's tabloids.'

'Fuck.' It was the first time I'd heard him swear. 'You're serious, aren't you?'

'I'm also waiting.'

The words came out bleeding and reluctant as pulled teeth.

'I have a certain lifestyle to maintain which can become . . . expensive,' he began, refusing to meet my eye. 'I admit that there are a number of occasions on which I may not have lived up entirely to the professional standards I and others expect of me.'

'Now you're talking like a lawyer. I'd better watch out or you'll start spouting Latin and talking about the party of the first part next. You want to give me an example instead?'

'Now and again I may have made extra copies of particularly sought-after photographic prints without the knowledge of the artist, and passed them on to interested parties. And I may have adjusted the odd percentage point in my commissions as I struggled to make ends meet.'

'Jesus, I am so dumb,' I said, shaking my head. 'And there was me all along thinking you were going to tell me you were the father of Alice's baby.'

'Me?' breathed Strange. 'There was never anything like that between Alice and me. Even had I desired her, Felix was always in the way. Felix was the only man for her. There's no point pretending otherwise now, is there? There are no secrets in death. Alice may have played around a lot in her younger days, but she'd grown out of it. She'd realised, I think, that all she wanted was Felix and she hadn't taken another lover for ten years. Nor had he before that little Gina Fox came along. Felix is the only one who could possibly have been the father of her baby.'

'So your crimes are financial rather than fleshly?'

'Please do not mock. This is ticklish enough as it is.'

Ticklish?

The man had a definite talent for understatement.

'Especially when I have,' he added, 'nothing to be ashamed of.'

'Then I'm confused,' I said. 'If you've nothing to be ashamed of, then why are you so anxious that the things you *may* have done don't become public? So anxious that you haven't even informed the police of the fact that God knows who is trying to blackmail you into becoming an arms dealer.'

'As I indicated, there has been a lot of negative publicity in recent days about Felix and Alice. About the pictures that were found in their house. I have my reputation to think of. I wouldn't want it to be thought that I was involved in any way with something underhand.'

'Heaven forbid.'

'It's just that people—'

'Wouldn't understand,' I said. 'You said something similar the first time we met too.'

'You can sneer,' said Strange, 'but I can already feel the disapproval out there drifting towards me since Alice died. It's like a glacier moving south. Clients have cancelled planned meetings, buyers have put off coming to the gallery or to Dublin to see me. If they were to find out that, in addition to their erotic activities, I had made certain errors in my accounting practices, things could become awkward for me professionally.'

'Why not ask your good friend Assistant Commissioner Draker to help out again?'

'There are limits even to friendship,' said Strange with a wry smile, 'and I think I may well have reached them. There have been a couple of incidents already.'

'Being photographed at a party organised by a gangster, for one. I heard about that.'

'Again, I did nothing wrong. I had no idea what Frederick Sheehy was involved in at that time. But people do have a tendency to draw the wrong conclusions. To be judgemental. And then there was another incident which there really is no need to go into now.'

'You mean giving Felix the gun with which he killed himself?'

'You know about that?'

His childlike astonishment was almost touching.

'Don't panic, I'm not going to start naming names to a Senate committee.'

'Well then, since you know already, there's no point trying to put a good gloss on it. It was a terrible misjudgement and I have suffered grievously for it. I lost a good friend. And the only reason I gave him the gun in the first place was because he threatened to expose the same mistakes of mine. We'd quarrelled about that some months back when he confronted me about . . . irregularities in his payments. That's why we drifted apart. And now here it comes again. My fear this time

291

is that I may fall foul of a crude three-strikes-and-you're-out mentality.'

'Maybe whoever called is banking on you being afraid of it too,' I said, as I looked up and noticed that we were approaching the bronze statue again where we'd begun our circuit of the park. 'But I still don't see what this has got to do with me. Why you've come to me of all people with this news.'

'I was hoping you could tell me that.'

'Why would I know anything?' I exclaimed.

'Because,' said Strange, 'the caller specified that it should be you who makes the drop-off. Hands the gun over. That was his only condition.'

I looked up through the trees at the buildings that surrounded St Stephen's Green, trying to pick out my own window and imagining myself up there, looking down at me.

Should I give myself a wave?

Imagined someone else standing here too, looking up in the same direction, waiting, watching for the moment I left and he could climb the stairs and let himself into my rooms.

Why me?

It could only be because of Felix, I thought. If it was the Marxman who'd called Strange, and I didn't doubt that it was, then he'd know I'd been investigating Felix's death. I'd hardly kept quiet about it. I can't keep quiet about anything. My tongue has a life of its own.

Did he think that I too was following his footprints in the snow as Felix had done? And if he did, what would he do if I just appeared, like he asked, and handed him Strange's gun?

Did I really need to ask?

'So what exactly,' I said, 'are you asking of me?'

'I want you to do what he said on the telephone,' said Strange, as if the answer was so obvious a child wouldn't have needed it spelled out. 'I want you to take the gun, I'll give you a gun, any gun, and I want you to give it to him.'

'You're crazy.'

'Don't say that. Think about it at least.'

'What's there to think about? You're saying you want me to give the Marxman a gun?'

'I'll pay you. I'll give you ten thousand. Twenty. I don't care.'

'Money has nothing to do with it,' I said. 'The man's a killer, Strange. You'd have to be loco to even be having a debate in your head about doing what he says. And why *should* I help you? I'm amazed you have the nerve to even come and ask me. From the first moment we met, you've done nothing but frustrate me. Put obstacles in my way. And now you want my help?'

'Is that what this is about? Getting your own back? No one would listen to you about Felix, so now you're going to turn me away when I need your help?'

'It's not that at all.'

'Then what is it? I just want him to go away. Can't you see? I'm desperate. Can you imagine how hard it was for me to get the courage to come and tell you this, not knowing what you'd do, what you'd say, how you'd react? But I had to. I'm in a hole and I want to get out, and I don't know how to get out except by simply doing what I'm told. I just want to be left alone. I want my life back. I don't know what else to do. If you don't do what he says . . .'

I almost felt sorry for him at that moment, but not so sorry that I didn't realise the risks he was willing to run with the rest of the population of Dublin in order to save his own hide.

'The fact that you're desperate is why you're not thinking straight,' I said. 'Can't you see how much worse it will be for you if it gets out that you've knowingly assisted a multiple killer? Whereas if you help the police bring him in, no one's going to care about a few dollars that found their way mistakenly into your back pocket. You've got to start thinking, Strange. I mean it. Don't you even care that more people will be killed if you do what he tells you?'

'Of course I care,' he said fiercely. 'I feel like a worm for even contemplating doing what he asks, but I'm over a barrel, don't you see? I can't be expected to take the responsibility for being a hero entirely on my shoulders. I have to think about myself. My own future.'

'Then think about yourself. Because do you really think this guy'll just vanish if you give him what he wants now? That he won't come back for more, and more after that? There's always something else to ask for, and you always ask the people who gave most easily the first time.'

'What else can I do?'

I tried to put the possibilities into some order in my head.

'When's he calling back?'

'About midnight. He's going to tell me the time and place the handover is to happen.'

'Then you're going to have to take the call,' I said. 'Act as if everything's OK, agree to whatever he says, just arrange the details, then call me.'

'What are you going to do?'

'You have to trust me. You came to me looking for help and I'm offering it to you. But you have to let me do things my way. I'll make sure your name is kept out of it as best I can.'

'You're not going to go to the police, are you?'

'Strange, listen. You're going to have to trust me.'

There was panic in his eyes as he stared at me.

And stared.

Then he nodded.

'What other choice do I have?' he said.

'There's just one thing I want in return.'

'Anything. Just name your price.'

'I want to see the photographs in the locker at Central Station.'

That obviously wasn't what Strange had been expecting.

'You know about that as well?'

'I wanted to know where they were,' I said, 'so I followed you.'

294

He sniffed with peculiar disapproval for a man who only moments ago had been suggesting handing a gun to a total stranger just to cover up his own bilking.

'I'm surprised you didn't just break in and steal them,' he said.

'I considered it. What can I say? I'm an inquisitive woman. But there were too many people about. I didn't know if the photos were worth the risk. Are they?'

'I wouldn't know,' said Strange. 'I never looked at them.'

'Come on.'

'You don't have to believe me. But as I told you before, Felix asked me to look after the photographs and that's what I did. For all my other faults, I am not a peeping Tom. I presumed he had his reasons for keeping them hidden.'

'What did you think they were?'

'At first,' he admitted, 'I thought the pictures might be of Felix and Alice together. That he'd got worried after the break-in at the house, realised how vulnerable they were, and wanted them out of harm's way. Then when Alice died too and the photographs of them were found . . . well, that didn't make any sense. You want to know the truth? The truth was I didn't know what they were and I didn't want to look. I was afraid of what I might find.'

'I'm not afraid. I want to see them,' I said. 'I need to know if they have anything to do with Felix's death.'

'Not that again. How could they?'

'Until I see them, how can I ever know?'

Chapter Thirty-Nine

We were in Fitzgerald's office and Draker was shouting, and I was enjoying every second of his discomfort. His voice shook the window like passing trucks. His words were variations on a theme, like he was some crazed maestro banging out angry chords on an untuned piano.

Who the hell do you think you are?

What gives you the right?

I'm afraid he wasn't very original in his ranting.

I tuned out his voice so that it merged into the background like a hum and he was a fly knocking itself in frustration against a closed window, unable to get out. I saw his lips moving, but the words broke apart and disintegrated before they could reach my ears.

'Time's running out, Draker,' I said when the lips stopped moving briefly.

'Have you been listening to a word I've said?' he asked.

'Let me think now. No.'

And that set him off again.

It was a simple deal. I'd told the Assistant Commissioner I was willing to pass on to the murder squad a tip-off about a possible handover of a gun tonight – so long as I was allowed in on the action. I wanted to be there. Plus – let's not forget the important part – I wanted to be the first to talk to the suspect.

It wasn't quite what Strange had had in mind when he came to me for help, but I figured he'd thank me for it in the end. Even if I couldn't guarantee that his name would be kept out of it afterwards. Whatever grief he got as a result, it was better than being in hock for ever to the Marxman.

Draker had a problem with my plan, however.

Two problems, I should say.

Problem One, which I could sympathise with, was that I was a civilian – as indeed he'd reminded me close on a hundred times since I walked into Dublin Castle with Fitzgerald a half-hour ago – and if anything happened to me tonight then he was the one who was going to have to go out in public and concoct some half-baked story to prevent the whole thing going bad faster than the morning's milk, all the time hoping the press didn't catch on to the lie, or he could kiss goodbye not only to the Commissioner's job but probably the one he already had as well.

Problem Two was that he didn't like me.

Never had.

Problem Two, though, wasn't my problem, and Problem One was non-negotiable, since there was no way I was going to just hand over what I had and let the police take control.

Besides, the caller expected me to be there.

I hadn't told Draker that part.

'Where exactly did you get this tip-off anyway?' I heard Draker asking irritably again.

'I'm afraid I cannot divulge that information,' I said, trying to make each word as irritating as possible. 'My informant wishes to preserve his anonymity. All I am willing to say is that I got a lead about a possible handover of a gun tonight somewhere on the northside and that I intend to be there. Whether your officers are there with me is entirely up to you.'

'And if I refuse to do what you want?'

'Then you'll never get the chance to find out if this man is who you want him to be.'

'You'd allow him to get away rather than back down?'

'There's no need for anyone to get away,' I pointed out patiently. 'All you have to do is agree to my conditions and then we all get what we want.'

'There are people dying,' Draker started again, his voice rising. 'It is your responsibility to hand over any information you have which might be of assistance to the Dublin Metro-politan Police in apprehending him.'

I found myself wondering if he talked in that pedantic way at home.

I pitied his wife if he did.

'And you,' I answered, 'are the one who's going to have to explain to the Commissioner why you let vital information go because of some personal problem you had with me.'

'I have a personal problem with *you*? In case you hadn't noticed, I'm the one who's trying to stop you getting killed here. You know what I should do?' he said with spontaneous insight. 'I should have you arrested. See how cocky you are after a few hours in the cells.'

'Then why don't you quit threatening and get on with it?'

Draker turned to Fitzgerald in exasperation.

'Chief Superintendent,' he pleaded, 'is there nothing you can do about this?'

I could tell from her face that Fitzgerald was trying not to allow her own enjoyment of Draker's dilemma show. She wasn't making a bad job of it either, but I wasn't fooled.

'Sir,' she said coolly, 'we are both in the same position. I have no more access to this information than you have. Saxon has already made her bottom line absolutely clear.'

He looked hard at Fitzgerald, as if sensing something in her which was relishing his discomfort, and defying her to let it show, but she didn't flinch, and he was forced to shift his gaze away. Back to me. And I saw that his energy for fighting was fading.

'You would let this man get away rather than back down?'

I nodded curtly, letting myself believe at that moment that I would, because it was the only way to make what I was saying sound convincing.

'You'd let more people die?'

'There's no *reason* why anyone else should die,' I said. 'Look. You can give me the how-dare-you speech again if you like. I'll sit here and listen to it all day. I'll even give you marks out of ten if you want. But it won't get us anywhere. Yes, it could go wrong and you'll wind up looking bad. Everything's a risk. Alternatively, you could bring this investigation to a close by the morning. It's too important to me to let this chance go. What about you?'

He didn't answer directly. Instead he asked me a question.

'Why does it matter so much that you get to talk to this fruitcake?'

'Because if it really is the Marxman who's going to be there tonight,' I said, 'I want to ask him what he knows about Felix Berg's death. I want to know why Felix died.'

'Not that again,' said Draker wearily. They were the same words Strange had used less than an hour ago when I'd asked him for the photographs. I seemed to be uniting the city in disapproval. 'I heard you were making a fool of yourself over that, but I never thought you'd let it interfere with your judgement. What's there to know? Felix Berg killed himself.'

'I want to hear that from the Marxman himself,' I said.

Draker turned to the window and looked out at grey clouds. The light was flecked with dark shadows, as if the rain that had fallen earlier on St Stephen's Green, unnoticed by me, was threatening to return. A solitary bird was making its way down to the river.

'Very well,' he said eventually. 'I agree. You get your way. You tell us where the handover's to take place and you can be there. You can make the first approach to the suspect. You can have your two, three minutes, whatever, to talk to him. But in return . . .'

He gave a thin smile.

'Yes?'

'You agree to let Seamus Dalton be your babysitter for the night.'

'Dalton?' I echoed numbly, and Fitzgerald began to protest.

'Seamus Dalton,' Draker repeated more loudly, to overrule both our objections. 'He's an experienced murder squad officer. He is familiar with the terrain on the northside. I also feel that he has been punished enough for whatever misdemeanours he's been accused of.'

'Dalton has not been punished,' said Fitzgerald. 'I have merely assigned him temporarily on to other duties because his personal problems have made it impossible for others on the team to work with him.'

'I didn't say what I just said as a prelude to a prolonged debate,' said Draker. 'I've made my decision. Take it or leave it.'

He was learning fast.

'Saxon?' said Fitzgerald.

'Dalton it is then,' I said.

'Are you sure you're OK with this?' said Fitzgerald for the ninth time. I know it was the ninth time because I'd been counting ever since she walked through the door. 'You sound funny.'

'That's because I keep having to shout so you can hear me,' I said.

'What? You'll have to speak up. I can't hear you.'

'See what I mean?'

She was in the shower, and I was sitting on the edge of the bath, watching her. She'd come round about ten minutes ago to freshen up ready for the night ahead – it was quicker than making the long trek to her place by the water – but seeing her had only made me feel more guilty than ever. I'd told her from the start that my information came from Vincent Strange, and what the caller had on him, but I hadn't told her that the caller had insisted I be the one who made the dropoff. That would have prompted too many difficult questions. About just what interest the caller had in me; I might have

300

even had to tell her about what had happened in my apartment on the night of Felix's funeral. I still hadn't got round to that.

Still wasn't sure what the connection was.

In addition, she was already concerned enough about my insistence on being there tonight. She'd even tried to talk me out of it, and I felt so bad watching her worry that I might have allowed myself to be dissuaded if it hadn't been for the fact that I had to be there, that that was part of the caller's deal with Strange. Anything else and the whole evening could unravel in our hands.

And I wasn't prepared to let that happen.

Not now, when it all might be coming to an end. When I might be so close to having with Felix what I'd never had with Sydney: answers. I had no choice. I had to be there.

'Here, hand me a towel,' she said, and I started.

I hadn't heard the water switch off.

I was getting quite a talent for daydreaming.

I reached over for a towel and handed it through the door to her, and watched as she wrapped herself inside it and stepped out, leaving damp footprints on the tiles.

As she rubbed herself dry she talked, trying to distract us both from our anxieties by bringing me up to speed on what had happened since that morning.

For once, it seemed, Fitzgerald had hit lucky. Within a matter of hours of the conference with Fisher and Walsh in her car outside Dublin Castle, they'd managed to put together a better picture of Tim Enright's dealings than had emerged during the initial investigation.

'Walsh brought back a huge box of stuff from Enright's office,' she said. 'Letters, email records, accounts, you name it. There was one name that stood out. Charles Mason, head of Mason & Vine, a wine import company with a warehouse down on the quays. Enright had kept an eye on Mason's investments for years, but the record shows he didn't take a cent from him last year.'

'Did Mason say why?'

'He did indeed, though not without considerable pressing. Last year, it seems, Enright asked him to bring in a package for him from the States, the deal being that Mason would pull some strings to get it cleared through customs, no questions asked, and Enright would work for gratis that financial year. It represented a big saving for Mason. He was one of Enright's biggest clients.'

'Did Enright tell him what would be in the package?'

'A rare vintage wine.'

'Wine? And he believed it?'

'Mason had no reason not to believe it. He'd known Enright for years, he didn't have a stain on his character. And Enright did collect vintage wines; apparently he had a fortune tied up in them. He simply told Mason he didn't want to pay duty on the purchase, which he'd have to if he declared it. He said the Revenue Commissioners were fleecing him enough already.'

'And Mason didn't mind helping him to defraud the tax inspectors?'

'Probably quite the opposite. Who wants an investment broker who doesn't cut the odd corner? That's like a hooker who doesn't do anything on the first date.'

'I guess so. So what do *you* think was in the package?'

'You know what I think was in it,' said Fitzgerald, hanging up the towel again and reaching for her clothes. 'A Glock .36 with a spotless ballistics history which now sits in our storeroom with a rather less spotless ballistics history. That's how the Marxman got the weapon into the country. Through Enright.'

'And that's why Enright had to die? It makes sense,' I said. 'If he hadn't been killed, the sequence could have all fallen apart at the start. He knew too much. But how come this Mason didn't come forward when Enright was killed? Didn't he think there might be a connection between him receiving some mysterious package from the States and him dying?'

'Not according to Mason, no. He says the police were briefing the media that the shooting was motiveless and random, which we were, and that there was no connection to organised crime. I don't think he had the slightest notion what was in the package, always assuming our hunch is right. All he felt,' Fitzgerald said, 'was relief because our conviction that the murders were random eased him of the burden of having to come forward and confess his peculiar arrangement with the dead man. It would've looked bad for him if it had come out.'

'And now with another brace of victims it's going to look even worse,' I reflected. 'But if Enright did give the Glock to the Marxman, then what did *he* get out of the exchange, that's the part I don't understand.'

'I don't understand it either,' Fitzgerald admitted. 'It couldn't have been money, there were no irregular payments into his bank account, we checked all that stuff out when he was first killed. Unless, that is, the payment was in cash, but again that doesn't really add up. Enright had plenty of money of his own, certainly enough to be immune to ordinary bribery.'

'So it must have been something else which persuaded him to risk bringing a gun into the country in his own name, if that is indeed what was in the package,' I said.

'Like?'

'Could be anything. Blackmail. Sex. Because he was threatened. To settle a gambling debt. To protect a member of his family. The usual reasons why people are persuaded to do stupid things against their better judgement. Look at Strange's photographs. Maybe the Marxman specialises in finding the weak spot of those whose path he crosses and exploiting it.'

'We found nothing in his background to suggest any reason he'd be blackmailed. No secret lovers, no hidden gay life. No unpleasant habits that needed covering up from his wife.'

'Then maybe Enright just wanted a gun for his own use, like Felix did, and the Marxman intercepted it and killed him before he could tell the police where it had gone.'

'You have a favourite out of that list?' asked Fitzgerald.

'That's the beauty of being a civilian,' I said. 'You get to throw tantalising suggestions into the air. You don't have to try and decide which one to catch when they fall.'

Chapter Forty

Dalton was regarding the inside of his empty pint glass regretfully and didn't even waste a look on me as I scraped back a stool, sat down opposite him and lit a cigar.

It was ten after midnight and I sensed I was going to need it.

'Drinking on duty, detective?' I said.

He blessed me finally with a look.

'Quit the detective crap. You trying to ruin my reputation round here?' he said. 'Detective, shit. Besides, officially this is my night off. I'm not on duty. I'm all yours.'

'Lucky me.'

'You want a drink?'

Opening hours were obviously a flexible concept in this bar.

'If you're buying,' I said.

'I'm buying. And since hidden somewhere inside that jacket of yours is probably the shape of a woman, I'm guessing a medium white wine?'

'I'll have a whiskey,' I told the barman who'd come over to take my order.

'Two,' said Dalton. 'And another Guinness whilst you're at it.'

I gave the bar the once-over while waiting for the drinks to arrive.

'Nice place you picked for us.'

He followed my gaze to where the only other customers

both sat staring blankly into some distant dimension. They looked like glue was their narcotic of choice. The bar was as dingy as the inside of a moviehouse before the lights come up. A place for those who prefer to dwell in semi-darkness. And at least it meant they couldn't see how dirty the glasses were.

What the eye doesn't see the heart doesn't grieve for.

'It's quiet,' said Dalton. 'That's good enough for me. No one will take any notice of us here.' And he drained his whiskey and belched quietly, before taking a long draught of his newly arrived pint, pausing for breath, starting another. Fitzgerald had said he'd been drinking since his recent problems in the murder squad, but I hadn't expected this.

Then again, I couldn't claim to be knocked out with astonishment either. Whatever energy Dalton had once had seemed to have fizzled out like a wet fuse on a firecracker.

'You not talking?' He interrupted my thoughts.

'In case you've forgotten, I'm not here out of choice. You simply happen to be Draker's pick for a date for me, and we both know he only did that to piss me off. I certainly didn't come here to provide you with conversation.'

'You make that obvious enough. Not exactly Miss Congeniality, are you? You never give away one thing about yourself. You got your whole life locked up tight like it's some big mystery. It's no wonder people don't take to you.'

'I've had that character sketch from plenty of people before,' I said, 'but getting it from you is something else. You're not exactly the winner of the Cary Grant award for charm yourself, Dalton. And what the hell difference would it make if I told my life story to everyone I met? You want to know where I went to kindergarten, what grade I got in math, who my first date was, my first car? It's an illusion that this stuff makes you know me any better. Either people take to you or they don't. Details don't come into it.'

'What *was* your first car, since you brought it up?'

'A 1971 Plymouth,' I said. 'Picked it up in a scrapyard on the southside of Boston with my first paycheck. Spent every night and every weekend for a year restoring it to life.'

'Nice,' he said, and it seemed like the first thing I'd ever said he approved of.

'You bet it was nice,' I said. 'Broke my heart when I went to college and had to sell it to pay my fees. There now, feel better? Think we're building some kind of empathy?'

'It all helps.'

'Except that, for all you'll ever know, I might've made the whole thing up right this minute because it was what you wanted to hear. So where's that leave your theory?'

Dalton looked disgusted.

'You've got a real bad attitude, do you know that?' he said.

'My attitude is my own business,' I said. 'I don't want to be your buddy, Dalton. I just want to get this over and done with. Don't you?'

'I'm here, aren't I?'

'You're here, but why are you here? You give the impression of not giving a shit. You can't even be bothered to keep your head clear by staying off the booze. If you've just come here to drink and gripe, why'd you accept the job at all?'

'Why did I accept it?' said Dalton. 'Because I've been shoved aside for the last – what? – year, maybe more, whilst I see young kids still wet behind the ears getting ahead. So I have a few disciplinary problems? Sue me. Doesn't mean I should've been left off the Marxman enquiry when someone like Patrick Walsh, who spends more time playing with his fucking Game Boy than he does building up contacts, learning his trade, is treated in there like he's the Second Coming. I've just had it with hitting my head against a wall. Policing today is like trying to pick up specks of dust with a forklift truck. The whole thing is just a chorus of birds twittering in my head. I don't have the patience for it, I don't have the subtlety to sift through the bits and pieces to try and find the few that might just fit together. I need something more definite. I need to be *doing* something. That's why I'm here. Because I've had it with being redundant. Because I want to get this thing done.'

I think it was the longest speech I'd ever heard Dalton deliver.

And there was something in what he said.

He summed himself up well.

'So what's the idea?' I said. 'You bring in the Marxman, get to be the big hero, give Grace, Healy, Walsh and the rest the middle finger and have everyone kissing your ass?'

'Sounds good to me,' said Dalton. 'You got any objection?'

'Got an objection to you trying to cut the ground from under Fitzgerald's feet when this is her case, she's been working on it for three months without a break, and she's stood by you a hundred times when you crossed the line and she could've hung you out to dry from the windows at Dublin Castle? Why would I have any objection to that? Besides, I knew what I was getting when Draker suggested your name. Knew it wouldn't be a pleasant evening.'

'Then let's establish a few ground rules, shall we?' said Dalton. 'Rule One. I'm in charge. You do things my way. I know this terrain. I don't just see it from the window of a train as it passes by. I can find my way round the northside blindfolded. I grew up there, guys I know still live there, they're not always on the right side of the law but they've been there for me more often than half the suits up in Dublin Castle.'

Workers of the world unite, you have nothing to lose but the mile-high chips on your blue-collar shoulders. Then I remembered I was meant to be biting my tongue.

So I bit it.

'Rule Two. You get your two minutes,' said Dalton, 'but if I detect at any point during those two minutes that things are going badly then I'm moving in and I don't care what deal you made with the Assistant Commissioner. Understood?'

'I got it, but I think Rule One covered that one too.'

'Don't get smart,' said Dalton. 'All you've got to remember is to back off when I tell you to back off and leave the rest to the big boys. And if it gets too much at any time for your delicate female constitution, then just say the word and I'll drop you off somewhere warm and safe where we can pick you up later.'

'And miss a golden opportunity to learn something from a legend like Seamus Dalton?' I said. 'I couldn't live with myself afterwards.'

'Then let's go,' he said.

He drained his drink and picked up the car keys from the table, and I followed him out into the parking lot to the unmarked vehicle that he'd picked up from the pound.

'So where's the switch to take place?' he said as we climbed inside.

I found myself hesitating. 'How do I know you won't just take the information, throw me out and leave me standing at the side of the road?'

'You don't,' Dalton answered bluntly. 'But a deal's a deal. Call me old fashioned, but I happen to believe in keeping my word.'

So I told him the address that Strange had given me at midnight over the cellphone, and he shifted the car into first and pulled out into the flow of the traffic.

I tried to keep a close eye on where we were going as we drove, but we soon moved out of the areas I knew well and into the badlands on the northside of Dublin.

At least that was how I saw them. Huge sprawling estates, as featureless as any wilderness or tundra, where there was nothing but drugs and crime to eke out the time till the end of the world. For all the surface prosperity Dublin had to offer the lucky few, there was still plenty of the city that had failed to taste the milk and honey, which still lagged behind, as distant from that other shining city of light and abundance as their ancestors in the decaying slums had been a century before. I simply sat back and let him drive.

And while we drove, Dalton got through on his radio to Fitzgerald to tell her where we were going to be, so that she could put back-up in place. She sounded anxious, but then I'd have been the same if it was her. The deal was that they stayed far enough out of the way to ensure Strange's caller didn't get suspicious, but close enough to be on hand if they were needed. In that margin, there was more than enough room for error.

'There it is,' said Dalton.

Through the window I saw the shadow of some derelict building, and a doorway under a broken streetlight where I was to stand and wait when it got to 1 a.m.

'We're not stopping?'

'Still too early. No point drawing attention to yourself.'

So instead we drove round the block a couple more times, and I didn't know whether to be reassured by the fact that I couldn't see any sign of the police back-up or concerned in case they hadn't gone to the right place. I felt my nerves tightening as the time ticked down. The only thing that stopped me admitting as much was Dalton's reaction.

I could imagine what he'd say.

Can't handle the heat any more, Special Agent?

Gone soft?

Eventually, with five minutes to go, Dalton pulled us over into a side street and we got out and walked the rest of the way. On one side of the street was a Dumpster, behind which he intended to lie in wait. On the other side was the doorway.

High walls rose all around, so that it felt like the road was cutting deep through some dark valley.

Yea, though I walk through the valley of the shadow of death . . .

'Now we go our separate ways,' Dalton said.

And I crossed the road alone and stood in the doorway beneath the broken light. The glass had been smashed and slivers of it were scattered on the path beneath.

It was midnight in Howth all over again.

310

The sound of footsteps came almost immediately – but as I turned in their direction I saw it was only some late-night straggler, muttering thickly to himself as they all do with too much drink in them, crossing the street at the far end; and the world returned to silence, shattered only by the squeal of a joyrider's tyres in an adjacent street a moment later. The noise made me flinch, but it made me more alert too, and now I noticed other sounds, like the clattering song of machinery in one of the nearby buildings. They were not all derelict then.

I checked my watch and saw that 1 a.m. had gone.

Had Strange's caller got cold feet?

Had he seen Dalton? The others?

Had he—

I felt myself go tense.

More footsteps, this time coming towards me, and, yes, there was a figure, illuminated by the working streetlights, approaching slowly.

Was this him?

He stopped a couple of metres from where I waited, but all I could see even now was only an outline, a shadow, because of the broken light, and when I made as if to step forward he said sharply: 'Stay where you are.' So I stayed where I was and he stayed in darkness.

'Have you got what I asked for?' he said.

Like Strange, I didn't recognise the voice.

'I have it,' I said.

'Give it to me.'

'How can I give it to you if you won't let me come any nearer?'

'Throw it along the path towards me.'

This was where things could get tricky.

I reached into the inside pocket of my jacket and pulled out the brown paper bag Dalton had given me out of the glove compartment. Inside was an imitation automatic pistol. It felt the same as a working gun. Weighed the same. In the

311

half-light he probably wouldn't notice it was a fake. At least that's what I was relying on.

I put the bag at my feet and kicked it across the ground towards him.

When it stopped, he bent to pick it up.

Pulled out the gun.

Nodded in satisfaction.

'Is it loaded, like I asked?' he said.

'Of course.'

With blanks, but let's not quibble over details. He must have been insane to think I'd seriously have handed him a weapon with the bullets already inside.

Did I look like a lemming?

'Then I think we're done here.'

'Just tell me one thing before you go,' I said quickly, afraid now that he would be out of here even before I'd managed to ask him my question. 'Did you kill Felix?'

There was no hesitation.

'I did,' he said. 'It was the best thing I've ever done.'

And he pointed the gun at me.

'I'm really sorry about this,' he said.

At that moment, two things happened.

The first was that a shout came from the other side of the street and Dalton emerged from behind the Dumpster, yelling: 'Police! Put down the gun!'

The second was that the scene was lit suddenly as if by a spotlight, and the stranger froze as the joyrider I'd heard in a nearby street took the corner at a squeal and came tearing down the centre of the road, swerving from side to side, the whoops of laughter bursting out from the open windows of the stolen car. Normally I'd have been wishing the nihilistic little punks just hit a wall and be done with it, but now I was glad of the light because it illuminated the place where I was standing, and in the instant before he threw up his hand to shield his eyes from the glare I had a chance to see the stranger's face for the first time.

312

I knew him.

I *knew* him.

But from where?

Then it came to me. He was the guy in pinstripes who'd been watching me in Burke's store the day after my apartment was trashed. And I'd seen him somewhere else, I realised. He was one of the three men in the photograph with Tim Enright, the one that Boland had snipped from a magazine and added to the victim's file.

Why hadn't I recognised his face in the picture? Because I hadn't been looking that closely at his colleagues, only at Enright, and out of pinstripes he looked a different person.

Out of pinstripes, maybe he was.

The stranger's face right now was a study in panic as he looked between Dalton and me, like he was trying to make up his mind which of us was more of a threat. And then, incredibly, he pointed the gun back at me even as Dalton was walking towards him.

I wasn't scared. Why should I be? The gun wasn't loaded. But even though I knew that, my blood was still ice as the stranger took aim and fired.

Chapter Forty-One

My ears sang. My eyes burned with the flash from the blank shell. But there I still was, standing, looking at the stranger with his arm outstretched, the gun still clutched in his fingers.

'Put your hands up and kneel down on the ground,' said Dalton. 'Don't bother trying to escape. You're surrounded.' And he barked into his radio: 'We got him.'

The stranger looked up the street, and down, as if confused by the emptiness, but he threw down the gun anyway, and didn't resist as Dalton finally reached him and told him to turn round. But as he turned, I saw his hand slip into his pocket and he drew out something that flashed like silver, and before I had time to cry out a warning, he spun round and the silver disappeared inside Dalton's jacket, and Dalton gave a gasp and fell to the ground on one knee.

The stranger turned and ran.

I hurried forward, and knelt down next to Dalton. He was clutching the jacket at the waist where he'd been stabbed, and his fingers were black with blood.

'I'll go and get help,' I said.

'Fuck help,' he said. 'They're on their way.'

'They should be here by now.'

'They'll be here. Just make sure he doesn't get away. Go on.'

I still wavered.

'You're losing him, for fuck's sake. Go! I'll be fine. I'll call through for help.'

So I ran in the wake of the fleeing stranger, feeling vulnerable without a weapon, without protection, hardly knowing what I was doing or what I'd do if I did catch up with him.

Hold him hostage with a lighted cigar until help arrived?

I could hear his footsteps in some side street, and turned the corner just in time to see him run into an alley on the other side. I followed blindly, and a cab sounded its horn as it narrowly missed hitting me, but didn't slow down or stop to find out how I was, just blared a horn in protest and hurtled on, the neighbourliness of a city captured in one brief second of shock.

Behind me I heard the sound of sirens as the police back-up finally arrived.

Where had it been?

But by this time I was over the road and moving away from the scene, and the stranger with the knife was even further ahead, dashing through one valley of dark brick after another, turning the city into a maze in the hope maybe that the pursuit would get lost; but I could see him more clearly now because he was among streetlights, and I ran as fast as I could, one of those times when I wished I had taken Fitzgerald's advice and got more exercise, for my heart was creaking with the effort of keeping up as I negotiated more streets, more corners, my furious footfalls amplified by the echo bouncing off the encroaching walls, more—

I stopped.

I was in a small square of abandoned, broken buildings, where people had once lived, right in the middle of all these factories and warehouses, frightened trees hemmed in by railings in a communal garden dead centre, and I was surrounded by watching windows, shards and shadow, and doorways boarded up and transformed into canvases for obscene graffiti.

He couldn't get out from here – unless he'd entered one of the houses.

Unless this was where he *lived*?

I rejected the idea as fanciful. He was hardly likely to lead the pursuit to the place where he lived. And no one lived here surely? Certainly not a man in pinstripes.

Was he merely waiting then for a chance to double back and escape?

Or luring me into danger?

I thought of Dalton and went cold. Coming here alone didn't seem such a smart idea now, but I couldn't turn round. Trying to keep my breath steady, I made my way slowly round the edge of the square, peering through what gaps could be found in the boarded-up doors and downstairs windows at the heaps of rubble within, pockmarked with the glint of used syringes.

Looking for movement.

There was nothing there.

Nothing there.

Nothing—

I jumped back as a filthy bird, disturbed from its sleep, flapped out of the shattered window of a house I'd just passed; and as I watched it circle against the stars and vanish, silence settling once more like snow, I looked back at the house and knew: *He's in there.*

Call it a sixth sense.

I retraced my steps, noticing this time that one of the planks that covered the doorway was loose. I moved it to one side, and a gap appeared, wide enough to squeeze through.

I wished I had a torch.

It was dingy inside.

There might be rats.

Might?

There was no might about it.

It was only when I was standing in the hallway, brushing the dust and dirt off my jacket, that I realised there was someone sitting hunched on the stairs.

I'd walked right into his trap.

But even now that I was here he didn't move, and he must have heard me enter.

He was sitting bent forward, arms folded, his head resting on the place where they were crossed. The knife dangled limply from his fingers.

Dalton's blood stained the edge.

'Don't worry,' he said, without looking up, 'I'm not going to kill you.'

'Why not? I thought you liked killing people.'

'I've killed enough of them,' he said.

And he started to laugh strangely, like it was the funniest joke in the world.

He lifted his head and looked me directly in the eye.

He didn't look like a killer.

Then again, which of them ever did?

I didn't know what to do. If I could distract him . . . try to cover the ground before he realised what I was doing . . . but no, it was a calculation I couldn't make.

One wrong move, and—

I could hear the noises of the city, dulled and distant, beyond the walls. I felt like I was in a belljar, like a trapped insect, with the air running out.

The sirens were far, far away.

I could hardly believe that I was here.

With the Marxman?

And as I watched him, I saw the same uncertainty in his eyes, like he was wondering what to do now – and then the next moment it was gone, it was a moon blotted out by a cloud, and he got to his feet and walked steadily down the steps towards me, and I had nowhere to run.

Besides, I wouldn't give him that satisfaction.

When he was about three steps away, he halted.

Lifted up the knife between us.

'It was nice meeting you,' he said. 'And I really am sorry about trying to shoot you.'

And he turned the knife round and pulled it hard across his throat.

I heard the scrape of it loud against bone.

When the police entered the derelict building a short time later, their arrival putting an end to the hidden scurryings that had begun to converge on the hallway, I was still standing in the same position. I hadn't moved. I couldn't move. I was staring down at the slumped body of the man who'd tried to kill me not a half-hour ago, sprawled in a spreading pool of his own blood.

'I can't believe it. Sometimes,' said Boland as he drove me back later from the northside to my apartment, 'I think I don't understand one thing that's going on any more.'

All the lights were red against us.

It seemed like a portent.

'I never liked Seamus Dalton,' he said, 'but it's hard to accept that he could have been killed out there tonight. That I might have come in this morning and he wouldn't be there giving grief to everyone like he always did. Wouldn't be there ever again. You know what he said to me the last time I saw him yesterday? I was standing at the coffee machine and he walked up and said: *Why don't you do some work for a change, you fat fuck, instead of standing around drinking coffee all day?*' That sounded like Dalton. 'Imagine if those were his last words to me. The last thing I had to remember him by. Not much of a memorial, is it?'

As it was, Dalton was going to be fine. He'd lost a lot of blood, and it was a long time before the paramedics could stabilise him enough to get him to hospital. But there'd be no permanent damage; the wound was messy, but the knife had missed the major organs. The doctors reckoned he'd be out within a few days if he took it easy and did what he was told.

They obviously didn't know Dalton.

He was already complaining about the bed, most likely.

I could understand Boland's reaction, though. I'd never known an agent who died in the line of duty, but I'd spoken to more than enough cops who'd lost colleagues to know how bad it could get, and tonight the murder squad had come pretty close. It was bound to come as a shock. The chances of a cop being killed in Dublin were still remote compared with other cities, but it was always a possibility, and tonight would make that possibility seem more real than ever.

'Still,' Boland continued, 'Dalton had a point. That *is* all I ever seem to do these days. Some days I think I've got more coffee inside me than the coffee machine itself. I've had enough of it.'

I hadn't really been listening to him up until then. My thoughts were back in that derelict house where George Dyer, as I'd now learned Enright's former colleague was called, had died. And back further than that in the street when I'd asked if he'd killed Felix and he'd answered: *I did.*

Now he had my full attention.

'You've had enough of what?'

'Of all this,' he answered. 'Being a detective. Everything. I realise that now. I'm going nowhere.'

'You can change. Healy changed. Look how he's leapt up the ladder this last year.'

'It's not about climbing any ladders. Healy knows what he's doing. Healy's a good detective. I'm . . . I'm just a fat fuck who spends all day at the coffee machine trying not to get in the way and wondering how I ended up here, hoping every minute they don't catch me out.'

I had no reassurance to offer. He wasn't wrong. He stood out in the murder squad like a nun in a brothel.

'So what you going to do? Shift departments again? Get a transfer to a desk job?'

Though in truth he virtually had one of those already.

'I want out,' he said. 'Totally. Not half in and half out. One hundred per cent out. I'm through with feeling like a waster for not being a better detective. For a long time now I've felt

319

I needed to be moving up, impressing the right people, or I was nothing, and I've been crushed when I couldn't do it. But I don't care any more. I never really did. Tonight's made me see that. I just want a job where I can clock on in the morning, finish my shift and clock off in the evening, get paid and go home and watch TV. Live a normal life. Spend weekends in the country fishing.'

'Policing's a hard job to leave behind,' I agreed.

'Cassie's been telling me that all along. If we're to have a chance, I need to be there for her. I wasn't for my ex-wife, Mary, and I screwed that up completely. Cassie already hates what I do. After what happened to Dalton . . .'

I didn't know what to say to him. Police work was tough on partners, tough on relationships. Dalton being nearly killed would make everyone jumpy, force them to rethink what they really wanted. Cassie wouldn't be the only partner begging their loved one to bail out once the news had spread.

Even so, the alternative Boland described – nine to five at some computer screen before going home and watching crap on TV – sounded like a living nightmare to me, and scarcely even a living one at that. But if it made him happy, and I suspected it would, it was his life.

And at least he still had one. Dalton so nearly had not.

Dalton would agree with me. Maybe we were more alike than I cared to admit. Obsessive, cranky, short-tempered, thinking everyone around us was incompetent, inadequate.

And where had it got him?

Where had it got me?

'I hope it works out,' I told Boland, and meant it; but I was glad when my apartment building came into view through the windscreen and I could climb out and be alone again.

Chapter Forty-Two

Apart from the blue incident tape slung across the gateway, where a police officer was standing guard, it looked like another unremarkable red-brick house in a street of equally unremarkable red-brick houses, each well set back from the road and with steps climbing to the front door.

Children rode by on bicycles trying vainly to catch a glimpse inside.

'What does Draker say about allowing me in?' I said as we pulled up the next morning in Fitzgerald's Rover.

'What Draker doesn't see can't hurt him,' she answered. 'Besides, you had as much to do with catching this guy as anyone. More. You have a right to see where he lived.'

He, of course, being George Dyer.

The Marxman? That was what we were here to find out.

'Plus I want to know what you make of it,' she added.

I saw what she meant when I got inside.

The house was completely anonymous, as though its only purpose was to keep up a façade of normality so that the man who lived there could hide his true self behind it. The rooms were bare as any monk's cell; in fact, it was hard to know what the crime technical team who'd spent the morning combing through the house could have found to take away and analyse.

Here was a front room with nothing in it but a single chair.

Behind that a room fitted out with bookshelves, but without any books, and certainly no copy of *The Foundations of the Critique of Political Economy* or whatever it was Burke had said Dyer had bought in his store that day.

There was no TV, no radio, no CDs.

In the kitchen, everything was kept to an icy minimum.

One cup.

One plate.

A handful of knives and forks and spoons.

All gleaming and perfect save for one small cracked window at the back.

'I like a man who knows how to party,' I said grimly.

We climbed bare wooden stairs to the first floor.

Upstairs were the same empty rooms.

A bathroom clinical as a mortuary.

A front room which smelt of paint.

The only furniture was in a room in the back where Dyer had slept.

The blinds were down here. It was a room where it felt like the blinds were permanently down. Fitzgerald pulled the cord, and the room shrank painfully from the light, revealing a single bed, the corners of the blankets turned down sternly and tucked into place, and a rail on which hung six identical suits and six identical shirts and ties. Socks and underwear were separated into neat piles.

Once again, the same absence of anything personal or intimate.

'Apart from this,' said Fitzgerald.

She handed me a photograph. It was an old picture, slightly curled at the edges, the colours faded like there was too much sun. A woman was looking at the camera, smiling, and above her head the word ONE was printed in block capitals on a sign.

'Dyer's mother?' I suggested.

'That's what I thought. The only other thing we've been able to find,' said Fitzgerald, 'is a small suitcase under the stairs, with a passport inside and some money inserted into the lining.'

'In case he needed to leave in a hurry?'

'That's the theory,' she said. 'What do you think?'

'About the house?' I said. 'It's almost perfect. Fisher said the Marxman would be orderly and you couldn't get much more orderly than this. There's only one thing wrong.'

'I know what you're going to say,' Fitzgerald said. 'There are no newspaper cuttings, no mementoes, nothing at all to connect him to the killings. Maybe he was just careful,' she suggested, playing devil's advocate. 'Forensically careful, I mean. Making sure there was nothing connecting him to the killings if he was ever caught. Or he may have all those mementoes safely stashed away elsewhere.'

A lock-up on the outskirts of town, say, or a rented room.

So that this house was kept pristine.

Untainted.

It was possible.

'Or maybe he feared that trying to buy a gun would bring him unwanted attention and he decided to destroy everything that could incriminate him beforehand,' she went on. 'Or maybe he destroyed it as he went along. There's a brazier out back and neighbours confirm he often burned stuff in it, but they can't say if the burnings coincided with the killings. At least some of them claim to remember, but I don't trust them. You know what witnesses are like for remembering what they want to remember rather than what they do. It's possible he burned all the evidence; everything that could be found in the ash has been taken away for analysis. But I'm not hopeful.'

'What you're saying,' I pressed her, 'is that you've got nothing to implicate George Dyer in the Marxman shootings at all?'

'Exactly.'

'No evidence of any interest in guns prior to last night? No gunpowder traces? Spent shells in the grass? Nothing to make forensics' day?'

'We're still looking,' she said, but she said it in a way that meant she didn't expect to find a thing; and looking round, that seemed like a reasonable expectation. 'Not that I trust half of them here. Sometimes I feel as if I'm the last practitioner of some meaningless rite called processing the crime scene. Don't touch this. Don't move that. Take these away for analysis. Healy and Walsh know what they're doing, but the rest of them blunder through with all the finesse of a rhinoceros on heat.'

'What did the neighbours make of him?' I said, as we walked back downstairs and out on to the front steps, glad of air after the suffocating atmosphere that permeated the house.

A white cat sat yawning on the path.

'He kept himself to himself. That's the phrase they're all using. He had no friends, no visitors, no women. He never used to speak to anyone.'

'Unpopular?'

'Not especially. They seem to have chalked him up as an eccentric. He was harmless enough. He never caused any trouble, just didn't seem to want to talk to anyone.'

'No sign of any family?'

'No birthday cards, no photographs, no phone book, no addresses,' she confirmed. 'He had no numbers stored in his cellphone. There are no obvious traces of any hair or fibres on the furniture other than those he left behind himself, and a few from a cat.'

The white cat on the path, presumably.

If so, it didn't seem too concerned that its master was gone and the house filled with strangers. Oh to be a cat and give so little thought to the mad bustle of the world.

'Cat aside,' Fitzgerald said, 'he was a complete loner. Utterly self-sufficient.'

'No man is an island.'

'Dyer was. Or a remote, isolated peninsula at least. And they said much the same about him at work. He didn't seem to leave much of an impression on anyone. He was aloof but not unfriendly. Quiet but not sullen. He never had visitors.

Never made or took personal calls. Never expressed any particularly strong beliefs or opinions. Rarely took time off.'

'No one ever thought all that suspicious?'

'Why would they? No one ever came here and saw how he lived. To them, he was what he appeared to be. A bit stuffy and lacking a sense of humour, they said, but you don't call the police and report someone because he doesn't laugh at your jokes. Well, *you* might,' she said with the first trace of a smile on her lips that I'd seen all morning, 'but no one else would. George Dyer just seems to have had an unrivalled knack for leaving a huge blank space in people's heads where they might otherwise expect their memories of him to be. They think they remember him and then, when they try to come up with some concrete recollection, they find they have none. He slipped off the surface of their lives like water. Which probably explains why we can't find out any more about him than he was willing to let us find out.'

'Did George Dyer even exist?'

'Only as a name,' said Fitzgerald. 'Officially there was never any such man. Even the qualifications he presented to Enright before he took him on were forged.'

'Erasing all traces of his real identity. Taking refuge in an adopted persona. Things would be a lot simpler if he *had* been a professional hitman. He certainly lived like one. But this,' I said, gesturing at the house, 'doesn't feel like the home of the Marxman.'

'That's why I brought you here,' she said. 'I wanted you to see it for yourself. I wanted to know it wasn't just me being paranoid by refusing to believe this was really over.'

'Could be we're both being paranoid.'

'Then at least we'll have some company in our paranoia.' She paused. 'There is one other thing. I didn't want to tell you until you'd had a chance to see this place for yourself. I didn't want to influence you one way or the other.'

'What is it?'

'The fingerprint we lifted from the gun the Marxman dropped round the corner from Mark Brook's house? It wasn't Dyer's. Healy gave me the results this morning. Now that doesn't necessarily mean a thing. Dyer could have always handled the gun wearing gloves and the print could be from someone who'd handled it previously, way back in the chain, even in the States. We've sent the prints on to be run through for a match. We'll know soon enough. And let's face it, this doesn't feel like the house of a man with nothing to hide. There's something unnatural about it. But even so, there's too much here that's missing. It doesn't feel like it's over.'

'Dyer was in this somewhere,' I said. 'He had to be. It's too much of a coincidence that his boss gets killed and then suddenly, when the Marxman loses his weapon, he's out looking to buy a gun and attacking the first cop that comes along. He must be involved.'

'Draker doesn't think so.'

'He wouldn't. What about Dyer's confession to me about Felix?'

'Two points there. First, even if he did kill Felix, that doesn't mean he's the Marxman. The only thing that connects Felix to the Marxman is his own interest in the case. Nothing else. Second, Draker's still insisting there's nothing to investigate in Felix's death.'

'Despite Dyer telling me that he did it?'

'Draker says you may have misheard. May have misunderstood. Wait up, Saxon. I'm telling you what he said, not what I said. He said that Dyer may have misheard or misunderstood too. He also personally called Alastair Butler and went through the autopsy report with him line by line until he was satisfied there was no way anyone else could have shot Felix.'

'Couldn't you get an exhumation order and have a second, independent autopsy?'

'That would be a great vote of confidence in Butler,' said Fitzgerald. 'He'd hit the roof, and rightly so. And even if I agreed to that, there's no way Draker would go along with it.'

'So we just let it go? Drop the whole subject.'

'No,' Fitzgerald said. 'What we do is bide our time. The investigation into Dyer's past activities will take weeks to conclude whether he was the Marxman or not. All we have to do is leave enough loose threads hanging for Draker to realise that he can't just sign off on the whole subject without at least attempting to sew them up. Then we explore the Felix Berg angle.'

'You've tried to dissuade me from following up my instincts on Felix ever since he died,' I said. 'You saying you agree with me at last?'

'I'm saying I think it needs to be looked at again. And that's as much as you're getting out of me, so don't push your luck,' she said. She took a deep breath before starting the next sentence. 'You can hardly blame me for not understanding why you wouldn't let it go, though, when you've never even told me about Sydney. That *is* what your sister was called, isn't it?'

'I swear I will kill Lawrence Fisher one of these days,' I said.

'Lawrence cares about you. And since I know you care about him just as much, I know you'll not give him a hard time about telling me. He just wanted me to appreciate what you were going through. Why this mattered so much to you.'

'I'm not mad at Fisher,' I said, and I was surprised when I realised that I actually wasn't. 'In fact, I'm glad you know at last. I never intended to keep it from you. I just wanted to keep it to myself, if you see the difference.'

'You keep too much to yourself. It's not good for you.'

'Like the sleeping pills and the bad diet, I know.'

'I guess it's a silly question asking if you want to talk about it.'

'I don't even want to think about it,' I said.

'Chief?'

We both spun round.

'What is it, Sergeant?'

'There's something here you might want to see.'

'I'll be right there,' she said. 'You care to join me?'

'I'd better be on my way,' I said. 'Don't bother about the car. I can walk back to town. I have some chips to cash in with a certain art dealer. He's expecting me and I'm already late.'

'Later then.'

'Later, yeah.'

Chapter Forty-Three

Strange had his nose pressed to the glass of his gallery when I got there, stepping back when he saw me approaching, unlocking the door without a word.

'Lock it behind you,' he said when I entered.

He crossed the floor and took up his place behind the desk, looking apprehensive. He was wearing a velvet suit with a scarlet cravat. Maybe in celebration that his secret had died last night. It had been the best of all possible outcomes for Strange. The caller couldn't disseminate any damaging allegations about Strange's errant dealings, but the art dealer hadn't had to put himself in an even more compromising position by turning Santa Claus with his guns.

But it had been no thanks to him that things had worked out.

If he'd had his way, he'd have handed a live gun over.

And I'd be dead.

Not that it would have changed my plans for the morning. I'd still have come round to the gallery as arranged. To haunt him, scarlet cravat and all.

I glanced at the wall again as I followed him to his desk, and saw that the pictures of the woman wound in chains and posing with knives had gone.

I can't say I missed her.

Strange gestured at the seat opposite, and I sat down whilst he struck the sides of his own chair with the palms of his hands a couple of times, deciding how to proceed.

'Is it him?' he said at last.

'You mean the Marxman?'

'They're saying on the news it's him,' he said.

'Must be then, if it's on the news.'

'But are they sure it's the real one?'

'It'll take time.'

'Time,' he said, and he didn't try to hide his disappointment. 'I just need to know that it's over. Finally over. That I won't get any more calls.'

'If you mean can your name be kept out of this, I think so. I did what I said I'd do. I took care of it.' Though to be honest, I wasn't so sure I could manage that as easily as I was pretending. Fitzgerald had already started making noises about pulling Strange in for questioning about what he knew. I figured she could be dissuaded so long as I agreed to keep it between ourselves about where I'd got my information, but even so I couldn't say for definite that he was out of the woods. I was only telling him what he wanted to hear in order to get what I wanted in turn. No change there then. 'Now I want to see the photographs,' I said to him, 'and then we'll both be happy.'

'You still want them?'

'Of course I still want them,' I said. 'Your friend last night told me he killed Felix. And he intended killing me too. He planned on shooting me, yes, I don't blame you for looking shocked. I wasn't exactly bowled over by the idea myself. But it does make me ask why, and the only reason I can come up with as to why he wanted us both dead is because we were skirting too close to some truth, maybe without even knowing what it was, and death was the best silencer. I can't ask Felix any more what he knew. But maybe I can see what he saw.'

Strange sighed.

'Sometimes,' he said, 'I think I should just have taken the photographs and burned them. I'm tired of thinking about them. Worrying about them. Tired of people asking about them. But I almost feel free now after last night. The hiding from shadows is over. I don't have to be drawn into this net that Felix's obsessions cast. You can have the photographs. You've earned them.'

He stood up and walked over to the coatstand. His fur coat was hanging there like a captured bear. He put his hand into the pocket and took out a small locker key.

He threw it towards me and I caught it in midair.

'Just tell me one more thing before I go,' I said. 'Who did take those sado-masochistic pictures you had hanging on your wall that first day I came here?'

Strange shifted his gaze to the wall as if he could still see them there.

'They were taken by Felix,' he said almost sorrowfully. It was the last answer I'd anticipated. I'd half expected him to say he'd taken them himself. 'He liked taking erotic pictures. He called it his release, though he didn't want anyone knowing about them. They were his secret.'

'I wouldn't want anyone knowing about them either,' I said, and I wondered if I'd ever be able to look at Felix's other work the same way again. 'But thanks for telling me, all the same.'

He waited till I reached the door before speaking my name. I looked back.

'I hope you find what you're looking for,' he said.

My hands were trembling as I lifted the key to the lock and fitted it inside.

Click.

That's how easy it is to get to the truth sometimes.

I pulled back the door and for a moment I was gripped by a certainty that there would be nothing in here. That Vincent Strange had double-crossed me, for what reason I couldn't begin to guess. Or even that there'd never been anything there.

But I was wrong. In the locker there was a brown canvas bag sagging into a heap like a sleeping animal, the shoulder strap curled up neatly like a tail, and I grabbed hold of it and pulled it towards me, carrying it to the nearest bench, sitting down, unfastening the buckle and reaching inside. I took out the first photograph that touched my fingers.

It was another snapshot like the one in Felix's papers.

Like the one dropped through Gina's letterbox.

Like the one on my wall.

Only this was no ordinary picture.

Here instead was Terence Prior, the judge, collapsed against his own door, the back of his hair slick and matted with blood. And this, as I lifted out another, was Finlay Hart, kissing a pool of blood that had gathered under his face, teeth obliterated by the force of the bullet.

My eyes shot up and caught sight of a young boy of about ten in a soccer jersey sitting on the other end of the bench, watching me rifling through the obscene photographs.

Had he seen anything?

I didn't know, but I felt guilty for taking that risk. Hurriedly I shoved the pictures back under canvas, tied the straps tight once more, threw the bag across my shoulder and headed for the stairs, walking fast down to the street again, relieved to be engulfed by traffic.

My plan was to return to my apartment for privacy, but I was so restless with the need to know by the time I crossed the river that I found myself looking for a café that I knew had tables on upper levels, grabbing a coffee, and almost running up the stairs till I reached a quiet corner.

I checked to make sure no one was snooping, then tipped the bag upside down. Photographs rained on to the table, scores of them, and I started to sift through them one by one.

There were only a handful of photographs like those I'd seen in Central Station.

Most showed the living.

There was a shot of Strange, hand on the handle of a bookstore door, about to go in, wrapped in fur as usual. Another one of Gina coming out of her apartment. There was Paddy Nye emerging from his shop – and another of his wife, taken through the glass as she walked from the counter into the short corridor that led to their garden, unaware she was being watched. There was one of Miranda Gray, too, in the doorway of the Abbey Theatre, fastening her collar. She had a frown on her face of equal parts irritation and puzzlement. The shot was slightly blurred, a passing car had dragged the scene into indistinctness, but it was still unmistakably her.

I soon lost count.

The pictures were always of people and always taken outside. None was looking directly at the camera; they weren't posing, or if they were then the pose was deliberately indifferent to the camera. Mostly they simply seemed to have been captured in the act of waiting.

Some were glancing at their watches with impatience.

Some craned forward to scan the street.

Others talked into cellphones.

Read newspapers.

Most of the people I didn't even recognise, but some were familiar to me.

That one there, for instance, was the proprietor of a small Italian restaurant out by the sea who always forgot my name but who adored Fitzgerald and fussed over her whilst she ate. This one was a Czech émigré poet who'd recently published his autobiography describing his years of imposed silence under the communists. The woman sitting glumly outside a café, her fingers folded round a cup of something that was probably going cold, was the Dublin editor of a French fashion magazine. *He* was a journalist specialising in long-winded, unreadable exposés of corporate skulduggery and political corruption. *She* was an actress I'd seen briefly on TV.

The photographs all had two things in common.

There was only ever one shot of each subject.

And the subjects were all standing in a doorway when

they were photographed, or were shot in such a way as to be framed by the shape of a doorway in the background.

I was bewildered.

Had Felix taken these photographs? Were they in some way his artistic response to the Marxman killings? Had his obsession become so all-consuming that he was acting out in each image what the Marxman had done in reality? Taking one shot of each victim?

Or were these the Marxman's work too? Was that why Felix had been killed, if that was what had really happened? Because he'd somehow found these pictures and realised what they meant?

But that didn't explain why he hadn't gone to the police. He might have held back if he wanted to be sure first before levelling accusations, but how much more proof did he need than pictures of the Marxman's victims immediately after death? Who else could have taken them?

I felt in the corners of the bag, checking whether there were any pictures I'd missed, and – oh, what was this? Not a photograph, but a book of some kind zipped into an inside pocket.

Of course. There was a journal as well. How could I have forgotten?

I swept the photographs back into the bag in case anyone came along, and then opened the journal and started to read. It didn't take me long to realise that Felix had had an obsession not merely with the Marxman murders, but with the murder of Lucy Toner in Howth as well.

The pages of his journal were lost beneath an intense flowering of scribbled notes and press clippings, each snipped out carefully and pasted inside, and there were so many that they frequently overlapped and I had to lift the edge of one clipping to finish reading another. Felix had obviously scoured every paper and magazine at the time for any reference he could find to what had happened to Lucy, and gone on doing so, for there were more recent commemoration notices published each year on the anniversary of her death. *Lucy, always remembered, your loving brother Brendan. Lucy, always remembered, your loving sister Katie.*

Lucy, gone but not forgotten, Patricia.

Page by page, the whole sad story of Lucy Toner had been re-created.

Police have appealed for information about the disappearance of a young girl in the north of the city two days ago . . . Police in Dublin have confirmed that the body discovered in Howth last night was that of missing schoolgirl Lucy Toner, 15, who recently vanished from her home . . . A man has been remanded in custody following the murder of 15-year-old Lucy Toner . . . Sources have confirmed that the man arrested by police over the murder of a teenager in the city last week was convicted paedophile Isaac Little . . . A 37-year-old man has appeared before the Central Criminal Court accused of the murder of a Dublin schoolgirl in July of last year . . . Isaac Little is today beginning a life sentence in Mountjoy Prison in Dublin for the murder of 15-year-old Lucy Toner of Howth . . . Flowers have been left at the scene of the murder of a young girl in Dublin on the second anniversary of her death . . . Judges are today expected to reject the appeal by a man convicted five years ago of the murder of a schoolgirl . . . Convicted paedophile and murderer Isaac Little is recovering in hospital following a suicide bid in his cell at Mountjoy Prison . . .

On and on it went, relentlessly, every passing reference to Lucy's death and its aftermath isolated, recorded, cross-referenced, her real life vanishing under a blizzard of details and names, her real suffering transmuted into little more than a list of appeals for information and arrests and court appearances. How easy it is to reduce a life to little more than its constituent parts.

But why, I asked myself, had Felix been so obsessed by this child's death?

There was one possible answer. What was it Alice had said about Felix? *He said the way to understand a city was to look at how the people in it killed one another.* I wasn't sure I accepted that. Spend an hour in any city in the world and you'd hear the same horrors. The ways of murder are finite, after all. But Felix had believed it passionately. Was this journal then his raw material for that study?

Yet this was no investigation of the dark side of the city, not really, only of one small patch of darkness in its long-forgotten past. Could his interest have been sparked then because he knew, or suspected he knew, that this was not the whole story?

Because he knew who really had killed Lucy Toner?

And even say he had, what did that have to do with the Marxman?

I took out my cellphone and called Fitzgerald. She was en route now from George Dyer's house to Dublin Castle for another scheduled press conference, at which she intended releasing a photograph of Dyer's face in time for the evening TV news in the hope that someone could identify the real man. I told her about the photographs, and she whistled softly.

'If Dyer is the Marxman,' I said, 'at least this might explain why there're no pictures or mementoes in his house connecting him to the killings. Because Felix managed somehow to get hold of them. To hide them.'

'Not so fast,' said Fitzgerald. 'You haven't heard my news. Remember the sergeant this morning wanted me to look at something in the house? Well, remind me to recommend the boy for promotion, because he'd taken a closer look at Dyer's passport and noticed there was a stamp for the date of Enright's murder showing that Dyer was out of the city on business at the time.'

'That can't be right.'

'According to his passport,' Fitzgerald said bluntly, 'he was in Vienna that night. Which doesn't mean he *was* there, I know, but if he really doesn't check out for that killing—'

'Then there might still be a vacancy for the Marxman,' I finished for her. 'But why should Dyer kill himself if he didn't do it? Why try to kill Dalton? It makes no sense.'

I was remembering, though, what he'd said last night when I'd caught up with him in the derelict house and taunted him that he liked killing people. *I've killed enough of them,* he'd said. And laughed. As if this was funny because Felix was the only one he had killed.

Or because – could it be? – he wasn't a killer at all.

But why kill himself if he was innocent?

Was he covering up for someone else?

'What we need to do is track down the people in these photographs,' said Fitzgerald, sensing my renewed despondency down the line and obviously feeling I needed to be given something positive to do to stave it off. 'We need to know why pictures of them have turned up alongside the pictures of the Marxman's victims. You can help me there.'

'Whatever you want, I'll do it.'

'Then you can start by dropping the rest of the photographs off in Dublin Castle. Healy's holding the fort there. I'll give him a call and explain what you found. I'll try and get a start made on having the people identified so they can be interviewed. After that, why don't you follow up with Miranda Gray? She might be able to tell you more about whoever took those pictures.'

Only when the call ended did I realise I'd forgotten to tell her about Felix's journal too.

Absently, I opened it up again and noticed for the first time that there were two pages stuck together right at the front. I eased a nail between them and prised them apart.

Inside there was an inscription, scrawled untidily in pen and written out like a poem. I began to read it. What in Christ's name was that all about?

Chapter Forty-Four

I tried calling Miranda Gray's office, but Elaine, the incompetent secretary she'd told me about, said she was out and she didn't know when she'd be back.

I tried calling her cellphone, but it must have been switched off.

Tried Fisher but he didn't have any idea where she was either.

Eventually I called back the secretary to ask if she'd any idea where Miranda could be and was told I could always try the Forty Foot.

'The bar?'

'No, the place where people go swimming, you know?' Elaine said. 'She often goes there if she's free.'

Now she tells me.

I did know the Forty Foot. I remembered reading something about it once. It was a heap of wild rocks a couple of miles further out along the road on which Fitzgerald lived, originally known as the Gentlemen's Bathing Place but now open to all, where people went swimming in the sea all year round, risking drowning and hypothermia in the name of tradition. They even used to do it naked, Fitzgerald once told me. Takes all sorts.

I drove out there and parked by a No Parking sign. Trusting to luck on both accounts because I had no way of knowing if Miranda was actually here.

There was a gate in a wall with the words *Forty Foot* woven in wrought iron in an arch across the top, and beyond that a stony path leading down towards a rough shore where I could see a few old men towelling their hair dry, their skin wrinkled.

Near the gate was a sign: *Togs Required By Order.*

That was a relief.

I pushed open the gate and walked down the narrow path towards the rocks. To one side was a flight of rough-hewn stone steps with a yellow railing up the side where swimmers could clamber out, and where a dripping old man was now stepping gingerly back on to shore.

A wind was whipping off the sea, too cold to be quite right for summer, not quite vicious enough for winter, and there was a dullness to the water. It would rain later. Clouds were gathering like a lynch mob on Howth Head across the bay.

A few heads lifted to look at me as I approached. I was looking round with a sort of lost expression, I guess, I didn't know where to start looking. Rocks fringed the sea and people sat about talking, but I couldn't hear their words. Rather there was a heavy silence like prayer enveloping everything. Every sense was dominated by the sea.

In the end, I asked the old man I'd seen clambering out.

'I'm looking for someone. Miranda Gray?'

'I know Miranda,' he said. 'That's her out there.'

He pointed back to the sea, where I could just make out a head bobbing like a buoy, or like a seal perhaps, lifting its snout and regarding the land like it was an alien element.

Was that her?

It must have been. She was the only presence I could see in all that waste of water. I considered shouting to her that I was here, but I would have felt foolish, and anyway the wind would only have snatched my words away and dashed them against the rocks; so instead I sat down with my back to a boulder and waited and watched her.

She must have been a strong swimmer to manage out there. She seemed so far away, and sometimes the waves rose around her and she disappeared entirely from sight and I was almost convinced she'd slipped below the surface too long – and then she'd appear again.

'It's rough, isn't it?' I said to the old man, but he only chuckled.

'This isn't rough,' he said. 'A milder day you couldn't have asked for.'

Was that what he called it? Mild?

It was only a few more minutes probably before the bobbing head began to make its way back towards the shore, and soon a figure was emerging from the water in a black bathing costume, smiling, hair in a swimming cap so that she was hard to recognise, climbing out with the same faltering steps as the old man, holding on to the yellow railing.

I rose as she got nearer.

The smile vanished when she saw me.

'Saxon? What are you doing here? Is everything all right? It's not Fisher, is it?'

'Fisher?'

'Something hasn't happened to him?'

'No. No. Nothing like that.'

She tiptoed past me and reached to another rock, where her towel was waiting. Wrapped herself in it and pulled the cap off, letting her hair tumble out.

'I just wanted to talk to you,' I said. 'I have to ask you something.'

'It'll only take me a moment to get dressed,' she said.

'I'll wait outside then, shall I?' I said. 'My Jeep's there.'

'I'll be quick.'

I made my back through the iron gate to the Jeep and sat inside, keeping watch. The old man I'd spoken to came out presently, then a woman I hadn't seen down by the rocks but who must have been there since there was no other way in or out that I could see.

I waited a while longer, and still there was no sign of her.

Eventually I climbed out of the Jeep again and began to hurry back. I reached out to the gate to push it open – but before I could touch it, it jerked back, and there was Miranda.

We both jumped.

The view behind her was dark with the sea.

There'd be no more swimming today.

'I'm sorry for keeping you,' she said. 'I couldn't find my shoes, and then I spilled my purse and there were coins everywhere and I was scrambling about for them.'

'You don't have to explain.'

'Sorry. Force of habit. I always explain myself too much.'

'And apologise.'

'Yes, I always do that too much as well. Sorry.' She smiled nervously. 'You made me feel a little shaky. When you appeared. I thought something awful must have happened.'

'Being in that water would be enough to make anyone shaky,' I said.

'You get used to it,' she said. 'It's the first shock. After that, it becomes easier. Every time it's easier. I find it takes my mind off things. I've been thinking about Alice a lot.'

I nodded. I knew what she meant.

'Let's get inside,' I said.

Soon as we were seated, I asked her straight out.

'Did Felix ever take your photograph?'

'Felix? Absolutely not. I wouldn't have allowed it. I was his therapist, he was my patient. It wouldn't have been right for me to start posing for him.'

'I don't mean posing. Just a snapshot. In the street.'

'No,' but a hesitant no now. 'I'm sure I would've remembered. Why do you ask?'

'It's probably nothing. Just a dangling thread that needs to be pulled. I only want to know if anyone ever took your photograph in the doorway of the Abbey Theatre.'

'How – how did you know about that?' she said.

'I've seen the photograph. Felix had a copy.'

'Felix? That can't be right. It wasn't Felix. I had a call, it must have been over a year ago. Someone called me and told me they were doing a series of photographs of people in the city who didn't belong, who came from elsewhere, who didn't quite fit in. They were going to call it *Strangers*, they said. There was to be an exhibition. They mentioned some people I'd heard of who'd already had their photographs taken. I was flattered.'

'So you agreed to have yours taken too?'

'Not at first. The man refused to say who he was, refused to give any details. That was part of the mystery, he said. All he would say was that it would take no time at all. All I had to do was be at the Abbey Theatre, it would be one shot and that was it.'

One shot.

'Finally,' she said, 'I agreed. Maybe I shouldn't have, but I'm a bit of a camera buff myself. The idea intrigued me. So I went there at the appointed time but he never showed. I hung around for half an hour, perhaps not even that, then I left. I was annoyed about it, as you can imagine. But I had no number to call, no name, no one to complain to.'

'And you never heard from him again?'

'Not a word.' She looked confused. 'And now you're saying a picture *was* taken?'

'One shot, like you said. It was among a collection of snapshots Felix had hidden in a locker at Central Station.'

'How did Felix get it?'

'You don't think *he* could've been the photographer?'

'Absolutely not,' she said firmly. 'How could I not know Felix's voice? The accent, the inflection, everything about it was all wrong. It couldn't be.'

'Maybe he got someone to call on his behalf.'

'Why would he do that?'

'You weren't the only one,' I said. 'There were scores of similar photographs. Each person must have had the same call, inviting them to be at a particular place at a particular time, only to turn up and find no one there, not realising a picture had been taken.'

And all of them *strangers*.

People who came from outside the city.

That was what the people in the pictures had in common.

And maybe Felix was one of them? He didn't come originally from the city either. Maybe he'd been told to go to Howth lighthouse; he turned up; his photograph was taken – albeit at a much greater distance than the others, which was why I'd needed to blow up his image before he could be recognised; and then – what?

Had it been sent to him? Had the Marxman made contact with Felix after all? All along I'd assumed it was Felix who had stumbled upon the identity of the killer, but maybe it was the Marxman who had chosen Felix, picked him for some role.

'Well,' I said, 'either Felix took the picture of you or he knew who did. That's why it's so important if you can remember anything about the man who called you.'

'I'm sorry. He wouldn't give me his name,' Miranda said. 'I know, it sounds stupid going along to a meeting with someone you don't know, but at the time the idea connected with something inside me. I've never felt I really belonged here. I liked the idea of being one of those strangers. Maybe you think it was silly of me to go.'

'I went out myself to meet Felix at Howth,' I pointed out. 'I have no right to be lecturing you about what you should or shouldn't have done.'

'I only wish I could help.'

'Think about it later when you get home, yeah?' I said.

'I won't be able to think about anything else.'

Chapter Forty-Five

'There was a man here looking for you,' said Hugh the doorman when I got back home.

'He leave a name?'

'No.'

'A number?'

'No.'

'A message?'

'No.'

Hugh was a man of few words.

Most of them unintelligible.

'He leave any lasting impression on you whatsoever?'

Hugh considered the question.

'He had a beard,' came the answer.

'We're getting somewhere,' I said encouragingly. 'Stay close by me now, Hugh. and I think together we can pull through this one. Tell me. Was the beard kind of short and all salt-and-peppered with grey?'

Hugh looked impressed with my clairvoyancy skills.

'It was.'

'And did the bearded one have a waistline that made him look in some lights like he was one of our larger planets which had fallen tragically down from space and ended up wandering the streets of Dublin looking for a new orbit?'

That was probably too many words for Hugh to take in all at once, but he worked his way through them one by one, chewing them over carefully like a mouse that had picked up too large a portion of cheese but knew its teeth could get through it given time.

'I didn't think he was *that* fat,' he said eventually.

'I do.'

It had to be Fisher.

I called him from the lobby, and it turned out he was in Brown Thomas, a big old-fashioned department store in Grafton Street on the other side of St Stephen's Green.

So as it was, I didn't get to go up to my apartment anyway.

'I was looking for something to bring back for Laura and the children,' he said when I caught up with him on the fourth floor.

'You going back to London?'

'Soon,' he said. 'I can't hang around Dublin for ever.'

'I'll miss you,' I said, and I meant it. 'But you know, you'll not find anything for Laura and the kids here,' I pointed out. 'This is the menswear department.'

'I know that,' said Fisher. 'I'm also looking for some new shirts. I'm running low. I didn't expect to be here as long as I have. I could really do with some clean underwear too.'

'Spare me the details.'

I ended up walking round the racks with him, picking clothes. Taking them off the hangers, making him stand in front of mirrors so he could see what he looked like with them up against him. Fitzgerald would have been astonished. Shopping had never been my thing. As long as I could find something that fitted and kept me warm, I was happy.

One pair of jeans was much like another, after all.

Though the peculiar thing was that choosing for Fisher was making me more fussy. I found myself irritably replacing shirts he'd picked out with a terse: 'Not your colour.'

What was happening to me? I was turning into a girl.

On the way to the counter, Fisher filled me in on what progress had been made in the last few hours. The murder squad, it seemed, had been able to identify over half the people in the snapshots and managed to speak to about half again of that number.

They all told the same story as Miranda Gray.

A man had called inviting them to be at a particular place at a particular time to have their photograph taken as part of a series of pictures to be entitled *Strangers*. All had made their way to the named location, only to find that the caller never showed. Each had been irritated, perplexed, but none had a clue who the mysterious caller had been.

And none had ever heard from him again.

Could it really have been George Dyer?

'There's certainly a similar type of thinking going on there,' said Fisher. 'Whoever took those photographs wanted to *shoot* the subjects as a trophy. Shoot them on film, in his case, but the methodology and language are uncomfortably close. He wanted to capture these people so that they became part of some collection. He was thinking like the Marxman. One shot per victim. It can't be a coincidence.'

'Shooting someone with a camera's a bit different from shooting them with a Glock .36.'

'Give me some credit,' said Fisher. 'All I mean is that you take something from someone when you take their photograph. They're in your power in some indefinable way. They're at your mercy. Even the American photographer Diane Arbus said once that it hurts a little to be photographed.'

I thought of the people in the snapshots in Felix's locker.

How vulnerable they'd looked.

The photographer *had* taken something from them, even if it was only their peace of mind for an hour. And then he had the record of their discomfort in his possession eternally.

To gloat over.

To enjoy.

Just as he must've gloated over the pictures of the other victims after they died.

'The only problem,' I pointed out, 'is that Dyer didn't

even have a camera. Didn't have one that we could find, at any rate. So if he didn't take the pictures, who did?' I felt frustrated, annoyed with myself. 'If only Dyer hadn't killed himself,' I said.

'It wouldn't have mattered,' Fisher said. 'He wouldn't have talked. Killing himself was a way of imposing silence on himself, but even if he had been arrested he would have embraced silence anyway. I've seen it often enough. Some perpetrators come in and can't wait to spill the beans; it's getting them to shut up that's the problem. Others never say a word about what they've done. I think Dyer would undoubtedly have been in the second category. Cutting his own throat was the ultimate proof of that. Maybe that's why he chose the name Dyer for himself. Dying was always going to be his final vocation.'

'Isn't it everyone's?' I said.

We paid up and I offered to make him dinner, because it was getting dark now and the stores were closing, and still he hadn't managed to buy any gifts for his children or Laura.

'I'll look again tomorrow,' he said as we walked round to my apartment. 'You should come with me. I see now you have a talent for shopping that you've never properly tapped.'

'Count me out. I've done enough shopping to last a lifetime.'

'Saxon! Fisher!'

'Fitzgerald?'

Her Rover had pulled up alongside the kerb suddenly and the window wound down.

'What's wrong?' said Fisher.

'Gina Fox is dead,' she said. 'Get in.'

She was pulling back into the line of cars before I'd even managed to put on a seatbelt. She was hunched forward on the wheel, willing the traffic to disappear.

'She was found about twenty minutes ago,' she explained in a rush. 'It's not clear how long she's been dead. I got a call from Walsh. He's down at the scene. He says whoever killed her must have fired about a dozen shots into her head from point-blank range. Blown most of her face away, according to him.'

'Where is the scene?'

'Strange's gallery. She was lying behind his desk, and the killer had taken another snapshot of her body and pinned it to the inside of the glass in the door. Someone passing noticed the snapshot pinned up, went closer to take a look, realised what it showed and called the police.'

'I'm not with you,' said Fisher. 'If this woman was killed in Temple Bar, aren't we heading in the wrong direction?'

'I'm not going to the crime scene. I'm going to Strange's house. Gina must have trusted the killer enough to go into the gallery alone with him. It wasn't even broken into. The killer locked up after he left. Where would he have got the key?'

'Are you saying you think Strange killed her?'

'I'm saying I don't believe he knows as little about all this as he lets on,' said Fitzgerald. 'We only have his word that he didn't look at the photographs in the locker. I want to talk to him now before he has the chance to weave himself a neat story.'

Strange lived in a huge house on a private road overlooking the sea in the shadow of Dalkey Hill, set well back behind huge gates and ivy-hung walls.

By the time we got out there it was fully dark, and yet, no, not fully because there was something peculiar about the sky as we turned off into his road.

Something still bright, like a comet.

It took me a moment to realise what it was.

A fire engine stood parked at the entrance, and figures in uniform and wearing oxygen masks were running in and out. Through the gate, I could see flames.

The dark was vivid with colours.

Fitzgerald pulled to a halt and leapt out. The firefighters at the gate tried to stop her, but she waved her badge at them and they stepped back to let her through, directing her as she requested to the senior officer, who was up close to the fire.

Fisher and I trailed behind her, forgotten in the madness and noise.

It looked almost as if the trees that lined the driveway up to the house were on fire too, but it was only an optical illusion caused by the fierce glow from the flames behind and the powerful arc lights which had been set up and directed towards the house to allow the firefighters to work. The air was rancid with black smoke that curled through the lights like drifting rags. It felt like it could peel skin from the eyes.

The house itself was huge, Gothic, with a turret growing up one side like a petrified tree. The windows all along this side of the house had been punched out by the great pressure within as the flames sucked dry all the air and the fire had nowhere else to go. Inside was a vision of warfare almost, drapes hanging on to rails only by fingers of flame. There was the noise of small explosions deep and distant inside the shell that remained, and the flames roared out erratically at anyone who tried to approach, like the fire was reminding them who was boss. Water was arcing from hoses into the shattered building and glistening almost prettily with the light shining through it; but it was obvious now that it was too late.

I could taste the flames in my throat.

Chapter Forty-Six

'That's where they found the body,' said Fitzgerald, and she pointed at the hearth.

Morning again, and the sky was drizzle.

We were standing in what had once been Vincent Strange's house and which was now a blackened, defeated, twisted husk. The stench of smoke was so powerful it was hard to believe the rain would ever wash it out of the air, that it would ever go away.

We were standing in what had once been the sitting room. There was a harsh crunch of glass and ash underfoot as firefighters came and went around us. The walls were thick with what looked like tar. The fire had exposed electric cables that now hung loose, bent into impossible shapes like snakes in the throes of agony. To one side a wall had vanished entirely, collapsing outwards so that, seen from the outside, it looked as though some great creature had bitten off the whole side of the house. The trees seemed to be crouching down to look inside at the destruction. The rain found a way in maliciously. Puddles of black water were pockmarked where the drizzle met the leftover water from last night's hoses. The chairs were skeletons. I could still sense the flames around me, though it was hours since they'd been extinguished.

Fitzgerald handed me a picture.

More photographs to look at.

It showed a fireplace and a hearth of sandstone with a high arched mirror above it. I could see what remained of it in front of me, shattered and buckled and fused to the wall by the searing heat. In the picture, Strange stood beside the fireplace, smiling.

'Where'd you get this?'

'It was taken by a photographer for one of those magazines where the rich and famous parade their houses for the pornographic delight of the masses. Strange's house was an eight-page spread last July. There's a whole series of them.'

She handed them to me one by one.

Here was the hall, with a great oaken staircase curling upwards.

Gone.

The kitchen laid with tiles, so she told me, from a twelfth-century abbey in Italy.

Not any more.

There was even one of Strange lying on his four-poster bed, wearing his fur coat.

And the walls everywhere were covered with paintings.

'They were said to be worth thousands,' she said.

Well, he did say he had a certain lifestyle to maintain.

'Did any survive?'

'Not that I know of. Saving them wasn't exactly a priority.'

'What will happen to the house now?' I said.

'There's nothing to save. The whole structure is unsound, according to the fire investigators who came round this morning. It will probably be knocked down and apartments built in its place. This is prime real estate territory. In fact, last night's fire is probably what property developers would call a result.'

'Do you know yet what happened to Strange?'

'By the time the fire was put out, there wasn't much left of him. I saw him at the mortuary. He looked like a piece of burnt meat. His face was like one of those things conkers come out of, what do you call them? Horse chestnuts. The lips were peeled back where the skin had blistered and split. It almost looked as if he was grinning. He was unrecognisable

351

really apart from a few pieces of jewellery. We're sending samples to London for DNA testing. We don't have the facilities here. The first firefighters on the scene thought he must've been overcome with fumes, slumped forward and died where he fell.'

Until the chief fire investigation team arrived. It had not taken them long to establish how the fire had started. The seat of the blaze was Strange's body itself. It had been doused in petrol and set alight. More petrol had been splashed through the hall, up the stairs, in every room, and the alarms deliberately disabled.

It was little wonder the entire house had gone up as fast as it had.

Suffice to say this was no accident.

As was confirmed when the City Pathologist carried out the autopsy on the few fragments that remained of Strange's body and found no evidence of any soot deposits in the airways, as would have been expected had he been alive during the blaze.

Suspicion was further pricked by the evidence of ante-mortem wounds to the skin around the skull. Butler surmised there was a strong possibility that the gallery owner had been struck by a sharp object, a poker perhaps, but as always he was hedging his bets.

The skin of fire victims could often split due to tissue contraction anyway, or sometimes because of the movement of the body during removal from the scene.

'Was he dead already when he was set alight?'

'Let's hope so,' Fitzgerald said grimly.

Thankfully, there'd been no one else in the house at the time of the fire. Strange had had a housekeeper, Amy, but she'd left hours before the blaze broke out.

'She's the one who owns the Citroën out front. Did you see it?' Fitzgerald asked me. 'She was here yesterday when Strange returned from town early in the afternoon. He must have shut the gallery shortly after talking to you. He went straight to his study, she says, and didn't come down until teatime. She'd made him something to eat. She sat with him while he ate, they had a glass of wine together, then he told her to go. She took a taxi back to town.'

'Why not take the car?'

'There was some problem with the engine. Strange had promised to look at it.'

'Strange was a mechanic?'

'You wouldn't know it to look at him,' she admitted. 'But he had a big interest in cars as well as guns. Vintage cars mainly. He'd a whole collection of them out back. About twenty in all. There's a stable block converted into a garage. Two Rolls Royces. An Alfa Romeo. He spent a lot of time tinkering with them, apparently. Couple of motorcycles too.'

'So he sent the servant away?' I said. 'Did he tell her why?'

'According to her, he was expecting a visitor.'

'Male? Female?'

'She didn't ask and he didn't say. But I hear it was well known that Strange swung both ways, so it could've been either. She said it happened all the time, her being bundled away when he had visitors. Special visitors. She didn't really want to talk about it.'

'Touchy subject?'

'You know what these old retainers are like. She's been with Strange for twenty years. Probably didn't like him having *special* visitors, if you know what I mean.'

'She must be upset.'

'Inconsolable would be nearer the mark.'

'Does she have any idea who might have killed him?'

'According to her, Strange didn't have an enemy in the world, though I'm not sure she knew that much about his life outside the house.'

'No one saw this special visitor arriving then?'

'No.'

'Which means you can't even confirm there *was* a visitor,' I said. 'An expected visitor, anyway, because someone

353

obviously turned up. Maybe Strange just told the housekeeper he was expecting a caller to get rid of her and free up his evening.'

'Precisely.' Fitzgerald stubbed her toe impatiently against a heap of ashes. 'I can't get my head around it at all. Strange is dead. Gina Fox is dead. The only one who knows anything about *her* is Boland, and he called through this morning to give in his notice and I haven't been able to reach him since for love nor money. I think he may have gone away for a few days with that new woman of his.'

'He's quit already? He told me he was thinking about it.'

'I haven't even had time to get down to the mortuary to talk to Butler about the gun that killed Gina. I spoke to him briefly on the telephone and he says it was some old piece like the one Felix Berg got from Strange, so did it come from here? It must have done. And to make matters worse, I'm supposed to be down at the hospital right this minute dropping in on Dalton and meeting his mother and various siblings to reassure them that their beloved was not stabbed in vain.'

'Dalton has a family? I didn't realise there was a danger of his DNA spreading. Do they drag their knuckles along the ground when they walk too?'

'Why don't you head over there and find out for yourself?'

'I think I'll give it a miss,' I said. 'I doubt Dalton would want to see me. He'd probably just take it as an excuse to start giving me aggravation again. And I certainly don't want to start getting it from his family too. They probably blame me for what happened.'

'You don't need to worry about them. I don't think they have any illusions about him being some kind of saint. Besides which, I think he's almost feeling humbled. He knows he'll get a bit of a carpeting over what he did the other night. Turns out that when he was hiding behind the Dumpster waiting for our friend to turn up, he issued fresh orders to the back-up team to stay well back so that he could have the glory of capturing the Marxman all to himself, and that's why they didn't manage to get there in time to catch him before he ran.'

'So it's safe to say Draker isn't in a great mood?'

'What do you think?' said Fitzgerald. 'This hasn't exactly helped,' she added, sweeping her arm round to include the burnt-out building. 'He's been going round shrieking about the whole thing like some old woman. Wants to know exactly what happened. Wants reports on his desk in five minutes or there'll be trouble. Every i dotted and t crossed, and the other way round as well. He's just pissed off. He thought the Marxman case had been closed down, and then this happens. He's wondering what next. He wants answers.'

'This is a worrying development, him learning proper policing.'

'I wouldn't go that far. Strange was a friend of his, that's all. He didn't mind signing off on the Marxman case and ordering drinks all round at the golf club with the Commissioner. But now Strange is dead, it's different. It's the old cliché: This time it's personal. Strange was one of the gang. He wants blood.'

'Mine, probably.'

'I wouldn't be at all surprised,' she said, and I almost laughed grimly in that dark, burnt-out place before seeing that she was serious.

'Christ, what's my motive for killing him meant to be?'

'Draker hates you. That's all the motive he needs. He also hasn't forgotten that Strange threatened to take out a restraining order on you when you were harassing him.'

'Not that one again. I already said I wasn't hara—'

'Also,' she held up a finger to stop me before I got started, 'he's already told Healy – in the strictest confidence, which was why Healy came straight over to tell me – that you could easily have got from the Forty Foot to Strange's house in time to set the fire.'

'How does he know I was at the Forty Foot?'

She shrugged.

'You must have been seen. It's a public place.'

'OK, but when the fire was lit, I was shopping for shirts with Fisher. You were the one who picked us up in town.'

'You looking for an alibi?'

'Might well be, if Draker has his way.'

'Then we'll negotiate when the time comes. But be warned, I strike a hard bargain.'

'Very funny.'

We walked back into what remained of the hall of Strange's house, and saw through the crippled doorway Sean Healy and Patrick Walsh standing talking to the chief fire investigator. They must have been asking where Fitzgerald was, because he raised a hand and pointed back towards the burned-out house.

Healy quickened his step when he saw us coming out.

'What have you got?' said Fitzgerald as he got near.

'A number of possible IDs came in this morning for George Dyer,' he said. 'Seven reckon it's their husband, despite the fact none of said husbands appear to be dead which makes it highly unlikely that any of them are our man. One reckons it's the US President. One claims it's the woman who comes to do her gardening. Figure that one out. But three say – are you ready? – that the man in the photo is definitely one Brendan George Toner, formerly of Howth.'

'Lucy Toner's brother,' I said.

'Is that the girl who was murdered all those years ago?' said Fitzgerald.

'When Felix and Alice lived in the house around the corner, the very same,' I said. 'Boland tried to track down the family, but he didn't have any luck. The parents were both dead, the sister was in care, the brother had dropped off the map, was how he put it.'

'Well, he seems to have reappeared on it now.'

An image came to mind of the faded photograph in the house of the man we'd thought of as George Dyer. The woman with the letters ONE above her head. That must have been the sign on the Toners' store on the sea front at Howth. It must have been his mother.

'That's all I need,' said Fitzgerald. 'Another complication.'

'Who did the IDs come in from?' I asked.

Healy consulted his notebook.

'One from a man who used to live in the same street as Toner and said he'd recognise him anywhere. An old woman who said she remembered going once a week into the shop the Toners ran down by the harbour, and what a pleasant, well-mannered boy Brendan was.'

'He certainly changed.'

'You can say that again. And the third,' said Healy, 'is from a woman who claims she used to go out with him.'

'That sounds more promising,' said Fitzgerald. 'If I need to find out about someone, I'd rather talk every time to the woman who used to sleep with him than the one who only used to go once a week into the shop where he worked twenty years ago.'

'Well, I don't know if she used to sleep with him exactly,' said Healy. 'They weren't much more than kids, by all accounts.'

'Since when did that ever stop anyone?' said Walsh.

'What's her name?' I said.

'Nye,' said Healy.

'Nye?'

He consulted his notebook again.

'Nye, yeah. Tricia. You know her?'

'We've exchanged scowls, put it that way. If it's the same one, and I'm guessing it must be. Nye isn't the commonest name on the planet. She's married to Paddy Nye, who used to share a house with Felix before they fell out. Paddy was the one who provided Felix with an alibi for the time of Lucy's murder. He even went out with Alice for a time.'

'Small world. This Tricia didn't seem to go out with Toner for very long, though. He wasn't more than eighteen when they split up, he moved away, and she never heard from him again until his face appears on the front page of the morning newspapers as the Marxman.'

'I think I need to go out to Howth and talk to her,' said Fitzgerald.

Chapter Forty-Seven

Burke wasn't in the store. There was a Closed sign behind the glass. Hare lifted his head nonchalantly when I rapped on the window, and blinked at me. But since I was no use to him out here, he quickly laid his chin back on his paws and went to sleep.

Or pretended to.

I envied him.

A single lamp burned on the desk, a sickly pool of light at its base.

I took a walk down to the river, thinking about nothing, which I generally find is the best thing to think about when I'm feeling low, but unable to stop the image of Strange's burned-out house swimming into my mind's eye. George Dyer had died and Strange had given me the photographs and now he was dead too. It was too much of a coincidence to believe that the three events were unrelated. But *how* they were related was another matter.

When I retraced my steps to Burke's store, the Closed sign was still there and the door was still locked, though it was only early afternoon, but another light had come on now in the back room and the cat had shifted from its sleeping place.

I rapped loudly on the glass again, and again, and the light went out, and Burke appeared in the doorway leading through to the back room.

He had a book open in his hands, and the cat trailing round his ankles, and his head was bent down to read and he didn't look up until I knocked again harder than ever – and then I saw that he was wearing headphones because he pulled them back and let them fall around his throat and smiled and came to the door to unlock it.

'I thought you were ignoring me,' I said.

'And lose my best customer?' said Burke, and he went over and laid the book face down on the desk, where I saw the title staring back up at me in the pale light: *Friedrich Engel's Essential Writings on Politics and Economics*.

Burke caught me looking at it.

'I'll lend it to you when I've finished, if you want.'

'That's OK. I'll just wait till the movie comes out,' I said, and I sat down heavily in the usual chair, only realising as I did so how much I ached, whilst that damn cat hopped up and started making itself at home with my person.

Burke pulled off his headphones and laid the Walkman on the desk next to the book.

'What can I do for you?' he said.

'Am I that easy to read?'

'Easier than Engels, that's for sure,' he said. 'I can always tell by the way you sit down whether you're here for coffee or whiskey or something harder to supply. What is it?'

I told him Strange was dead.

That Strange had been murdered.

I told him about the photographs.

I told him about the *Strangers* series, and all the while he didn't say a word in reply. Didn't even wonder aloud why he hadn't had an invitation to have his photograph taken too. He did that sometimes. Just listened whilst I ran on complaining like an overflowing bath, not spoiling things by interrupting or offering unwanted solutions to problems like I tended to do.

Finally I told him how Paddy Nye's wife had recognised the photo of Dyer . . . Toner . . . whatever he chose to call himself.

'Now ain't that a coincidence,' he said.

360

Which was how I knew, if he was interrupting me, that it must be important.

I watched him as he got up and walked back behind his desk.

'You have something?' I said.

'I made it my business to have something,' he said, 'since you mocked my ignorance about the subject last time you came in.'

'I don't even remember talking about Nye's wife.'

'We didn't,' said Burke. 'We were talking about the book on the Ireland's Eye murder.'

'And what's she got to do with it?'

'She wrote it.'

I was about to object when I realised what a simple mistake I must've made.

P.F. Nye.

And Nye's wife was called Tricia. Short for Patricia. Why had I assumed the P stood for Paddy? It was just as likely to have stood for her name.

'She's quite a well-known local historian,' Burke said. 'That's how she got it together with Nye. They shared a mutual interest in the island.'

'Who told you all this?'

'She did,' he said.

'You went out there?'

'Thought it might be worth a journey.'

'You obviously got on better with her than I did. I got the full forty degrees below zero treatment. Got the impression she wouldn't spit on me if I was on fire.'

And then I cringed inwardly as I realised what I'd said.

Bad analogy.

Burke had the decency not to point it out.

'How did you get her to talk?' I started again.

'Some people have it, some people don't. You don't because you're too prickly. Too quick to start a fight. I prefer the smooth approach. So I appealed to her vanity. Said I'd read her book and admired it hugely. That usually does the trick. Soon she was singing like the proverbial canary. I'm quite an expert on old Howth murders now. Reckon I might write a book about them myself.'

'But did you learn anything *useful*?'

'Knowledge is useful for its own sake,' Burke said. 'Did they never teach you that in school? However, if you insist on taking a strictly materialistic approach to the subject of wisdom, then yes, I guess I did. I learned, for one thing, that Tricia Peel, who's now Nye, used to play together with Lucy Toner when they were kids, and that Felix and Brendan were like blood brothers, never out of each other's company. And I also learned for another thing that she's always believed it was Felix Berg who killed her friend. I think maybe that's where she got her interest in long-forgotten miscarriages of justice. Now why aren't you looking as surprised as I expected you to be? You hear what I'm saying?'

I heard.

But it wasn't what I was hearing that kept me silent, it was what I was seeing. I was seeing again what I'd read yesterday in Felix's journal.

Why hadn't I brought it with me?

'Do you remember what it was about?' said Burke when I explained what was bugging me.

'There was something about a corpse being planted in a garden,' I said, 'and whether it was blooming or not blooming, and then something else about the frost disturbing it. Or maybe it was a dog. I dunno. It just sounded like garbage to me.'

'It's people like you give Americans a bad name. That garbage just happens to come from one of the greatest poems of the twentieth century.'

'Says who?'

'Says everyone.'

'Well, you know my brain isn't wired for poetry. You going to tell me what it is?'

'I'll do better than that. I'll show you. Wait here.'

He switched on the light in the back room again, and his voice drifted back like an echo as he read aloud through the names on the spines of the books, until—

'Here.'

And his shadow was returning and handing me a thin book that looked less substantial than a leaf in his huge hands.

The Selected Poems of T.S. Eliot.

'Those words you half remembered sound to me like they come from *The Waste Land*. I told you to go read it.' He opened it flat and pointed triumphantly to a page. 'There, I was right. Part One, *The Burial of the Dead*, line seventy onwards.'

I read where his finger pointed and recognised at once the words from Felix's journal.

And a few lines further up there were more words that I recognised. Felix hadn't just got the title of his own book, *Unreal City*, from any part of *The Waste Land*, but from this very same section, with its forgotten corpses buried and disturbed in gardens.

And all of a sudden I felt so cold it was almost like it was winter again.

Chapter Forty-Eight

Fitzgerald wasn't impressed by my theory, to say the least.

'You think Felix Berg killed Lucy Toner?'

'Don't jump down my throat,' I said. 'Just hear me out.'

She took a drink and replaced it deliberately.

It was coming on for late afternoon. We were sitting in a bar, catching up. A jukebox was playing too loud, but for once I was glad of it. It meant we wouldn't be overheard.

Telling Fitzgerald was bad enough without an audience as well.

'That's what the quote meant at the start of his journal,' I said. 'All the stuff about a corpse being planted in the garden, about it being disturbed. Lucy's was the corpse that was planted in the garden. Hers was the body whose rest was disturbed. What else could Felix have been talking about? Why else would he fill his journal with those press clippings? What were they for except to feed his appetite to relive what he'd done? Why else would he call his book *Unreal City*?'

'Because Eliot borrowed it from Baudelaire and Baudelaire's line about ghosts in daylight clutching at passers-by fitted what he was trying to show in his work—'

'That's only what we were meant to think,' I said. 'Doesn't it make more sense to see the title of the book in the context of an ongoing pattern of confession? He told Vincent Strange he used to live in a house with a murderer. Paddy Nye says Felix constantly said one of them was a murderer. He even visited Isaac Little in prison and told him he believed he was

364

innocent. I don't know what his reason for doing all that was, whether he was tortured with guilt for what he'd done or simply liked playing with people's minds, playing with fire, risking exposure; but you can't deny that he *did* it.'

'Fisher says artists don't become killers,' said Fitzgerald firmly.

'No he didn't. He said there hadn't been many examples of artists becoming killers, but he accepts they're as likely to become killers in the right circumstances as anyone.'

'Let's say Felix did kill Lucy Toner,' she said. 'I saw the report on her murder. I saw what was done to her. The soil in the mouth. The rape. You're not saying that Felix Berg did that and then just got up, dusted himself down and got on with leading a normal life as if it had never happened? Because as a generality, men who rape fifteen-year-old girls and fill their mouths with soil until they choke don't tend to be able to hide what they are for ever.'

'Of course I'm not saying that.'

'Then where did it go in Felix Berg?'

'I think he was able to sublimate those urges into his work. Into his pictures. Remember how the introduction to his book said his early work was considered violent, highly erotic, some even said semi-pornographic? I think he knew what they revealed about him, which was why he tried in later years to buy back his earlier work. They were like a pane of glass stretched across his skull. Anyone looking at them could have seen right into his mind. He didn't want them to know what was in there. I don't believe artists who produce those sorts of extreme images are just exploring *issues* to do with sex and violence in contemporary culture, like they claim. I think they produce them because, to put it simply, they get off on them, because they make some dark place deep inside them sing.'

'I'm with you all the way on that,' said Fitzgerald. 'But surely Felix had stopped producing those violent pictures?'

'No, he hadn't. He was still taking sado-masochistic

photographs. He took the ones that were hanging in Strange's gallery. I saw them. I saw how disturbing they were. And even in his mainstream work, you heard what Fisher said. How it was detached from normal human feeling. Dissociative. Even Strange talked about the rage in Felix's work. He was like a drug addict getting methadone, a killer by instinct and appetite making do with a substitute, and in his case the substitute was the imagination. Killers often use sick, violent pornography as a kind of self-medication. Felix was producing his own supply.'

'Killers do often consume other people's images of cruelty and pain when they can't make their own,' acknowledged Fitzgerald, 'but it never serves to dampen those feelings down. It only fuels the fantasies. Why would Felix Berg have been any different? It's too risky a strategy. By flirting with those urges, wouldn't he just risk accentuating them, taking them to a point where he couldn't control them any more? If you're right about Lucy, and I'm not saying you are, then he'd already killed once. He'd know he had it in him to do terrible things. Wasn't he risking being drawn to killing a second time?'

'Maybe that's what he secretly wanted,' I said. 'Maybe he wanted to fuel his fantasies whilst pretending to himself that he was controlling them, so that when they did spill over he could tell himself he'd tried his best, it wasn't his fault, he'd been unable to stop, he'd done everything he could. Or maybe the urges were so strong that he was forced to try *any* method of controlling them or they would've taken over his life.'

'But they didn't spill over, did they?'

'Didn't they?'

'I don't know,' she said, looking confused. 'That's what I'm asking you, isn't it? You're the one with all the theories.'

'They're not theories,' I said.

'If they're not just theories, where's the proof?'

'About a year ago, Felix was out working on the streets,

middle of the night, when he was knocked on the head and left for dead.'

'It was in the obits. I remember.'

'Where he was hit,' I said, 'is the most vulnerable part of the head. The skull's thin, there's no protective fluid keeping the brain safe from harm. I spoke to Felix's doctor earlier this afternoon and he confirmed that Felix sustained significant damage to the temporal lobe region of his brain. Not enough to stop him carrying on a normal life, but enough to mean he'd have serious problems afterwards with self-control. In anyone this would be a problem; in someone like Felix with what you can only call an extreme, violent sexual fantasy life, it could be disastrous. Violent people, people who kill repeatedly, have often been found to have sustained damage to the very part of the brain where Felix was injured.'

'Just because he took a blow to the head doesn't make him a killer,' Fitzgerald said. 'Or do you want me to go and arrest everyone who went to hospital in the past five years with a sore head on suspicion of being a potential murderer?'

'I'm not talking about *everyone*, I'm talking about Felix. His doctor told me Felix suffered blinding headaches following his attack. He had black-outs, periods where he didn't know where or who he was. This was rather more than the breakdown Alice said he suffered. He was raving. Threatening suicide. Attacking her even. That's why she and Strange decided that the best thing to do would be to take him away to the States for treatment at some private clinic the doctor recommended. That's where they spent last summer. But—'

'How did I know there was going to be a but?'

'It didn't work out quite the way they expected. He was leaving the clinic for no reason, going drinking. Next thing Alice discovered he'd been visiting a gun club. You remember he told Miranda the same thing? And now it turns out that even the patrons of the club thought he was a bit odd, erratic, talking to himself, shooting wildly.'

'How do you know all this?'

'I got Burke to call the county sheriff and spin him a line. He's good at that. He gets people to talk who haven't even talked to themselves for years. They talk without knowing they're talking. Seems Felix had become something of a local legend over there. It didn't take much persuasion to have them recounting all their stories about him.'

'So Alice and Strange brought him back home?'

'Yeah, and she said he was doing well, that he was on new medication, that it was working; but shortly after he returned people started dying. The Marxman was in business.'

'I still don't see what your point is. Felix killed Lucy Toner? OK, if you say so. He took a bump on the head and turned into a one-man version of *Wacky Races*? I'll buy that too. I always told you he was probably screwy, which is precisely why you shouldn't have got involved. But why's it so urgent all of a sudden that we have to sit here and discuss it when the whole world seems to be falling apart around us? Felix is dead.'

This was the difficult part.

The part I'd been dreading.

The part I'd been building up to all along.

'What,' I said, 'if he isn't?'

'Isn't dead?'

It was like I'd told her I was an extraterrestrial.

'I didn't see his face that night at the harbour,' I insisted before she could start objecting. 'It could have been anyone. Does Butler know what Felix looked like? How could anyone say that the man hauled out of the water that night was Felix Berg? Half his face must have been blown away by the gunshot wound through the eye.'

'But why would he *want* to pretend to be dead?'

'Because he needed to disappear.'

'Why?'

'Here goes.'

Deep breath.

'Because Felix Berg is the Marxman.'

The howl of the jukebox filled the long silence from Fitzgerald that followed.

'Saxon,' she said at last, 'I really think you've flipped this time.'

'Why is that so unbelievable? He killed Lucy Toner. He'd been behaving erratically, violently before he went to the States. He visited gun clubs whilst he was there. The start of the Marxman killings coincided with his return to Dublin. Maybe Gina's even right about the Tarot, I don't know. He did introduce her to the cards, and there are even references to it in *The Waste Land*.'

'You were the one who said the Tarot was nonsense.'

'It *is* nonsense, but if it's a nonsense that Felix believed in then maybe we need to look at it again. Think about it. We have the testimony of his sister that Felix was obsessed by the killings. He had the pictures of some of the crime scenes on the wall of his latest exhibition. He even told Miranda Gray straight up that he was the Marxman.'

I was trying to batter down potential objections with words, and it was working. Fitzgerald still wasn't convinced, but she wasn't putting up a fight.

'But Alice identified the body in the water as her brother,' she said simply.

'I know. The only thing I can think is that she must have been in on it.'

'Why would she do that?'

'Because he asked her to, because she loved him, she wanted to protect him, because she suspected she was having his baby. Who knows? Besides, she had those drippy bleeding-heart notions about redemption and second chances. Whatever he's done, she probably thought, Felix is a good person. He will get better. All he needs is time and treatment and the love of a good sister.'

'Even if more people die in the meantime?'

'Even if that. Because that's not his fault, remember? He's sick, he's ill, he's a tortured genius, he took a knock on his

369

head and it played havoc with his hypothalamus. There are no end of excuses to find once you start looking for them. But at the back of it all is the real reason, which is simply that she needed Felix, she was imperfect and incomplete without him. She said once that they were really two parts of the one person.'

'So you're saying she did what?'

'She agreed to identify the body found at Howth as Felix's. Felix would arrange for me to be there, and when I saw a body in the water I would instantly assume it was him because of his call to me. I would tell the police when they arrived that it was Felix Berg, and they would go and fetch Alice. No one was going to question the word of a grieving sister. Felix would be free to go into hiding, maybe go abroad, where she could join him later when the fuss had died down. Only he had other plans. He wasn't going to stop being the Marxman, he liked it too much. Plus maybe he never had the slightest intention of being with Alice again. Maybe that's why she killed herself. When she realised. Anything rather than be without him.'

'It's a brilliant theory, I'll give you that,' Fitzgerald said, 'but if the plan was to make the world think Felix was dead, why did Alice keep pressing you to investigate his death? We were happy to put it down as a suicide. If that's what they wanted, like you say, why would she take the risk of you uncovering the truth?'

'For the same reason Felix called his book *Unreal City*.'

'You're saying she had an urge to confess too? To play with fire?'

'Why not?'

'Why not? Because there are too many loose ends, that's why not. Such as, if it wasn't Felix who died that night, who was it? Such as, how did they manage to make a murder at the harbour, if that's what it was, look like suicide? Such as, why is it that when Miranda Gray investigated Felix's activities, she discovered he'd been out of the city at the time of the first murder?'

370

'*How* did Miranda know he was out of the country? Because Alice told her, remember?'

'You still haven't explained how all this connects to Brendan Toner. If Felix Berg was the Marxman, why did Toner confess? Why would he be willing to kill himself and cover up for a man who you say murdered his sister? Just because they were thick as thieves when they were children doesn't mean he'd conceal something like that.'

'I'm not saying I have all the answers,' I said. 'All I'm saying is that there are questions that need looking into further. Like the break-in at the mortuary the night Mark Brook was shot. You said you thought it was just kids looking for drugs, but even addicts aren't fried enough to think there'd be drugs in the filing cabinet of the City Pathologist. What if it was Felix looking for his own autopsy report so that he could destroy it, just in case suspicion ever arose about his supposed death?'

'Stop!' she said. 'Just stop, please. I can't get my head around this. I can't . . . I can't believe . . . I don't even know what you want me to *do*.'

'Get an exhumation order, like I asked before,' I said. 'Have the body in Felix's grave tested to see if it's him. That way, the matter will be cleared up immediately. It's not like Felix has any troublesome relatives who'll kick up a stink about it.'

'How am I supposed to get an exhumation order? I can't just start ordering a judge to let me dig up bodies all over the city on the say-so of some lunatic American.'

'First get the autopsy X-rays from Butler. Like I say, Felix was knocked on the head pretty badly and suffered severe damage to his skull. If the fracture doesn't show on the X-rays Butler took at the time of the autopsy, then an exhumation order should be simple.'

'OK. I'll do it.' She put down her drink. 'I'll call Walsh and send him over there. I'm not saying I believe you. As a matter of fact, I think it's crazy, and I'm even crazier for listening to you. But I'll do it to put your mind at rest. So that you'll see

371

at last that what you're saying is impossible. And in the meantime, you and I are going to talk to Paddy Nye.'

'Why?'

'Because if you're right and Felix Berg really did kill that little girl in Howth ten years ago, then I want to know why Nye gave him an alibi for the night it happened.'

'Didn't you already speak to Nye's wife today about Toner?'

'I wasn't able to, as I might have told you if you'd let me get a word in edgeways since we sat down. According to the neighbours, they've taken their boat out to Ireland's Eye to spend a few days away from it all whilst their son stays with his grandparents.'

'We're going to talk to them by cellphone?'

'They never take them to the island. Reminds them too much of the modern world.'

'Then how *are* we going to talk to them?'

'I'll give you three guesses.'

Chapter Forty-Nine

Being a Chief Superintendent had its advantages. Fitzgerald was able to requisition a boat within five minutes of arriving at Howth. Though now that we were sitting in it making our way across the dark water to Ireland's Eye, I wasn't sure it was an advantage.

Especially since it had started drizzling again.

I sat huddled in the middle of the boat, my hair getting wet and wishing I'd brought a coat, whilst Fitzgerald perched up straight at the back, working the outboard motor.

Like she was born to the life.

The boat made alarming noises as we went, creaking and complaining like the ancient thing was resenting having to make its way through the water when it had thought its work was finished for the day. I tried to take my mind off the racket it made by watching the island getting closer. By degrees it was turning from being little more than a smudge against the rain, with no more substance than a fallen stormcloud, to having a definite shape.

Soon I began to make out individual rocks at the edge of the isle.

See the contours of the land.

The journey couldn't have taken more than a half-hour, but by the time we were pulling into the landing place where a small sandy beach stretched and curved like a crescent moon along the edge of the land, overlooked by a ruined tower with a door halfway up the wall and a rope dangling out to climb, I almost felt I'd forgotten what solid ground felt like.

I was never a very good traveller.

We tied the boat fast next to what must have been Nye's own boat, and stood still for a moment, listening. The birds were restless in the growing dark. We must have disturbed them as we came in. The outboard motor had made a mockery of any idea of arriving quietly. The birds wheeled and screeched round a great stack of rock in the cliff.

Fitzgerald saw me looking at it, and said: 'That's Puck's Rock.'

'Puck?'

'People used to say it had been carved by the Devil.'

Nothing would surprise me.

'Surely they must have heard us arriving,' I said.

But no voices called out, no one came to see who we were.

'Where did they say they were going to be camping out again?'

'Round by a place called Long Hole,' said Fitzgerald.

'Long Hole. That's where that young woman died all those years ago.'

I'm not sure I'd have wanted to sleep there.

'Come on,' she said.

'You know the way?'

'I checked the map at the harbour before we set out. There's a path that leads directly to the main beach on the other side. It shouldn't take long to find. The whole island's only half a mile square. Watch your feet for rabbit holes, though,' she shot back as a warning, and not for the first time I wondered what I was doing here.

My preference would have been to leave the island for a couple of centuries and come back when they'd replaced the rabbit holes with sidewalks and buildings and there was somewhere warm I could get a strong drink. Instead here I was stumbling along a path in the darkness after Fitzgerald, with nothing to stop me tripping and breaking my neck but the fitful beam of her torch dancing across the rough grass and picking out the way ahead.

I understood now what Paddy Nye had meant about the wildness of the place. How having it so close was an escape from the city. My only quarrel was that, for me, it was places like this I needed to escape from. It felt oppressive. I could tell Fitzgerald didn't feel like that at all. Her mood had been lighter since we'd arrived here, like she felt the same relief Nye talked about. I'd never understand it. Being too long in a place like this would drive me mad.

There are only so many times you can look at the sea and the sky without growing sick of them, and soon with yourself, and after that with everything bar none.

I looked ahead and saw Fitzgerald had stopped.

'What is it?' I said.

'I see them.'

We'd reached some kind of summit. The island swept down at our feet towards a beach below, where flakes of white foam were licking the land and – what was that?

A fire.

For a moment I remembered Strange's house, and the ghost of a panic touched my brain, then my eyes adjusted and I saw it was only a small campfire down on the beach.

'Let's go,' said Fitzgerald, and she was whispering, I noticed, which was strange, as if the sky was listening. It was so quiet all that could be heard was the soft phut-phut of another boat as it moved, invisible in black water, alongside the island's margin.

As we got closer, details began to come clearer. There was a tent pitched on the level sand between rocks; a couple of rucksacks heaped alongside; the fire was burning low.

There was no sign of Nye or his wife.

'Inside sleeping?' I suggested to Fitzgerald.

'Without putting out the fire?' she said. 'Didn't you ever go camping as a kid?'

'I was too busy shoplifting and smoking weed.'

'I can believe it.'

The sand felt cold through the soles of our boots as we walked towards the tents. And then it felt colder still as I saw a shape lying unmoving on the ground beside the fire.

Nye.

'Grace.'

But she'd seen him already. She shone a torch down on to Nye's white face – and then we both started as Nye, who we'd obviously feared was dead, let out a confused mumble, threw his hands to his face to keep out the light, and said: 'What the—'

'Easy, Paddy,' said Fitzgerald. 'It's the police.'

Nye sat up, rubbing his face roughly.

'Shit, I must have fallen asleep,' he said, and he looked round, eyes squinting into the dark, hand still shielding his face. 'Hey, switch that off. There's enough light with the fire.'

Fitzgerald thought about it a moment and then switched off the torch. We'd need it for getting back to the boat anyway. The beach rearranged itself under a different glow whilst across the water hundreds of lights pricked the dark land we'd recently left.

'Where's your wife?' said Fitzgerald.

'She went to fetch some more wood,' said Nye. 'What's it got to do with you?'

'I came to talk to you about Felix.'

'Not again. How many times do we have to go over this? Felix is dead,' said Nye.

'So is Lucy Toner.'

'What has she got to do with anything? That one there,' he said, pointing at me roughly, 'came round asking about her too. I told her the same thing.'

'You didn't tell me you'd given Felix an alibi that night,' I said.

'Did I?'

'You know you did,' said Fitzgerald. 'Quit playing games.

376

We're not going to start charging you with anything now. We just need to know if he really was with you.'

Nye got to his feet and walked a couple of steps to one side, lifted a handful of something from the ground, heather maybe, or moss, and threw it on to the fire. The fire delighted in the company, blazing fiercely as he added more and more handfuls.

'I don't understand,' he said, looking down at the flames. 'I thought it was Brendan Toner you wanted to know about. My wife already told the police on the phone everything she knows about him. What has this got to do with Felix? Felix is dead.'

'You already said that,' I said. 'Are you really so sure he is?'

He stared at me in confusion a moment before finding his voice.

'He was buried,' he said. 'That's usually a pretty good indication.'

'Maybe not this time,' I said. 'We think – OK, I think that it might not've been Felix's body which was in the water that night. That Felix might still be alive.'

He looked at Fitzgerald.

'Is this true?'

I could see she was still struggling with the idea, but she simply said: 'The autopsy reports are being double-checked back in Dublin to make sure it really was him who drowned. They're going to call me as soon as they have an answer.' There was a fear in Nye's eye that needed to be built on, so she continued: 'We also suspect he may have killed Lucy Toner.'

'Felix?' He shook his head firmly. 'That's impossible.'

'Because you really were with him that night?'

Nye's mouth opened to lie, but the words wouldn't form. Instead he sank down on the sand and stared into the flames.

'How did you know?'

'About the alibi being false? You can call it a lucky guess, if you like,' I said. 'Felix's behaviour all along suggested he killed Lucy, but if he did kill her then that could only mean he wasn't really with you the night it happened. Unless you did it together?'

'You don't honestly think that I could do something like that?'

'Do you think Felix could have?'

'Yes,' he said flatly. 'I think he could. There was always something hard about Felix. They didn't call them the Ice Bergs for nothing. But could's not the same as did. I wouldn't have given him an alibi if I'd suspected for one moment he'd murdered that girl.'

'Why *did* you lie for him?'

'He'd spent the night with another woman and he didn't want Alice to find out about it. He said she'd kill him if she knew. She could be very – protective of Felix.'

'They were sleeping together even then?'

'Alice slept with everyone, I told you that,' Nye said to me. 'Felix doted on her. Never went out with other women, even though she slept with anything on two legs. Then one day he told me he'd met someone a couple of nights before, the night Lucy Toner was murdered, and that he'd spent the evening at her place. He was desperate for Alice not to find out, and he feared that if he told the police the truth then it might all come out.'

'So you agreed to say he was with you?'

'It didn't seem to matter,' Nye said. 'They'd already arrested Isaac Little. No one had any doubt he did it. It was just a small white lie. It never crossed my mind that Felix would have . . . that he could have done something like that. I still can't believe it. Though . . .'

'What?' said Fitzgerald.

'I remember he had a scratch on his face,' said Nye. 'The price of passion, I remember him telling me. We laughed about it.'

And that made it seem almost worst. If only they'd taken scrapings from under Lucy's fingernails . . . if only they'd matched them to samples from men in the area . . . if only someone had seen Felix's face . . .

What ifs. There was no point regretting them now. Those were primitive days, policing-wise. The important thing was to get better. To always keep moving on.

'Why did you never come forward and tell the truth, even when he was taunting you through the mail?'

'I told you. Because I thought Isaac Little was guilty. Even during all those times when he was tormenting me, I never for one moment thought that he'd done that.'

'Your wife thought so.'

'Don't you see that was the problem? She was always going on about how she was convinced it was Felix who had murdered Lucy. How he'd got away with it. How much she loathed him. How could I admit to her that I was the one who gave him an alibi, and that the alibi wasn't even genuine? Can you imagine how that would have made her feel?'

'She's going to find out now, whatever happens,' Fitzgerald said.

'Don't remind me,' he said miserably.

He looked back up the beach to see if he could see her coming.

I wondered where she'd got to.

'I still don't see why you came out here at this hour,' Nye continued. 'Even if it was Felix who killed Lucy. Even if Felix really isn't dead, like you seem to think. What does it have to do with me?'

'It has everything to do with you,' I said. 'As far as Felix knows, you're the only one left alive who knows that his alibi that night doesn't count for anything. Alice knew probably, but Alice is dead. Brendan Toner is dead. Even Felix himself is presumed to be dead. And if he could find a way to stop you from talking—'

I was jolted suddenly from my thoughts of Felix by an unexpected sound.

'That'll be Walsh,' said Fitzgerald, and I realised it must be her cellphone ringing inside her jacket, but the noise of it sounded so alien out there that it hadn't registered as real in my mind.

She took out her phone and pressed the button.

'Walsh? What have you got?'

I watched her face as she listened to what Walsh had to say.

'Repeat that,' I heard her say. 'I can't hear you too well.'

Then: 'Shit. No, Walsh, no, you did good. I'll call you later.'

'What is it?' I said impatiently when she turned off the phone.

'Walsh got the pathologist to show him the report again.'

'And?'

'It was Felix,' she said. 'He's dead. The fractures matched. Everything was correct. Walsh even went round to his doctor's house and showed him the still photographs from the autopsy. Saxon, it was Felix.'

I couldn't believe it.

'I don't get it,' I said. 'If it wasn't him who was doing all this, then who was it?'

'I think you'll find that it was me,' said a voice from the other side of the fire.

Chapter Fifty

And we both turned to the fire, and there stood Paddy Nye – but that couldn't be right, surely, because the voice hadn't sounded like his. It had been more distant, and anyway Paddy was turning his head in his turn to look behind him, and there—

There was a figure silhouetted behind him on the hill.

And it had the voice of a woman.

'Tricia?' said Nye.

The figure who stepped off the hill into the circle of light wasn't Nye's wife, though.

It was Gina.

She wasn't looking bad for a woman who'd been dead for the last twenty-four hours.

Was hers the boat I'd heard phut-phutting as we stood on the hill a short while ago? Must've been, I guess. It never occurred to me that another boat might be coming to the island.

I thought only an imbecile would come here.

As I'd proved.

I wondered why I didn't feel more shocked to see her standing there with a pistol.

'It's a Derringer,' she said, catching me looking at it. 'Nice piece, don't you think? I stole it from Strange's house. I thought it might come in useful. It's old but it will do the trick. Which is more than I can say for Strange. All that bad sex I put myself through with him lately in the hope he'd give me the key to Felix's locker, and in the end he just hands it to you. Talk about ingratitude. Still, I think he learned his lesson. And what else could I do? I'd tried softening him up by sending him threatening letters and breaking into his gallery, and still he said it was his duty to keep Felix's worldly goods safe from harm.'

'As a matter of interest,' I said, 'who exactly did you kill in Strange's gallery?'

'I haven't the faintest idea,' said Gina, as though the thought had only just that moment occurred to her. 'I'm sure she'll be reported missing soon enough. I just waited in the street until someone who could pass for me at a pinch appeared, and then I pretended I'd been attacked. Put on a big act. Crying. Sobbing. I was rather good at it, I must say. I told her I was afraid of being left alone and would she please, please, pretty please come with me to the gallery whilst I got a glass of water. I told her I worked there. I'd actually stolen the key earlier from Vincent. I let us in, she helped me over to the desk, and then, bang bang, how's that for a touch of impromptu facial reconstruction?'

'What are you all talking about?' demanded Nye. 'Who is this?'

'Don't you remember me, Paddy?' said Gina.

He stared at her blankly.

'Why should I remember you? I've never seen you before in my life.'

'She's Katie Toner,' I said. 'Lucy's sister.'

'Well figured out,' said Gina. 'What finally made the penny drop?'

'I should have realised it as soon as we knew that the man we thought was the Marxman was Brendan Toner. Who else would he have been willing to cover up for? Who else would he have been willing to die to protect but his little sister?'

Nye was staring at her now even harder.

'Katie? But,' he said numbly at last, 'I thought you were dead.'

'Everyone seems to think I'm dead. Katie and Gina both. That was the general idea. I *wanted* to be dead. To be invisible. Life's easier when you're invisible.'

Still Nye shook his head, like he didn't want to believe it.

'What are you going to do now?' I said. 'Kill us all, like you killed Felix?'

'*I* didn't kill Felix,' Gina said with a laugh. 'It was Brendan who killed Felix. Poor foolish Brendan, who wanted to protect me from myself. And look where it got him. He thought I was crazy when he realised I was the Marxman, but he still wouldn't turn me in. He remembered what happened to our mother, how she'd spent half her life in institutions.'

'Being mad seems to run in the family,' I said.

'I guess so, Special Agent. But then stupidity obviously runs in yours. When I think of your face that day I called you, weeping down the line, to tell you I'd been sent a threatening picture. When I think how you rushed round, so earnest, so concerned.'

'Whilst you were the one taking the photographs the whole time.'

'That's right. The *Strangers* series was mine. Quite a good idea, I thought. I'd never felt as if I really belonged in this city. I got Brendan to make the calls for me, arrange the meetings, then when the subjects turned up I shot them. In a manner of speaking. I used to get such intense pleasure from being able to control people in that way. Say be here or be there, and they'd just do it. And they'd never know what it had been about. That's how I got to meet Felix too,' she said. 'I called him myself and suggested we meet at the lighthouse. I knew it meant a lot to him, that he'd spent hours there as a child. I figured he'd be intrigued enough to come. And he was. Unknown to him, I took his photograph. Next day I sent it to him with a note inviting him to lunch. Our first date, just as I described it, Saxon, on *our* first meeting.'

'Where you seduced him.'

'How could any man resist? Look at me. Felix was mine. I always knew it. It wasn't Felix and Alice who were two halves of the same person. It was Felix and me who were that.'

'How can you talk about him like that?' I said. 'He killed your sister.'

'So she was my sister. She meant nothing to me.'

'He raped her.'

'I know,' she said. 'I watched him do it.'

'You were there?' said Nye.

'I suppose you could say it was my first sexual experience,' said Gina. 'I was hiding in the garden and saw it all. How he pushed himself into her. How he filled her mouth with earth until she choked. How he buried her. I saw it all. I didn't tell anyone what I'd seen, but I thought it was incredible. Exhilarating. It's the only word. I also knew that what I'd seen created a sacred bond between us. A sacred and unbreakable bond. It didn't work out quite that way, of course. Mother killed herself and I was sent away to stay with relatives, and when that didn't work out I was put into care, passed around like a piece of meat. But I hardly cared. I knew Felix and I would be together one day. That kept me going. I kept cuttings about him by my bedside. That we shared the secret of what he'd done to Lucy – even if he didn't know we shared it – fused us together. It was only a matter of enduring. Of waiting.'

'Waiting for what?' said Fitzgerald.

'For when we'd be together. I told you, everything I did was for him. Soon as I left care when I was sixteen, I headed for London. I knew Katie had to die, Katie had to disappear. That's why I had Brendan tell everyone I was dead. I became Gina Fox instead. I even picked the name Fox because it reminded me of Felix, and I worked, you don't know how hard, to be able to afford the plastic surgery I needed if I was ever really to leave Katie behind. I was taking night classes in photography too, just getting myself ready for the day I was finally back with Felix, so that I could be worthy to take my

384

place in his life. I even flew back once or twice to Dublin, testing the waters. And gradually I realised that everyone had forgotten about Katie Toner. Forgotten about Lucy Toner too, because what's one small murder? The world is full of murders. I was free to return.'

'When did you come back?'

'Just over a year ago,' Gina said. 'I found myself somewhere to live. I managed to manoeuvre a meeting with Felix by sending him the photograph. We became lovers. And yes, before you ask, it was everything I wanted it to be. For him too, I think.'

'He recognised a fellow dark heart,' I said.

She laughed. 'Yes, maybe that was it. He gave himself fully to me in a way he never could to anyone else. Not even to little Alice. We began to spend more and more time together. I brought out something in him. It was me who persuaded him to take those photographs you saw at Strange's gallery; I posed for him, I encouraged him to hurt me, and I could see that he was beginning to enjoy indulging that side of himself again, the side he'd repressed too long.'

'Did he know who you were?'

'Not then, no, he didn't guess. Why would he? It was a long time ago. I looked different. And I wanted to know he was totally in my power before I told him the truth.'

'But you hadn't accounted for Alice,' I said.

'Alice wanted to split us up,' Gina said with bitterness. 'She wanted Felix for herself and she got her way. He stopped returning my calls. Sent my letters back unread. Then they took him away, Alice and Strange. Sent him to the other side of the world. As if I'd gone through everything, gone through hell, just to have him snatched away from me like that.'

'What did you decide to do?'

'I decided to kill them all,' she said. 'Felix. Alice. Strange. I could imagine them all laughing at me. I couldn't bear the thought of anyone alive being a witness to my humiliation. All I needed was a gun. It had to be a gun, I don't know why, though I think I know what the psychologists would say. And luckily, that's where Brendan entered the picture. George Dyer, I should say. I'd tracked him down soon after returning to Dublin. He was working for Tim Enright and he knew I needed money, so he pulled some strings to get me the commission to take a few pictures of them for some corporate magazine. Which is how I met Tim. He didn't know I was Brendan's sister. We started an affair. No one knew about us.'

'And you got him to arrange for the gun to be smuggled in by blackmailing him?' said Fitzgerald.

'There was no need for blackmail,' she said contemptuously. 'You think I'd take a risk like that?'

'Then how did you get him to do it?'

'I asked him – and he did it,' she said.

'Simple as that?'

'Simple as that.' She shrugged.

'He must have fallen for you big time.'

'Men seem to make a habit of it,' she agreed lightly. 'Once I'd got the gun, I waited till I knew Felix was back in town, but it was hard getting close to him even then – Alice was still watching him as if he was a child – and I could feel the tension building inside me. I needed to release it or I'd explode. And it was whilst I was feeling like that that I heard that Felix's new exhibition had opened in Kilmainham. So I went there – and I *saw* them. Saw those pictures which he'd taken the previous winter when he was mine. Every night we'd walked the city together, in snow and rain, and there they were. I'm the one whose hands and feet and shadow you can see in the shots. I'm the reflection in the water. And I just knew that this was Felix's message to me. He wanted us to be together again. All he was waiting for was a sign from me. So I didn't kill him. I gave him the sign he asked for.'

'Tim Enright,' I said.

'It had to be Tim. I didn't want him becoming suspicious of me. He knew I had a gun. He'd got it for me. He knew what kind it was. So I lured him out to O'Neill's Place on a promise of something suitably filthy to celebrate my birthday, and I killed him there. Then I shot the judge in the square. I didn't know he was a judge at the time. I just chose the place because that was in one of the photographs too, and he was the one who came along. But the press put two and two together and got five and decided that I had some great political motivation. That I was the Marxman. So I decided, why not? Might as well be that nickname as any other. And besides, have you ever seen what's written on the side of Marx's grave in London? *The philosophers have only interpreted the world in various ways. The point is to change it.* That didn't seem such a bad motto. That's what I thought Felix and I could do, if we were together, if we were true to ourselves. Change the world. So each time I killed, I sent Felix cuttings from the press about the killings with the names of the places where the victims had died underlined, hoping he'd realise they were from me, that these were the places we were together last winter, that these were the places in his photographs.'

'And he confronted you.'

'He came round one day to my apartment and demanded to know if I was the Marxman. It was the first time I'd seen him since he went to the States. It was so good to see him again, it just confirmed to me that I wanted to be with him, that he was the man for me. I confessed gladly. I even showed him the photographs I'd taken of the victims after they died.'

'Why?'

'I hoped it would turn him on. That he'd be inspired by what I was doing, want to join me. I told you, I'd seen what he did to my sister, I knew his urges, his appetites, I knew he still had it in him to be the man I desired, I knew he'd called out to me in his photographs. I hoped we'd be able to share this, the same way we had the *Self Portraits*.'

'But Felix didn't react the way he was supposed to?'

'Are you kidding me?' she said contemptuously. 'He told me he felt nothing for me any more. He confessed that yes, he had bad appetites inside him, that was how he put it, he always had, but he was learning to control them. The only reason he'd put those photographs into the exhibition was because they were all he had, it was as if the medicine he was on had suppressed that part of him, he said, and he didn't care any more, he was ashamed of everything he'd been. He wasn't going to let me destroy his life. He wanted to be with Alice. Whine, whine. Witter, witter. Are you getting the picture? And to make it worse, he said he was also going to tell the police that I was the notorious Marxman.'

'What did you do?'

'I used my nuclear option,' said Gina. 'I told him who I was. I told him I'd seen what he did to Lucy. I reminded him of details even he'd forgotten. There was no point him denying it. And I told him that if he exposed me, then I'd expose him.'

'How did he react?' said Fitzgerald.

'He went very quiet. He told me he needed time to think it over. What I didn't realise was that was just a front. He told me he felt dizzy. He asked for a glass of water. And while I was in the kitchen getting it for him, he grabbed hold of all the photographs I'd taken of the *Strangers* series and the victims, put them in a bag, and fled. He called me from his house and told me he'd say nothing about me being the Marxman, but that if anything was to happen to him or his sister in the meantime, then the photographs would go straight to the police.'

'And to be sure,' I said, 'he asked Strange for a gun to protect himself and Alice.'

'I didn't care about that. All I cared about was getting those photographs back,' said Gina. 'They were mine, I needed them, I wanted them. So I persuaded Brendan to go to Felix's house, break in, and find them for me. My brother knew I was the Marxman by then, of course, but he didn't know what to do. He begged me to stop, but when I said no he had nothing to threaten me with. I was all he had left. He couldn't turn me in to the police. He'd only lose me that way. So he agreed to try and get the photographs back.'

'He was the one who broke into their house that time?'

'He was, but he didn't find the photographs. What he found instead,' she said, 'was Felix's journal, filled, so he told me, with charming clippings and quotes about our dear sister's departure, and he realised that Felix had killed Lucy. He'd always trusted it was Isaac Little and now, by utter chance, he discovered the truth. He was so shocked that he forgot to even bring it with him when he left. But it wasn't as if he needed it any more. He had all the evidence he wanted. Everything that had gone wrong in our lives, so far as he was concerned, stemmed from the moment Lucy was murdered, and now he had the chance to put it right.'

'It was after the break-in that Felix decided to give the photographs and the journal to Strange,' I said. 'He knew they weren't safe at his house.'

'Especially when Brendan started following him, and calling him up in the middle of the night and telling him he was going to kill him for what he'd done to Lucy. I tried to make him see that it was no use, that he might be wrong, but he just knew.'

'I still don't see how he managed to kill Felix.'

'Well, I can only tell you how Brendan told me it happened. He said he took the Glock without my knowing and followed Felix to the harbour that night. But Felix did something unexpected. He pulled a gun on Brendan too. It was the old piece Strange had given him, a bit like this one, I suppose. So there they both were with guns pointed at one another, and that's when Brendan told me he came up with the perfect plan to kill Felix. He told Felix they could shoot it out if he wanted, but he had a Glock and Felix had an old thing that hadn't been fired in fifty years and who knows how it would turn out? He said they could do that if Felix wanted, but if Felix died and Brendan lived, then he would find Alice, rape her, strangle her and fill her mouth with soil until she choked, just as *he'd* done to Lucy. Or—'

'Or,' I said, suddenly understanding, 'Felix could shoot himself.'

'Exactly. He could put the gun to his own eye, pull the trigger and die there, just like our mother had done. And if he did, then Brendan promised to let Alice go unharmed.'

'How could Felix know your brother would keep his side of the bargain?'

'He couldn't know it, but what else could he do?' said Gina. 'The Glock was pointed at his head. He knew he was going to die one way or another. His one way of keeping Alice safe was to do what Brendan told him. So he had to make a choice. And he did.'

'Weren't you furious that your brother had killed this man you claimed to love?'

'Not really,' said Gina. 'Lucy meant nothing to me, but I understood Brendan's need for revenge. When he told me later what pleasure he'd got from standing there and watching Felix put the gun to his eye – stand there, shaking – then pull the trigger and blow his face away . . . well, let's say I recognised that pleasure. And at least Brendan did something. Felix only talked. The only thing Felix ever shot was pictures. I told you, he wasn't the man I thought he was. He'd failed. The very fact that he'd do that for her, for that snivelling bitch, just showed how pathetic he was. How could he prefer her to me? How could he think that dried-up cow was worth sacrificing his life for?'

She glanced up at an unexpected noise, but it was only the dying driftwood shifting in the fire, sending out a brief bright burst of light. The light sparkled along the barrel of the gun.

'As for that,' she added, 'what was done was done, I wasn't going to spend my life brooding on it. I was the Marxman now, I'd outgrown him. I had work to be getting on with. I didn't even need to make things fit Felix's pictures any more. I was free. I was a little careless at the church, but that's because I was so furious with the newspapers for saying Felix was killed by the Marxman. By me. How stupid could they be? I had to show them. I didn't realise by that point that you already knew Felix had shot himself, otherwise I'd have waited till I was better prepared. I made a mess of it, I admit. That's why I picked the magician next time and whispered that dumb message in his ear. So I could slip the card under your door, Saxon, and spin you that ridiculous line about the Tarot. I was just trying to buy more time while you went haring off up one blind alley after another before you clicked it was baloney.'

'We never believed it for one moment,' Fitzgerald said, and I saw Gina bristle with annoyance. 'The only thing that really threw us was how the killer knew where Brook lived.'

'That part was easy. I'd taken his picture too,' Gina said. 'He came from Germany as a kid, didn't you know? His parents' original name was Bruch. Like the composer. He was another of my *Strangers*. The only thing that messed it up was losing the damn gun.'

'But big brother rode to the rescue.'

'Like I say, he thought I was *ill*. He felt responsible for me. Especially when I insisted on getting another gun. I knew I could get one from Strange. Felix had told me about Vincent stealing money from his artists. But Brendan wouldn't let me go and get the gun myself. He said it was too dangerous in that part of town, can you believe that? He said he'd go instead. I agreed – on one condition. That he killed the woman who handed over the gun. And that was going to be you. I know you were beavering away at Felix's death, trying to figure out the truth. I didn't want to take the risk that you might get to it. That's why I broke into your apartment and left the photograph on your wall. To try and scare you off.'

'You did *what*? Saxon, is this true?' said Fitzgerald.

'I didn't want to worry you,' I said, avoiding her eye. 'It was the night of Felix's funeral. I came home and found the place trashed. I didn't want to make an issue of it.'

'An issue?' echoed Fitzgerald in disbelief.

'That hadn't worked anyway,' said Gina. 'You still wouldn't let it go. So I realised you had to die. Brendan didn't want to do it, but he wanted to protect me more, and I made him see there was no other way. But you were one step ahead and he must've panicked.'

'Did you care about *him* any more than you cared about your sister?'

'I cared about his white cat. Gorgeous creature. Have you met? I'm surprised you didn't recognise it, Saxon. I took rather a lot of pictures of it at one time. Don't you remember looking at them on the table that first day you came round to ask me about Felix?'

The white cat.

I did remember now. Too late, but I remembered. Mainly how I'd been glad the cat was only in the photographs and not curling round my feet and tripping me up like Hare.

Why hadn't I remembered when it might've helped, like when I was standing in the garden of the man I thought of as George Dyer, watching it sit on a path?

I remembered other things too.

A wooden staircase.

A window cracked like a web.

Why hadn't I recognised them?

'Don't you even feel ashamed that he sacrificed himself to save you?'

'Why should I feel ashamed?' Gina said. 'It was his decision. It was his throat to cut. Don't get me wrong. I can see what you're saying. He obviously thought that if the police believed the Marxman was dead, they'd leave *me* alone. I guess it was a nice gesture when you put it like that, but I still think he was nuts.'

'*He* was nuts?' said Nye. 'I think you're *all* nuts.'

'Maybe so,' said Gina, 'but I'm the only nut with a gun.'

'So what do you intend to do with it?' said Fitzgerald.

'Do you really have to ask?' she said. 'I intend to protect myself.'

'By coming here after Nye?' said Fitzgerald. 'Why? He has nothing on you.'

'I didn't come here after Paddy,' she said dismissively. 'I can deal with him later. I came here after you two.'

And she raised the gun and pointed it at Fitzgerald's head.

'No!'

The cry escaped without thought from my lips, and I took a step forward.

Gina just smiled to see how she'd got a reaction from me – but she didn't smile for long. At that moment a shadow rose behind her, holding something ragged against the light, and the shadow brought the ragged shape down on to Gina's head, and Gina slumped suddenly to the sand and dropped the pistol. Fitzgerald kicked it out of her reach before she could clutch hold of it again, and Gina just tutted and raised her hand to her head, and then looked at her fingers in the firelight where they were covered in blood.

'Ouch,' she said sarcastically. 'That hurt.'

'Fuck you,' said Nye's wife, and she dropped the driftwood to the ground.

I'd been wondering how long she was going to be gone fetching that wood.

Chapter Fifty-One

It was late. The sky was scattered with stars and reddening at the edges, and I was on the balcony, catching a moment, when I saw Lawrence Fisher finally arrive.

The cab pulled up on the other side of the road and he clambered out, waiting till it had pulled away before crossing over. He didn't look up. He didn't see me.

I pulled open the glass door and went back inside. Fitzgerald was talking to Miranda Gray on the couch whilst Healy listened. Thaddeus Burke was pouring drinks, enjoying the experience of making free with my whiskey for once instead of me making free with his.

Walsh had skipped an invitation. He had some woman he wanted to take out. 'Can I help it if I'm irresistible to women, babe?' he'd said when I told him about the party.

If you could call what we had here a party.

'He's here,' I told them, and instantly they fell silent and got to their feet, and I crossed the room to open the door for Fisher.

He came in a few moments later, looking tired, sombre.

'She wouldn't see you?' I said.

'I saw her all right,' he said with a mock shudder. 'That's what's wrong.'

'I'll get you a drink,' said Burke as Fisher pulled off his coat and filled an armchair.

'Sit down,' he said to everyone. 'You're making me nervous.'

So we did.

Fisher had spent much of the day with Gina. He'd been sent for because, ever since being caught, she'd refused to speak a word to anyone, including her own defence lawyer.

Though what *was* there for her to say? Her fingerprints had been matched to the gun used in the Marxman killings and to the photographs which were found in Felix's locker. Forensics were pretty sure they could connect her to the fire in Strange's house. Under her clothes they'd even found a necklace threaded with the spent shells from the Glock, and there was gunpowder propellant residue ingrained into her clothes. The rest was joining the dots.

Fitzgerald still felt there was more that could be learned about Gina. She wasn't idiot enough to think there was anything which could explain what Gina had done, which could provide a straightforward why. She just wanted to know what Fisher made of her.

Fisher looked up as Burke brought over the whiskey.

'I shouldn't really,' he said. 'I'll not sleep.'

But he didn't look like he'd get much sleep that night anyway, and he took the glass and sipped the whiskey, lost in thought.

'If you'd like to leave this to another time . . .' I said.

'No,' he said. 'Let's get it over with. Not that Gina seemed to find the experience particularly stressful. She spent most of the time laughing at my new shirt.'

'A mad bitch *and* no taste,' I said.

'In my experience,' he agreed, 'the two tend to go together.'

'Did she talk?' said Fitzgerald.

'She talked.'

It turned out that Gina had talked plenty.

'I think maybe she was impressed by who I was,' Fisher said. 'Intrigued that I was intrigued. She'd seen me on TV, she said. I guess she thought she was getting some second-hand celebrity status from being interviewed by me.'

'Your biggest fan,' growled Burke.

'The worst kind,' said Fisher. 'Frankly, the problem wasn't persuading her to talk. The problem was getting her to shut up.'

'She talked a lot out on Ireland's Eye too,' I said.

'The only time she really let me in on the conversation,' Fisher said, 'was when she asked what I thought of her, of what she'd done.'

'What *did* you think of her?'

'That was the problem,' said Fisher. 'I told her I thought she was quite a common case, psychologically speaking. I don't think she took too kindly to the notion of being un-extraordinary. I guess it's not very flattering to the ego.'

'Every killer likes to think they're unique,' I said.

'Common?' said Healy. 'Getting pleasure from watching your sister die is certainly what I call unique.'

'Not even that is so unusual,' said Fisher. 'Everything goes back to childhood. Research shows that violent offenders have often had violent fantasies from as young as seven years of age, sometimes younger still. Children can take it further and kill too. If they can do that, why be so surprised by Gina? Sometimes people do bad things because they're born that way, they're primary psychopaths, but mostly it's just because something happens to them in childhood, a confluence of events which makes them what they are.'

'Innocence gone bad,' said Healy.

'Exactly. You take a paradigm of a normal, happy childhood and then you see how it can be bent, skewed. If something goes wrong along the way, then what we call normal starts to become distorted, and who knows what comes out at the end? Not a normal, happy adolescent anyway. And Gina's childhood was screwed up long before she saw Felix kill her sister. She had the classic signs. A dysfunctional home. Psychologically damaging parenting.'

'What was wrong with her parents?'

'According to what Gina said to me tonight, both she and Lucy were forced to watch their father screwing their mother throughout their childhoods. His behaviour towards them was very sexual. He never actually raped them, but he touched them, made them touch him, touch each other. He used to beat them too and make them watch as he beat their mother. So it wasn't as if seeing Felix rape her sister was an entirely new experience.'

'Did no one know about this at the time?' said Healy.

'From what Fitzgerald tells me about the records,' said Fisher, 'it seems not.'

'Is Gina telling the truth?'

'We'll never know that,' said Fisher. 'We can only guess at the past by looking at what happens in the future, and what she went on to do seems to me to be consistent with what she says happened in her childhood. The neglect, the emotional and physical abuse. Then, when her own sexuality began to blossom, there was little chance that she would be unaffected. She didn't know what was normal behaviour. Didn't understand about affection. So when she saw what was happening to her sister, she didn't have an alarm in her head that told her it was wrong. The only question was, how would her sexuality develop under those circumstances? And I think we have our answer. She found it exciting. Sexually stimulating.'

It's always the same. Killers turn natural, healthy qualities into diseased ones. Sexual desire becomes depraved lust. A need for money becomes corrosive greed. The need for self-assertion becomes a compulsion to destroy whatever undermines it. Discipline becomes obsession. They take normal appetites and heighten and distort them.

'What made matters worse here,' Fisher went on, 'is that she looked up to Felix already. The Bergs were well known in Howth. Wealthy. Educated. Cultured. They were what many people wanted to be, certainly Gina with her life revolving round the store, the lower-middle-class life. She idolised them. It never occurred to her to question what Felix did, especially when it concurred with so much of what she'd already been taught at home. So she turned what had happened into a sacred thing they had in common and spent her whole life trying to get back to him, trying to re-create that moment, trying to share in that power.'

'And maybe she would've managed it if it hadn't been for Alice,' I said. 'Do you think Alice knew about Felix and Gina working together?'

'Again, who can say? It seems likely that she knew there was something unhealthy about Felix's relationship with Gina. Maybe she saw the pictures Felix had taken of her and realised Gina was stirring something in him that was best left unstirred.'

'Little realising,' I said, 'that Gina wasn't the sort to take being thwarted lightly.'

'Killing all those folks is some over-reaction to being dumped,' said Burke.

'Not so uncommon,' commented Fisher. 'I talk to prisoners all the time in jail who've killed their partners and often other members of their partners' families simply because they tried to break off a relationship. Men, mostly, but women too. You have to remember the sequence of things. Her father starts to mess with her mind as a child, she sees her sister murdered and finds that she enjoys it, she then sees the family broken further and is passed around from one unsuitable place to another, in some of which, she says, the same pattern of abuse and mistreatment and inappropriate sexualisation continued. It fuels in her a thrill for what is warped but also a sense of injustice that she has been treated badly by life. Put them together and – well, it's a lethal combination. She told me that she used to dream of what she calls revenge. Of walking down the street and killing every single person she passed. Of blasting the smug idiot grins off their faces and making them realise what life was really like. She imagined destroying the whole city. That's fairly common too, having a rich fantasy life wherein you take vengeance on the world. She drank heavily, I think she's probably an alcoholic like her parents, so her inhibitions were lowered. You said, Saxon, that she drank plenty that afternoon you went round to her apartment. And she had suicidal tendencies. Depression, instability, violence all ran in the family. She suffered sleep disorders. Feelings of withdrawal and persecution. Killing became her way of reversing the pattern of childhood, of turning feelings of powerlessness into feelings of absolute power.'

'What about her brother? Did he share those feelings too?'

'Put two people through the same experiences and they'll still react entirely differently. There's always a mysterious X factor that makes the difference and I doubt we'll ever know what it really is. But as it happened, Brendan Toner had a different experience. He was never initiated into his father's sexual games. The traumatic event of his childhood was what happened to Lucy, and he seems to have reacted to that by shutting himself off from the world. Shutting down. The pain was easier to deal with that way. Of course, he reinvented himself too, like Gina did. He became George Dyer. But once he'd done that, his way of dealing with the trauma inside him was to keep a tight hold of his mind. You can see that in his house. How he needed to keep everything emotionless, impersonal, under wraps.'

'What I don't understand,' said Fitzgerald, 'is why Felix didn't respond to Gina's attempts to lure him into her way of thinking? I mean, after what he did to that child . . .'

'You think because he'd killed once, he was programmed to do it over and over again? No. I think he knew what he was capable of, the darkness inside him, he saw it in himself every day, but he was also capable of control, of sublimating his urges. He wanted to get better. He lost control for a while when he was hit on the head and nearly killed, and he allowed himself to fall into Gina's world again, the world of his own fantasies which he'd tried to keep a lid on all those years. But he was saved by Alice, and slowly, like she told Saxon, he came round and began to get better.'

'It must've come as a shock to that control when he found out who Gina really was.'

'Yes,' said Fisher, 'and we'll never know for sure how, inwardly, he reacted to finding out what she'd seen him do. He may have flirted artistically with the idea of revelation in the past, dropping a hint of T.S. Eliot here, a tale about his life in a house with a murderer there, playing with Isaac Little's mind for the pleasure of watching him squirm, skirting the edges of the truth in his earliest pictures, but this was different. This wasn't some self-referential game he was involved in with Gina. This was war. He must've known that whatever happened now, she would most likely kill him anyway. He was living on borrowed time. Stealing the evidence of Gina's crimes bought him some time, but not much. Before he knew it, Toner was harassing him too, following him, calling him up in the night and telling him he was going to kill him. Which is when he contacted our friend Saxon.'

'Why'd he do that?' said Burke. 'I don't think I get that still.'

'Once again I don't think we'll ever know what went through his mind,' Fisher said. 'My guess is that at some point Felix decided he'd had enough. He called Saxon, probably for the same reason Gina demanded to see me, because we're some name they'd seen on late-night TV, and arranged to meet her. He was going to tell her everything, about Lucy, about Gina, the Marxman. He was going to confess and let whatever would happen happen.'

'How can you possibly know all that?' said Burke.

'I can't,' said Fisher. 'And if you like, you can dismiss it all as Grade A bullshit for which I haven't got the first scrap of evidence. But I think it ties into what we know about the rest. I'm paid to investigate behaviour, I'm not a mind-reader or a psychic, and that's what I think happened. He must have known he couldn't run for ever, so he decided to stop the hunt himself, only Brendan Toner – George Dyer, call him what you will – intervened, and Felix realised he had to make a choice to save his sister. And maybe he knew about the baby by that point too. He knew he was going to die. The question is, what happened after that? His one hope of ensuring that Alice was safe was to do exactly what Toner told him to do.'

'It must've taken a lot of courage,' I said, seeing another side of Felix than the one which had dominated my thoughts since I realised he'd killed Lucy Toner so brutally.

'Even killers can find nobility in them when they need it,' Fisher agreed. 'And never underestimate how much courage it needs sometimes to take your own life.'

I knew what he was telling me in his own Fisher-like way.

'Do you think Toner *would* have done to Alice what he threatened?' said Miranda as Burke came round with the whiskey again and poured everyone huge shots.

'I doubt it,' said Fisher. 'He doesn't seem to have been a bad man really. He was an unhappy man, and a man who couldn't really cope with ordinary life, and he panicked and lashed out when Dalton tried to take him in. But that's different from what he said he'd do to Alice. I don't think he blamed her for what Felix had done. Even if she had covered up for him, he was covering up for Gina too. They were two sides of the one coin. Both understood the meaning of loyalty. The only thing he wanted was to see Felix suffer for what he'd done. And he did. What he didn't know was that his loyalty to Gina would cost him his life.'

'I'm just glad you finally caught her,' said Miranda.

'Well, it was Nye's wife who caught her really,' said Fitzgerald. 'Right on the back of the head with a large piece of driftwood.'

'Though sadly not quite hard enough,' I said.

Chapter Fifty-Two

Everyone was gone and I was alone once more with Fitzgerald.

'I guess that means Isaac Little gets out now,' I said.

'You're not responsible for that.'

'Might even be paid a fat lot of compensation for his time behind bars. Enough to start again somewhere new. Buy a nice house. Near a playground maybe.'

'Stop torturing yourself,' she said. 'What are you saying? That you wish you hadn't found out the truth about what happened to Lucy Toner?'

'Truth doesn't seem that wonderful if all it does is benefit monsters like Little.'

'Single acts have unforeseen consequences,' Fitzgerald said matter of factly. 'Some of them are bound to be bad. If you never did anything for fear of the bad consequences, you'd never do anything at all.'

'And what about Alice?' I said. 'No one's mentioned her in all this.'

'Alice simply killed herself.'

'Simply?' I said, thinking about Sydney.

'You know what I mean. There's no mystery,' she went on. 'She was having a baby, the baby's father was dead, the baby's father was her brother. And anyway—'

'What?'

'We found a tape. In Alice's house.'

'What kind of tape?'

'A video Alice made the night she died. I didn't know whether to tell you,' Fitzgerald said, 'didn't know if it was the sort of thing you'd want to see. Then I figured you were bound to hear about it eventually. You get to hear about everything eventually.'

'When was it found?'

'I heard about it yesterday morning after the fire in Strange's house. A friend of Alice was round at her house clearing away the last few things. She found the tape inside the video player. Purely by accident. The video player was turned off at the wall. When the uniforms were searching the place for a note, they never thought to look for a video.'

'What's on it?' I said.

She hesitated, then walked over to her bag that was sitting on the table and reached inside and took out a video. Walked back and held it out.

'I had a copy made for you,' she said.

I looked at it for a long time, almost afraid to touch it.

Then I reached out and took it.

It didn't bite.

'Have you watched it?' I said.

She shook her head.

'They told me what was on it,' she said. 'I didn't want to see it.'

Did I?

I wondered what I would do if someone told me there was a tape of Sydney's last moments. If I could watch her leaving the house and walking down to the railroad track.

Would I watch it?

Yes, I realised, I would. I wouldn't be able to stop myself. I'd want to know.

That was my weakness.

I always needed to know.

Fitzgerald didn't ask me what I was going to do. She had that perfect gift for knowing when to talk and when not to talk. When to leave things alone. Since the other day, she'd never even asked about Sydney. She knew if I wanted to talk about it I would, and if I didn't think the time was right then there was no point trying to make me do it. I wish I had that gift, but I always push and badger and don't know when to let things go.

'Thank you,' I said, and I laid the video on the desk.

We had another drink and talked about Gina. She was due in court tomorrow, where she'd be formally charged and a date set for her hearing. That was the worst thing about law enforcement. An investigation ended, but the paperwork never died.

Fitzgerald also made just the right sardonic comments about how well the apartment was looking since I'd cleaned up after Gina's impromptu visit.

'I'd better get off,' she said finally when I offered another drink. 'I've things to do.'

Tactful as always.

I was sad to see her go, but I knew I needed to be alone for this; but even then, it was some time before I could take the tape out of the case or slot it into the machine; and I don't know how long it was after that before I pressed Play.

But there was Alice.

I'd watched tapes of people dying before. Men. Women. Even a child one time. The FBI made us view them during training and I'd learned to watch without flinching, pretending it was science, even as the victims begged and cried.

This was different.

Alice had no one to beg. No one to plead with. She was alone in the house and the camera was trained only on her, watching her raptly as she took the bottles and shook pills out on to the table, where they rattled and bounced, and then she sifted them with her fingers, separating them out according to some pattern in her head only she could fathom.

One by one she began to take them, white, blue, yellow, pink, lifting them to her lips, letting them dissolve on her tongue; washing them down with something that looked like water but might have been vodka, how could I tell? And every so often she got up and danced and skipped round the room, slowly separating from her real self until it was almost like there were two people there on the tape, Alice and another woman who looked like Alice but who wasn't, and the two of them circled one another warily, quiet and secret and suspicious as cats meeting for the first time, until the pills really took hold, and then she was more like a cat which had met its reflection for the first time and was momentarily alarmed and determined to ignore this other presence. And then Alice was swallowing the pills two, three at a time, and more, until there wasn't a single one left, and there was only the glass stuck to the table by its own spills.

And Alice sat and stared at the camera, through the camera, like she was looking straight at me, or not *me*, simply whoever it was on the other side of the lens. Staring with a kind of puzzlement as if we were the same mystery to her as she was to us. As if she was sorry for everyone who was watching her, not the other way round.

Then she reached forward and switched off the camera.

White noise replaced her.

A hiss like rain.

I stared at the white noise a long time, seeing patterns that weren't there, before I too flicked a switch and sent Alice's last wordless testament into oblivion.

Like her.

Like Sydney.

I turned off the video and walked to the window, opened the doors wide and stepped out on to the terrace. The stars would be summer stars soon. It was about time. The air would be warm with scents, and the names of plants tripped through my head, meaningless, but I never knew which plants were which, they were only the words reminding me that summer was finally here, that the scent I could so nearly smell was summer, whatever flavour it had, and though I preferred the cold I was still glad it would soon be over for

405

another while, because it had been a dark season and I didn't want to extend it. I looked down at the city and almost felt as if I understood Alice's resignation, her surrender. To die, to sleep.

But death wasn't sleep, that was just some foolish lie, it wasn't slipping into the next room, as some fool once described it; there was no next room; death was nothingness. I'd seen it too often to pretend that it was otherwise, that it could be prettified. But why choose that when instead there was this: the lights of the city I could see before me, a siren blazing as a squad car turned the corner of St Stephen's Green and made its way west, out of sight. As I stood there and thought about Alice, I felt a fierce burning in me for all this chaos and noise. It never ended, never ended, and it shouldn't otherwise there really was nothing.

Take away that and there was only the dark.

But still I was tired; it was late.

I shut the doors and went into the bathroom, opened the cabinet and found the sleeping pills, the ones Fitzgerald had told me to flush away all those days ago.

I took out two and placed them on the edge of the sink, and the rest I upended into the lavatory, watched them fizzle for a while and then flushed them away.

I didn't need them any more.

Tomorrow I wouldn't need them, that is. But just for tonight I was going to enjoy the last two. I was going to set the alarm, but not too early, then I was going to let them dissolve on my tongue and lie down in bed and think and dream of nothing because sometimes that's the best thing to think and dream about; sometimes the light is too much.

I was going to let the dark take me.

Just for a while.

Just one more night.

The dark was welcome to me.

The Dead

Ingrid Black

It's five years since Ed Fagan disappeared, and since then nothing has been heard from the serial killer known as the Night Hunter. Until now.

A Dublin newspaper has received a chilling letter claiming to be from Fagan that promises a new reign of terror. But it's not until the body of prostitute Mary Lynch is found that the police become convinced the Night Hunter has returned.

Saxon, a former FBI agent, was writing a book about Fagan when he disappeared. She is absolutely certain he can't be responsible this time. So while Detective Chief Superintendent Grace Fitzgerald and her team sniff at a cold trail, Saxon has to convince them to look beyond the obvious.

But Saxon is running out of time . . .

0 7553 0702 X

<u>headline</u>

Watching Out

Ann Granger

Fran Varady fell into private detective work by chance. Now she's got a 'real' job at a trendy pizzeria, she's back on track with her acting ambitions, and she's even found a nice flat to rent. But things aren't as straightforward as they seem.

The job, for a start: there's something sinister about the way the pizzeria is run. And the play rehearsals are riddled with problems. On top of all this, Fran has rashly undertaken to help a young boy, illegally in the country, find an elusive people-trafficker called Max.

When the trail Fran is following is tragically inter-rupted by a horrifying death, she finds herself up against dangerous men and a ruthless organisation. Fran's in big trouble this time . . .

Praise for Ann Granger:

'A good feel for understated humour, a nice ear for dialogue' *The Times*

'Ann Granger's skill with character together with her sprightly writing make the most of the story . . . she is on to another winner' *Birmingham Post*

'A delight. Darkly humorous but humane . . . fluent, supple and a pleasure to read' *Ham and High*

0 7472 6802 9

headline

Now you can buy any of these other bestselling
Headline books from your bookshop or
direct from the publisher.

FREE P&P AND UK DELIVERY
(Overseas and Ireland £3.50 per book)

Chapter and Verse	Colin Bateman	£6.99
Mandrake	Paul Eddy	£6.99
To The Nines	Janet Evanovich	£6.99
A Place of Safety	Caroline Graham	£6.99
A Restless Evil	Ann Granger	£6.99
Inside Track	John Francome	£6.99
The Cat Who Talked Turkey	Lilian Jackson Braun	£6.99
Fallen Gods	Quintin Jardine	£6.99
Petrified	Barbara Nadel	£6.99
No Good Deed	Manda Scott	£5.99
Oxford Proof	Veronica Stallwood	£6.99
Bubbles In Trouble	Sarah Strohmeyer	£6.99

TO ORDER SIMPLY CALL THIS NUMBER

01235 400 414

or visit our website: www.madaboutbooks.com

Prices and availability subject to change without notice.